FOXES & POISONS

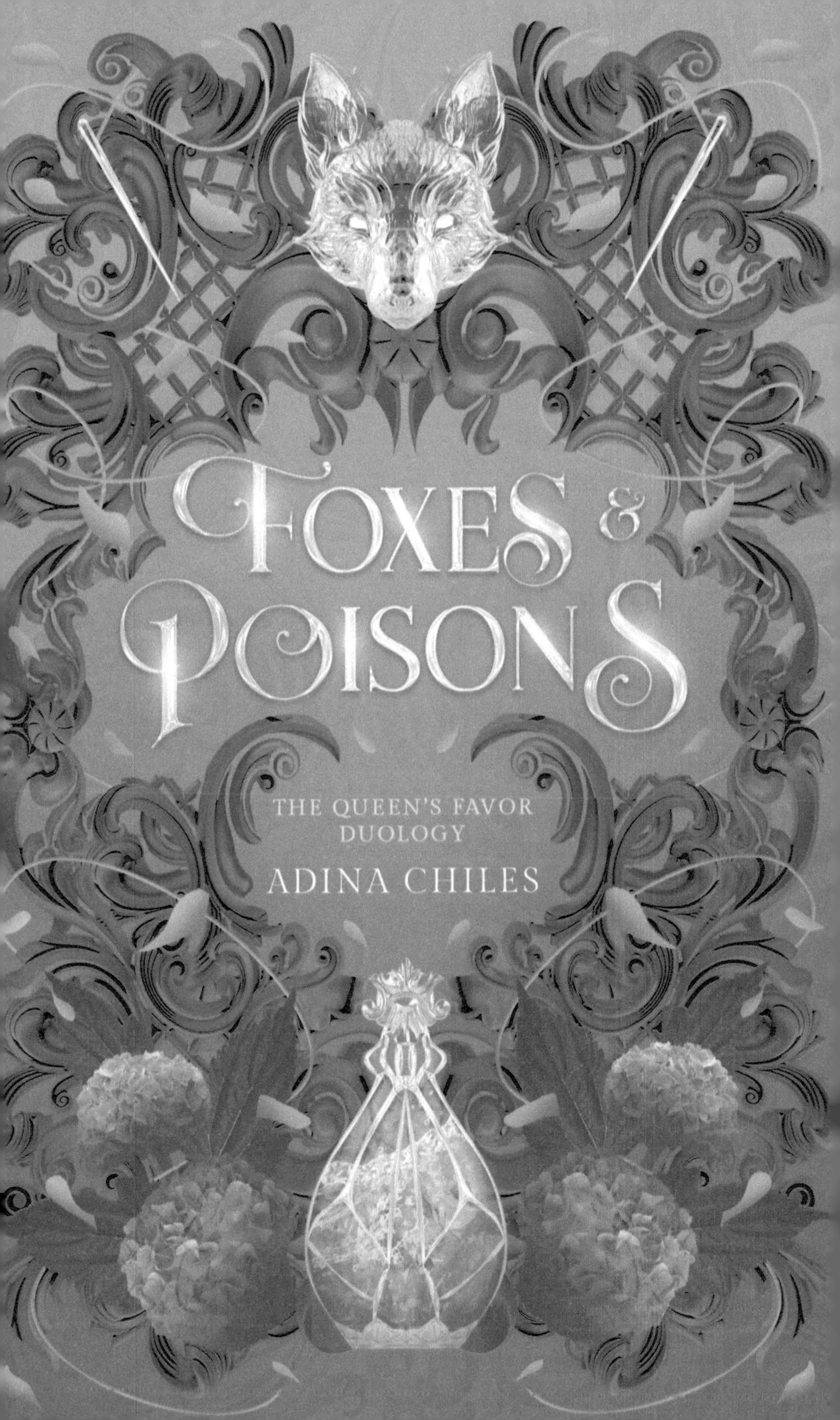

FOXES & POISONS
THE QUEEN'S FAVOR
DUOLOGY
ADINA CHILES

Foxes & Poisons
First Edition, 2025
Copyright © 2025 by Adina Chiles

Published by Never & Ever Publishing | @neverandeverbooks
Edited by Joyce Fernandez | @rejoyceliteraryediting
Cover & edge design by Lexie | @selkkiedesigns
Cover & interior artwork by Natascia Mora | @moranatascia
Interior artwork by Dezaray | @oblivionsdream
Map by Centaur Maps | @centaurmaps
Interior formatting by Brindi Quinn via Vellum | @brindiful
Digital edge formatting by Painted Wings | @paintedwingspublishing

Hardcover ISBN: 978-1-967709-13-7
Paperback ISBN: 978-1-949222-68-5

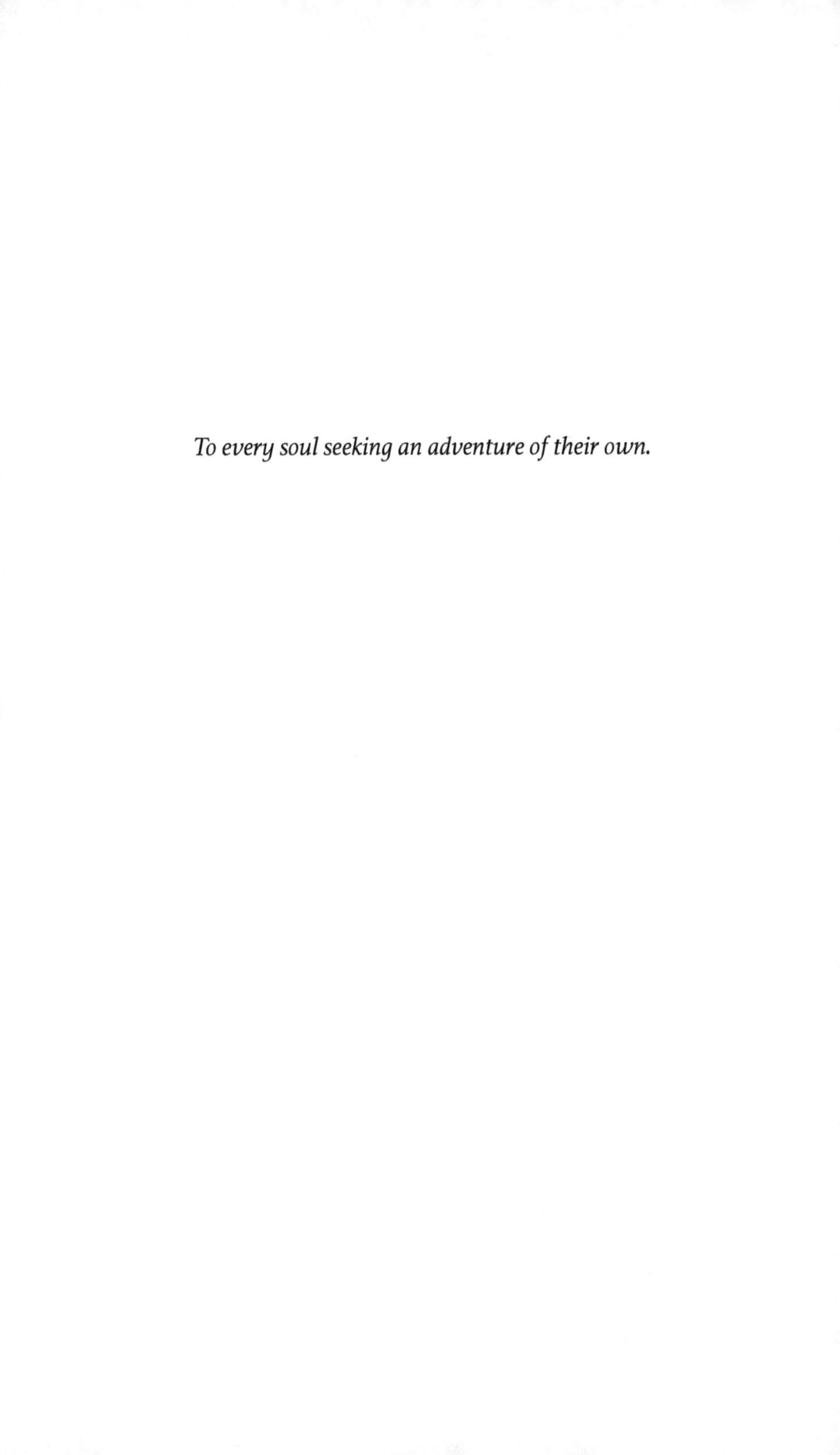

To every soul seeking an adventure of their own.

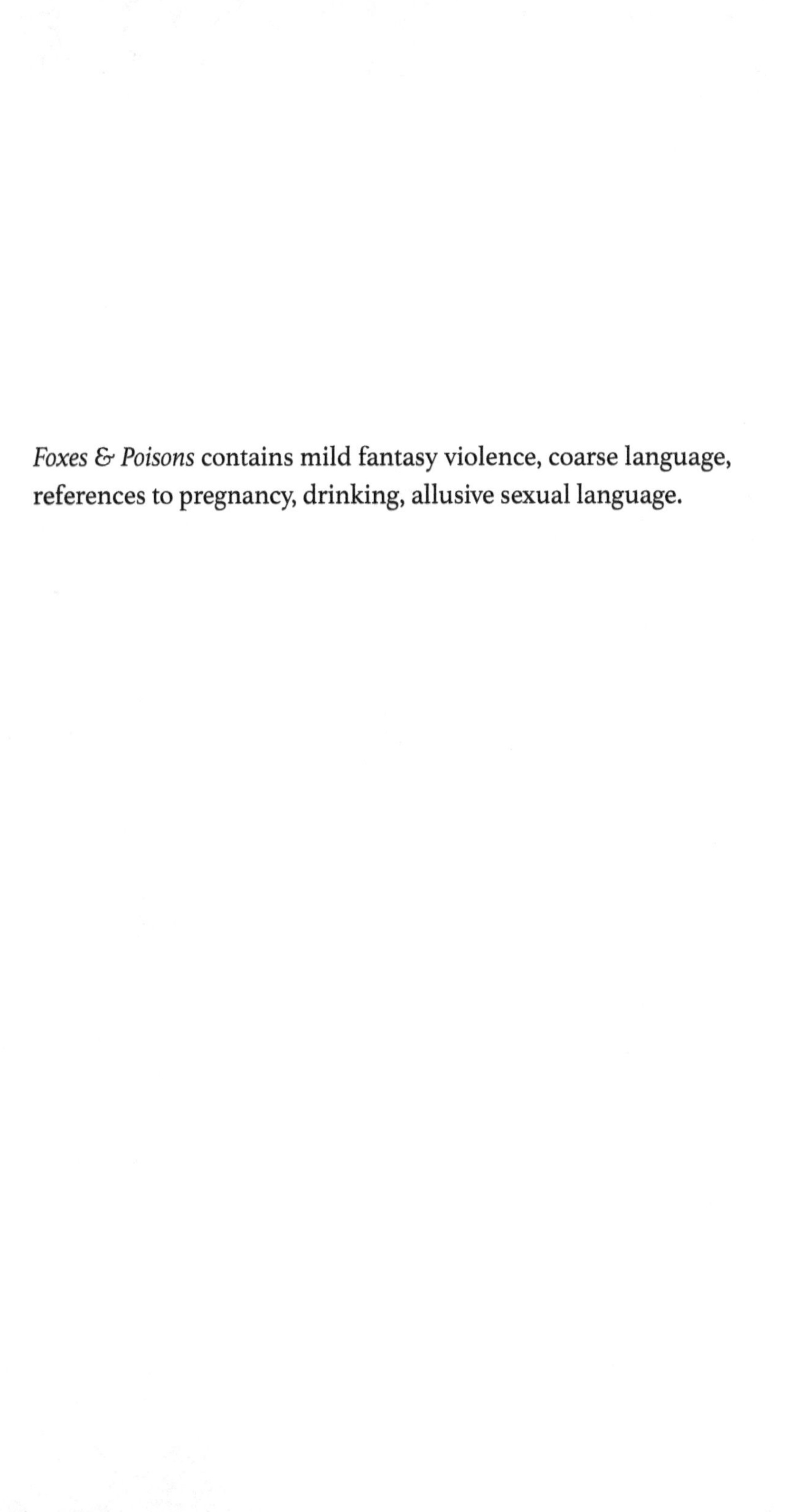

Foxes & Poisons contains mild fantasy violence, coarse language, references to pregnancy, drinking, allusive sexual language.

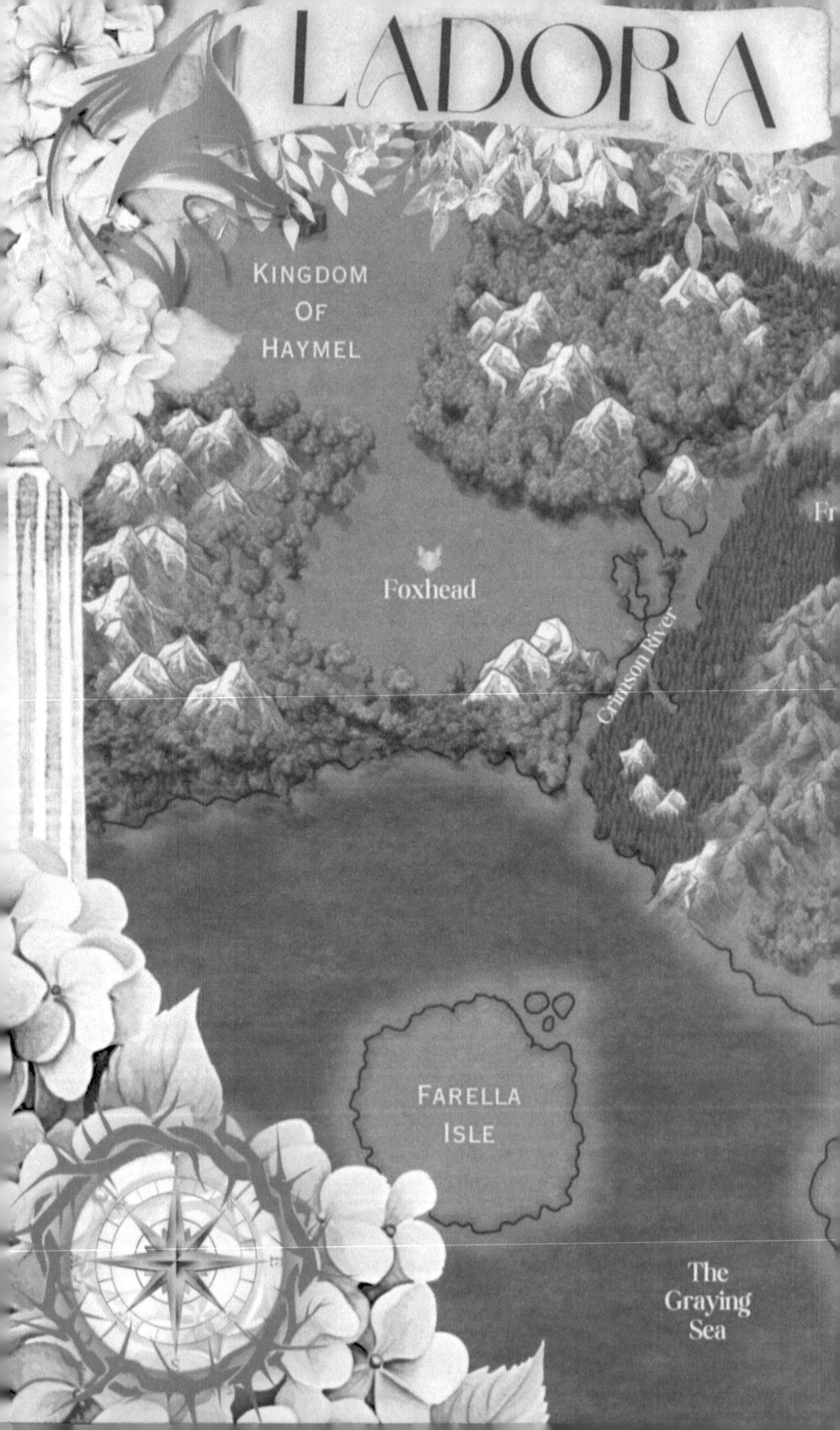

LADORA
KINGDOM OF HAYMEL
Foxhead
Crimson River
Farella Isle
The Graying Sea

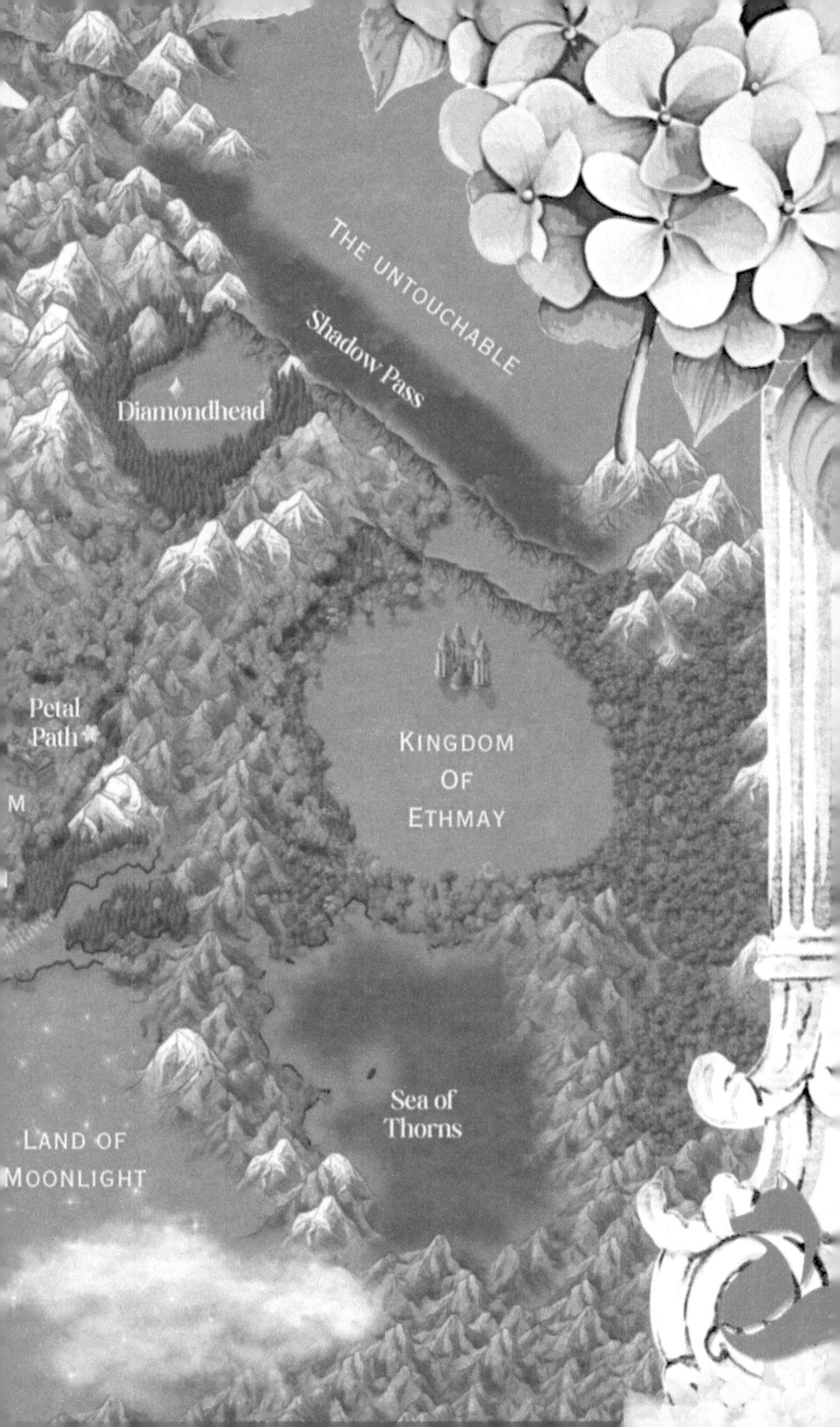

THE UNTOUCHABLE
Shadow Pass
Diamondhead
Petal Path
KINGDOM OF ETHMAY
Sea of Thorns
LAND OF MOONLIGHT

CONTENTS

PROLOGUE

Lovers' hearts are equally powerful, as they are pathetically weak. The bond formed between individuals is one difficult to sever, but if managed, it can cause destruction to not only one heart, but two.

Queen Cayleen knew this when her most loyal spy and her greatest apothecary fell in love. She saw it before they ever did —in the slightest of glances, the way they tensed when the other's name was spoken, even in the sly touches exchanged as they passed one another in the corridors.

It came as no surprise when the couple had requested to marry and live out the rest of their days away from court.

Anger exploded inside the Queen, for all members of the Foxes knew love was against the rules. She knew her response had to be calculated. Any sign of condemnation and she could destroy two yearning hearts. Of course, she cared little for their affection, but a saddened heart would wither away their skills, skills that made them ever so valuable.

Instead of denying their request, she granted the couple permission to marry and leave court, but they had to stay within the boundaries of her kingdom. As payment for her graciousness, she made them vow that if ever there came a time, whether a year or a hundred from now, in which she needed their assistance once more, they would offer it with no hesitations.

The couple agreed, but love is blinding and gives little visibility into the future. In their adoration, they forgot that all debts must be paid, especially a debt with the Queen of Haymel.

PART ONE

PROPOSITIONS

1

ARIAH

Over a dozen available chairs take up space in the near-empty lobby of the council building, and of course, my soon-to-be husband takes the seat next to me.

We aren't officially betrothed, but I refuse to pretend that's not our purpose here. The saddest part about this situation, other than a lack of consent on my end, is that I don't even know his name. Nor do I want to. And despite living in a fairly small village, his face is not one I recognize. He is an utter stranger to me.

Tugging at his chamomile yellow overcoat, as he adjusts in his seat, particles of dust rise from the patches of soot scattered on his clothing.

The man sneaks a peek at my embroidered design as my needle slips through lilac linen, finishing another daisy. While I work the needle, he begins sucking at his teeth.

It's a rather vexing noise that he incessantly carries on with. When the sucking isn't enough, he uses the nail of his right pinky, an exceptionally long nail, to pick at his teeth. Even with its length, he struggles with whatever object is between the crevices.

Wanting him to stop, I dig through my bag and find my old worn canister of needles—a necessity I always carry with me.

"Here." He frowns at the metal sliver I point at him. "Might work better than your nail."

His smile is weak, but he takes my offer and digs at the disturbance in his mouth. With a flick of his wrist, he gives one final suck.

Just as my hand begins working my needle again, something wet and green hits my arm.

Absolutely disgusting.

Flicking it away, I fall back in my seat.

He doesn't notice the old food particle he flings onto my skin, and therefore makes no attempts at apologizing. Instead, he hums a little too loudly while watching passersby out the window.

Side-eyeing him, I take in more of his frame and realize his coat is a few sizes too big, swallowing him whole. It's probably not even his. It looks second-hand and rather dated, perhaps something he borrowed from his father or an older brother.

His skin reminds me of the raven trees that grow around the back of our cottage. When I was a child, my father used to make the finest furnishings from their dark, enriched trunks. I'll give it to him, his skin is nice, like black silk. However, his brightly colored clothes completely drown out the cool undertones of his complexion, and while it shouldn't be an issue for me, it is. He needs something more like a cobalt blue or dark gray. I bet even a deep purple would do well. Before losing myself in color palettes that would suit him, I pull myself out of those thoughts.

He clears his throat, and my eyes drop to the marble floor before he catches me staring. He releases a few coughs, and then the sound of hacking has me staring again. Much like my cat, Ella, it sounds as if he has hair of his own stuck in his passageways. The hacking is phlegmy, and I suddenly realize what he is trying to cough up. He stops when mucus pools into his mouth. With nowhere to spit, he lets it go back to where it came from, and I think I'm going to be sick.

The thought of having this man touch any part of me makes me want to regurgitate every meal I've had for the past week.

"*You have to be open to the idea,*" Jaleese, my older sister, advised me before coming here. And to that I had said, "*The hell I do.*" I don't want any part of this. The system may have worked for her, but my doubts are solidified and I want out.

"Ariah Tyddle," an older woman summons me, poking her head out of the grand doors of the lobby. She has a smile that beams like the sun. Warm and inviting. At least one of us is happy. "It's your turn, dear. Council will see you now."

Before I can stand, my husband-to-be is out of his seat and standing next to me.

Her eyes drift over his lanky frame before speaking, "Are you Miss Tyddle?"

He lets a snort slip and follows it up with a couple of huffs and puffs. "She is my wife. I have every right to be in there."

Acid hits the back of my tongue. All I picture is a scrambled egg and porridge mess on the floor, and I hope this poor woman doesn't have to be the one to clean up after me.

There is a tightness in my chest, but before things get worse the woman speaks again. "You don't have a wife. And if you don't sit down and wait your turn, I assure you never will." She points a finger at his empty seat until he finds his way back.

I don't know who this woman is, but I want her to be my best friend. It's like she's in my head and saying all the things I want to.

Put in his place, the man clunks down in his seat. His dark color transforms to red, a red that makes me think he is about to blow. Wanting to avoid further annoyance, I slip into the room and let the woman shut the door behind me.

To my surprise, we don't enter a room. It's more so a large hall with towering columns. Thick stone pillars line both sides, forming arches above that hold warm light from high windows. Pockets of gold guide us to another set of doors.

Between the pillars are stone figures of Haymel's greatest divinities, or so legends say. Supposedly, divinities were once beings with supernatural abilities who ruled over our world and shaped a lot of kingdoms we know today.

Whether or not I believe in the legends, my favorite is, and has always been, Panntra, the divinity of night, who was also said to be the ruler of what we now call the Land of Moonlight. In all the images I've seen of her, she is portrayed almost thief-like—wearing a mask that covers everything on her face but the eyes.

The statue in the council building is different, though. Not only is she over ten feet tall, but a skintight dress snuggles curves and holds crisscrossed beaded material that runs up and down her body. Her face, like usual, is covered. Floating above an open palm of the large statue is a diamond. Moving farther into the hall, I catch fragments of light bouncing from a cobweb-like string that suspends the massive gem, and I wonder if the stone is real or a fake one only meant for display.

Pulling my gaze away from Panntra, I examine the other divinities and notice a quietness about the room, one that makes me wish I brought my sketch pad. The number of outfits my mind can conjure up in such a tranquil place would be infinite.

"An abhorrent practice," the woman mumbles.

Pulling my attention away from the details of the grand structure and craftsmanship of the walkway, I register that she is speaking to me. "I'm sorry, what?" My voice comes out a little more creaky than usual.

"Young ones having to be married off well before their time. And for what, the promise of land and moinlings." She stops quickly, creating a screech that echoes around us. "My name is Ivy. Ivy Mayfoot."

Everyone knows members of the council like to target unmarried people over the age of twenty and use them as bargaining pieces for trade coins, what we call moinlings in our kingdom. All of which helps them fund this *glorious* institution they have created, and I'm sure the plush lives they live outside of it. At an unwed twenty-two years old, I'm just ripe for the picking.

"Has anyone ever denied council?" My question causes immediate regret as I watch her eyes widen like moons.

"Deny?" Her face returns to normal as she processes the question more. "I mean, technically, the Queen has not signed off on these marriages, therefore they are not law. But I don't think she would be against such arrangements, if presented to her. These men were appointed by Her Majesty, they act in her name. Plus, people are too afraid of the power the council holds to turn down such unions. There is only one person I know to have refused council. Kyla Lahorn."

"Lahorn? Like lonely Lady Lahorn?" She is the village spinster with an awfully bad attitude. I never considered why people call her that, but if she did turn down the council in her day, then that would make sense.

"Yes, and she's still reaping those consequences." Ivy places both her hands on my shoulders. Wrinkles run over her dark skin and her hold on me is a bit weak. "I won't be the one to advise you in taking a stand against council. They are bitter old men with nothing better to do than make your life a living hell if you revolt. In the end, you're the one who has to live with the consequences of your decision, so make it for yourself."

I nod and see my voluminous curls bounce in her iridescent green irises. "Have you ever had to make this decision?"

She pulls away and her face drops like I've just offended her. But it only takes a half second for her to find a smile again. "Yes, I have. It's been many years since I was in your shoes. A moment that undoubtedly changed my life." She exhales gravely before continuing, "Deep breaths, Ariah. It will be over in no time." But as good-natured as she's been, the words fall short, and I don't find the comfort she intends.

Before entering, I start digging in my pockets. My chest tightens even more when my hands come up short. I always carry it with me. Why can I not find it when I need it most? A frustrated exhale catches the attention of Ivy, but before she can ask what's wrong, I dig a little deeper. Resting beneath an extra hair tie and my canister of needles, I find my medicinal spray bottle.

I release a quick spritz of the bottle's contents into my mouth and hold my breath. My father says his concoction works best if I hold it in and let the mixture move into my lungs.

My eyes slip shut as I exhale, but when I open them, Ivy is staring, not rudely, but she watches me with concern. Once my airways loosen, I give her a nod. Not because I'm ready for what awaits me on the other side, but because we've stalled long enough.

She knocks twice on the glossy oak and seconds later the double doors swing wide, revealing strangers who know exactly who I am.

Inside, there are five men in total, and immediately I pick out features that stand out in each of them. Terrible toupee, mole under left eye, snow beard, receding hairline, and monocle. All are decrepit and look rather annoyed with how slowly I stroll into the center of the room. But can they blame me for taking my time? They want to sell me off to a man whom I've only met this morning and have no desire to marry. They act as if I'm some kind of livestock they can barter with and then have the nerve to be bothered by my leisurely pace.

Every movement is like making my way through a labyrinth of thorns. My body pricks with pain the closer I get to my judges.

Each of the men sit behind what looks like a pulpit. Beyond them are windows that take up most of the wall and allow in yellow rays that cast light on marble sculptures. All of it seems too sanctified for the men who occupy the space.

"It's about time," the man straight in front of me mutters. He pushes the golden rims of his glasses higher on his nose, before smoothing the snowy white of his mustache and following the hair down to his beard. "I don't like waiting, Miss Tyddle."

A pitter-patter of feet rushes across the floor, and I catch Ivy scrambling to a desk where she picks up a quill pen and begins scribbling on her paper.

"Neither do I." I feel a slight discomfort settle in my chest. It's too early to tell if I need more medication or if the pressure is fear.

All the men gasp as if never having heard a woman speak.

"What did you just say?" This time the question comes from another man, one who has deep, rich brown skin, similar to my own, and is completely bald.

My eyes drift to Ivy who is still writing away but releases a smile of approval.

I clear my throat and stare at the men. "He said he doesn't like to wait, and I said, nor do I. I have been sitting out in the lobby for nearly an hour, waiting for all of you. I'm late for work, which means I'll have to stay well into the night to make up the moinlings from missed hours. Now I am here, still waiting for the meeting to start." Adrenaline pumps through me as I hold my stance.

"Well, Miss Tyddle, let's not make you wait any longer." The man in the center, the one I'm certain is the leader, speaks again, "You have been brought to the Council of Foxhead because you are ordered to marry Morren Beetlerum." *Ariah Beetlerum?* The thought stays in my head where it belongs because the name is just an awful one. "He and his father own a considerable size of land west of our village, and they have amiably offered to part with some of it to expand the Queen's Road." *Of course, they have.* "In a week's time, the village will provide a small but pleasant ceremony, and from there you shall live in, and be a part of, the Beetlerum Estate. You will no longer need your *little* job and you will be more than *compensated* in your new life."

The foolery that has just been uttered makes my blood boil and I'm not even sure which issue to address first. *My little job.* Dressmaking may not mean anything to him, or anyone else, but it is mine and something I have worked damn hard for. And even if I agree to this futile practice, why would I have to give that up?

"*Think and then speak. Anger fuels nothing but stupidity.*" My father offered this advice before I left our house this morning. Unlike my mother, he always takes a gentler approach to things. While Mother's fire is often needed, and I rarely hesitate in harnessing it, I think about my response and try to gain as much clarity as I can.

"No," is the only word that gets sifted out from the many that want to be shared.

The response makes the leader's pasty skin flash with a red warning, and the others start whispering amongst themselves; I can only imagine the *pleasantries* being passed around.

"Miss Tyddle, I don't think you quite understand how this works," he says as calmly as his rage allows.

"This practice is not an official kingdom rule. If you want me to marry the person of your choosing, I need to see documentation from Queen Cayleen herself. If you do not have any,

I would like to go to work now. Some of us have to make our own money."

"You ungrateful girl," someone shouts.

"No one has ever questioned us before," bellows another.

The leader holds up a hand. "Very well, Miss Tyddle. Though I am displeased with your decision, we shall choose someone more *worthy* of Mr. Beetlerum." He leans forward, placing his hands on his stand. "However, we will match you with another, and next time I assure you, you will be married, even if the Queen of Haymel has to come here herself." The sound of doors opening comes from behind me. "Now, get out. You've wasted our time."

Terrible toupee, mole under left eye, snow beard, receding hairline, and monocle—I memorize the men who have threatened me once more and gladly take my leave.

Ivy puts down her pen, no longer needing to take her notes. I toss her a quick smile and though she doesn't return it in front of the men, her thoughts shout at me with approval.

I take in the grand hall on my way out and wish I had visited under different circumstances. While I would love to be in the beauty of the building again, if it means I have to see any of those men, it's not a chance I'm willing to take.

Opening the door to the lobby I inhale the freshest air I've ever known. That is, until Morren gets up from his seat and blocks my exit.

"They did a pretty good job selecting a wife for me," he says. Morren isn't the worst-looking guy in the world, but he's far from my type, plus I have no desire to be married, at least not now. "I had my doubts when my father told me, but you'll do nicely."

Just when I thought my breakfast was starting to settle back down, it starts creeping up. "About that...they decided to go with someone else."

His head cocks back. "What? They said I would be meeting my wife today. I'm not really in the mood to wait for another."

"Sorry." I give him a shrug and maneuver around him.

Extending an arm, he keeps me from leaving yet again, and the motion boils my insides. "Why don't we go tell them they don't have to find anyone else? You and I can be married by morning."

I grimace. "Absolutely not."

With a final push, I move his arm out of the way and leave. Not once looking back.

2

IANN

The scent of iron merges with salty sea air as a pool of blood soaks into the deck, accompanying stains of piss and vomit.

When we travel by ship, it starts off in pristine condition, but after months of harsh weather mixed with drunk nights, little clean water, and no proper waste disposal, it needs a good scrub.

"Get him!" someone shouts at the sound of bones cracking, followed by a hard thud to the wooden floor.

As the crew catches sight of me emerging from the captain's quarters, their huddle disbands, leaving behind two sparring individuals.

One is Kalen, who holds himself in a bloody mess on the floor. Kalen has been part of my crew for years and not once has he caused me issues.

The other is a newcomer by the nickname Twigs. Twigs is a tall, lean man, mid-twenties like myself, but is the cockiest bloke I've ever had in my crew. He was also not hand-selected by me, and is a *friend* of my eldest brother. As a favor I agreed to

"

take Twigs along. An abysmal agreement on my end, but who am I to argue with the future king?

The knuckles of Twig's right hand shine bright red, carrying drying blood that doesn't belong to him. He tosses me a smirk that makes me want to punch him and send him to the ground, aside Kalen.

"Is there a problem?" My voice hits a deeper tone than my usual one as I extend a hand to help Kalen up, but I aim my words at Twigs.

The crew remains quiet, as do the crowds waiting for us beyond the dock. Just my luck, these two begin fighting just as we arrive at the port back in Saden.

"He shorted me on my payment, and I want what is mine before we get off this ship." Twigs spits a thick, brown liquid to the ground.

"Is that so?" I draw closer to Twigs, and while I dread confrontation, this is a moment that's been building for months, and I can no longer ignore it. Friend of my brother's or not, Twigs needs to learn his place, and I might have to be the very person to teach him. "I give Kalen the amounts for each crewmate. I assure you that all in my crew receive what is owed to them." I take another step closer to him, right as palace guards approach. Their presence aboard my ship, instead of waiting on the dock as they should be miffs me, but I focus on one problem at a time.

"You are lazy and condescending. You drink more than you work, and you did little to help us during this expedition. I gave you what you deserved."

Twigs goes from a pale white to a raging orange-red, and had I, Prince Iann, third son to King Marcel II, not been standing before him, he would have tried to pummel me the same way he did Kalen. Part of me wishes he would try.

Guards move closer, but with a simple wave from me, they back off, waiting for my command.

"If you desire more payment, then you are to clean the entirety of this ship top to bottom. It's mostly your mess, so I assume it shouldn't be an issue."

"Piss off." He dares to take a step closer and cocks an arm back. Before I can react, guards rush in and seize Twigs.

"Get him off my ship and take him to a cell to sober up," I order, making sure to have the final command. It may be my father's army, but this man is part of my crew, even if he's a terrible crewmate. "The rest of you"—the crew stills—"your King will be pleased at our findings. Your service, as always, is most appreciated. Now, get off my ship and go enjoy your families."

With their laughter and payments in hand, they each depart the vessel that's been home to us over the past several weeks, with me following right behind them.

Every time I disembark, I find the final step off the ship onto the dock is the hardest. In the matter of one second, I go from explorer to prince, and it's a bittersweet moment that hits like a boulder dropping to the pit of my stomach.

I find the notion that going home is the best feeling, to be nonsense. I propose that the greatest feeling is found in grand adventures. Made all the better, if accompanied by the right crew. It is a feeling I crave daily and a high not always easy for me to achieve, especially not in court.

While I adore my family, I always feel distance from them gives me a greater appreciation for all they do, at least for most of them anyway. My excursions allow me opportunities to truly miss them.

But after a two-month exploration of Diamondhead, in search of precious stones that we ended up uncovering, immersed in the mountainous terrain, I'm finally back in my home kingdom of Saden. Not just that, I'm back to being a full-time prince, and with all the draining duties attached to it.

At the end of the dock is a familiar man who instantly

draws out a smile from me. His deep umber skin soaks in the kingdom's rays and his balding head glistens with his bow. "Pleasure to see you again, Your Royal Highness."

"You've been with me for over fifteen years, Esha. How many times must I tell you to simply call me Iann?" Forcing him to drop my bags, I wrap two arms around him. Hugs have never been something I hand out with ease, but Esha is more than my courtier, he is family.

His head only comes to my shoulders and he stands awkwardly with his hands at his side, also not a fan of hugs, but eventually, he caves.

"I've told you,"—he pulls away and picks up my bags before I have the opportunity—"your mother will have my head if I do such a thing."

She and other family members never show up at the docks, or any other arrival location. They much prefer to greet me back at the palace. It's easier on all of us this way, city goers make much less of a fuss about it, and there are rarely any dreaded crowds.

"What do you have on the agenda for me today, Esha?" I climb into a carriage.

"A special breakfast has been arranged for your return. Your mother ordered your brothers and grandmother to be in attendance."

"Very well." I am not in the mood for a family breakfast, but time together will not be all bad. I'm sure my father will use it as an opportunity to find out what new resources I've discovered to benefit his kingdom. "Anything else I should know?"

He clears his throat. "Lady Thana has requested a meeting with you."

Hot, pestiferous air flows from my nose, but even with the irritation at the name of my former lover, it somehow makes me smile. "Couldn't let me have one day back before subjecting me to that name?"

Esha's lips twitch. "I only report, your highness."

"And did you ask what she wanted?"

"I did." He fixes the collar of his coat. "She told me I should stay focused on my own business and that you can request her anytime."

"Sounds about right. I'll deal with her. Thank you, Esha." It is a small lie because my way of dealing with her is always the same. Ignoring her is rather easy, and a benefit of having royal guards is that they are useful in keeping unwanted people away. One slipup with Thana and I can easily become undone; our separation is much needed.

Hating large crowds and endless gawking from strangers, I'm thankful when the driver takes the back way to the castle. Most of the time, meeting the people leads to disappointment, all on their end, when they learn I'm only the third son of King Marcel—never the prince they are pining for. They undeniably prefer to see my brothers over any other royal in Saden. The reality of my royal standing comes with a mix of relief and dejection.

With the start of a new week, I know that also on the agenda, next to a family breakfast, are meet-and-greets. Meetups that go on longer than they should, as we listen to the concerns of our people. The latter one is the only part I enjoy. Listening to the struggles of the commoners is a humble slap in the face most of us nobility need, especially members of my own family.

Inside the castle, my boots thud against the pristine floor as I make my way to the dining hall. The marble tiles reflect the colossal chandelier suspended nearly fifty feet above, and two curved staircases lead to the upper levels that overflow with blinding light. It's all just as I left it.

"Your Highness." Esha rushes to my side with a bouquet of hydrangeas wrapped in scented paper, explaining, "I figured you didn't have time to grab anything since your arrival was pushed back, so I thought I would get your mother flowers for you."

I never forget a gift for my mother, but the flowers are a nice touch. "Thank you, Esha. It will go perfectly with what I brought her."

At my approach, palace guards open double doors that are triple the height of my tall frame. A table, large enough to seat over twenty, runs through the center of the room. Windows that overlook the palace fountains line the entire wall on the left side. On the opposite side of the room is an enormous fireplace with a family portrait hanging above the mantle. The portrait took nearly three weeks to perfect and consisted of hours having to stay still, all while being a restless eight-year-old. Nearly fifteen years ago, and I'm still fickle about having to sit still for so long.

My mother's braids fall over her rose gold dress and onto her chair. Snuggled between her braids is her canary diadem. It's her favorite headpiece and was a gift my father presented to her on their wedding day.

From behind her, I offer a single kiss to her right temple before placing the hydrangeas on the table. Next to the flowers, I place a diamond I discovered on my trip.

She catches my face before I pull away and plants a kiss on my cheek. "Good morning, my youngest child." She softly pinches the hair on my chin and moves my face about while studying my appearance. "I beg you and your brothers to stop aging. It only reminds me that my time is getting shorter." She leans in close and drops her voice an octave or two above a whisper. "Maybe your next trip should include locating the Ivian Flower. Bring me back a bit of that immortality people claim it possesses."

She pulls away, laughing at the legend of the flower that is supposed to bring eternal life. I join her, but our interaction is cut short when it sounds like my father is choking from across the table.

He coughs a few times and chases his food down with wine.

Seeing he's okay, I offer him a bow. "Good morning, Father."

A servant slides out a chair for me and another brings forth a golden plate filled with eggs, meat, a variety of fruit, and my favorite, cinnamon cakes. It's been months since I have had the addictive, flaky pastries and oh, how I missed them. I inhale one as a servant pours me a drink.

"I see your brothers are late, as usual," my father says. "You've been gone for nearly three months and still manage to make it on time."

"Glad to know nothing has changed," I retort, tossing in another bite of one of the cakes.

"Tell us, Iann, did you find anything new during this trip?" My mother's eyes grow eager for information.

So do my father's, but his reasoning is different. Mother actually enjoys listening to my stories, while Father appreciates them, but cares more about the findings than the experiences.

"Yes, brother," Deean, my older brother and middle child, says. "Please tell us all about your travels." He drops his body weight against me, providing a hug meant for annoyance. He then drops his lips near my ear as he whispers, "Please tell me you spent time exploring the beds of the women in Diamondhead. I hear they have a special taste for us, Saden men."

"Heard or know?" I mutter, pushing him away.

Stealing a slice of melon off my plate, he chucks it in his mouth and lets some of the juice dribble down his chin. "If I knew, you would have certainly heard about it."

"Am I suddenly invisible to you?" Mother remarks, trying to get Deean's attention. "Or have all the manners I taught you been forgotten?"

I would say the latter, but I keep my mouth shut. Deean has always been the wildcard of the family. One to do as he pleases, with little to no repercussions. The fact he is second in line to the crown is a detail he doesn't hide and many times uses it to get what he wants. This mainly comes in the form of women or extravagances.

Deean gives our mother a kiss on her forehead. His skin matches the sepia brown shade of hers and they share the same rigid jawbone.

He drops a diamond bracelet into her hand. "So, you'll always be reminded of your favorite child."

She only shakes her head. "Then I shall think of all of you when I look at it."

"Deean, stop messing around and take a seat," Father orders.

Deean offers me a slap on the back of my head as he passes, but eventually finds his seat. It's hard to think he's nearly two years older than me.

"Where is your other brother?" Mother asks, taking a sip of wine.

Deean shrugs. "The last time I saw him was with…"

His sentence dies when Marcel, our oldest brother, strolls in. It's not his presence that keeps us quiet, but the woman he strolls in with.

She is full-figured with most of her hair pinned up, only leaving a few curly strands to wander over the deep complexion of her skin. Her lips are painted a deadly red and she has on a dress to match.

Deean raises his eyebrows at me when I look back and together our gazes float to our mother.

"Family," Marcel announces himself, adjusting a button on his black coat that runs wild with gold stitching.

Marcel looks more like my father and me. Same russet skin and thick black eyebrows that arch over hazel eyes.

The woman bows and goes to sit in the chair across from me, next to my brother. She doesn't get halfway before a cane occupies her seat.

My grandmother, appearing out of nowhere, blocks the woman from joining us at the table.

My mother raises her eyebrows at me as she takes a sip of wine, covering up a grin.

"Marcel," my grandmother says, "did you miss the part about this being a family breakfast?"

My grandmother's lips thin out as her eyes focus on my brother. Sensing how vexed she is, he answers quickly, "She simply wanted to know what breakfast in a palace was like. What's the issue?"

"Because she hasn't had that experience before?" Deean whispers while cutting into a sausage, but Marcel waves him off.

"Are you, his wife?" Gran asks her.

The woman looks around the room, flustered. "No, but—"

"Betrothed?"

"Not yet, but—"

"Did you get an invitation to this breakfast from either my son—your king—or my daughter-in-law—your queen?" The girl doesn't try answering this time. "I thought so." My grandmother turns to a guard. "I'm sure you're a lovely girl, but this is a family affair. This man will escort you out." The woman looks towards my brother, who looks to have forgotten her entirely as he eats like he's the only one at the table.

The girl doesn't wait to be escorted out, she gives a half bow before running out of the room.

Gran takes her seat and cuts her eyes at Marcel. "Must you be so careless?"

"You're the one who kicked her out. I cared enough to let her at least join us for breakfast." Marcel licks a finger.

Gran mumbles under her breath. We all know she isn't in favor of Marcel taking the throne after my father. His every move has been the subject of her scrutiny. But if a part of him cares, he's good at not showing it.

"Good morning to you too, Mom," Father says, directing the conversation to something more positive.

"Iann my boy," Gran shouts, ignoring my father and waving off the servant who offers her wine. "It's been too long. Tell us what you found in Diamondhead."

"Yes," Marcel says before taking a sip of wine. "Do tell us all about your grand adventure."

Gran doesn't turn to him, only exhales loud enough for us all to hear.

My eyes lock with Marcel and his annoyance subsides. "No really. Tell us, brother."

This time, he says it with sincerity. I straighten myself in my seat, ready to share every detail. "At first, we thought the entire trip was a waste. Found nothing for two months and every clue we had about the diamonds hidden deep in the mountains led to nothing but dead ends."

"So, you found nothing?" Deean interjects. "That's rather boring."

"We thought we found nothing," I clarify. "After listening to local stories, we found the coordinates to be off. The diamonds weren't in the mountains at all. They were buried deep, near the edge of Shadow Pass."

"Tell me you didn't enter those lands?" my mother asks with a mix of horror and intrigue.

Shadow Pass leads to the Untouchable, a land no one has ever explored.

"No, the diamonds were near it, but we didn't actually enter it."

"And what about...?" Suddenly my father's courtier appears at his side, interrupting Gran.

After a few whispers my father gets up from the table, and we all stand with him.

"Marcel and Deean, accompany your mother and grand-mother to hear the people's concerns. Iann, follow me."

All eyes drift to me, but no one interjects and we each do as we're told, with the others heading out of the room, and me going in the opposite direction after my father.

The tail ends of his coat flap back as he flies through the halls. Paintings smear across my periphery, trying to keep pace with him, and if the speed is alarming, his lack of speech turns a tighter knot in my stomach.

Coming to his study, he barges in and crosses the room in a few strides. He keeps moving, but I stop.

Stacks of books line the floors and maps inked with scribbles are sprawled out on the walls. There is an old musty smell and I spot dishes that look to be untouched for days. He pulls on a book snuggled into a shelf. The movement sets off a series of clicks and we watch as the shelf retracts from the wall and forms a strip of darkness.

It's similar to hidden doors all around the palace, but never have any of us entered my father's hidden rooms.

"Don't stall, boy, keep up." he warns before descending spiral steps. Not daring him to repeat himself, I follow.

At the end of the staircase we come to a room that is already lit by a fire, and standing at the other end is a man who leans forward, exerting weight on to a cane. Wrinkles pinch his face as he offers us a smile, a smile so trustworthy it could make anyone confess their darkest secret.

"Iann, meet Rolley Mackall. He is an explorer like yourself."

Rolley bows. "Your Royal Highness. It's a pleasure to finally meet you."

My father sits in a black cushioned chair and gestures to two empty seats on the other side of the desk. "Tell me, my son, what do you know of the Ivian Flower?"

Taking my seat, we stare at each other for a good minute and when he doesn't offer clarification, I find an answer for him. "Umm...you mean the mythical flower that's a part of a fable you and Ma told us as children?" My father's face grows with excitement and I am clueless as to why. "That's it. It's a fable. A delusional quest people have gone on, only to return with crushed dreams or worse, not to return at all."

My father pulls out three glasses from his desk, followed by a bottle of apple bourbon. The apples are grown in the orchards that surround the castle and are known as Saden's sweetest. A crisp tang hits my nose before my father slides the glass across the desk. Alcohol has never been something I acquired a taste for, but there is something about apple bourbon that I enjoy. A refreshing, yet burning sensation, prickles the inside of my mouth, but that doesn't stop me from taking another swig.

"As I was saying—" My father gets out half a thought before downing his glass. "What if I said it was all true? What if a flower like that truly existed? I know you well, my son. There had to have been a time when you thought it was more than just a fable."

He isn't wrong. Beyond my nursery years, there have been several times in life when stories have troubled my desires to set out on the dangerous expedition. But the thing with legends is they are all stories that come from people with no proof. The ones with potential proof are dead and unable to leave stories behind.

My gaze goes to Rolley, who hasn't taken a sip of his drink and still carries some of the weight on his cane. "I assume you know something about this?"

Rolley smiles. "I believe my great-grandfather may have discovered it. My great-grandfather looks no older than His Majesty, but was born nearly one hundred and fifty-seven years ago. He outlived my grandfather, my father, and I reckon he will outlive me. He has stayed hidden most of his life to keep speculations low. There isn't a soul outside my immediate family that knew of this secret. Well, so I thought."

"Why isn't he here to tell us himself?" I pry. "That might make your case stronger."

Rolley nods. "It would. Unfortunately for us all, he was taken. The only thing the captors left behind was this." He tosses what looks like a black fur ball onto the table. My father doesn't seem the least bit surprised, so I assume this is something he has already seen. I touch the item, immediately recognizing it as fox fur, the tail no doubt. "I was setting out to look for him when His Majesty's men arrived. Turns out the news of the flower and my great-grandfather's connection with it isn't as much a secret as I'd hoped."

My father's chair slides back and he rises to his feet, causing Rolley and me to stand with him, Rolley taking a little longer than everyone.

"Thank you, Mr. Mackall. I would like to speak to my son alone now." Rolley bows and takes his leave, but my father stops him one last time. "The plans we discussed earlier are still in motion. Departure is in three weeks.

Rolley nods and makes his way up the steps. My father and I sit in silence until we know the door is shut.

"Do you honestly believe him?" I ask my father, who pours himself another drink.

"Do you not?" His lips curl into something wicked, but once the glass hits his mouth, it vanishes. "Can you imagine the power Saden would gain if we had access to something like that?"

"I don't think anyone should live forever." My retort rids him of any pleasurable thought he has. "And that's if it even exists."

A finger traces the rim of his cup. "Fear has a knack for persuasion." He leans forward, tugging on my attention. "I've asked you to go on many expeditions for me, and just like all the other times, this one is no different. I need you to team up with Mackall and find the Ivian flower."

A deep sigh slips out and my grimace meets the desperation in his eyes. He's asked me to go on several expeditions, most of which are fueled by a blend of power and greed with a dash of wonder. This time is different. He looks like he might wither away if my response is no, and that alarms me.

"Where does he think it is?" My question comes out dry, but I would be lying if I didn't want to know where the legendary flower resides.

"Farella Isle."

"Farella Isle?" It is not the place I expect him to say. "Going on a hunt for a flower that may or may not exist is one thing, but you're telling me it's located on an island, not only owned by your greatest enemy, but by a queen ruthless enough to kill us on sight?"

My father finishes the contents of his drink once more before slamming the glass down on the desk. "Your one and only task is to find the flower. Let me deal with the Queen of Haymel."

3
ARIAH

My head has never held itself higher than today. An exultant grin keeps forcing itself on my face, even with me making attempts to hide it. I just denied council, making me the second person in all of Foxhead to ever do so. Knowing they will try to make my life a nightmare should come with fear, but I can't find it. I'm utterly buzzing.

Walking the cobblestone path of Foxhead Village, I am nothing but smiles. I'm even tempted to dance through the streets, but knowing that's a foolish move keeps my feet planted on the ground.

Even the air smells different, fresher in a way I never noticed before. My nose picks up on the scent of panicle hydrangeas, along with a mix of honey and rum that escapes Lady Emm's Sweet Treats shop.

The walk to work is how I imagine taking a stroll through the clouds would feel. A blissful weightlessness, with not a single burden to anchor me to this world.

Drawing closer to the dress shop, I pick up on the not-so-subtle glances of the blacksmith across the road, Tristen Marden. He's a few years older than me and works under the apprenticeship of his uncle. It's not the first time I've seen him, but it is the first time I notice him, noticing me.

I'm surprised the council hasn't tried to play matchmaker for him. My bottom lip slips between my teeth as I lightly bite down. I wonder if it had been him sitting in there with me, if I would have been more swayed to say yes. Despite the sage green of his eyes that I wouldn't mind being trapped in, or his smile that holds an obnoxious dimple on his left cheek, I would have still denied council. *I think.*

Pulling myself from the distraction across the street, I slip through the door of the dress shop. A bell chimes, and I'm bombarded with heat from the lit fireplace in the small sitting area off to the right.

None of the oil lamps are lit and besides the light of the fire, the rest of the shop is cloaked in darkness. Not even the OPEN sign has been turned over, despite the door being unlocked.

"Mrs. Kimpol!?" I shout, heading to the sewing station at the back of the shop. "Are you here?"

A loud thud from the floor above causes me to jump, nearly knocking over a box of crystal beads that would have taken me forever to clean up. There are more footsteps and then another loud thud at the top of the stairs. Grunts and heavy breaths get closer until a door swings open and a suitcase is tossed into the shop.

"Mrs. Kimpol?" I ask once more, seeing a body emerge from the threshold.

The person descending the stairs jumps back and screams. A package they are holding falls to the ground along with a basket that tips over, causing bread and some dried fruit to roll out onto the floor.

"Ariah," Mrs. Kimpol says between shallow breaths. "What are you doing here? I thought you would be off with your betrothed."

My face scrunches as if inhaling a terrible stench. "Why would you think that? I told you I would be here. And why are you still closed?"

Picking up the food that escaped, she sets her things down on the worktable. "If you must be nosy, I decided to close for the day. Rarold and I will be heading to Picktum Creek to enjoy a nice getaway." Walking around the table, she comes to me. "Ariah, why in all of Ladora are you here?"

She doesn't have on her usual shop attire. On most days, she wears an ordinary cream dress that suits the deep rich undertones of her skin, with a marvelous mossy-green apron with hand-sewn flowers, created by yours truly. I had originally created it for my sister for her twenty-eighth birthday, but once Mrs. Kimpol caught a glimpse—she twisted me into selling it to her.

Today, she is in a fancy dress as is she has no intentions of working at all.

"I denied them." I straighten my back and light the oil lamp on the table.

"You did what?" She stops me from walking away. "I heard that they selected Morren Beetlerum for you. Do you know how much that boy's family is worth? They own most of Foxhead. You mean to tell me you turned that down?"

Dara Kimpol is a sweet woman with a slight obsession for moinlings. Her husband Rarold runs Foxhead Bank and is known to possess quite a bit of coin himself. Dara, like several others in this village, had a marriage arranged for her. She was quite adamant that I take whatever offer they give to me, and now I can see why. Despite not knowing her husband before they met, they are extremely close, I would have never guessed their alliance was one arranged for them.

"I already told you, Mrs. Kimpol, I want to travel outside the boundaries of this village. Maybe even see beyond this kingdom. I want to know who I am before knowing anyone else. I don't even know all the things my heart desires. How do a bunch of old men?" Mrs. Kimpol sighs and gives me a defeated smile before I continue, "When I marry, if I ever marry, it will be because that's what I want. In the meantime, council can go bug someone else because they get nothing from me."

"As you say, dear." She pats my arm, and I know that's her way of disagreeing without offering further argument. She collects her items and starts heading to the door. "The shop will remain closed for the next three days. Go spend time with your family. Isn't your sister about to deliver any day now?"

"Three days? I can keep the shop going for you." I rush to her side like a dog begging for a treat. "I'll keep it up and running. That way, you wouldn't have to miss out on any earnings."

She *shoos* me. "Oh, I'm not worried about that." She stops with her hand lightly on the doorknob. A finger goes to her chin and she mumbles inaudibly to herself. Suddenly, she begins searching her pockets until she finds one she likes. She then pulls out a floral coin pouch and holds it out for me. "This should cover the next couple of days. No need to have you miss out on moinlings because I want to have a little fun."

She perks up and swings the door open. My fingers feel along the pouch and I don't even have to open it to know this is much more than my wages for three days.

"Mrs. Kimpol, I can't—" She gives me no time to finish before I feel her pushing me out the door.

"Hush girl," she orders once we're outside. "Take it and go enjoy yourself."

She locks the door to the shop and checks it once more to make sure it is secure. I help carry her bag to her wagon, and she plants a kiss atop my head before climbing up.

With the reins in hand she gives me one last look. "I know you don't want to hear this, but if I were you, I would see if I could get council to offer me the deal once more. Once you get to be my age, comfort and stability are what you will depend on the most, and if someone is willing to offer it, I would take them up on it. And who knows, dear, you might end up falling madly in love with him later in life." She fixes her sights ahead and flicks her reins. "See you soon, dear."

"I doubt it," I mumble before stuffing the coin purse in the pocket of my dress.

With nothing else to do with my day, I begin walking through town, making my way to the outskirts of the village. I dread the opinions my sister will unwarily share, but I make my way to her anyway.

The day is still a glorious one. The weather is perfect and the sky is bright and clear. Poking out above the various homes and shops are the Rosewood Mountains. The snowy peaks tease me with exploration. Just another place on my list to visit. Feeling the coins jingle in my pocket, as if a reminder of what I just acquired, I wonder if I have enough to go on an adventure of my own. Surely that journey would take more than three days, and I highly doubt Mrs. Kimpol would mind. She probably would push me to concede and give in if given the chance.

I spot a large crack on the cobblestone path. One invaded by a moss that is my favorite shade of green. I jump over it, much like I did when I was a child. A game Luna, my best friend, and I used to play as children. There was never any point to it. Just something for us to do.

Up ahead, I spot Shea's trolley. He is a wild old soul and the village florist. As usual, I rush to my favorite section. Every day I stop and touch the hydrangeas in his cart. Having a garden of my own I never purchase anything, but his are too pretty not to admire.

"How many times do I have to tell you, Ms. Tyddle, you either buy them or keep your grubby little hands off?" he says in a Saden accent as he comes around the corner with a wink and a grin. He looks around to make sure no one is near. "Have you seen the new ones yet?"

He doesn't have to tell me twice before I start scanning the flowers. All I see are the usual ones. "Where? If you're referring to the green ones, I saw those the other day. Stunning, but not as pretty as the...baby...blue." My sentence slows as he pulls flowers from behind his back. He and I both know my obsession with hydrangeas, and he's just shown me the most beautiful ones I've ever seen.

The petals are like butterfly wings and the color looks like it's been painted with rose gold and sprinkled with crushed diamonds. I take them from him without permission. "How did you get them like this?"

He leans in close before sharing, "Crushed eggshell in the fertilizer and I let loose magis worms. Harmless to the plant, but that nasty, shimmer goop they leave behind does wonders."

My head snaps up with the perfect idea. "This is a good inspiration for a dress. How much?"

"For you? Nothing. Plus, I heard what you did at council and that alone deserves free flowers—for life."

"How did you hear about that?" Suddenly, I'm all too aware of others roaming the village.

"You think you can deny council and there wouldn't be talk about it before you even left the building?"

He takes a watering jug to a row of multi-colored tulips. A few streams don't pour as easily as the others, so I snatch it from him and dig in my bag for one of my needles.

"I think those men should concentrate on more important matters." My needle pokes through the clogged holes until the flow matches the others. "And people should learn not to fuss over matters that have nothing to do with them."

"Ariah!" A dour voice beckons to me from down the cobble path.

Shea snatches the jug from me. "Looks like fuss is heading your way. You two take it away from my cart please.

Thankfully, it's only Luna who waves me down; and doing as he orders, I meet her before she can reach us.

I toss Shea one of my newly acquired coins. "I said it was free," he calls out after me, dropping the Saden accent so others can't hear.

"Put it towards your shop."

Shea has been trying to get a place of his own for years. Being from the rival kingdom of Saden, opening his own business has been difficult, and not many want to take a chance on someone they believe could betray them at any moment. Shea never would, but people have little trust nowadays.

Luna stands in the distance, tapping her foot against the stone and holding her hands against her hips. This can't be good.

A faded blue dress, the shade of her favorite color, ripples along the ground and tightens perfectly around her bewitching curves. Her dark skin holds patches of flour and she constantly looks over her shoulder, checking the bakery she helps run with her parents.

"What have you done?" she whispers.

"What are you talking about?" I play stupid. "Shouldn't you be working?"

"Shouldn't you be married?" she snaps, but then lowers her voice as a couple walks by whispering to each other, and I bet all the coins I have that their exchange is about me. "Is there something you two would like to say aloud?" Luna gives them a cautionary look. "Go on. Share it with all of Foxhead then."

Taking her arm, I pull her to her parent's bakery, dragging her inside. "What is wrong with you?"

"Me? Ri," she calls me by the nickname only she uses. "Do you know what you've done?"

The scent of fresh bread rattles my stomach, and for a second, I forget about the conversation entirely.

"I don't see why other people care. They act like I'm the first person to ever say no to council." I take a seat behind the counter, flopping down on sacks of flour.

"Umm, you're the first person in decades to do so. The last is now a spinster that the town is afraid of. Is that what you want to become?" She folds her arms across her chest, and I know I'm going to have this very conversation at least two more times with my sister and parents. "So, what happens now?"

"They will try to marry me off again. I have no doubt about that. But until the order comes from the Queen herself, my answer will remain no."

She clunks down next to me. "So, how pissed off were they?"

"I imagine they are preparing a spike for my head to sit upon at the village entrance as we speak."

She nudges my shoulder. "You'll be okay." Her voice falls to a whisper. "My parents think you are a fool, but I have your back no matter what."

"You seemed pretty upset outside." I chuckle.

"Upset? Never. Surprised is more like it. Those men are relentless. They are coming after Ma and Pa for over ten thousand coins. They say the bakery broke some kind of tax regulation, but Pa swears everything owed to the Queen was paid. Pompous bastards. Pa thinks the real reason is because we screwed up one of the council members' orders last month. Well, actually, his wife's order. She had her monthly garden party..."

"That one where they get together wearing those big, ugly hats?"

"Exactly. And they all think they look really good. But anyways, she ordered orange blossom scones. I remember clearly, because I was the one to help her. When Pa took the delivery to her she griped about having asked for vanilla cream."

"Ten thousand coins for scones!" I shout and feel a warm palm over my mouth.

Ten thousand moinlings is a lot more than this shop makes in a year. I'd be surprised if it has made that since its establishment.

"Why didn't you tell me?" Dropping my voice to a whisper as the bakery's little bell chimes and a shopper comes in.

Luna shrugs. "It was around the time when you got your letter requiring you to show up at council. I figured you had bigger issues to deal with." She stands up and smooths her apron before offering me a hand.

"That is huge news. You could have told me. No more secrets. Promise?"

Extending my right arm, I hold my hand sideways with my palm facing the left. She looks at it, unsure what to do, but then I see a sly grin on her face and she holds out her hand. We slide our arms together until our palms meet and then wiggle our fingers.

"You're so childish." She playfully pushes me. "No more secrets, though. Promise."

Someone intentionally clears their throat trying to get our attention. When I turn to the stranger across the counter, my heart forgets how to function and a snow-white beard is the only thing I can focus on.

Crap.

4
IANN

"Who here thought azaleas would be a good choice for tonight's celebrations?" my mother snaps, and there isn't a soul that would dare interrupt the Queen while on a tangent. "Tonight is to celebrate our freedom from the tyrannical reign Haymel held over us for decades. You think displaying their kingdom's flower is what people want to see?" She snatches a handful out of a vase. "I want every last one burned and replaced with the hydrangeas and long-stemmed black grass I requested."

Scattering like ants, servants panic, dropping everything in hand to empty all the vases in the grand hall.

"Shame more people don't think like the Queen," I tease, approaching the table she's examining swatches of fabric at. "Would have saved you some energy from losing your temper if they all had a mind like yours." I offer a bow once she sees me, before picking up an azalea that has yet to be sentenced to its fiery fate.

"Ha." Her dour laugh makes no attempts at caring for my humor as she holds out a piece of sapphire blue fabric with a gold diamond pattern for her lady-in-waiting to take. "I have

43

yet to show them a memorable temper. I don't think it's difficult to select the right flower. We filled the grounds with hydrangeas. One would think it would be a mindless task to clip them and put them in water." Done with the swatches, she gets up and starts inspecting the silverware.

"I think they're quite pretty, if you ask me." I twirl the stem, watching the white petals dance between my fingertips. "Some might say prettier than our kingdom's flower."

She cuts her eyes at me mischievously. "Don't be a fool. Plus, I imagine you've seen prettier ones with all the places you've ventured to." She waves her hand, releasing her lady-in-waiting. "Tell me, what did your father want?"

Growing up, I would have described my parents' marriage as an envious one. Never perfect, but always balanced. With the blazing temper my mother can carry and my father's calming—sometimes almost too slackened—demeanor, their alliance was destined to be a testy one. Sometimes there were days when they couldn't stand the sight of each other, but it never once got in the way of the crown. Even in their deepest anger, they have always remained loyal to each other.

"He's heard whispers of great treasures in the south," I answer, only excluding part of the truth. Unsure of how much he's told people about this mythical flower, I try to keep most of the details to myself. "He just wants me to do a bit of research and find out how true some rumors are."

"So, he hasn't mentioned anything about me?" She examines my face like she's waiting for any detection of a lie.

Chuckles release when I see the worry on her face. "No. Should he have told me something about you? Have you been up to no good?"

Worry melts away and her posture loosens. "I'm always up to no good. But I have something planned and I don't need that big mouth father of yours to go spilling it."

Footsteps trail in behind me.

"Your Majesty, and His Royal Highness." Miriam, my mother's head lady-in-waiting and first cousin, bows. Her hair is graying and her skin has collected a few more wrinkles since I last saw her before my most recent exploration. She smiles, rising from her curtsy. "Your request is complete, ma'am. They...it awaits you in the greeting room."

My mother claps her hands, braids bouncing when she jumps with excitement. "You"— she pushes me to the nearest exit—"go get ready for the party tonight. I must attend to prior commitments." A sudden shouting travels in from beyond the garden windows. "Before you do that, go check on your brother. I can't imagine what he's doing."

"Which one?"

She squints towards the window as we hear more shouting and we both know she is referring to Deean.

"I thought his antics would grow thinner with age, but that boy knows exactly how to do all the wrong things." She gives my left shoulder a squeeze and then follows Miriam out of the room.

I'm tempted to leave Deean to his mischief, but no matter how hard I try to fight it, I always seem to do as I'm told. Even as a grown-ass man.

Warmth coats me once I pass through the wide doors that open into the great hall. They lead me to the palace gardens. A trickling of water sounds in the distance providing extra serenity amongst the array of colors. Once I hit the fountains, my inner calms disappear as my ears pound with more shouting.

The scent of rose infused with orange peel permeates the air, and I'm certain small notes of cinnamon and clove mix with it—a scent I've smelled a hundred times.

To the left, near one of the open fields, I spot Deean who carries a crossbow in his right hand and a glass containing a deep red liquid in the other. The drink is also the source of the smell. As usual, he entertains a couple women, both perking up with my approach.

"Ladies, let me introduce you to my younger brother and your Prince, Iann." He leans in close to one of the women, hovering just above a deep slit of cleavage. There are streaks of pink shimmering in her wavy brunette hair and her eyes appear cut with emeralds. "The explorer I told you about." She bites the corner of her lip and gives a slow bow, never breaking eye contact with me.

"Pleasure." I force a half-hearted smile. "Would you both mind leaving us for a minute? There is something important I need to discuss with my brother?"

They stay silent, and even if they want to, they know they can't refuse without repercussions. Both offer another bow before they leave us.

"So, what would you like to talk about?" Deean spins, chugging his wine.

"Nothing." Heat seeps through my pants as I sit on the stone flower bed. "Mother was worried."

He takes a seat next to me and hands me his drink. The blend smells too tempting not to try and even though it's early in the morning, I take a sip of the mulled wine and enjoy the spice that burns my throat.

Breathing heavily, he looks out over the grounds. "Mother is always worried. Especially when you're not here. She always expects the worst." He takes back his cup and chugs some more. "Can I ask for a favor?"

I shrug. "Do you deserve one?"

"You've been gone for months and this is the attitude you return with." A sly grin creeps across his face. "The place father is sending you, I want to come this time."

My head cocks to the side as he holds the same sly grin, with two of the faintest dimples resting on either side of his cheeks. "Why do you think father is sending me somewhere? I just got back."

He scoffs. "He always sends you on wild adventures, does he not? I want...No. I need to go on the next expedition. Being stuck here is driving me mad and I swear, if Mother tries to arrange another marriage for me I will disappear from this place forever."

"Don't be dramatic," I say, spotting some workers carrying in decorations for tonight's festivities.

Today marks the forty-fifth year since driving out the enemy kingdom of Haymel. Though my family has ruled for hundreds of years, there was a moment when our monarchy nearly collapsed at the hands of our greatest rival. My grandfather fell ill when my father was in his first year of life. Once Haymel learned of his sickness, their king sent soldiers to infiltrate our kingdom and claimed the land as their own. For a brief period of time, Saden fell to the hands of the enemy.

According to my grandmother, who I'm sure has fluffed the story over the years, she composed a secret group of loyalists determined to overthrow Haymel's new king and queen at the time, and ultimately assassinate them. It took nearly ten months to drive out all Hamelians, and then another year to restore Saden back to its original state prior to the invasion. During Haymel's short rule, several people had been sentenced to death, robbed of their land, and stripped of their titles. Today is in remembrance of what we rightfully claimed back.

Deean snaps his fingers in my face. "You still listening?"

"I hear you."

"So, what do you say then?"

I have no issue with Deean. Sure, he can be eccentric and self-centered, but overall, he's good fun, and I have no doubt he would bring some lightheartedness to trips that can last months at a time. But if I am honest with myself, there is a part of me that doesn't want him stealing any attention that's reserved for me. Being the third son to a king means I am overlooked a lot and often forgotten by everyone around me. These moments of exploration are my own and in some selfish way I want them to remain so.

"I'm not sure it's a good idea," I finally muster up the courage to answer. "I think you would get bored after a few days, and Mother would have my head. You think she annoys you now, wait until you disappear for chunks at a time."

His gaze deepens, and I swear he can detect the half-truths.

"Would you allow me to go if I found you more information about that precious flower of yours?" He smiles as my body stiffens. "I know a lot of things, a lot of people, and a lot of secret places."

As soon as he mentions the flower, I know he's been hiding in the tunnels connecting to Father's study. As bored, energetic children growing up in a castle, we learned the ins and outs of everything. Especially the secret passageways.

"What could you possibly know about it?"

"Unlike you and our brother, I actually mingle with the people of our kingdom."

"You mean drink and gossip with them in taverns?"

He can't fight off his smile. "Drunk or sober, the people tell me things. I've heard many stories about that flower. Some utter nonsense but others are different, and I can feel a bit of truth in their stories. I might even have a lead on where you can get a map of the isle."

"Impossible."

"Is it? You think over the span of thousands of years, no one has ever ventured there or charted the land. I know you're smart enough to know better."

I release the tension in my jaw and let a hefty breath loose. "And where is this *map*?"

"You only get to know if I'm promised a spot on this expedition." He holds out a hand for me to shake.

"And how do we know if this map is legit or not?"

He withdraws his hand and thinks it over before surrendering a shrug. "We don't. Just like our father has no clue if this man who brought him news of the flower is telling the truth. We're all going in blindly. But if the map turns out to be real, it would get us one step closer to finding the mystic flower." He holds his hand back out, "Come on, brother, it's one trip. Some brother bonding time will do us good."

I am really going to regret this, but if what he is saying is true, then the map could make everything easier. Putting my hand in his, we shake on it. "You better get that map. If I don't see it by the time we board for Farella Isle, I will leave you at the port and wave goodbye."

His eyes grow childlike, filling with utter delight. "We have a deal."

5
ARIAH

My mother finishes peeling her fifth potato while I still scrape at my first. The way the blade in her hand effortlessly glides over the skin is smooth, like she doesn't touch it at all but manages to remove the cleanest layer. Once she has enough potatoes, she moves on to peeling the carrots, again skinning four before I even touch my first.

She doesn't speak to me. Not even a subtle glance or a hint of a smile is pathetically tossed my way.

After seeing Luna and running into one of the council members, I wasn't in the mood to deal with my sister, so I went to the creek for a bit. It allowed me to work on some of my sketches using Shea's flower for inspiration. I spent a good three hours there, but I could only stall for so long.

Once I hit the outskirts of the village, I took the road of Willows Path until my parents' cottage came into view. I noticed a familiar carriage parked outside. It took me all of two seconds to realize my sister had already heard the news and so kindly shared it with my parents before I could.

Now, Jaleese sits in the corner of our kitchen with one hand on her ballooning belly and the other pops persinp berries into her mouth. The berries are as yellow as the dress that tightly clings to her swollen frame. It's not my favorite color but it does suit the red undertones of her dark umber skin.

She wears a white fabric bracelet embroidered with flowers that I had given her on her wedding day. She doesn't wear the bracelet often, and I can't help but think this might be a small slight to me and my decision.

"So, Ariah, I saw that Mrs. Kimpol's shop was closed. Where has she gone?" She continues to rub her belly and leans back in the chair. She doesn't say it in a nosy tone but like she's trying to break the tension she's caused.

"Her and her husband went up to Picktum Creek, and she gave me a few days off."

"I miss those days. Jerimi and I haven't taken a trip in a long time. Nothing but you, nature, and your loved one. The best things about life if you ask me." This time she smiles, and I feel the snub she undeniably throws my way.

"Aww"—I pretend to pout—"I hope you enjoyed them. Probably won't happen anytime soon with the baby coming and all. Can't have too much fun after having a child."

This only makes Jaleese smile more.

Despite our disagreements with each other and the routes we take in life, I don't feel any less loved by her. She has found something that works for her and I'm happy. It may not happen as soon as I'd like, but I know one day she'll understand my position.

"Ariah," my mother says dryly, causing both Jaleese and me to jump. It's the first time she has spoken to me since I've been home. "Can you get one of the smaller wine jugs and then tell your father supper will be ready in twenty minutes. He's been in that room all day. Can't imagine what those fumes are doing to his mind."

One thing accepting the proposal would have given me was

the chance to run my own home. I love my parents, but I'm itching for a place of my own. Maybe with the coins Mrs. Kimpol gave me today, I can start to save for a place. It would be frowned upon for a woman to live on her own unless widowed, but how much more could council hate me?

Making my way to the small cellar where we keep wine, oils, and other nonperishables, I find one of the smaller wine jugs. It weighs no more than fifteen pounds and I carry it up the steps easily, using my foot to shut the door behind me.

Instead of going back to the front of the house, I make my way to a shed-like building my father built. It also acts as a greenhouse and it's where he does most of his apothecary work. Not bothering to knock, I let myself in. I set the jug down on a nearby desk and follow the music notes of a piano farther into the space.

There is a maze of plants, and the walls are covered in bookshelves that possess hundreds of books and glass vials. The deeper inside I go, the more the air fills with a rotten egg scent and I cover my nose to keep from gagging.

Rounding one of the corners, I come face to face with a large birdcage and one very yellow cockatoo named Lemon.

"Ariah's coming. Ariah's coming," Lemon squawks to alert my father. There is no surprising him with Lemon around.

"Thank you for the introduction," I whisper near the cage and pet his head.

At the sound of my name, I see my father's head pop up from behind two beakers he is working with at his desk. In one beaker rests a red-colored liquid looking like over-soaked berries. In the other is a toxic, green mixture that emits an even greener mist, and I wonder if that is where the awful smell is wafting from.

Removing a round set of eye protectors from his face, Father tosses them on the table and comes to me with arms wide open. In one fluid movement, he wraps me in his arms and squeezes me in a comforting embrace, much like the ones I used to get as a child.

Pulling away he grips my shoulders and searches my eyes. "Well? How did it go? Who's the lucky fella?"

His eyes are puffy, either from wearing the protectors too long or messing with late night experiments. There are little green leaves that stick out of his dark hair, and despite messing with different substances all day, he smells like fresh rainwater and cucumbers.

"Jaleese hasn't been in here babbling?" He shakes his head. "Oh, well, I told them 'no.'"

"No?"

"Yes."

"Yes, you told them 'no.'" I let him take a few moments to process the news. "And does your mother know?"

"She does," I say with irritation.

"*Jaleese*," we both utter at the same time.

He lets go of my shoulders and takes a step backwards before giving me a big smile. "Good on you. No one deserves you anyways." I exhale like I've been holding my breath for several minutes. "And your mother will come around. She just wants a good life for you, that's all."

"I think I have a pretty good one." This makes his smile grow.

"It's not too bad is it." He tosses me a wink. "I assume you're here to tell me it's time for supper."

"You assume correctly." I wander over to his desk. "And what have you been working on?"

"Mr. and Mrs. Simol's newborn has an unusual heartbeat, and they asked me for something that might help. I'm trying to use the gentlest ingredients I can think of, but now it's all about..."

"Finding that seamless combination," I finish his favorite saying.

"Exactly." He gives me a wink and then points his head to the door. "Best to not keep your mother and sister waiting. Come on." He pushes my head playfully and takes the wine jug. "Should we grab the bigger one to make it through supper?"

"Not a bad idea."

To my surprise, inside Jerimi, Jaleese's husband, is waiting at the table. His sleeves are up and utensils are in hand. All he needs is food.

Jerimi is a boulder of a man, his colossal frame looking like he is about to snap the wooden chair in half. He works at the village quarry and is one of the kindest souls I've ever met. Far too good for Jaleese, but I won't tell her that.

We eat in silence, and anytime someone starts a conversation it is short-lived and about as dry as the wine I brought in from the cellar.

Just as I'm about to take another sip, I see my mother put her fork down and dab at her lips with a napkin before looking my way. *Oh boy.*

"So, Ariah," she begins, and I watch a slight line form between her eyebrows. "You've made your decision. No one will give you a hard time for it." Her eyes drift to Jaleese and then back to me. "But have you thought over the consequences? What will you do if you see any of the council members again?"

"Too late," I mumble, stuffing in a bite of rabbit stew.

"What?"

"One came into Luna's shop when I was there." I pile in another bite. "Not long after the rejection."

I go for a third bite, but she reaches out and pushes my hand down. "And what did he say?"

I shrug. "Nothing really. He got some pastries and said, '*I'll be seeing you soon, Miss Tyddle,*' and then he left." My family passes glances at each other. "I just need people to trust me." Exhausted with all the talk about today, I plead my last case.

My mother exhales a long breath before taking a sip of wine. "Fine," she utters after setting the cup down. It's subtle and creeps up slowly, but eventually she offers me a smile. A genuine one. "We trust you. And from here on out, no one"—her eyes drift to Jaleese—"and I mean, no one, will pester you about your decision."

"Really?" I ask, with a potato hanging halfway out of my mouth. It's not the reaction I was expecting.

"Really."

Jerimi leans over and gives a small punch to my arm. "We got you."

"Thank you..." The potato bursts in my mouth and I chew on it, slow and confused as to what just happened. "That's it?" And now I'm the one bringing it up. "You're not going to tell me how foolish I'm being or how I'll never be able to find a respectable man after this?"

My mother looks at me from above the rim of her cup and sets it down torturously slow as I wait for a reply. "Do you think you're being a fool?"

Jaleese coughs, but we all ignore her. "No."

"And do you think this decision has ruined your chances of finding someone?"

"Maybe here in Foxhead," I answer with a quick certainty.

Her lips twitch. "Good thing the world is bigger than this simple village." Her reassurance soothes me.

"Maybe we could—" Jaleese's comment falls short as she grips her fork and places a hand to her belly. When her breathing returns to normal she tries again. "Maybe we—" She hunches over without finishing the thought and her head hovers above the plate of barely touched food.

She's been having labor pains all day but now they appear to be occurring more frequently. Lifting herself up she takes in a deep breath and a sip of water.

"Sorry, I don't—" This time she cries out before her body

lurches forward and her forehead rests against the table in pain.

"The baby." Jerimi stands, knocking the table with his brawny body. Cups and pitchers spill over and liquid pools on the floor at the side of the table.

"Quick, get her into Ariah's room!" my father shouts, taking her hand and helping her up.

"My room?" I protest. "Absolutely not." It sounds selfish, but the fluids that accompany childbirth are ones I would rather not have soaking into my bed.

"You want her to have the baby on the table, then?"

My mother rushes to the other side of the room, pushing both my father and Jerimi out of the way. "Have we forgotten this used to be her home, too? She has her own room. Galen"— she calls back to my father, heading to the back of the cottage— "get herbs and anything that will assist with pain. Ariah, get wet cloths and sanitize a blade."

"A blade?" Jaleese, Jerimi, and I respond in syncopation.

"The cord, my dear." My mother smooths Jaleese's coarse curls and rushes her away.

I gather the supplies and take them to my mother in Jaleese's former bedroom. My father comes in seconds later with an ample amount of his many concoctions, but then we are both forced out of the room.

We wait and pace outside, both restless, the constant screaming is our only update.

"Ready for that to be you?" my father jokes as I stop pacing and take a seat next to him.

"Absolutely not. Not anytime soon," I reply without a thought, and that only makes him laugh.

"She's so tiny," I say to Jaleese, who looks outright obsessed with her new arrival. "Do you have a name yet?"

Jaleese was in labor for over fourteen hours. Enough time for the night to come and go without one of us getting any rest. Well, all but the newest arrival.

"Peace," Jaleese answers without looking my way.

"Peace Lily Tanden," Jerimi adds.

I have several peace lily plants sitting in my room, and my father has placed an abundance around the house. They aren't consumable, but they help with my breathing.

"Beautiful," I whisper.

"Ariah," my mother says, coming into the room with a piece of paper. "Go into town and get these items, please. Your sister will be here for the night, and I want to make sure we have enough."

"Yes, ma'am," I reply, before giving my sister a kiss on the head. "Congratulations."

"Thank you." Her face is glowing when she looks at me. "Get me something sweet, will you? And don't tell Mother."

"Our secret."

Letting the others get their time in with Peace, I disappear and head into town. The sun is still rising, painting the sky a vibrant purple with hints of fuchsia splattered throughout.

Despite the lack of sleep, I'm wide awake. The crisp morning air rolls over my skin and I can't help touching the fresh dew on the tall grass as I near a bridge next to Willows Path.

Mornings have always been my favorite. Soaking in the serenity is when I get all of my greatest ideas. Any ideas, really. Inspiration for dresses, thoughts of adventure, better under-standing of the meaning of life, and so much more. Today is no different. My thoughts are of my niece and what life with her will be like. Will she like me? Honestly, though, does she really have a choice? Jerimi has no siblings so I'm kind of her only option.

From the bridge, it's only another ten minutes until I reach Luna's parents' bakery. Of course, my mother put their bread and cream puffs on the list. Maybe I should surprise Jaleese and Jerimi with a cake. Luna's mother does make the most delicious orange sponge I've ever tasted. The perfect treat for the perfect celebration.

Inside the bakery, warmth wraps around me and doesn't let go. Behind the counter, I see Mr. Trivy stacking some jars of honey for display and Mrs. Trivy isn't far behind him, sweeping up the morning crumbs.

"Good morning," I call out, hearing my echoes bounce around the room. "Is Luna here? I want to tell her about my new niece."

Mrs. Trivy's eyes round out like moons too big for her sockets. One second, she's behind the counter and the next she's wrapping me in a tight embrace.

"Congratulations to you and your family. Darmen," she calls out to her husband. "Pack up anything this girl wants. Today is a fine day if you ask me."

Mr. Trivy takes the list and starts collecting my mother's items. Luna's mother and father take turns asking me questions, and I'm about ten answers in when I realize there is one person who is not here to share in the joy.

"Is Luna up yet?" I go to place a few coins in Mr. Trivy's hand, but he closes it before I can drop them in.

"This is on us."

It's a kind gesture, but knowing their situation it doesn't feel right not to pay.

"Luna was summoned to council," Mrs. Trivy's shrieks out, excitement overflowing from her. "The divinities have seen our struggle and have sent us aid."

"What do you mean, summoned?" My mouth dries and

items around the shop vibrate in my periphery. It takes several blinks for my vision to return to normal.

She retrieves a scroll from her apron pocket. "They sent an order this morning. She left for council an hour ago. They usually like to space out the marriages, but considering they didn't get one yesterday, they continued down the list. Our precious girl will save us."

"No." My head shaking prevents me from reading anything on the paper. "They can't."

"Don't be irrational." She grabs my hand, her tone soothing. "This is a good thing for us all."

I can't listen to her, and shove the scroll back her way as I run out of the shop and into the street, where I nearly collide with a wagon going at full speed. Narrowly escaping a tragic end, I keep going and make my way to the village center where the council building is located.

Slowing near a fountain, I hear bells chime. I hear eight rings before the dongs stop. Nearing the building, I spot Morren Beetlerum out front with an older man who looks an awful lot like him. Morren has on a finer suit today, one that looks like he's ready to marry in this instant if given the chance. That thought alone sends my heart into hysteria and my chest becomes tight, as if a thousand pounds have just fallen on it.

Digging in my pockets, I fish for my spray and take in two puffs. As I get closer to the entrance, I see one of the doors open and out comes Luna. My eyes drift to Morren, who grins wildly.

Luna, is in a rose gold dress that sweeps over the cobblestones, making it hard for anyone to miss her. Her hair is pinned in a tight bun with a few loose curls. The color of ripened red berries sweeps her lips and coal dusts her eyes. Through the decorations on her face, she holds a look that suggests she's ready to kill.

She walks up to where I wait and then straight past me, purposely ignoring me.

"What happened?" I whisper, struggling to keep up with her pace.

"What do you think happened?" she spits out bitterly.

Tugging on her arm. "Well, you said no, right? They can't do that."

"They said my parents' debt would disappear and I would be given a life people only *dream* of." No wonder her parents were so cheerful. It doesn't sound like a bad deal for people in their position, but I know Luna doesn't want this.

My eyes roll back. "Council should be ashamed of themselves."

"Them?" She stops and spins before taking a step closer. She's only a few inches taller than me, but at this moment she stands over me like a towering tree. "All you had to do was say yes. I wouldn't be in this position so soon if you had just stuck with tradition."

"That's unfair." I too, take a step closer ridding any intimidation, and we are both crossing the line into each other's spaces. "They would have come after you, eventually. They go after everyone."

"Maybe so, but they saw us together yesterday and that moved me up on their list. If he couldn't have you, then I'm sure the best friend will do." When she's done, she sucks in a deep breath, as if she's trying to keep calm. "I have to go. I have to go tell my parents the *good* news."

"I really am sorry." She stops with my whisper. "I didn't think it would lead to this."

"Me either." Her eyes fill with water, but she holds her tears in. "I have to go. I'll see you around...maybe."

She leaves me standing there. We could easily walk back together since my home is in the same direction, but I know she doesn't want to.

"Miss Tyddle," a familiar voice calls from behind me, spreading a fire inside. I turn to see the man with the snow-beard. My hand clenches into a fist and I'm tempted to let it loose. "Good thing I caught you. Just wanted to inform you that a request was sent off to the Queen this morning. After your defiance yesterday, we realized that *all* marriages should be overseen by that of council. Why have people choose and worry about marriage when we can assist and make it easier? Of course, your dear friend will take your place in the Beetlerum house, but I assure you we will find you another match."

I want to slap the grin off his face. "How *kind* of you. I hope the Queen takes it under a long and thoughtful consideration."

He tips his hat to me. "Must be off now. I have wedding plans to attend to."

6

IANN

A blade comes crashing down onto the butcher block, severing a leg from the unfeathered bird. The carcass is far too large to be that of a chicken or even a pheasant. I'm thinking, turkey. It's a waste, in my opinion, the driest bird I've ever eaten. Not enough sauce in all of Saden can redeem the bland meat.

The chef whips his head in my direction and quickly offers a bow as I enter the kitchen. Others in the vicinity follow suit, offering a bow of their own.

"Excuse me for intruding," I say, moving through the kitchen as it's the fastest way to my study. Going through the halls would leave me exposed and at risk of being found by my mother.

Once the party began, she let me enjoy a whole hour of it before pulling me aside and dragging me off for a *surprise*. That surprise being a room full of gorgeous, and most *importantly*, eligible women. It's a pure fantasy to most, but I saw the mask of well-intention for the trap that it was.

My mother's two primary focuses in life are one, to worry

about her children and two, make sure my brothers and I are married off and produce heirs as soon as possible.

While I have every intention of meeting a woman and marrying one day, I would like to do it on my own terms and in my own time. Not by selecting one from a room full of strangers, in front of my mother nonetheless. If it was up to her, she would arrange a marriage for me herself. But just as my parents married for love, they vowed to let us do the same.

As soon as she began interviewing each of the girls with pointless questions, I took it as an opportunity to get away and snuck out when she wasn't paying attention. I give her a few more minutes before she sends Esha after me.

I can now see why Deean wants to leave so badly. This is the first time she's pulled something like that with me, and I can't imagine how many *coincidental* rooms full of women Deean has had to endure. Although, something tells me he fancies the opportunities more than I do. A room full of women who would do anything for the opportunity to be close to the crown, and him at the center of it all.

Passing through the kitchen, I pocket some cheese and bread. Right before I reach the exit, I spot a bottle of apple bourbon next to some mini tarts. Both placed there with temptation.

A drink isn't usually what I resort to when stress arises, but what could it hurt? I snag the bottle and a few tarts before making my exit.

The hall is quiet. The only sound that drifts my way is the distant music from the ballroom. It's another thing I'm glad to be getting away from.

Finding the stairs, I make my way up. A few guards stop and bow, but none of them dare question where I'm going. I pass the painting of explorer James Iann Venark, the very explorer my name derives from, and continue my ascent.

Walking in the opposite direction of my room, I follow the

golden carpet to the end of the hall. Verging right, I come to a hidden set of stairs behind a large statue of one of the divinities. Unlike the other set of stairs, these are crafted of stone instead of wood and allow the coldest air to bounce between the narrow hallway's walls.

As a child I was terrified of coming up here, but the older I got, the more I realized that its seclusion and mystery were the best parts.

Darkness greets me when I open the door. "I've missed you," I whisper into the room. It's the first time I've been up here since being home and what better time to visit than when my family is hosting a ball.

Cautiously making my way to a table in the dark, I set the bourbon and food down and proceed to stumble a few more steps to a fireplace.

Along the mantle I feel for the two nille stones—stones taken from deep within the Kryten Mountains—they cause massive sparks when struck together. They also work well when struck with iron, but I find the best results are with two of the same stones. Their smooth exterior rests in my hand as I bend down and hold them over pieces of wood in the fireplace. It takes no more than two scrapes before sparks shoot out and ignite the top log that quickly spreads to the others.

Light stretches out over the darkened room, and I use the fire to help me light lanterns and candles. If I wanted more light, I could ask some servants to help with the candles on the chandelier, but that would disrupt the solace of this place. It might also alert my mother, so no, thank you.

If I'm going to hide away, I might as well make my time useful. Snacking on the bread and cheese, I wander to my bookshelves. There aren't a lot of books on the Ivian Flower, but I do know of a few that mention it.

I take *The Forbidden* by H.R. Loving. It's not so much about the flower but his attempts to study plants native to Farella Isle.

Then there is *Everlasting* by B.E. Quinn, which documents accounts of people who have claimed to be immortal. The last book, and the one covered in the most dust, is *Petals of Time* by Donohue Stephens, which is a children's fictional story about a boy and his mother who get stuck on the island because of a shipwreck and discover an edible flower that gives them remarkable powers. The author completely made it up, but I grab it anyway, secretly hoping it might hold some truths.

With the dim light from a lantern on my desk and bourbon in hand, I dive in with *The Forbidden*, marking anything about the isle that could be helpful. The parts about the plants are most interesting. It's been years since I've read this book and I've forgotten a lot of the specimens he documented. Some are even located here in Saden, ones I use for my own apothecary purposes. I'm not nearly as good at apothecary as I am at being an explorer, but it's still a passion of mine.

An hour later, I slam the book shut. There is no mention of a mysterious flower or details about the island. Judging from the pages' contents, he didn't even make it far enough onto the island to discover anything worth mentioning. Stayed near the shore and left before fate could get the wrong idea. Smart, but unhelpful.

Defeated, I move on, but as I reach for the next book, a creaking sound from across the room pulls my attention. My head flies up to see a shadowed figure and my hand drifts to the top drawer where I keep a spare dagger, unless someone has touched things in my absence.

As the figure moves closer, I stop the pursuit of the blade and any short-lived fear begins brewing with anger. Light cascades around curves, curves I once knew all too well.

Thana.

Her dress is composed of a tight, copper corset that makes up the top half. Extremely fitted. At the hips, the material begins to puff out and there isn't much of a difference about it compared to all the other gowns the women in court wear.

Reaching my desk, she curtsies but never severs our gaze. "It's good to see you, my precious Iann. Thought I'd find you hiding in here." She strolls leisurely to the other side of the desk, approaching my seat. "You know how I always get so worried when you go on your *little* adventures." The belittlement strikes a small nerve, but I don't stop her from moving nearer. "Why didn't you send word you were back?"

"Didn't realize I was supposed to," I say, pouring myself another glass. "I certainly don't know your whereabouts. Why would you want to know mine?"

She falls into my lap once I have my drink. Her brown skin glistens with tiny gold particles that she has applied, and I wonder if they can be found on every inch of her body.

The thought of tearing off her dress crosses my mind, but I keep one hand gripped around my glass and the other on the arm of my chair. She is no longer mine and I'm assuredly, not hers.

"We can change all of that," she whispers into my ear while playing with my collar. The scent of jasmine and musk sends my mind into a frenzy. She moves her hand to my face and cups my cheek while her thumb faintly brushes over my bottom lip. I fight the temptation not to nibble at it. "What do you say, my precious Iann? You and I were great together. I know I made mistakes, but I promise to give you everything you desire." She moves my head until I'm forced to look into those soul-sucking hazel eyes. "And I mean *whatever* you desire."

Pulses tap throughout my body and my heartbeat knows no end, or a steady speed for that matter. Between my father's impossible request, Deean's demands to join in on said impossible request, and my mother's constant push for marriage, my nerves are spiked, making me realize why I prefer to stay away from Saden. But what if, for one night, I bury all my worries in her? *Just one night.*

Once upon a time, all Thana Hagens had to do was look in my direction, and I would have given her my father's kingdom if that's what it meant to keep her. But pain hardens one's heart and time may not always heal, but it definitely makes me more skilled at recognizing one's deceit. And Thana was, and still is, full of it.

I could have my way with her, she and I both know that. Satisfy that ever so small craving and be done with her—tossing her aside like she's done with countless others.

Taking her wrist, I pull her hand from my face. "I see you haven't changed much. My brother, turn you down finally?" The question stings us both, but she'll recover.

"Don't be like that." She moves in, pulling herself to my lips, but she only meets my cheek. Her soft lips brush my skin. "Fine." She pulls away and moves from my lap.

There is coughing that comes from the door and we both find Esha standing there uncomfortably. "I'm sorry to disturb you, Your Highness, but your father, the King, is requesting you meet him in the war room."

Finishing my drink, I set it on the desk and stand. "Thank you, Esha. Tell him I'm on my way." Esha bows and takes his leave.

Without a word or glance, I move past Thana.

"You will never find someone like me," she calls after me, like it's some kind of threat.

Turning to her, for a split second, I see the brilliant woman my heart once pranced for. But there is no prancing, no more critters that used to stir my stomach, or breaths that used to be caught with a simple look.

"Oh, I don't know about that. I'm awfully good at finding things." The corners of her lips twitch upwards. "But you're right. I won't find someone like you because...I'm no longer looking for you." And then her smile vanishes.

Before she can retort, I walk away and head to the war room, leaving her alone.

"There he is," my father shouts from across the grand room, his echoes traveling to me.

The war room is always the chilliest place in the castle. The space is nearly the same size as our main ballroom and could hold a few hundred people if given the opportunity. But I've never seen more than twenty in here at a time; a mix of ambitious people, ready to offer their opinions to the King.

Vast statues occupy the spaces on the blackened stone walls. All are replicas of the rulers who once controlled Saden. My father has one nearest the large, round table, and I imagine Marcel will have one of his own when the time comes.

Approaching the table, I see Marcel, my father's advisor Kinnry, and one of our army commanders, Devona.

Kinnry and Devona stand and bow before I take my seat. Both are dressed up tonight. Like everyone else, they came for a celebration and didn't shy away from fine linens and gold jewelry.

Despite the numerous fireplaces burning, a dark ambiance fills in the room, and I think that's what the designer intended. This isn't a room for the weak.

Taking a seat, my father holds up a letter. The envelope on the table next to him is empty, the wax seal is a deep orange—a color closer to red. The symbol on it is that of a fox with a crown on its head. It's not a seal we see often in this kingdom. It's one that could get someone killed if they aren't an active member of the King's court. It is the seal of Haymel, and only those with official crown business are allowed to send and receive anything from the enemy territory.

"Queen Cayleen would like to arrange a truce between our kingdoms," my father starts, and both Kinnry and Devona shift in their seats. "She has written in great detail what she requires and what she's willing to give up if we agree to this truce."

"Rich of her," Devona says, under her breath before adjusting once again in her seat.

"She's killed countless soldiers and citizens of ours and audaciously sends a letter demanding things of us?" Kinnry chimes in.

"We are kings and queens. We always make demands," my father retorts. "Of course, this will open up conversation for us to make demands of our own. It will also provide opportunities for trade and allow for easier travel between the kingdoms." Reading further he continues, "She has also extended an invitation to a ball hosted in our honor. She wishes me to be in attendance."

Devona leans forward in her seat, shifting in a dress that was made to look like armor but is much easier to move about in during events like these. Her eyes are as clear as Lake Alma, an immense blue spreading throughout. "If you don't mind me being forthright, Your Grace." She waits for my father's acknowledgment before continuing, "You, walking into Haymel after all these years, is a death trap. Surely, she will limit the number of guards we can send to protect you. She will have the advantage and Queen Cayleen will certainly use it."

Leaning back in his chair, he props his elbows on the arms of his seat and folds his hands under his chin.

This opportunity is perfect for getting access to the flower. He can even use it as a bargaining chip in the truce. Giving Haymel access to trade and travel might allow us access to Farella Isle in return.

My father doesn't speak, but I know that's exactly what his

mind is on. But I have to agree with Devona on this one. He would be walking into an ambush.

"Marcel," he calls to my brother, whose gaze is caught in the silver swirls of the black wooden table. He wears clothes similar to our father—a cream-colored coat embroidered with gold to match the crowns on their heads. My father's, of course, is bigger and carries stones far more precious than anything in the room. "What would you do? Make peace with our enemies in the west or continue the division to ensure protection?"

He's testing him. Always has. Deean and I would get a few political lessons here and there but never to the extent Marcel has received from him. As future king, he is to know all things about our way of life, and I wonder just how much my father has shared with him about this upcoming expedition.

Marcel clears his throat and pulls his eyes away from the table. "I cherish and miss our grandfather dearly, but the war between our kingdoms started with him and Queen Cayleen's father. Not even she had anything to do with it. Maybe it's time to show our enemies redemption." He struggles to find a word.

"Redemption?" Kinnry grumbles, clearly against the extended truce. "Surely that will be seen as a weakness on our end."

Marcel only smiles.

Looking back at my father, I can't tell if he agrees or not. While redemption is a route someone like me would take, it doesn't feel right coming from Marcel. I know my brother, and letting things go is not something that comes easily to him.

He once stopped speaking to me for an entire year because he thought I had destroyed one of his favorite telescopes when we were kids. In actuality it was Deean, and it's still a secret I haven't shared to this day. But Marcel only started speaking to me again because he wanted to play with my new toys.

Even after the incident with him and Thana, I didn't resort to stooping so low. I adjust in my seat before memories bring forth such cruelty; clearing my throat, I turn my attention to my brother. "Let's say we offer them redemption. You still think it wise to send our father there to potentially be attacked, or worse, killed?"

"No, I don't," he responds like he already knew this question was coming. "I agree with the Commander. I think instead of sending the King, we aim a little lower."

Instantly understanding his point, I interrupt him. "You? You'll go in his place?"

"I'm less of a threat and not as important. I think it's our best move."

Kinnry and Devona eye each other, their expressions hard to read. Then a thought comes to me. It's not something I want to do, but if I'm to go after the flower, it makes the most sense.

"Send me," I say, turning to my father. "I'm not your direct heir and therefore not nearly as valuable, and I'm not a threat to her. I could convince her to open all of her roads and passages for trade." The words come out slowly, making sure he gets the emphasis on what I'm trying to say.

My father leans his arms on the table, thinking over the opinions of everyone in the room.

"You will both go." Marcel and I stare at each other in bewilderment. "Sending two of my sons shows her there is no threat and no fear. If she wants to meet with me, then let this interaction be a test. Commander Devona will accompany you. I shall write the Queen of Haymel back and confirm your attendance at the ball. You depart in three weeks, so make the proper preparations. Now, go enjoy the night before it's over."

Kinnry and Devona are the first to leave. Marcel takes his time but eventually exits the war room.

"Three weeks," I say, sitting back in my chair. "Exactly the amount of time you told Rolley we would depart."

My father grins. "The Queen's letter arrived a few days after Rolley showed up and shared the story of his great-grandfather.

The timing couldn't have been more perfect. I didn't make this clear before, but no one is to know of the flower or of your mission in Haymel. You must convince the Queen to let you journey to Farella. Lie. Scheme. Cheat. Do what you must. If she forbids it, then you have my permission to travel there without her knowing."

Shock ripples through me. Going there without her permission is a death wish and he seems to have no concern.

His eyebrows burrow together and he leans away from me. "Sorry," he whispers. "Don't put yourself in danger." He reaches out and places a hand on mine. "Just promise me you'll try to convince the Queen?"

"What's going on? You don't even know if this damn flower exists and you're willing to risk your sons for it? Why this sudden obsession?"

"I wouldn't ask you if it wasn't dire. I can't tell you anything, but I need this. I need this to be true."

"Are you dying?"

"We're all dying."

My eyes roll. "Don't be a smart ass. And that's not a no."

He chuckles. "No, I'm not. Just trust me on this."

Again, he's cryptic and there has to be something bigger at play here. Why do I always find it difficult to say no?

"I will go to Haymel for you. I will try to get permission to cross the Queen's waters, but if she says no, I am coming back. I will not risk my life for a secret you're not willing to share."

"Fair enough." He digs in his pocket and pulls out the black foxtail Rolley had given him. "And while you're there, do some digging on who may have left this. Whoever works for the Queen and entered our lands without permission, is likely to know the whereabouts of Rolley's great-grandfather." He stands, placing a hand on my shoulder. "Go have fun before the night's over. Pretty sure I saw Thana Hagens roaming about."

"Already saw her, and no thanks." I tuck the foxtail into my pocket.

"For the best, I suppose. She kind of scares me. And your mother's not too keen. Maybe you should let your mother try to find you a suitable match," he teases.

"She already tried, but I snuck out when she was occupied with interrogating the women." His laughs boom throughout the room, and I have little doubt he already knew of her plans.

"I thought her and her sister were up to no good. They've been sneaking about for the past few days."

"Thanks for the warning." His laughter continues to echo. "Goodnight." I turn my back to him before I crack a smile, and leave him with his humour.

7
ARIAH

It has been four days since my fight with Luna, and less than a day since a messenger delivered her wedding invitation. Council wasted no time spreading the *happy* news. Greedy bastards. I wonder what they'll be getting out of this beloved union.

The solicitation came in thick, expensive parchment. The type one only splurges on for the most important things. It was bound by a lace ribbon and held a single azalea—not because they are Luna's favorite flower, because they aren't—because they are Haymel's kingdom flower, and how dare they not represent the Queen in a practice she hasn't officially put into law.

The invitation read:

> To the Tyddel Residence,
> Galen, Adreena, and Ariah Tyddel, you are cordially invited to the union ceremony of Morren Beetlerum and Lunessa Trivy. The ceremony shall be held at the Beetlerum Estate on the eleventh day of

*Hellera at seven o'clock. It will be an evening of
pure joy.*

 In celebration,
 The Council of Foxhead

It was short and straight to the point. A waste of paper, in my opinion.

Today marks the tenth of Hellera, and in only a day my best friend will be married off to a man she doesn't know. A man who was meant for me. I hate that she's in this position, but is it bad to be glad it's not me?

Ella, my black-and-orange striped, chubby cat, nibbles at the silk wrap around my head, the way she does every morning, and I know it's officially time to get up.

The sun is slowly waking; a few rays of light break through my window, but the corner of my room furthest away still remains in the shadows. I'm surprised after last night's rain to even see the sun coming up.

Pulling myself out of bed, my nightgown drags across the floor until I reach the fireplace, where I take a bellow to the dying fire, breathing new life into it. The flames illuminate the remaining dark corners and spread a needed heat throughout the room.

Mornings are usually easy, but the past few days have been difficult. Last night, I stayed up far too late sketching and stressing.

Not ready to get dressed for the day, I sit at my desk and play with yesterday's drawings. My newest piece is a midnight-blue gown, tight in the bust and around the hips, resembling that of a mermaid, with a long train running down the back. Crystal-like beads are sewn all over. The hardest part is the embroidered design I want on the torso. Everything I've tried seems overdone and not worthy of the piece.

A knock at the door sends Ella jumping into my lap. A second later my mother stands in the doorway.

She has on a moss-green dress that compliments her complexion. Her braids are tied up and she has placed golden clasps within her tresses. She looks like a walking embodiment of a divinity.

"Your father left for the Simol's early this morning. Their baby is having a hard time." She traces a finger over my design. "Beautiful as always."

"Thank you." I place Ella on the ground. "I should get ready for work. Mrs. Kimpol should be back today."

My mother holds out a letter for me before I can get up. "Came for you this morning."

She squeezes my shoulder at my heavy breath. It's a letter from Mrs. Kimpol telling me she and her husband have traveled to another city and she will send word when she returns. No wonder she gave me so much money.

"You can come with me to see Jaleese and Peace. She has a physician coming in to make sure Peace is nice and healthy. She trusts your father, but our new mother wants to be certain." She lifts my head up to her. "You can't hide in this room, Ariah."

"I'm not hiding." Only sulking, but she doesn't need to know that. "I'll go see them tomorrow. I think I might take a walk."

"Good. Maybe you can stop and see Luna while you're out?"

"I don't think she wants to see me."

She takes a seat on the edge of my bed. "Luna made her choice. She may have had to make it because you turned them down, but still, she had a choice. Just like you had one. I don't think one is right over the other, but you must each deal with your decisions. It's called life. Throwing away a lifelong friendship isn't worth it."

Maybe she's right, but it means one of us has to admit we

were wrong. Both of us are far too stubborn for that. Maybe I can bend this one time.

"Why Foxhead?" I ask, and see the confusion on my mother's face. "The amount of villages in Haymel and you had to choose this one."

She releases a pathetic laugh, and I watch her eyes drift to the window and become distant. "Your father and I weren't given much of a choice. Plus, Foxhead isn't the only village with these practices. Even the Queen arranges marriages that benefit the crown. Us common folk are no different."

My parents rarely talk about life before they moved to Foxhead. I know that they used to live within the city limits of the castle. My father ran an apothecary shop with an elderly gentleman and says my mother used to come in everyday and pretend she was buying something for her family.

She claims she was truly buying something for a sick family member, but I once got her to confess that my father was the primary reason for her visits. She said he had the greenest eyes she had ever seen and with one look, knew he was the kindest soul in the entire world. She couldn't rationalize it, but she knew right away that their fates would forever be intertwined.

She pats my hand and pulls herself up from my bed. "I have to get to your sister's. Go get some fresh air. Clean. Cook. Write. Do something to distract yourself."

Leaving me behind, she takes off for Jaleese's, and I take her advice and stop sulking inside.

I don't make my way to the pond as planned. Instead, Ella and I steep a cup of tea and tend to the garden I have been neglecting for days. A few of the tomatoes are ripe for picking and I get a few good cukes for supper tonight, which I should probably have ready by the time my parents get back.

Once I'm done with the vegetables, I move to the flower section of the garden. We have rows and rows of assorted flowers. As always, I check on my babies first. We have four different beds of hydrangeas. Each one with different types of soil, or as my father would say, "Soil with different levels of acidity." The different acid levels help produce different colors in the petals.

I wonder if I let a few magis worms roam free, as Shea suggested, if the blossoms would turn out like the ones he had given me? I'm certain my father has some in his study.

Many have warned me about my love for hydrangeas—they're just flowers. And yes, I know the flowers represent our kingdom's greatest threat—Saden—but just because those in power have issues with our neighbor doesn't make those people my enemy, too. I snip a few pink blooms and pair them with some tall astilbes. Perfect for the vase above the sitting room mantel.

By the time I leave the house, the sun's position is high in the sky. I can't decide if I just want to take a stroll to clear my mind or if I want to sit by the pond.

In case I decide on the pond, I brought along some food and a sketch book—I'm thinking a belt of sorts would be a pleasant touch to my latest piece. Also in my bag is my medicinal spray. While the temperature is perfect, not requiring a coat or the need to remove a layer, it creates the perfect opportunity for creatures and critters to roam around carefree, as they should, and most leave particles in the air that can sometimes make it difficult to breathe.

When I was younger, Luna and I went on one of our many grand adventures. It wasn't too far from my parents' cottage, but at the time, it had felt like we had traveled for miles. We came to rolling fields covered in pastel purple flowers. Ones I had never seen before at that age. After exploring the field, my chest became tight. The running didn't help either. That was the day I learned lilacs and I would never be friends. It was also the day my father started making the spray mixtures for me to carry. If it wasn't for Luna's quick thinking and running to get my parents, I would not be here.

The pond is near a bridge that connects the village with other homes on the outskirts. Approaching the water, I see a few people fishing and farther off, kids are playing tag near a grouping of trees, some of the trunks covered in mud from last night's rain. Then I spot one lonely soul who sits on a blanket shaded by one of the grand oaks.

Luna.

She looks up in my direction, making it impossible to walk away unnoticed. Her face is stern and suggests she wants to be alone. That is until it melts and puddles into a smile. I don't deny her one back and I'm thankful she's even smiling at all. I suck in a breath and walk her way.

"Mrs. Kimpol's shop was closed again this morning," she says, and I notice as soon as I reach her blanket, she is fiddling with her hands. "I thought the pond was the next best place to find you."

"You were looking for me?" I sit next to her and look out at the pond. Sensing her about to respond, I speak quickly. "I'm sorry the consequences of my decision impacted you. You have to know that was never my intention."

"I know." She nudges me. "It came with a shock, is all. My parents would have probably disowned me if I told the council no. I wanted to though." We look at each other and she puffs up her chest. "I told myself if Ariah could do it, so can I. It was on the tip of my tongue until they brought up my parents' debt. Said they would add on another ten thousand moinlings to their dues if I declined. They don't even have the first ten thousand. The thought of them working their lives away and then it falling on me, and future generations, until it's all paid up was agonizing to think about. A crushing weight that would destroy anyone. They offered to make it disappear if I agreed to marry Morren Beetlerum."

"We could disappear, you know. Go east, sneak our way into

Saden or maybe even Ethmay. O-o-oh, we could venture into the Land of Moonlight. No one will find us there."

She laughs and I join her until I see tears fall. I waste no time wrapping my arms around her. Salty water seeps into my top and I'm pretty sure some snot is mixed with it, but I don't care. I hold her until she wants me to let go.

She sits in the comfort of my arms for a few minutes until she pulls away, wiping any evidence of sadness from her face. "While those are all wonderful options, we would miss our families too much. Plus, I hear you just had a niece. Congratulations, Aunty."

A heavy breath flows out as I sit back down. "You're right. I would miss them too much. And thank you. Her name is Peace."

"Awe, that's a pretty name. I bet Jaleese is obsessed."

"Utterly."

She locks her arm with mine and we watch ducks waddle to the water.

"Now that we're talking again, I want to ask you for a favor."

"No, I do not want to meet your betrothed. I met him once and that was more than enough."

A snort slips out when she laughs. "No, that's not it. I need a dress for tomorrow."

"You don't have a dress? What have you been doing these past couple of days?" I tease.

"Brooding and waiting for an apology from you," she teases right back, and I know our little conflict is over and gone.

"I certainly can't make one from scratch overnight, but I might be able to touch up something I already have. You're about Jaleese's size before the baby. I'll see if she's got anything I can work with."

She pulls me close and plants a kiss on my forehead. "I owe you. My mother found one but it is ghastly—like wearing a fishing net. Made my entire body itch."

"Fine," I cave. "I got you."

My mind starts spinning with ideas. Her ceremony is a day away and I have to make something perfect.

Jaleese has an old, lavender dress. That's definitely Luna's style, and it goes with the marriage custom of *the brighter the better*. The event is close to dusk, so something with longer sleeves will help with any cold the night brings.

Luna and I part ways after a few hours. She needs to get back and help with last-minute arrangements the council is forcing her to do, and I need my workspace.

Taking the same path home, I'm struck with glee. Not because of what Luna is about to embark on but because we're speaking again, and a slither of that happiness is because she asked me for help with the dress. If one thing is going to be perfect about tomorrow, it will be the blushing bride.

"Move girl!" A loud, deep voice calls out from down the road.

Too occupied in thought, I didn't see the carriage speeding my way, and despite me still standing in the road, they make no attempts to slow down.

Jumping so they can pass, I lose my balance and fall into tall grass. I know the grass is going to trigger wheezing, but before I can dig in my bag for the spray, the carriage passes and rolls into a puddle where it then shoots out water from the wheels, spraying my clothes and face. This not only happens once but three times, as three different carriages go by.

You have got to be kidding me. I wonder if all of it has to do with tomorrow.

I curse after them, but they are long gone.

8

ARIAH

Dry mud clings to my skin and clothes. Afraid of what I'll discover, I don't even risk touching my hair. I just had my wash day too. This better not dry out my curls.

Furious with whomever was driving the carriages, I trudge home, role playing exactly what I will say to them and how I will deliver it.

Up ahead, I see my front garden and come to a full stop. Outside my family's cottage are the same three carriages that nearly ran me over.

Continuing on, I get a close-up view of the impeccable condition the carriages are in. The outsides are a metallic brown with a copper finishing, and elegant filigree designs run over the top, doors, and wheels. Each carriage also has an area where bunches of azaleas and fern have been placed as adornments.

There is no way these belong to anyone in Foxhead. We have wealthy villagers, but no one comes this close to this level of rich. Not even Morren Beetlerum.

My hand floats out to the shiny temptation, but suddenly a figure pops up and blocks me.

"What are you doing?" They wear a gold-and-black uniform with a symbol of a fox with a crown on its head. Royal colors and symbols.

Looking the carriage over once more, I inquire, "Who does this belong to?"

"What's it to you? Keep moving."

They turn to walk away, but I place my hand on their shoulder, stopping them. It isn't my wisest move, considering the glimpse I catch of their hand going to their sword, but I have questions. "Firstly, you and your fellow guards need to learn that when someone is walking on a path you are traveling on, it doesn't mean you just keep going at full speed, secondly, be appreciative that mud washes out. Thirdly, I live here, so kindly inform me of what you're doing here."

A head pops out of a carriage window. A woman, with large earrings that brush her shoulders, eyes me with caution. She is in all black with the collar of her frock wrapping tightly around her neck. Golden buttons form a single line from the collar all the way down to her chest, where they disappear and become blocked by the carriage door.

"Your parents are Galen and Adreena?" Her voice is light and alluring, almost like she's trying to trap me in a trance.

I nod. "They are."

"Leave her, Borric." He does as he's told and walks away. She then looks back at me and says, "You can go in now. Enjoy your time...while you can."

"What is that supposed to mean? And who are you?" A smirk is the only thing she gives me before settling back into the carriage.

On the other side, near the gate that runs along the perimeter of the cottage, I find more guards. Seven in total. I speed through the garden and up a few steps, swinging the front door open. Two more guards apprehend me, but a woman from another room tells them to let me in.

Making my way into our dining area, my father meets my gaze first, his eyes widening with concern. My mother, on the other hand, looks furious. She sits across from a woman who has her hands folded. I know my mom's looks, and she's enraged.

"Ariah, dear." My father gets up and gestures to the guest before him. "We have company." *Yeah, no kidding, Father.* "Come give Queen Cayleen a proper greeting."

My throat closes up and I'm unsure if it's from my condition or because the Queen of Haymel is at our table.

My feet move, I think. Edging closer, it's almost as if she's getting further away. Is the Queen really in my home?

Once I'm at her side, I offer the best curtsy I have. I've only ever had to bow to a lord who visited our village once. He was a distant cousin to the Queen and a complete ass.

"Your Majesty." My voice trembles as I bend, but I manage my way through it.

Queen Cayleen stands, and my parents rush to mimic her. "Your mother has talked an awful lot about you and your sister, and let me not forget that new niece of yours." This makes me light up, but when I look at my mother, she's incensed, and all my excitement withers. I even notice my father secretly dropping his hand to squeeze hers. "Ariah, is there somewhere we can go to speak privately?"

Speak privately? My heart works overtime. The Queen of Haymel wants to speak to me alone?

"You may use my study," my father answers. "Right outside. No one will disturb you."

"Thank you, Galen. Ariah can show me the way."

My eyes and mind stay glued to my mother. Something isn't

right with her. When she notices I'm still standing there, ignoring the Queen, she fixes her face. In an instant she smiles, but we both know she's only pretending to be strong.

"Ariah, my girl, go take Queen Cayleen out there so you two can talk."

I nod. "Right this way."

I lead us out of the cottage and to my father's workspace. My mind churns with thoughts that only spiral into more thoughts when suddenly it strikes me why she's here. Council has told her I turned them down. She has come to make it official. But why not just send a letter? She wouldn't come all this way for a girl in a village she doesn't know, let alone care about. Surely posts take longer than five days to arrive. But then it depends if it went by bird or person. I count on my fingers. Yes. Yes, it's only been five days. There is no way she knows. She just can't.

Convincing myself she's not here because of my defiance is one thing, but determining what else she might want is different, and I have nothing.

Walking inside, we pass Lemon who says my name and then calls the Queen "stranger." This brings a faint smile to her face, but it's quick to disappear.

We move closer to my father's desk to be near the fire and with nowhere else to go, we both stop and wait in silence.

Her hair waves like flames in a darkened sky, burnt-orange strands alternating in the darkest night. She makes no attempts to smile back at the pathetic one I offer her. I'm not even sure it constitutes a smile, it is a more nervous twitch that keeps me from saying something stupid in the presence of royalty.

There isn't a soul in this village that hasn't wondered what the Queen of Haymel looks like. There are portraits that have circulated through the years, but the ones I've seen don't measure up to who stands before me. Folding her hands in front of her exquisite hand-beaded gown, she eyes me with all the hesitancy in the world.

A hard swallow gets stuck on the way down and that's when I realize how dry my throat is. Instantly, my eyes dart to the pitcher of water and glasses on my father's desk, but before I can offer her a drink and relieve the ache in my own throat, I see her hands move. Moving to her hips, she displays fingernails that are perfectly shaped with the slightest tip. All nails have been dipped in black and dusted with gold. It's not a particular color I would choose for myself, but it does go well with the cream dress clinging to her amber skin.

She walks, hands still glued to her hips, and does a few circles around me.

"Your parents once served me in court."

What the...Surely, she's at the wrong home. But I think about how scared and upset my parents looked when she arrived. They looked like death showed up personally to collect something they had stolen.

I can't help but chuckle, which makes her stop and tilt her head.

"You think I traveled all this way to be mocked by a little girl?" With three steps closer, she gets within arm's length and places my chin between two fingers. The pressure she forces on my jaw makes me certain she could crush it. "Your parents owe me a debt. One we agreed I could cash in on at any time."

That sounds like a personal issue to me, but with my face still gripped between her fingers, the words are best kept in my head.

"I'm sure they have no problems paying it." My words come out of a crooked mouth as she pushes one side of my face up with her nails. "We aren't destitute."

"I am the Queen of Haymel. I have more money than all the people in our realm combined. Your family's money means nothing to me."

My heart flutters and my shoulders rise higher. My airways narrow and all the gulps in the world aren't satisfying my need for breath.

Seeing me struggle, she lets go of my face and backs away.

"What in all of Haymel is wrong with you, girl?" she shouts with equal parts worry and annoyance.

Digging deep in my pockets, I search until my fingers find the diamond shaped glass container and I immediately draw it to my lips. I spritz the contents in my mouth and inhale deeply before releasing a vast breath. A few minutes later, I'm able to take deeper breaths and my chest doesn't feel as tight.

Sensing eyes on me, I look up and find the Queen staring. "I have difficulties breathing," I explain. "It happens when I panic or exert myself too much. Sometimes even the slightest weather change can set it off." I lift up the once perfume bottle. "My father, being the apothecary that he is, played with different plant extractions and put them in these containers for me. They are an enormous relief."

She blinks a few times, but her eyes are glazed over, her expression hard to read. "Sounds like him." She takes a step closer before continuing on. "Tell me, Ariah, what skills do you possess?"

That's an odd question for a queen to be asking a commoner like me.

"Well...I am a seamstress and work for Kimpol's shop. My dream is to design dresses, though. I made this one, and the one my mom is wearing. Oh, and my friend who is getting married tomorrow, I'll be making her dress." Her lack of emotion crushes my enthusiasm.

"Is that all?"

Ouch, that one stings.

"I mean, I can cook. Sometimes." She's really making me think here. Should I be concerned that I can't think of any other skills?

"How about your apothecary abilities? Do you take after your father?"

"I know very little. Chemistry is something I struggle with."

"And your use of a blade?"

I hesitate. How am I supposed to answer that? "Normal? Mainly just for cooking."

"Archery?"

"I skipped those lessons as a kid."

She begins circling me again, like a bird waiting for their prey to die. "And how about sneaking in and out of places undetected?"

"I...don't...know. I've never tried. Why are you asking these questions?" I spin to her as she passes between me and the desk.

"Have you ever killed someone?" she continues, ignoring my question entirely.

"What? Absolutely not."

She leans against the desk and stares at me, her eyes drift from the hem of my dress that brushes the wooden floor up to my dangling earrings. "Your father's hands shook when he poured my tea." My eyes draw close together, not understanding what she's getting at. "And all your mother did was talk about her children. I didn't think time would make them so fragile. You see, Ariah, I came to collect."

"Collect what?" Her words are not aligning for me.

"Your parents were once a part of my Foxes. Your father could mix the kind of concoctions all other kingdoms were envious of. My favorites were his poisons, though. He once created a mixture that slowly burned a man from the inside out. His flesh began to boil and melted straight off his bones during a coronation. And your mother, well, she was something special. She moved with the night and could track down anything I asked of her. I reckon she has a body total that's more than all the workers in the brothels in Haymel combined.

Though I suspect they brought a different kind of pleasure. A different kind of lust."

Bodies. Poisons. Blades. Is she mad?

Instinctively, I step away from her. I've thought about what it would be like to meet the Queen before, but never something like this. Slowly, the questions and her little monologue set in, and the more it all saturates, the more I'm disturbed.

"Are you calling my parents murderers?" It takes a few attempts to conjure up any kind of coherent sentence, but finally I get it out.

She smiles. "I call them loyalists. You seem to be taking a little longer to get this than I'd like. Your parents are older and have lost some of the qualities I look for in my Foxes. Yet, they still owe me. Instead, I'd like to make a deal with you."

"Me?"

"I promised your parents a safe life here in Foxhead. The chance to live out their love." She looks like she's going to be sick when saying that word. "Under the condition that at any time I could come back and ask for a favor. I didn't think that favor would take nearly thirty years, but here we are." She pulls something from the pocket of her dress, making her ensemble even more desirable. Holding up a letter, she continues. "Ariah Tyddle, I am giving you the opportunity to pay off your parents' debt. If you come back to the castle with me, train under my Foxes, and serve me in court for the next year, I'll consider their debt paid."

"And if I say no?" I ask, trying to get a better glimpse of the paper in her hand.

"Then I say yes to this letter, which will then grant the council of Foxhead permission to marry you off to the highest bidder, which I assume is something you don't want since you denied them." Dammit, she knows. Moving closer, she draws a finger and points it at me. "Better yet, I'll make it a law. Everyone in Haymel shall be forced to marry for the convenience of their village councils. A way for all to serve the crown." She pulls back, thinking of her own words. "That's actually not a bad idea though..."

That's a terrible idea, and to know my "no" would set the new law in motion is sickening.

"Alright, what if I say yes and fail at being one of your so-called Foxes?"

"Then you keep trying until you succeed, or until you or your parents die."

"I want to make conditions of my own." She stays quiet and almost a little too still. "If I do what you ask, you not only make their debt disappear, but you make this absurd practice vanish. No more elders intruding on another's life. And..." I really have nothing else but might as well see what I can get. "And I get to make a dress for you to wear to your most attended event."

"Is that all?"

"You clear my best friend's parents' debt so she doesn't have to marry Beetlerum."

"That one isn't possible. I'm going to attend her wedding tomorrow. It would cause too much of a fuss, and since I have no real reason to end their union, it's a waste. However, I will agree with your previous terms. Your parents' debt, erasing strategic practices, and you may design a dress for me. The two extra promises come with two extra years."

Three years in servitude to the Queen, I should have known she would counter with her own stipulations.

Never in my wildest dreams did I think I would get to meet Queen Cayleen, nor did I think our meeting would result in finding out my parents were in some kind of a cultish group that served her and potentially lead them to do unspeakable things—things the Queen might ask of me.

She makes her way to the door, but before she knocks for her guards, she looks back at me. "No need for an answer right now. You can give it to me tomorrow at your friend's marriage ceremony. Your demands are high and could cost my kingdom a lot, especially that marriage clause of yours." She knocks twice before a guard opens, and she slips away.

And just like that, I must make a choice again. This time between two options of which I have no desire for either.

9
IANN

My carriage vibrates as I shake my leg. No one brings it to my attention, but if it's strong enough to annoy me, then I can only imagine how irritated the driver must be.

Gripping my knee, I force the nervous tic to stop. I don't know why I'm uneasy. I shouldn't be. Can't recall anything I've done that may have solicited attention, but there is something about having a discussion, especially one with my grandmother, that makes me wary.

She isn't cruel, blunt undoubtedly, but she has always been kind to my brothers and me. I would even go as far to say that I compete to be one of her favorites. The other being Deean, of course. She respects Marcel because she has to as her future king, but I would bet all of Saden's coins that she would rather have someone else be the future figurehead of the kingdom.

Esha told me this morning that she requested me to accompany her into town today. Unlike the rest of my family, she and Deean are the two who interact with the townspeople the most. Maybe that's why she has a fondness for him. It's often a thing the two of them do together. I wouldn't mind joining them more often, but being away for great lengths of time makes it difficult.

The carriage door swings open and there is a sudden sway of the box, causing me to shift in my seat as someone joins me inside.

"What are you doing here?" Deean's face scrunches at my presence, and he looks at me like I don't belong. Pointing his head to the seat in front of me, I take the hint that I'm in his spot, and with a quick eye roll, I move.

"Does it really matter where we sit?" I adjust my coat, trying to get comfortable.

The carriage moves yet again as he plunks down. "You're a guest on this little trip of ours, so you sit where I tell you. Remind me again why you're here. I thought you hated going into town."

"You're getting me confused with our brother. Grandmother asked me to join, if you must know." We bicker like we did in childhood. "Where are we going, anyway?"

He folds his right leg over the left, resting it on his knee, before adjusting the button of his coat. "You'll find out."

After the last conversation with our father, I've concluded that even if Deean can locate a map of Farella for me, he can no longer accompany me. If stopping in Haymel is first, it would be unwise to take all three Saden heirs. Right as I'm about to tell him, the carriage door swings open once more and my grandmother gets inside.

She gives Deean's hand a pat and then sees me in the seat across from them. "Glad you made it, Iann." She gives the roof two quick thuds, signaling to the driver to leave, and gives me an anxious expression. "We have a special treat for you."

This better not be a repeat of last night. Between my mother and the unexpected visit from Thana, I've had my share of surprises.

Deean and my grandmother gossip the entire way. Some of

it is interesting, but most a waste of breath. As they continue, I gaze out the window. Part of my mind watching the pristine cobblestone streets and the other, picking up small pieces of their conversation.

Just beyond the gates of the castle lay the city streets. Saden isn't the most colorful place I've seen. The buildings alternate between an eggshell and cream color, each with a bronze or copper roof that shines for all of Saden to see. The neutral simplicity is still a breathtaking view.

City streets bustle with people who make way as we pass, leisurely strolling about without a care, visiting and chatting amongst each other like they have time to spare. Most dress in a similar style to the designs of the city. Nothing vibrant, yet still elegant. My favorite hues are those of evergreen that mix in with the peachy browns or washed-out golds.

Deean is talking about one of our many lords being caught with his wife's sister, but I stop listening as the carriage comes to a halt.

Outside is a shop called Iffa's Collectibles, painted in gold leaf on an eggshell canvas with sage green trimmings that run along the window and door frames of the two-story building.

By the time I turn back to the two gossipers, they are already out of the carriage and waiting for me on the path that runs in front of the building.

There is a light breeze outside but nothing that requires a coat, and across the road is the sound of trickling water where several small waterfalls flow down beyond a bridge.

My grandmother takes the lead, as she always does, and Deean and I follow her into the shop.

"What are we doing here?" I whisper to Deean, but he only waves me off.

There are a few antique shops in Saden. Several of which I've sold items to that I've brought back with me from my trav-els. My favorite has always been Adrick's, but Iffa's is new to me and that brings with it an excitement I didn't think I'd experience on this outing. A chance to find something new.

Inside is toasty, and despite the sun that beams in through the windows, the atmosphere is darker, gloomier than most other shops around here. I suspect the black painted walls are the cause, but the items add a bit of eeriness on their own.

"Your Graces." A bodiless voice travels down to us.

Searching the room, I can't find anyone beyond the endless trinkets that fill the space. That's until a ladder, connected to a rail running across the room, moves and I spot a figure descending the rungs.

The image of them disappears behind an enormous, hand-crafted ship that takes up a sizable area of square footage, and all I hear are their shuffles as they move around the display.

A man with pale white skin and dwarfism comes before us and offers a bow. His head is eye level with my hips, and he steps on a stool to get a better view of us, and even then, his full height comes to about the top of my ribcage. He twirls one end of his long mustache. He looks enthusiastic about our visit, like he's been itching for this moment, but I catch a single bead of sweat on his forehead, which is not surprising. Most people are nervous to meet royals, and usually, when they do, they don't get three of them at once.

"You must be Bennum Iffa?" my grandmother says as she plucks off her gloves.

"You may call me Benny," he offers, and finally dabs away the solitary drop of perspiration. "That's if you'd like to. Ben... Bennum is fine, of course."

"Very well, Benny." I see some nerves fall away. "Do you have what my assistant discussed with you?"

He nods and points his head towards the stairs. We follow behind him, allowing me to take in more of his shop. It's every collector's dream. Old books, furniture, clocks, crystals, plant specimens in glass jars, and insect collections. There is a corner with rolled up maps sprawled over an oak table and another area with timeworn boxes, and I wonder if any are filled with treasures of their own.

Reaching the stairs, instead of going up, we go around to a door that isn't visible to shoppers.

Benny leads us inside an office, one brighter than the rest of the shop. The ceiling is covered with a painted map of Ladora, like the one in my bedroom. In the center of the room is a long table covered in books and parchment, and shoved in the corner is an equally cluttered desk. All the walls have more parchment covering them. Clearly, it's the room of a researcher.

"Is this Crispin's work?" I ask, pointing to the ceiling.

Benny's mouth twitches up. "It is. Crispin Iffa, my son. Did this for his dear pa when I opened the shop. He always pushed me into entrepreneurship, and I probably wouldn't be here without him."

Deean looks closer at the ceiling. "His paintings are all over the palace. One hell of a talent."

"Thank you." Benny pulls something from his desk and meets us at the table in the center. "After your assistant came in, I did some research and spoke with a few locals about stories they may have heard."

Deean and my grandmother eagerly wait for him to continue, but I interrupt, "Excuse me, but what are we talking about here?"

"Your Royal Highnesses inquired about a map." He sets the box on the table as my eyes fly to Deean.

"And this map leads to?"

"The Ivian Flower. Isn't that what you're after?"

"It's not meant to be public knowledge." My glare still rests on Deean.

My grandmother places her hand out for the item, "His Majesty the King, my son, is many great things, but a secret keeper he is not. I've known about his desire for the flower for many years. Since you both were babes. Now Iann, would you like to continue asking your questions or would you like to see the item that will help lead you to the greatest discovery of your life? The greatest discovery in all of Ladora?"

The proposition makes me reconsider. Helping my father has been the main reason for doing this, but if the flower is more than a myth, then my name will be forever tied to it. People will tell my story for years to come and it won't be because I'm the third son of King Marcel II. It will be because of my doing. My efforts. My legacy.

"Proceed," I tell Benny, and I feel Deean's hand on my shoulder, gripping it in approval.

There is still the matter of telling him he can't join me, but how can I crush his spirit now? He actually may have come through on his end of the bargain. But with Marcel now going, it's sheer stupidity to send all Saden heirs to Haymel.

"If it makes you all feel better," Benny says, digging for a key in his pocket and then placing it in the lock of the box, "I was discreet in my search and whatever happens between my clients stays between us."

"You're a good man," my grandmother replies, as he takes a golden item from the box and hands it to her.

I don't know Benny from any other stranger but I accept his word, for now.

"That's the map?" Deean holds out his hand as my grandmother passes the figure to him. "Not quite what I was thinking." Getting a better view, I see that he holds a tiny golden anchor.

Benny races across the room and stacks a few books in his arms before coming back to the table. They drop with a thud before he's off again and snatches a few pieces of paper off the wall.

"How did you acquire it?" I ask, taking the figurine from Deean. "I'm surprised it's even in Saden of all places."

"I won it off a drunk. He claimed that it belonged to his great-great-grandfather who had come here from Haymel. Claimed this grandfather once sailed with Fraya Vellen."

"Fraya Vellen?" My mouth dries.

"She sounds intriguing," Deean chimes in. "And who is she?"

"She was a captain known to have accompanied H.R. Mates on his journey to Farella when he did his study on plants native to the island. And this was hers?" If the story is true, I can't believe I'm holding something that once belonged to Fraya Vellen. A legend in her own right.

"According to the man, his ancestor stole it from her." Benny comes around the table and lays a book before us. "After some research, I learned Fraya had a map created in Haymel shortly after her expedition. And not long after, there are accounts of it being stolen. I'm not certain if this is a clue or some kind of key to finding the map, but it is something she had made, and there are several references to the map and the item found in these."

He then offers us a stack of parchments. All taken from Haymel. There is a report she made with city guards after the trinket had been stolen. It cites two missing items in total. Then there are sketches of the anchor that look to have been drawn by a blacksmith, except one sheet is missing half its contents.

"It is illegal to travel to Haymel without approval from the King." Deean examines one of the sheets.

"I didn't travel there," Benny is quick to refute any speculations.

"So you just randomly had documents from there on hand. Specifically of this Fraya person, in connection with the flower?"

Benny wipes away more sweat. "I've studied Fraya and the flower for a long time. I also have great connections. I was just doing what you required of me."

"And there is nothing wrong in that." Turning to Deean, I give him a cautionary look, one that suggests he leave it be. "Do you happen to know where the rest of the image is? It looks torn." I ask, hoping for more clues.

"That's all I was given. The rest is missing. But you may have all of these to look over as well as the anchor, of course."

"And the deal is still a thousand moinlings?" my grandmother confirms, which seems significantly too low for what he's giving us.

"Yes, Your Grace." He bows but then turns from her sheepishly before he gets the courage to ask, "I was wondering though, if we could add something?"

"Trying to play us?" Deean grabs the anchor out of my hand like he can protect it best.

Benny holds out his hands, placatingly. "No. No, of course not. You see, I grew up listening to legends of this everlasting flower. A single petal that can conjure immortality. It's death's worst nightmare and every wonderer's dream. I just thought that if Prince Iann is successful in finding it, then maybe my name might be credited in assisting in the discovery."

Smart man. The moinlings will surely vanish with time but his name in history will last forever. If that's what he wants, then we have a deal.

I nod to my grandmother and Deean, who give subtle nods of their own. "That's fair and will be granted if it's found." I push the books on the table back to him. "Better yet, how about you join us?" Deean and my grandmother make no protest to this idea. "I have yet to assemble a proper team and I have a feeling you'll be of great use. You can continue your research on the journey. What do you say?"

He stumbles back into the table pinching his head. "I'll have to find someone to run the shop. And my wife will be excited and then furious. I'll have to pack." He begins mumbling a to-do list to himself.

"I'm sure we can help with accommodations." My grandmother gestures to one of the guards near the door who brings over a jingling sack. "You can keep this and my grandsons will help arrange the rest." She plucks the anchor from Deean and locks it back in the box. She hands our new clue off to the guard and instructs him to put it in the carriage. "It was a pleasure meeting, and working with, you, Benny. I look forward to our future endeavors."

Benny offers a bow, and Grandmother walks out. Clearly, it's time to go.

"Deean will be your point of contact," I inform both of them and ignore the interruption Deean is about to offer. "This is a great start, but we still need a map, and our deal still stands."

"Fine," Deean huffs. "Benny and I will figure it out."

I'm sure Benny will. I think, in this situation, Deean isn't offering much help.

"Benny"—he looks up, his amazement still doesn't have him fully grounded—"it was a pleasure. Departure is in a week. We'll see you then."

Deean and I take our leave. The anchor is still a mystery, like every other part of this venture, but maybe with Benny we can learn of its use. It's not much, but it's something.

10

ARIAH

T he ceremony was beautiful given what it was. Luna was as stunning as ever, and I would argue, it would have been a breathtaking event had Beetlerum not been there.

Like most traditional marriage ceremonies in Foxhead, there isn't a disparity of color. Bright and gallant, starting with the lavender-colored carriage that transported Luna and the purple hued flowers that adorned it. All but lilacs, Luna made sure for my sake that there wouldn't be one present. She had stepped out in Jaleese's old dress that had to be let out slightly, but I made it work in the little time I had.

I added sheer flowing sleeves to help with any bitter cold the night would bring. She wore a fitted corset that looked tight but was held together by loose ribbons in the back. Luna made it clear she wanted to breathe and was not sacrificing comfort for vanity. I commented that if she did faint they would likely cancel the wedding, but she said that would only prolong the inevitable. I was also able to get handmade flower patches sewn on the bottom half, each a different color and all connected to the forest green thread that ran all over the dress to give the appearance of flower stems. The bottom half rippled down like the sea with more lavender ruffles.

Luna borrowed her mother's pearl drop earrings, matching a necklace that sat splendidly against her deep umber skin. Her hair was loose, coarse curls roamed free, as they always should.

In traditional Foxhead style, the ceremony began shortly after dusk when the sky was illuminated with an abundance of stars. Thousands of tiny lanterns were strung from ropes that ran all around the gardens of the Beetlerum Estate. The central fountain radiated with seafoam-green water and held swans and floating iridescent flowers. The Council, and predictably the Beetlerum family, spared no expense, all of it made more extravagant by our guest of honor.

Everyone buzzed and gawked and gossiped when Queen Cayleen made her entrance, one nearly as grand as Luna's. She took her seat at the front to observe the couple she had never met before.

My family sat a row behind her. My parents remained silent and not once looked in her direction. They were furious with her and even more at me for not immediately declining her offer. When I told them what my "no" would bring it seemed to silence them both, but anger remained.

Occasionally, I caught the slight glances of the Queen's eye, but she never stared long. Once the sacred words were exchanged the event took on more of a festive feel and food and drink started flowing in abundance.

I currently move underneath a vine-covered arch that's crawling with roses. Behind the secrecy of the bushes and arch, I rearrange my drawers that cause itching near my thighs. Once I'm fully adjusted, I ensure no one has seen me; thankfully, it seems no one pays me any mind. From afar, I observe everyone seemingly enjoying themselves. Even my parents crack a smile as they dance and mingle.

Behind me I get a good view of the Beetlerum Estate. The

home could easily house most of the people who reside in Foxhead judging from the bits I can see in the light. And to think this all could have been mine.

"Ariah." The call of my name sends me spinning around.

An anxious Luna and her new husband come walking up. Well, it's more like Luna drags Morren along. He clearly has no desire to speak to me and I'm in agreement. But this is not my day I remind myself, so I perk up and muster the best smile I can.

"Morren," Luna begins. "I know you've met before, but I would like to properly introduce you to my best friend and sister, Ariah Tyddle."

He and I enter a staring match and it's a question of who will outstretch their hand first.

This time Morren isn't covered in soot, but his clothes are still a few sizes too big. I now know his family has money and I suspect his ill-fitting apparel is a personal choice, which I can't find fault for. At least this time his evergreen vest not only looks nice against his skin, but goes well with the thread I added to Luna's dress. His black tailcoat compliments the overall aesthetics of tonight nicely.

Luna's glances bounce between us, with everything I've put her through, I give in first and stretch out my hand for his.

"Pleasure to properly meet you." He's reluctant at first but eventually surrenders as I continue, "It was a beautiful ceremony."

"Mmhmm." Is all I get from him.

"Luna!" Mrs. Trivy calls for her.

"Excuse me while I go assist my mother." Morren moves to go with her, but Luna stops him. "You two should speak. Get to know each other."

Get to know each other? If I wanted that then I would have married him myself.

"You and your family have a lovely home." I utter the first bit of small talk that comes to mind.

"We do," he says coldly and straightens his tailcoat. "Bet you regret your decision now."

"Excuse me?" I exclaim, not entirely surprised.

"Luna has hopes that you and I can make amends, but I'm not so liberal with forgiveness. I will tolerate you for her sake."

Oh, how kind. However, shall I repay him.

"Ha!" I let out a pathetic laugh, one to let him know just how amused I am. "You don't owe me any forgiveness because there is nothing to forgive. My decision wasn't made with regard to you." Only partially true. "It was what I wanted." I take a step closer to him until we're almost nose to nose. "And whether you tolerate me or not, I will always remain Luna's friend. And I swear if I hear you are ever unkind to her or if you hurt her, I will kill you myself."

He holds my glare, and I can see his nostrils flaring.

"Is there a problem?" A woman says from behind him. I recognize her from the ceremony and know it's his mother.

"No ma'am," I answer for the both of us.

"Ariah and I were just admiring the decor, Mother." Morren spins on his heels and walks off to join his guests.

Gravel crunches behind me and I turn just in time to see Queen Cayleen step from around a bush.

"Lover's quarrel?" she asks before grinning. I bow as she comes closer and notice she extends a hand to me holding a glass of pink champagne. "I saw you two arguing from afar, thought maybe this would help settle the anger. Or maybe ignite it. Either one is useful I suppose."

Taking the glass, I watch a few bubbles rise to the surface and I discreetly try to sniff it for any poisons.

"Don't insult me." Queen Cayleen takes a sip from her own glass, leaving a deep red lip stain behind. "Killing you would provide me with nothing."

I down the drink in one go. The fizz satisfying a craving I didn't know I had.

While I finish my drink, she opens the massive locket around her neck and her touch sets it aglow. I double check my glass and sniff again for poison, before blinking a few times to make sure my eyes aren't deceiving me.

"It's enchanted." Queen Cayleen examines whatever she's viewing with intensity. "It's how I know what's going on within my castle walls without being present." She snaps the locket shut. "It's good to know powerful enchantresses and be Queen. A lethal combination." I knew there were enchanters, but never have I met one or seen their work. "Tell me, Ariah, do you have an answer for me?"

I've thought about nothing more over the past day. If only I could know the tasks she's going to give me. Are they requests I'll be able to handle?

Stealing, while not ideal, is something I can get past. Spying surely, I suppose I could do that too. Lies don't feel great after they're told but it's something I've done several times without getting caught. My issue isn't any one of these things. It's with the deeper vices this all could lead me too. Actions that would be hard to come back from.

"Sort of." I look back at the festivities, thankful my parents are still distracted and not watching me. "Why me? Why not just have them pay a different way?"

"You remind me of your mother. In looks and attitude." She moves a curl out of my face. "I'm skilled at reading people and I wouldn't ask you to join my elite Foxes if I thought you would represent them poorly. Plus, with your new demands, this is your opportunity. One you will never get here in this small, pitiful village."

There is an unnerving feeling in the way she speaks. So convinced of everything uttered out of her mouth, though I suppose one would have to be quite confident to rule thousands. What I hate most about what she says is how much it's true. I have nothing but family here, which in many ways is enough, until it's not. There has always been a nagging feeling deep within. One I've ignored despite its growing intensity. I want more. I want to see beyond this village, beyond Mrs. Kimpol's shop, beyond my parents' home. I want experiences I'm so afraid of missing out on.

The more I stand there thinking over my answer, I realize I already know what it is. I've known since her proposal and there is no use in stalling.

"I'll do it." Queen Cayleen's lips form into a smile that is equal parts satisfied and sinister.

She extends an arm as she says, "Welcome to The Foxes."

Reluctantly, I take her hand and we shake to either the wisest decision of my life or the most reckless.

PART TWO
THE FOXES

11

ARIAH

"All Foxes must follow three simple, yet integral, rules while carrying out a task assigned by the Queen. You are to remain unseen—cloaked in the shadows—and unidentifiable to all. You must be unheard, those you pursue must never hear you coming. And then you must be untraceable, leaving nothing that can tie you, or the Queen, back to the act. Unseen. Unheard. Untraceable. The moment there is a single rumor about you being a Fox, you're as good as dead, and my advice would be to disappear before Queen Cayleen can catch you." My mother's instructions have been a constant echo in my head since she began training me.

As expected, she hates that I accepted the Queen's offer. She even threatened to go herself and pay her own debt. But although she didn't say it aloud, we both know she has much more to lose than I do if something were to go horribly wrong. Plus, I doubt the Queen would allow it at this point.

At the wedding, Queen Cayleen made it clear she would be sending a carriage in a week's time to retrieve me and insisted I soak in as much as I could from my parents. It took some convincing, but once they both got quickly on board, my days soon filled with lessons in apothecary and my nights reserved for all things in espionage, theft, and weapons.

Listening to my parents explain their former roles as assets to the court in great detail, showing clear expertise for the skills they possess, makes me see them in a different light. The experience has forced me to envision the life they had before all of this. Before Jaleese and I were ever a thought. Probably even before they knew each other. It is undeniable that they were… are, masters in their craft.

The more they show me, the more I understand why the Queen didn't want to give them up. Their skills demonstrate why she granted them the freedom to marry as long as they stayed within her kingdom, with the condition that she could ask for a favor at any moment. The only thing she did not consider was time, and tied to that are the natural changes that come with life and the inevitable increase in age. While I think my parents can carry out any task the Queen assigns, she decided it best to change the rules, and the deal is now my sole responsibility.

My father started teaching me about healing elixirs right away. They are most important to know, given they are what I use to assist me with my breathing issues. For a single bottle of mine he uses twenty-five crushed elderberries, two pinches of mullein, a dash of ginseng, and four leaves from an elmonk flower, boiling it all in heareth liquid. When I asked what heareth liquid was, he proceeded to tell me it was slime from a particular type of slug. I stopped him immediately, not wanting to think about spraying that into my mouth. He said the liquid isn't necessary, but it helps.

Today, he continues with elixirs. Ones that can help with stomach aches, cramps, different infections, wounds, even some that can rid the mind of nightmares.

"The more healing someone needs, the more magic is required. And plants that hold magical properties are rare and often difficult to find," he says, adding a drop of a toxic green liquid into the beaker. "It's best to work with things that are simple."

"Can any of these elixirs give you immortality?" I study his every movement and watch him drop in three grains of sand and a pinch of moss before stirring.

"No." He chuckles. "You think I would have that sitting in my office and not tell anyone?" He pushes my head playfully. "Although, I suppose the Ivian Flower could. If it truly exists."

I've heard my father tell many stories about the fabled flower that several people in history have looked for. All of them have been unsuccessful in finding it.

"What about poisons?" I ask, growing bored with the elixirs. "The Queen mentioned a poison that melted someone's skin off." My father's body tenses, the only part of him moving is his shaking hand, and I see what the Queen was referring to. I place my hand on his and stop the contents in the beaker from splashing out. "She mentioned it was one of your creations."

"Lord Corrgen," he whispers, almost like he's not talking to me at all. His mind giving way to the past. "I had called it Azaethel. My first deadly concoction."

"Why him? What did he do?"

"I was only asked to create it, the *why* is not my story to share. You're going to have to ask Queen Cayleen if you want an answer. And that's not something I recommend doing." We laugh before he falls back to reality and sets the beaker down. "I can go on for days about poisons. Unfortunately, your week is up tomorrow." I force down a hard swallow.

"I'll send you off with a few books, I know how much you love to read." He gives me a teasing wink and suddenly his eyes fill with tears. I don't even have time to ask if he's okay before he pulls me in and wraps me up. "Ariah, promise me that you will do what she asks and then you get the hell out. If any pursuit is too great to bear, you come straight back, and we will figure it out as a family."

"I promise," I whisper into the crook of his shoulder. "I do this, and she will get rid of that stupid tradition, and you and Mom will never have to deal with her again. It's what we all want."

He squeezes me tighter and his silence is stabbing, filling me with fear and guilt. They spent years being the Queen's aides. Years of learning who to cheat, steal, kill, and do all kinds of unspeakable things to, on her behalf. A week is nothing. Enough time to hear stories and be shown a few things, but not enough for me to stew on what it all means. With my luck, I'll forget it all by the time I arrive at court.

It was just before sunset when my mother told me to meet her at the council building, in the center of town, within an hour's time.

All she said was, "Don't be late and remember, you must be unseen, unheard, and untraceable."

Our nightly lessons are usually conducted at home and this is to be the first time out in the open. Keeping the rules in mind, I dress in all black to make it easier to remain unseen. Ditching my dress, I pull on fitted pants and a flowing black top that I tuck into the waistband of my pants. She told me to always stay armed, so I insert a dagger in each boot where I created a place to conceal them. The only other items I take with me are my medicinal bottle and canister of needles.

My mother had gone over several weapon choices, showing me a box she kept hidden under floorboards of our sitting room. It was another surprise at the time, but the shock from their past lives has begun wearing away and I'm becoming more and more numb to the details they share.

Out of her weapon stock, I had been most drawn to the ring swords. She had two, both with a wooden grip and a glistening, silver blade that wrapped into a circular shape. The only difference between the two was that one had metal spikes, while the other did not.

I end up taking the one without. The spiked one felt more advanced—for people far more skilled than I am or would ever like to be. I want to keep it simple and pray that I will never have to use it in the first place. I think of it more as an accessory to go with my new ensemble, and a great accessory is something I can get behind.

As I cross the bridge that connects our home to the larger part of the village, I spot a few people still wandering the streets. Unsure of how unseen I am to remain, I decide to take the backways to circle all the buildings.

It is dark and there are very few patches of light, making it easy for me to go unnoticed, also making it harder to see things.

The scent of roasting chicken and herbs smacks me in the face and my stomach instantly grumbles. Moving along I pick up traces of stew followed by quail and potatoes.

Ignoring the tempting scents, I move along to the council building. I ease out of hiding, cautiously, but the sound of giggling, followed by low moans, sends me back into the shadows.

The area appears empty. I can't spot anyone or anything other than darkness and patches of moonlight, but voices are getting closer.

"Over here," a low, hungry voice beckons.

At first, I think my mother is signaling to me but then there are more light moans and...kissing? Oh, no.

The noises are of lips interlocking and mouths trying to smother moans as a couple explores one another.

"Why can't we go back to my home? My father is away in Verrum to attend to his dying sister. He'll never know who has been in my bed." A soft voice pleads before they suck in a quick breath of air.

Yes, why can't you go home? Why do this here, and now of all places? I think to myself.

"Too dangerous," the deep voice grunts, before the kissing picks up again.

Ugh! I'm not about to hear anymore from these two. I don't have anything on me, but my hands search the ground for a rock or pebble, anything small enough to throw.

My hands land on a small pile of rocks. The noises come from somewhere to my left, so I dash one of the rocks off to the right.

"What was that?" All seductive noises stop and all is still.

Carefully, I toss another rock. Without a word or an investigation to see where the noise is coming from, the couple runs out of the darkness into a patch of light blue moonlight.

Tristen Marden perhaps? I'm not certain who the young woman with him is, she has beautiful, dark flowing hair that ends about mid-back, but I've seen her around before.

The blacksmith's apprentice looks around. Trying to see if he can spot anything in the dark. My head goes back to resting against the stone wall that's hiding me. My chest tightens and my shoulders rise ever so slightly.

As I concentrate on regulating my breathing, I hear movement.

"I thought I saw something," Tristen says, and I hear him take a step closer to my hiding place.

"It's probably one of the mill owner's pesky cats. Let's go before someone sees." The girl with him pulls at his arm.

Footsteps scurry over the stone path, and I wait a few minutes until it all falls silent around me again. When I don't hear or see another soul, I cautiously make my way to the steps of the council building.

I am too visible, even in the cover of night, so I move to the other side where the council garden is located.

Suddenly, a figure dashes across my vision running from one bush to another. "Mom?" I whisper and move closer. "Is that you?"

There is no answer, no movement, no sound, and it's like my eyes saw nothing at all.

"Mom?" I whisper again.

"Why don't you just scream my name through the streets." I jump at the sound of someone's voice behind me.

Turning around, I jump again. With the light of the moon, I make out a figure wearing what looks to be a fox mask and think the divinity Panntra has reincarnated before me.

"Mom?"

She whips off the mask. "Yes, It's me Ariah. What happened to the rules?"

"I just saw you run across the bushes, that's not exactly remaining unseen."

"I wanted you to see me so you knew I was here."

"Yeah, well, that message didn't come through," I loudly whisper back. "And why are you dressed as Panntra?"

"Panntra is the divinity of the night and someone I modeled myself after when I was recruited into the Foxes. Now, no more questions. Follow me."

I do as I'm told and follow her to the outskirts of the village until we approach a familiar house. It holds the same gardens Luna was married in. It's the Beetlerum Estate.

The windows are illuminated with a yellow light and together my mother and I watch figures dash in and out of various rooms in the house.

"There is a study on the third floor in the right wing." I follow my mother's finger. "It belongs to Sabbien Beetlerum,

Morren's father. There are whispers that he plans to reconstruct Foxhead, build more industrialized buildings for advancement. Uproot houses that have been here for hundreds of years, meaning dozens may lose their homes and will be forced to relocate to neighboring areas. I want copies of these papers, and you are going to be the one to get them."

"What!?" I whisper too loudly, and feel her palm against my lips. Only when she removes her hand, do I continue. "How do you even know that?"

"I've been watching him for a while. The entire family actually." She places a hand to my cheek. "I knew who the council had selected for you months ago. I learned everything I could about the Beetlerums after that. I also know you, and knew you were never going to go through with a forced betrothal, but I still had to make sure you would be safe regardless. It scared me at first because I know what men like Sabbien are capable of. But you're a bright woman. If Cayleen wants you in her circle, it means you're much more capable of things not even you know yet." My mother doesn't refer to her as a queen and says her name like an old friend, or possibly foe. "This is the final task I have for you. The last thing I can teach in our limited time. You must sneak in and find those papers. The rules remain. If you can't do this simple task Ariah, you will be useless to the Queen and that won't fare well for you."

Suddenly, several figures collect in one room of the house. Silhouettes dance past the curtains.

"Okay," I whisper. My chest tightens and I make sure my spray is tucked away in one of my many pockets.

My mother hands me her mask. "They have just begun supper. Now is the perfect time. They have three guards who roam the grounds. Four servants, who I suspect will be in the dining room with the family or in the kitchen, and two maids with undisclosed locations. You'll find the papers within an

office and know exactly what I speak of when you see them."
She nudges me and I put on the mask. "Foxes are to remain..."

"Wait," I hold up my hand connecting all pieces. "You know exactly where the papers are and won't tell me?"

"You think the Queen is going to spoon feed you while you're in court? I've given you the assignment. It's your job to figure it out. Now, Foxes are to remain..."

Taking in a deep inhale before releasing it with a bit of uneasiness, I reply, "Unseen. Unheard. Untraceable."

12

ARIAH

Around the perimeter of the Beetlerum Estate grow enormous elm trees that I run to and hide behind, as I draw closer to the right wing.

I stop when two guards near one of several fountains emerge and start chatting yards away. Gossiping about two people named Saffria and Issa, who conned a poor bloke out of hundreds of moinlings. I don't know if their actions were justified, but staying to hear the full story is not prudent, and I take advantage of their distraction and quietly continue through the trees.

Making my way towards the back of the estate, I vaguely make out a terrace with a large, vine infested wooden arbor. Underneath the arbor is a door, and above are several windows.

Good! I have multiple points of entry.

The windows on each level are dark, increasing my chances of the rooms being vacant.

The two guards are still standing yards away as they continue to chat with each other.

My mother had said there were three in total. I don't see the other one and hope they are by the other wing of the house.

Quickly, I cross the yard of the estate and head straight for the arbor. Drawing my ring sword, I prepare to use it to help get the door open, but to my surprise, it's already unlocked.

I suppose, given how rich the Beetlerums are, they live assured that no one is foolish enough to steal from them. I am either a fool about to fall into a trap or about to teach them a lesson to always lockup.

Slipping inside, I'm greeted with more darkness and a set of stairs.

Perfect. Up is where I need to go and this all feels a little too good to be true.

The first step creaks under my weight as I make my ascent. I pause until I feel comfortable enough and then take another step.

To enhance my stealth I move on to my tippy toes. I'm not sure if it's actually helping, but I feel more relaxed, so I keep it up until I have ascended the first flight of stairs.

At the base of the second floor, I gaze out and see a lifeless and nearly lightless hall. The carpet runner crawls with a white light halfway down the corridor and then fades into absolute darkness.

Although, afraid someone will pop out of the dark, I continue up the stairs and make my way to the third floor which is identical to the second.

A musty scent wafts through the air, clinging with dust and the absence of life. Not necessarily the smell of death, but the lack of bodies that stay on this level and perhaps the limited cleaning attention it receives. It is a perfect place to hide valuable things.

I begin with the first door in the hall. Of course, my mother could tell me how many guards, cooks, and servants there are, but not what room these documents are in. Another test, I assume. If she knows about the papers, she certainly knows what room they are kept in. Better yet, she could have nicked them herself. But this is my last lesson, not that there have been many in the past week; but this is a chance to prove to her that I can handle this.

The first room has a small archway I pass under before reaching the door. My hand goes back and forth, contemplating if I should rush in or knock.

Why the hell would I knock? Just go in, Ariah.

I end up having a full-blown conversation with myself before I decide knocking is a dumb idea and summon the courage to open the door.

Gradually, the door swings back and, like the hall, there isn't much light inside the room.

Straight ahead is a window, and the little light that creeps in reveals a hope chest set near the foot of the bed.

Immediately, I shut the door and move on to the next. This time I don't argue with myself, and I open the door. The next room is like the first. There is a bed, but instead of a hope chest, there is a tiny rocking horse, along with a rocking chair near the window.

All I find are bedrooms, with the exception of one painting room, but it still isn't the office my mother is referring to. Of course, she could have helped me more by providing the exact location of the room instead of being ominous about it, but it's useless to stress, I already have enough nerves coursing through me.

As I'm about to enter the seventh room on this floor, I hear footsteps traveling up the stairs, and I catch the faintest glimpse of candle light flickering against the wall before I tuck into the archway.

"Remember this is a secret for Morren." It's Luna's voice, and I tuck farther into the wall between the door and hall. The last thing I need is for her to find me. "Just set it in the room and he'll find it in the morning."

We haven't spoken since her wedding. I would have thought

she would be traveling by now, enjoying time with her new husband, but maybe the plans changed. The thought of him reminds me just how much his words bothered me at the wedding. I wonder if he told Luna of my not-so-little threat if he misbehaves. I would tell her about the incident myself, but I don't want to taint their relationship, if there is even one at all.

Three bodies walk past me and I sink farther back into the shadows.

Luna stops midway, sniffing the air. "Strange."

"Is something wrong with My Lady?" one of the voices asks from farther down the hall.

"Sandalwood, amber, and peonies," she mumbles. My pits sweat knowing she is picking up the scent of the perfume my father has specially mixed for me. Without making a sound, and moving with the speed of sap down a tree, I get the door open and slip inside. "I thought I smelled something."

"Only your husband and Sir Beetlerum come to this side of the house, ma'am. I'm sure it's just cleaning scents left behind by the maids."

"You're probably right." Luna turns to continue on and together they finish up what they were doing.

Waiting in the dark, I listen. I hear them go into one of the furthest rooms in the hall and then come out, walking back towards the staircase.

"Once he goes into his office, he's going to be so surprised, ma'am," another girl says as they pass the door I'm hidden behind. Her voice is almost childlike, and I can't imagine she's over the age of fifteen. Must be a servant assigned to Luna.

She does offer good insight though. If Morren's office is all the way down the hall, then I would bet some moinlings his father's isn't far from it.

"Oh," Luna says, as they hit the steps. "I forgot something. You two head back down and help with supper. Let the others know I'll be there momentarily."

"I can fetch it for you," the younger one pleads.

"I got it. As I said, you two head back down."

My heartbeat quickens. Why isn't she leaving?

The sound of footsteps trail downstairs and then the hall falls silent.

Now would be the time to go for the study, but I know Luna is still around. Giving it a minute, I still don't hear anything and wonder if she went back to Morren's office.

Slow and steady, I create a gap in the doorway and peer out into the corridor. There is nothing in my line of sight. It doesn't mean that Luna still isn't on this floor. If I go now, then we could easily bump into each other.

A creaking noise sends me flying back, away from the door.

"Ariah?" Luna's voice is cautious.

New rule, no more perfume while on assignment. Definite violation of the untraceable part, especially when you have a custom scent.

The door swings open and Luna comes in with a candle in hand. She sees me and jumps back, the candle falling and the flame grabbing hold of the tassels on the carpet.

"What's wrong with you?" I shout as we both stomp to put the fire out.

"Ariah?" She scurries to what looks like a dresser and lights the candle once more before coming over and pulling the mask that I forgot was on, off my face. "What in the hell are you doing here? How did you even get in?"

"The back door was unlocked."

She lowers the candle and examines my clothes. "What are you wearing?"

Had this been a task assigned by the Queen, I know what would be expected of me for being caught, and the thought makes me ill. Thankfully, the Queen isn't here, and neither is my mother. Besides my family, Luna is the only person I would trust with my life. With my family's secret. Our honesty has fueled our friendship—lying now might destroy it all.

"Promise me you won't say anything." She nods without question, just as I would. "Not even to Morren." She nods again, a little more hesitantly this time, but it's a nod nonetheless. "I leave for the Queen's court tomorrow." Her eyes and mouth widen, but I finish before she can interject. "It's a long story that I promise to tell you about when I have more time, but right now, I need to get into Sabbien's office. Can you show me where it is?"

She stands there, reluctantly waiting, and I can't fault her. If someone wearing a strange fox mask, lingering in the dark, asked for my help, I wouldn't offer it either.

"Let's go!" I'm right behind her as she charges down the hall —her candle flickering with the speed of her gait. "He keeps it locked."

"No worries." Instinctively, my hand goes for a needle in my pocket and I use it to twist the mechanism of the lock until I hear that beautiful click. It's another useful skill my mother has taught me over the past few days.

Once unlocked, she stares at me, a million questions swim in her eyes, as she allows me to enter first.

Taking another candle near the entrance, she lights it and hands it over. "This is his office. An office he hates people going into, so hurry up."

I plant a kiss on her forehead. "Have I ever mentioned how much I love you?"

"Well, anyone willing to kill someone who hurts me must love me."

She hits me with the threat I gave Morren. "He told you about that?"

"He did." She waits a minute before giving into a smile. "I laughed when he told me. I don't think he liked that very much, but eventually I broke him down. He won't be impolite to you anymore."

"Thank you." I give her hand a quick squeeze. "And you have my word that I will try to get along with him."

She lets out a breath that seems like she's been holding in for days. "Alright. What are we looking for?"

"Papers. Plans. Anything about Foxhead." She heads off towards a table on the left and I take the desk. "My mother is convinced he has intentions of reconstructing Foxhead."

"Can he do that?"

"You tell me. He's your father-in-law."

The desk is pristine, not a pen out of place and no papers. I find a journal, but it's only filled with names and moinling amounts. Suspicious, but not what I'm looking for.

The drawers are the same, most are filled with random trinkets. Everything is perfectly organized. The only issue is there aren't many papers. There are a few notebooks, but each is unused.

"Ariah." Luna stays fixated on a sheet as she unfolds it before her. "I think I found it." I cross the room in three quick strides. She holds out a map of Foxhead. "That's your parent's place." Luna points to a cottage that has been circled with red ink. "That's my parent's shop and their home." Both are circled with the same ink. "What does this mean?"

Shaking my head, I reach for the other papers on the table. The top document is addressed to Queen Cayleen. The contents are too long to read now, but the last line is for her signature.

"I'm taking these." I fold them as best as I can and shove them in the back of my pants.

"He's going to know they are missing." Luna cleans up what she's touched.

"Good. Let him. I will give them to my mother so she can take a look, and she'll sneak them back in."

"Your mom?"

"Yeah, that's part of the longer story. Now, what's the fastest way out of here?"

It might be cheating having her show me, but I've been here too long.

Following her out, we don't go back to the stairs at the end of the hall. Instead, we run to the next room. She shuts the door behind me and then leads us to a wardrobe. There are a few coats she shoves to the side and then she pounds on the top right corner. The back of the wardrobe separates, allowing her to push it open, like a door.

"This path leads to stairs that will take you to the back gardens. No one really knows about this passageway, so you won't get caught."

"How do you know about it?" I move past her and take the candle that she holds out for me.

"Ummm...Morren showed me." There is too much bashfulness in the reply.

"Yeah, what else has he shown you?" I tease, and then hold the light up to her face and she can barely keep eye contact. "So, Morren has been taking care of you."

"Stop." And there is no hiding her grin, even in near darkness. "He's actually a really good man."

I lean in close. "How good?"

Her smile still beams and she bites the corner of her lip. "Really good."

We both laugh until we realize we're meant to be quiet.

"I'll write to you. I want to know everything. You take care of yourself."

"Wait!" She tugs at my arm before I can pass through the door. "When do you leave?"

My eyes dart away before I whisper, "Tomorrow morning."

"Tomorrow?" She hits me in the arm. "You were going to leave without saying anything?"

"You have just been so busy I thought it would be better to write to you once I got there."

"Unacceptable." She wraps her arms around me. "Once you get there, you better get to writing and don't leave out a single detail. Be careful."

Luna and I haven't been apart for longer than a week since we were children. I want nothing more than to stay behind and have her tell me about what life is like for her now.

There is a fear of losing her. A chance that my role in her life has fallen a position or two. There is a strange wave of jealousy, and I can't figure out if things will ever return to how they once were, or if they're even supposed to.

We let go of each other's embrace and I do everything I can to retain my tears. This isn't a goodbye. I assuredly will be seeing her again, but there is an ache in not knowing when that will be.

With the papers tucked in my pants and a smooth exit down the clandestine staircase, out into an unoccupied garden, sneaking away isn't as difficult as sneaking in.

13
IANN

Everyone in the palace lines up outside to offer their farewells and well wishes to Marcel and me as we set out on our journey to Haymel.

We take four carriages in total, one is for Marcel, his courtier, and Rolley; another is for me, Esha, and Benny; one is for my expedition crew; and then a final one is for luggage. Then there are a total of ten guards on horseback and four footmen who also join us.

At some point, I had to fess up and tell Deean he couldn't join. He became fixated on finding the map and learning the functions of the anchor. The more I watched his passion grow, the more I knew I had to tell him before he became too emotionally invested.

To say he was pissed is an understatement, and had Benny not been present, I'm sure the fist he took to my arm would have been in the face.

He's so angry he's not even here this morning to send us off, and I haven't seen or talked to him in a few days.

"Make sure he stays away from the bottle," I whisper to Gran as we lean in for a hug.

"I'm worried he may have fallen into one. I haven't seen him in over two days." Pulling away, she squeezes my shoulder. "Don't you worry, I'll find him. You and your brother have more important things to fear than a grown man pouting because he can't go on a trip."

She makes sure our eyes lock when she states, "Now remember, Queen Cayleen is a callous, stone-hearted individual just like her mother was. Rumors have it that she has spies all over court, so be careful who you interact with. This may be a peace offering but be cautious of anything she offers you, especially in the form of a woman. The last thing you need is both your heads and heart tied to a Haymelian."

"Lovely. Please, don't spare any details on how much you hate her." I laugh.

"I mean it, Iann. A Haymelian can't be trusted. And you and your brother are walking targets once you cross into their territory."

I nod. "I'm sure there has to be one who can be trusted." She swats at my sarcasm. "But I understand."

She lets me go so my mother can have a turn. My mother goes back and forth from kissing mine and Marcel's heads. Her tears are uncontrollable.

"For goodness sake, Evie dear, they aren't babes." My grandmother rolls an eye at all the affection. "Stop with all the kissing and crying."

"It's a long journey." She sucks in a breath and wipes a few tears. "I just want them to be careful is all."

"They will be fine, my darling." My father plants a kiss on her right temple. "They will go make peace and we'll all be better off." He claps his hands. "Now! There is a schedule, and the Queen expects you soon. It's departure time, my sons."

Marcel and I offer him a bow and head to our carriages.

"Nice to see our brother couldn't bother to show up. Might be the last time he sees us for a few months and he's nowhere to be found. Probably buried deep in a bottle, or a woman." Marcel tosses me a dry smile and a wink.

"Nice to know the future king is so optimistic. Must give the people so much hope." But my reply only brings out a laugh from him.

Before we part ways, Marcel holds out a hand, blocking me from heading to my carriage. "What do you know about this man Father has instructed to join us?" Over his shoulder, I catch a glimpse of Rolley waiting. "I know you will be going off on your next adventure once we're done in Haymel, so I get the need for your crew, but he doesn't seem like he's with you."

Unlike Deean, Marcel is unaware of the flower and our father's obsession with it. "He knows the area I'm meant to explore well. Father thinks he belongs."

"And do you think he's of use?"

"Potentially." Giving Rolley another glance, I catch him looking back, offering me a slight grin. "He is either a man of his word or a leech that has made his way to our father. Either way, we will find out."

"Very well." I don't know if that's the answer he's looking for, but he doesn't ask anything further and offers my arm a squeeze. "This is gonna be fun, little brother." We separate and prepare to leave.

My father granted permission for us to use the larger carriages, and they are proving much more spacious and with softer cushions, which I'm grateful for on this long journey. I also made sure workers placed coats and blankets inside each carriage for when we approach the mountains. It might be perfect weather now, but the temperature will begin to drop drastically once we reach the mountain range.

Cheers and shouting erupt as we depart and continue through the city streets. It isn't until we are out of the castle's territory, and beyond the gates, that the air around us falls silent and the real journey begins.

Benny's storytelling is spellbinding and lasts hours without a single ounce of boredom. Before opening his emporium, he too, traveled and studied the lands of Ladora. He was once assistant to Hargo Vello, someone I met while in the kingdom of Ethmay, studying the land known as the Thistlebane. Hargo is also accredited for his most recent discovery in Diamondhead, where he and his crew dug up scrolls said to be left by King Tuhan.

Esha wasn't as enamored with Benny's stories, not until he brought up his studies in the divinities. Particularly the divinity of Mathemous, the one who is said to have crafted Saden and is widely known for his elemental powers, especially that of nature.

Although Esha has been with me since my adolescence, there are only a handful of things I have been able to pry out of him. One being his piousness to the divinities, and I know he always carries the symbol of Mathemous with him around his neck.

Benny's eyes dart to the side cart that carries the alcohol and back to Esha. It's the tenth time since leaving Saden that he's glanced at it.

"You can help yourself," I interrupt, and lift up the lid, revealing the selection of liquors. "I'm certain Deean stocked it himself when he still had intentions of coming."

Benny doesn't go for it immediately, but within a few minutes, the lid to the bottle of whiskey is off and a glass is in his hand.

"Can I get you two something?" He stops from serving himself.

"I don't drink, but thank you," Esha responds, before leaning back.

"Thank you, but my goal is to finish this book before we hit the mountains and that will make me see double," I say.

"I shall have the double for you, Your Highness. There was once—" Benny is cut off when he goes flying into the air. Whiskey and the glass going with him.

The seat beneath him rises and I draw a knife at the sight of a hand coming at me.

"Don't you dare touch my Hennessy." My eyes hit the back of my head when I recognize the voice.

Deean flies out of the storage space beneath the seat. Once he's fully out, I grab him by the collar and place the knife to his throat.

The carriage goes silent, and Benny settles back in his seat after practically being thrown in the air.

"What the hell is wrong with you?" Even with the metal at his neck, Deean offers up nothing but smiles. "I told you that you were to stay back in Saden."

Deean shoves me off, knowing I don't have the guts to do something. "We had a deal. I followed through and I'm going. Father can come fetch me if he wants me back." He pours himself a drink. "Though he doesn't. Probably won't even notice I'm gone, and if he does, he'll think I'm off drinking in some unspeakable place with unimportant people." A tinge of guilt comes over me. It's a thought most of us had when he didn't show up for the send-off.

The knife gets placed back in the sheath. "Technically, your end of the deal hasn't been fulfilled. You still owe me a map."

He nods and then wraps an arm around Benny. "And we are working on it. Aren't we?"

"Only if you don't scare me like that again," Benny says, eyeing Deean's glass. "And only if you pour me one."

Deean wastes no time and gets Benny the drink he's been longing for.

Esha clears his throat. "May I give my opinion on something?"

"No one really asked, but why not?" Deean settles back in his seat, placing a blanket over his legs. The heat quickly dropping, just as I said it would, the more we move through the mountains.

"It was already dangerous traveling with two Saden princes," Esha begins. "You now want us to carry on and take the entire line of succession into enemy territory?" Deean raises an eyebrow.

"He's right," I confirm.

"People won't know. Only those traveling with us know what I look like. I'll simply be another servant to you. A second Esha if you will." He stretches, and I wonder how long he was stuck in that storage compartment. "If it makes you feel better, I'll throw on some kind of disguise. Just to make sure people can't see a resemblance." It does little to comfort me.

"You would pretend to be the help just so you could get away from a palace that has everything one could need and people to wait on you night and day?" Esha makes the clarification for his own good. People would kill to live the lives we have, and to give it up for a taste of exploration is unfathomable to some.

"This must be your first time away from court." Benny chuckles before taking a swig and grimacing at the burn. "There is nothing better than discovering something new. No matter how glorious or treacherous it turns out, the high getting there is all the same. Feeds your soul, much like praying to Mathemous probably does for yours."

"Yes, only one has better outcomes, and it ain't a dead divinity," Deean chimes in.

There is a thud when my boot collides with Deean's foot. "And what about Marcel?" I pull everyone's attention back to the issue at hand. "You think he'll let you carry on once he finds out?"

"Stop worrying," Deean says with agitation. "Worrying is boresome. For someone who has experienced so much of life and the unexpectedness that comes with it, you care far too much about getting caught. Father will not blame you. Mother will not blame you. Marcel will not blame you. So why are you so worried?"

Done with arguing, I flip open my book and read the same sentence ten times before trying to get the last word. "Do what you want. And I'm not boring."

Deean smiles. "Never said you were. I'm certain I said worrying was boring."

Suddenly, the alcohol glasses jingle violently and our bodies sway uneasily, bobbing back and forth. We each cling to the seatbacks or whatever we can grab for stability, while the carriage driver tries to garner back control.

The carriage tips over, balancing on the wheels on the right side, and just when I think gravity is about to win and take us down sideways, the weight shifts and we are pulled back down on the left and become balanced again.

The driver stops and curses as he tries taming the horses.

Esha stops me from opening the door. "I'll go see what the issue is, Your Highness. Everyone stay here."

As he opens the door it slams back, sounding like it rips off the hinges. A strong flurry invades the carriage. Esha struggles to close the door behind him, but manages to do so with the aid of Benny and me.

A few minutes later, the door swings open again and Esha jumps back in, covered in snow.

"We traveled right into a snowstorm, and it covered a bed of rocks that nearly took us out. Originally, we were heading to a town called Alphen where we have accommodations for the night, but it's another few hours away. The driver says there is a place about ten minutes away where we can potentially stay and put the horses up for the evening. It's either that or stay here and freeze to death. Prince Marcel has already ordered us to keep moving and go to this not-so-far-off inn."

"Thank you, Esha." I turn my attention to Deean. "I advise you to work on a story as to why you're here. There's no hiding out here all night unless you wish to be ice by morning."

14

IANN

"You're a selfish soul that deserves to be left behind in this frozen, pathetic little town." Marcel grips the collar of Deean's shirt and pushes him against the carriage door. "If you think you're actually going to make it to Haymel with us, you have lost all sense."

Deean sucks in a sharp breath as his head slams into a glass window that I'm surprised doesn't shatter.

Deean was meant to stay hidden a little longer, but no one suspected Marcel would come over to our carriage. Once he opened the door, he saw Deean first and went red before pulling him outside.

Like the rest of us, he knows Deean being here is dangerous, but beyond that fact, he knows his presence comes with a level of managing.

In many ways, Marcel has always been Deean's protector. Their antagonistic behavior towards each other might not always suggest it, but there was once a time when they had a relationship stronger than any one of us. This bond, of course, intensified the more I found myself away from home, but one day I came back, and it was different. Their care for one another became tolerance. They never speak about it, and I do my best to never ask.

"I'm selfish? Ha. Shall we list the things you've taken just because you can?" Deean squirms under Marcel's weight. "I'll stay out of your way and you out of mine," he pleads, as Marcel places his hands near his neck, pushing his fists into his collarbones.

The crew traveling with us watches the interaction and begins whispering among each other.

Marcel's muscles are hard as boulders when I reach for his arm. "Maybe we should discuss this privately."

Marcel takes in the staring faces and releases Deean. "He is to go back to Saden as soon as we depart for our lodgings in Haymel." He leaves us and walks into the inn.

Deean doesn't need an *I told you so*, so I don't give it to him. He stands there, seemingly a bit distressed, as he fixes his coat. He takes a lot of crap from people, which would make me feel bad, but I know he also gives a lot.

"You, okay?" Benny steals the words from me.

Deean smirks. "Always."

We follow the rest inside and get out of the cold.

Harpen, Marcel's courtier, a no-nonsense, middle-aged man whom I've never seen smile, comes over to where we wait with Marcel. "They are fully booked, Your Highness. With the exception of one room." He looks back at the innkeeper and then leans in closer. "He is willing to force a few out of their rooms to free up space. That's if Your Royal Highness would like to do that?"

Marcel thinks it over, taking too long to respond.

"Absolutely not," I interject.

"And where do you suggest our men sleep?" Marcel whispers through his teeth.

"You want to remove commoners, some probably children, so that we have a place to sleep?" I'm astonished that he even considers it.

"That's what it sounds like to me," Deean adds unhelpfully. "I'm not surprised."

"I saw a barn next door," Esha interrupts before Marcel can kill Deean. "The princes can take the room and the rest of us can stay out there. There will be complaints, but it's either in there or in the snow."

Thank you, I mouth to Esha.

We are assured that our crew will be given food and spare bedding material to keep comfortable through the night. A few of them grumble, but Marcel offers them the carriages or outside to sleep if they want to complain. It shuts them up. At least the inn has a tavern on the lower level. I'm sure some will even sleep in there after a few rounds.

The innkeeper gives us our key and Esha and Harpen help us carry a few bags to the room. We climb up creaking stairs with loose planks—each could use another nail or two. Up two flights and down a long, dust-plagued hall, we come to room fourteen.

Harpen opens the door for us. A single window allows in dim light that is enough for me to make out the ten-feet by ten-feet room. The ceilings are short, and another two feet and my own six-feet, two-inch self would be scraping the top. There isn't much inside but a bookshelf with torn and worn-down books that I don't recognize. There is a small mantle with some nille stones for lighting a fire and next to that is a wardrobe that can only fit a few outfits. On the far wall, sitting in the center, the main focal point of it all is a large bed, the only one in the room.

Esha and Harpen take their leave and head back downstairs to the others.

"Dibs on the bed," Deean says, tossing his stuff in a corner.

"You should be in the barn with the others." Marcel moves over to a chair in the opposite corner. "There isn't a hell's chance that you are getting anywhere near that bed unless it's on the floor next to it. If you want a warm bed to sleep in, go find a wench you can share with."

Deean's eyes turn to slits. "That's not the worst idea you've had, albeit demeaning to those hard-working folks. Bet they wouldn't have an issue sharing."

"A prince and a sack of moinlings." I pick up the books on the shelf. "I think it would be hard for them to turn down." With not much to do in the room, I rummage through my bag and retrieve a few books along with notes I've been making. I know Benny is doing his part, but there is one person I have yet to have a conversation with. "I'll be downstairs if anyone needs me."

"Drinking already?" Deean perks up. "I'll come with you."

"Not drinking. Some of us actually came on this trip to work."

"Perfect, we can do both."

"Wait!" Marcel stops us before we can reach the door. "You two are working together?"

I look at Deean, and his eyes scream at me with desperation. He knows once the weather clears, Marcel will send him right back to Saden. He also knows that I might be the only one to save him.

Loosening the muscles in my jaw, I face Marcel who is still waiting for an answer. "Before Father ordered us to go to Haymel, I may have promised Deean he could go on my next voyage."

"Why the hell would you do that?"

"He's clever when he needs to be." My defense isn't so much in favor of Deean as it is in Marcel's opinion of my decisions. "It's one trip Marcel. It's not going to hurt anyone. In Haymel he stays out of sight so the Queen isn't suspicious, and once we are finished, he comes with me and is out of your way."

"You both know I'm not some underage brother you have to pass around and take care of," Deean interjects.

Marcel nods. "Yeah...we'll see."

"Pain in the ass," Deean whispers and leads the way out of the room. Down the hall, he grabs one of my books. "So, who do we have to speak to?"

"I need to speak to Rolley."

"Ah, yes. The man who claims his conveniently kidnapped great-grandfather is immortal. And why do we need to speak to him?"

"Again, I need to, not you." I snatch back the book. "I have questions for him. Plus, he's the only member of our crew who I don't know very well, and thanks to your escapades he's now aware all three Saden princes are about to cross into the land of our greatest rival. I need to be able to trust him."

Downstairs, we make our way into a nearly empty tavern that will surely get busy within the next couple of hours. The innkeeper is kind enough to get Rolley for us as we take a seat at one of several tables in the tavern.

There are two servers near the bar. One fixated on counting his moinlings, and the other lost in a letter he's reading. Every other second, I catch one corner of his mouth tugging upwards. I've seen, and been a victim of, those looks before. It's a love letter, no doubt.

Someone from the kitchen brings out a tray with various meats, bread, cheeses, and fruit, along with two pints of ale.

Rolley enters as Deean shoves a few cold cuts in his mouth and guzzles it down with half the ale.

"Your Royal Highnesses." Rolley bows and then sits when I gesture to the seat across from me.

"Thank you for joining me."

"Us," Deean corrects me.

Ignoring him, I continue on, "We didn't have time to speak when we first met, and I just wanted to make sure we were on the same page. Plus, I have a few questions that my father may not have addressed with you."

"Of course, sir. Ask away." Deean slides the tray to him. Rolley reluctantly plucks a few grapes and a slice of cheese from the assortment. "Thank you, sir."

I push the ale in his direction. "You may have that as well." Flipping through my journal, I open it to a blank sheet and search for the pen that I keep on myself at all times. "Now, I'm not sure if you've properly met him, but Benny may have found something quite valuable on this trip. He is still trying to figure out how it works, but I have no doubt he'll get there."

"We'll get there," Deean interrupts again, making me realize exactly why I prefer to work alone. "He and I already have some great leads, I'm sure we'll know more once we set sail for Farella."

"That's great to hear." Rolley folds his hands on the table. "May I know what it is you've found?"

"You may, once we learn more about it. Right now, there isn't much to tell."

"Very well, sir."

I proceed with my questions. "Why was your great-grandfather on Farella in the first place? It's not a common place to be and Haymel has always owned it. What was a Saden man doing there?"

"He wasn't from Saden. Born and raised in Haymel and eventually became a prisoner for theft against the Queen. He escaped their prison and was a stowaway on one of their trading ships. He thought it was going to the Land of Moonlight. At least that's what he claimed the sailor said. Hiding in a barrel, he was thrown out to sea and washed up on an unknown island, well, unknown to him. It was Farella." Rolley takes a long drink and then taps on the glass with his fingernails—nails, rather long and pointed at the tip. "He said he had no choice but to go farther onto the island. The island was too far from another land mass to swim, and staying near shore meant no fresh water and limited food."

"That's when he found the flower?"

"Soon after that. He said the flower gave off an intoxicating scent. Pulled him in much like a magnet, the scent growing stronger until he found the magical plant. One minute he's hiking the land and the next he's consuming the flowers."

"He just ate it?" Deean's eyebrows nearly hit his hairline. "What kind of person shoves something they have never seen before, let alone tried, into their mouth?" Two women walk by whispering amongst each other and tossing Deean and me a quick wink. Rumors about princes being here must have spread. "Don't answer that question," Deean proceeds. "But your father..."

"Great-grandfather," I correct.

"Who cares? One of his family members could have been ingesting poison for all he knew."

Rolley laughs. "Can't say I blame you there. Bloody idiot, if you ask me."

"And what happened after he ate it?" I jot down a few notes.

"He blacked out. Doesn't remember a thing. He said he ended up back on shore somehow. A few days later, he came across pirates ready to loot the land. My great-grandfather said he could show them treasure if they provided space on their ship and took him away from the island."

"I'd like to believe I'm a pretty optimistic guy, Mr. Rolley, but a prison escape, immortal flower consumption, and benevolent pirates—sounds like a bunch of horseshit to me." Deean reaches for a slice of turkey. "Why should we believe you? The said immortal has supposedly been kidnapped and isn't here to offer us proof, so what else you got?"

The same ambivalent emotions I felt when my father told me of the flower creep up. It all sounds like malarkey to me, too. A fool's quest, as we travelers say. I'm not against a challenging adventure, but this one feels near impossible.

"The King believes me. Is the King's word not enough?"

Deean's grin grows wild. "It would be, if he wasn't our father? We can read him better than most and I don't think even he is fully convinced. There has to be something else you can give us."

He's bluffing. Even he thinks there is something out there or he wouldn't be here. He wouldn't be excited to help Benny or stupid enough to hide in a storage space just to come along.

"We do appreciate you bringing this to our father's attention." I play along. "But I believe what my brother is getting at is for more information that can help us. Did your great-grandfather leave any journals, maps, letters, anything that can help?"

"His possessions were raided by his kidnappers. I understand how ludicrous this all sounds. Trust me, I do. I have grown up hearing this story, and if I'm honest, I'm pretty sick of it. All I can offer you are stories he told me growing up and hope that from there, you get nuggets of information that might be useful." He taps his hands on the table. "I put it on my great-grandfather's life, on the legend being true. The Ivian Flower is real."

Setting my pen down, I lean away from the table and eye Rolley before giving him a grin. "Betting the odds on an immortal man? I'm not too sure that counts. But while I don't have enough evidence to prove you're lying, I also don't have enough to prove you're not. My father may have ordered you here, but like all the people in my crew, you will earn your keep. Get better acquainted with Benny and Deean. You will work closely with them." Deean shoots me a sly side eye. "If you find anything, remember helpful accounts from your childhood, or have any concerns, you are to run them by Deean."

"In Haymel, we shall query about your great-grandfather. From there, Deean will be the one to decide if you continue on with us or return with Marcel back to Saden. After all, we don't really need you to continue on to Farella." Rolley cranes his neck to the right and then to the left, releasing a pop with each movement. His lips thin out and his nose twitches slightly. "Is that a problem?"

"No, Your Highness. I have no doubt that together we shall find the flower. Whatever help I can conjure up, I'm willing to give you freely."

The scent of roast and potatoes enters the rooms, along with a few more bodies. Out of fear of being heard, we end our conversation and join the others in our party for supper.

15
ARIAH

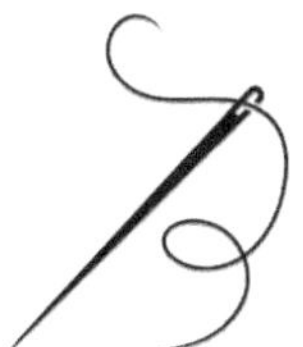

The road from Foxhead to the castle is an easy one and doesn't cause an ounce of trouble. The Queen must have ensured it this way so she could travel across Haymel comfortably. Hell, if I had her power and financial resources, I would do the same.

Accompanying me on the trip are Yanz, the driver, and Haya, one of the Queen's ladies. Yanz is a quiet man who is clearly only here to do as he's instructed. Every attempt I make at starting a conversation with him is shut down, and he walks away without a care for any of my questions. Haya, on the other hand, is a chattering beast and gossips nonstop. My mind tries to keep up with all the names she throws at me, while the information isn't useful now it may prove to be so once I'm at court.

When Haya isn't talking, sometimes even when she is, my focus sinks into the newness outside the carriage windows. For the first time, I get to witness scenery beyond my village.

All of nature's colors bleed with a new vibrancy. Forests hold glorious canopies, each with pockets of iridescent light, and I'm certain magic runs through the streams. The water is far too turquoise and refreshing for it to be ordinary.

The number of times the thought of running off to find out exactly how far the mountains in the distance are, or to know the feeling of a sea breeze coating my being, are alluring dreams I've had many times. But the deal I made with the Queen is set, and she doesn't seem like the type to care about my desires, so running away seems like a death sentence.

On the second day of traveling, Haya is in the middle of telling a story about her sister who is ill, when the road beneath us changes. It goes from smooth dirt to bumpy terrain, as if rolling over an unending number of cracks. Looking out the window I realize the forest disappears, and we are now traveling through busy city streets.

Growing up, I thought the council building was the largest building in Haymel, but the castle perched on the hill up ahead is nearly ten times its size. No singular person should be allowed to own something of such unnecessary stature.

"Gorgeous, ain't it?" Haya stops her story when she catches me suddenly hypnotized by what we're casually passing through. "Wait until you see the inside."

Lush reds and oranges cover the city, accenting the white castle.

Once we stop, Haya leads me inside where I discover she isn't exaggerating. The outside is nothing compared to the grandness of the interior. She takes me through several corridors before showing me into a room with tall, wide windows.

"You can wait here, in the study. I'll go see what the Queen would like to do with ya."

She leaves through one door as another door to the right of me opens, and three people make their way in.

"Who the hell are you?" asks one who wears a venomous-red lipstick and pearls in her long, voluminous curls.

She circles the room of the study, holding on to the sight of her prey, and I don't dare look away. She moves in a manner that sways her hips, drawing attention to her shapely frame; and if that hadn't captured my gaze, her use of bright colors that complement perfectly brown skin surely would've. Confidence seeps out in the way she moves, the way she speaks, even in what she wears.

"Play nice, Vera." A man wanders to the desk, cracking open a book, never giving me the time of day. Occasionally, I catch his lake-blue eyes glancing up at Vera, landing on her chest or hips, but he never stares for too long.

"Did you know about this, Skyleen?" Vera folds her arms over her chest. The man, who I assume is Skyleen, gives her a simple shake of his head. Vera's attention then turns to the woman, off to the right side of the room. "Did you, Chana?"

Chana leans against a wall playing with a string between her hands and intertwining it between all her fingers. She wears mostly black, her deep purple lipstick almost just as dark. Her skin is swarthy and rich, and I assume she isn't originally from Haymel. A fringe swoops over her forehead and her hair is chopped right below the ears, barely grazing her shoulders. I catch sight of a dagger in her boot and when she follows my gaze, all she gives me in return is a smirk.

"She's the newest recruit," Chana finally gives Vera a reply. "The fifth Fox."

"She's no Fox," Vera spits, seemingly disgusted by the thought of new blood in her precious group.

Chana also said fifth, given there are currently four of us in this room, I wonder where the other is.

The doors suddenly swing open, and it is my first time seeing the Queen since Luna's wedding.

Everyone stands up straight, even Skyleen, who slams the book shut and tucks it into his coat, before offering a bow.

The Queen's dress is cerise, like it has been immersed in blood, with gold beads trailing over the swirling patterns on the corset and over the hemlines. The sleeves are long and puff out at the shoulders. Her red hair is pinned up tight, and she enters carrying what looks like a kit, asleep in her arms.

"Ah, good you're here. I see you all met Ariah Tyddle. Ariah's parents, like yourselves, were once some of my most trusted Foxes." Skyleen looks at me for the first time, his eyes burning holes in me. "She will be taking turns training with each of you. You will show her all your ways, exactly how I like them." The Queen spins in my direction. "There is another Fox, but I'm afraid I sent her off to Ethmay to deal with an urgent matter. You'll meet her when she returns. Chana will be your mentor of sorts. You can work out times for your lessons with Vera and Skyleen. We have company arriving in a few days and I need you ready." She leans in close, the scent of azalea wafting off of her. "Remember, you need not only succeed for yourself, but your parents too."

Most of the lessons come from Chana, who on my day of arrival, showed me every inch of the castle, including select hidden places few people know about. She also showed me my new room, which is bigger than I imagined. Definitely more spacious than my room back at home.

Over the next four days, I'm at her mercy. Chana is what I would call a watcher, and unlike Vera, who does most of the mingling with court guests, Chana prefers to be in the background. Not just because it gives her a better vantage point, but because she seems to prefer it.

Every day she gives me names of various advisors, lords, ladies, servants—anyone we pass—and any information tied to them.

Today isn't any different. "You'll learn who everyone is soon enough," she says, sorting through a stack of letters without her name on a single one. "One of your many jobs will be to observe everyone associated with court. Any abnormal activity is to be investigated. Most actions lead to nothing serious, but if anything in any way involves the Queen, you are to report to me." Pulling a blade from her pocket, she slices one of the letters open. "Last year, we caught a lord planning an assassination attempt on the Queen. You'd be surprised what fools think is safe in a letter."

My finger slides between the collar of my dress and my neck. Heat suddenly fills the room. I make a mental note to be discreet in my letters home.

She tucks away the letter and rolls her eyes, seeming unamused by the contents.

My mouth opens wide and before I can stop it, I suck in a deep breath and try to hide my yawn. "Not used to staying up late?" Chana snickers at my yawn.

"Not at all. I would usually be waking up in a few hours."

Chana looks at the wall behind me. "Crap. I forgot about your lesson with Sky." She swipes her arms in the air, pushing me out. "He'll be waiting by your room. Hurry!"

Rushing out, I race to my chambers trying not to look suspicious. And just like she said, he is in fact, waiting.

"I'm sorry." My hands go to my hips, the stance somehow making it easier to breathe. "Chana and I were…"

"I didn't ask." Sky starts walking away. "Keep up."

We move out of the corridors and pass the gardens, not stopping even when we hit the boundaries of the woods. He moves quickly and I almost have to run to keep pace with him.

At the start I think I'm going to meet my end, or far worse, be taken advantage of. But like all the other times I've interacted with him, he mostly ignores me. That's until we reach a massive tree that would have taken four of me to wrap my arms around the trunk.

"It's a tannum tree," he says, dropping his bag. It is the first time I've heard him speak a full sentence. The bass in his voice startles me. "The roots rise up and stick out of the ground just before dawn." He points to a sea of upright roots that emerge from the soil. "They are strong enough to cure the deadliest poisons. I add some to most of my antidotes."

Antidotes was a lesson my father didn't have time for, and I wonder if this root can be found in any of the books he gave me.

"Are they only native to Haymel?" I pick at the thin, long roots then cut with one clean swipe of my blade and shove them into my bag.

"No. This tree was imported from a forest near the kingdom of Ethmay. The locals near there call it the Forest of Thornes. The Queen had to pay a hefty price to get it here. Don't grab the bent ones!" he warns, seeing me going for one. "Those are rotting, and the healing properties fade with it. Some contain dangerous toxins."

"Good to know." I move on to another that is sticking upright. "Do they heal everything?"

He shakes his head. "No. They have their limits like every-thing else. But they are a great antidote to most poisons your body may be exposed to."

"So, you're an apothecary?"

"That's obvious." He points off to the right, like he didn't just give me sarcasm. Lucky for him, I bite my tongue. "Go for the thicker ones."

"You know, my father is—"

"Yes," he huffs, stopping me. "Your father is an apothecary. I'm well aware of who your parents are. Collect two more so you can go. Your next lesson is approaching."

At a slower pace, I drag out picking two more roots. It takes everything within me not to respond to him.

"That's two. What's next?"

Sunlight creeps onto the tops of the trees and the tannum roots are already crawling back into their hiding spots.

"The gallery room on the second floor next to the library. Vera will be waiting." He grins. "Good luck."

"That's it?" The lesson is rather short and I don't see the point in it.

"For now, yes." Sky continues picking roots. "As long as you learn something new with each lesson, I consider it a job well done." He stands straight, his tall frame nearly touching a branch of the tree. "Did you know about tannum roots before today, or did your father teach you that?"

My tongue clicks instinctively. "He did not." I lift my shoulders and scrunch my nose. "Job well done." I almost add in a *good boy* but I'll keep it for another time. He's bound to be an ass again.

He walks farther into the forest, swiftly disappearing out of sight.

Good thing we didn't go too far from the grounds. Finding my way back is easy, but my stomach turns at having my first lesson with Vera.

Hopefully, it's a little more enlightening. I can't say that plucking branches from the ground taught me a lot. The time would have been better spent on sleep.

Still new to the castle's layout, I head up to the second floor and immediately become lost. People pass me in the grand halls, whispering at the new face they see in court.

My favorite part of being around so many people is seeing the multitude of different outfits and eventually getting to wear them. Trends run rampant in court and, unlike in Foxhead, the people here actually care about what they're wearing.

Buttons and lace must be the newest trend. So many people are wearing buttons that serve zero purpose, but I don't hate it, not one bit. As soon as I can find some free time—if I'm ever allotted any—my first goal is to find material and sewing supplies. Designs slosh around in my head given my pen and pad were replaced by a dagger, I'll just try to mentally keep track of them all.

Along with the choice of custom-made, jewel-encrusted weapons, which in my opinion is too much, I was told to choose a few dresses and various outfits to wear in an attempt to blend in around court.

The story is that I am a daughter of a distant relative of the Queen, here to assist her with courtly duties. There are a lot of people in court with those types of roles, so no one really questions the legitimacy of it all. Plus, if the Queen says it to be true, then that's the end of the conversation.

I peek into each room until I come across a library and know the gallery room is close.

A large arch creates the entrance, it is the only room on the level without doors. Inside, small groups wander around looking at the hundreds of paintings and sculptures. According to Chana, this part of the castle and the throne room are the only two areas open to certain, more sophisticated, members of the kingdom.

It's an odd place for training. I don't even know what Vera is supposed to train me in.

Outside of people-watching, Chana has gone over weapons, much like my mother, only more in depth and with a greater passion. If there is one thing Chana loves, it is a sharp blade and a steady hand. She speaks of her weapons as if they are people and cares for them much more.

I catch a glimpse of an emerald green dress fashioned with bronze buttons that run up the bust to a covered neck. That's when I see red lipstick and dark eye shadow. Vera.

"There you are!" She waves me over.

Her face is bright, lit up like she's been waiting all day to see me. This newfound, friendly demeanor is off-putting and stops me from moving closer. Vera made it clear the first day I met her, that she doesn't care much for me, and I don't have the highest opinion of her.

Vera continues to wave to me and people soon give me strange stares for not acknowledging her.

Play along, I repeat internally and move to her.

At my approach, she leans in and plants two kisses, one on each cheek. Pulling away, her eyes drift up and then down, examining my black dress with a puffed-out skirt that I happened to pair with a long-sleeved lace top. A single chuckle is let loose. "Ariah, dear." She tries to hold on to the chipper sound she possessed when I first entered the room. "Has someone died? In court we usually refrain from wearing black unless necessary."

"Not yet." I copy her perkiness. It feels grotesque pretending. "Some say the divinities would often wear black as a symbol of power. Plus, I like it. Is my preference an issue?"

"Good morning." A young woman dips her head at the sight of me and Vera.

Lady Arranella Gallor is what Chana had called her. She is also someone Chana and I have been spying on the past couple of nights, which is a rather creepy thought, but then I remind myself that is our mission, given to us by the Queen. She is the wife of Lord Theo Gallor, who is an old, stuffy man, and because of it, his wife has a knack for seeking out attention from several people in court, and I mean several. All of whom she sneaks out to meet in the late hours of the night. I don't particularly care about who she does or doesn't spend her nights with, but Chana says the Queen is convinced she has other motives outside of pleasure. Treasonous acts. Ones that could send her straight to the gallows.

"My Lady," Vera says as she curtsies, and I do the same.

"Vera. It's a pleasure to see you this morning." She eyes me. "I know we have met once but I'm dreadfully awful at remembering names. Do remind me."

"It's Ariah, My Lady."

"That's right," she says with a burst of energy. "You're one of the new ladies-in-waiting to the Queen. Pleasure."

She shifts her attention back to Vera. "Only a few days left of my little getaway. I'll be hosting a farewell party the night before my departure, in the Rose House. You must join. You as well, Ariah, and any guest you wish to bring." Her accent differs from most of us at court. It's higher pitched and sometimes she speaks so quickly words get jumbled into one large one.

"Such a shame you have to leave so soon. The castle is less dull when you're here." Vera exaggerates her words and laughs when Lady Gallor does.

"I'll have to come without my husband next time. He instantly sucks out all the air in the room when he's around. Floppy old geezer needs to let death win already." I summon a fake laugh and catch Vera giving me a look when it comes out too forcefully. Lady Gallor waves to someone else in the room. "I must be going, but remember, my last evening here in the Rose House. I expect to see both of you."

"We'll be there," Vera calls out as Lady Gallor takes her leave. With a quick spin, Vera interlocks her arm with mine. "Walk with me, Ariah."

Together we stroll the room, examining the paintings but never speaking. People come in and out of the room until Vera and I are the only two left inside. It isn't until the room falls silent when Vera stops.

She lets go of my arm and moves in front of a portrait. I am way too concerned wondering what this woman is up to, to notice the portrait is of a group of people on a summer's day. There is a lake in the background with swans floating atop it. In the front is a gazebo covered in blooming flowers, and two women are painted on the steps. One of them is my mother, and the other has long, wavy hair with deep red lips.

"Is that your mother? Our parents were friends?"

"Partners." Vera's tone is cold, and all the light is gone from her face. I knew it was too good to be true.

"Your first lesson. Never let personal feelings get in the way of the job. Your loyalty is always to the Queen." She steps closer. "A lesson your mother didn't comprehend."

There is about an inch of height difference between us, and we nearly come eye to eye when I close the gap between us. "Speak of me as you will, but my parents are off limits."

She laughs at something sinister. "And is Ariah Tyddle going to be the one to stop me? Foolish girl," she spits out mockingly. And before I can reply, she pulls a dagger from her sleeve and locks her hand deep in my curls, spinning me around and pulling my head back so she can have easier access to my neck. The metal is cold and stings my skin. "Ever threaten me again and I'll have your blood stained on the floor before you can utter a sound. I'll do what my mother should have done years ago."

My head cocks at an uncomfortable angle, staring straight at a ceiling I didn't notice is painted—I'd have more appreciation for its beauty if there wasn't a blade to my throat.

Though out of sight, I recall a sculpture of a bird with a rather long neck resting to my right, which would now be on my left. I could try searching for it with my hand, but there is no guarantee I could reach it before Vera has her way.

I don't doubt her ability to kill me. The Foxes have all been trained to carry out such deeds in a multitude of ways. But she's not daft enough to risk the Foxes' exposure to carry out some harbored vendetta.

There are sudden footsteps, and she pulls my hair tighter at their approach.

"I recall the Queen telling us all to play nice." Chana sounds as if she's used to this constant behavior. "She's ordered all of us to her study. Alive."

"And lesson number two"—Vera releases my hair and

removes the blade before pushing me forward—"be like Chana here, and always show up for your partner."

She pushes past Chana and me.

My scalp is burning and there is an alarming sensation around my neck. My shoulders rise and I feel my airways tighten. My hands can't decide if they want to hold my neck or chest, so one rests on each.

"Ariah?" Chana's voice is growing distant, and I take a few steps away from her.

In my pockets I dig for my spray. I release one spritz and hold it in. When I release my breath it's as if a thousand pounds fall from me.

"Ariah?" Chana calls again and this time it's clearer. "Vera likes to put borga on her blade. A poisonous algae she makes Sky go searching for. It numbs the skin and surrounding area but it's not deadly." I feel her hands at my neck. "It didn't get into your bloodstream. You should be okay."

"She said the lesson was about not taking things personally. That felt personal to me." I find my composure.

"Vera is what I like to call the Queen's mask. She's good at making people trust her. She wears many different faces and uses the best one to get close to her target. Secrets are far easier to unravel the closer you are to a person." She tips her head to the exit. "The Queen hates belatedness. We should go."

16

ARIAH

A ten-foot tall birdcage is set in the middle of the room—the golden bars house birds of various colors and sizes, jumping from branch to branch of the tree within the boundary.

Walls are lined with bookshelves and tables. Atop each table is some form of art—ceramic ware, paintings, sculptures—or terrariums. There is an overwhelming number of terrariums in the room, which adds life to the chamber. I was expecting gloominess. Dark colors for a dark soul, but it's suspiciously bright.

Rounding the birdcage, I see Vera and Sky waiting on steps that lead up to a desk the Queen is writing away at.

Vera looks over and tosses me a malicious grin, but I cut it off with a bow I offer the Queen.

"King Marcel II of Saden has declined my invitation to join us for a ball to end our kingdoms' long-running rivalry. However, he is for ending the feud. In exchange, he is sending not one, but two of his sons. Prince Marcel and Prince Iann." She stands, displaying another jaw-dropping outfit that is more elegant than all the outfits I've seen yet in this kingdom.

Bending over, she scoops up the same kit I saw her with when I arrived. "We are scheduled to receive them tomorrow, and the ball shall be in a weeks' time. Vera, you are to escort Prince Marcel during his time here. Show him everything Haymel has to offer." I catch the side eye Sky throws Vera's way but my vision snaps back to the Queen when she calls my name. "Ariah, congratulations, you have your first task. You are to be Prince Iann's escort during his visit. Like Vera, your only goal is to focus on him, and him alone. You both are to keep the princes happy at all costs." She descends a few steps.

At all costs?

There have been stories over the years of the three Saden princes. Each with a hunger for sovereignty and a thirst for riches and an appreciation for late night company. Bedding anyone they please just because they can. Possessing both women's hearts and an overabundance of great treasures.

I've known one man my entire life. A drunken, foolish mistake I made nearly three years ago. So awful and not worth the memory because I can't even recall the poor bloke's name, and I remember almost everything. I want to say it was Timothee...no, Thorton. Whatever it was, the two things I can't get out of my head are the scent of strawberry wine and vomit, a sickening combination. I grimace, tossing the memory away once again.

"While this visit seems like a promising one for our kingdoms, my excitement is reserved. The former Saden king and his vile wife were responsible for the deaths of my parents. I was named the 'Orphan Queen' because of them." A vein twitches in her neck. "I have no issues ending the feud, but I don't trust anyone from Saden, especially those in line to rule the kingdom. If they are plotting against my crown, I want to know everything. You are to intercept their letters, listen in to conversations not meant for you, and drag out any possible secrets that might pose a threat to Haymel. Sky you are to tamper with their drinks and food, causing them to have looser lips. And Chana, do what you do best. Find things hidden in the shadows." Simultaneously, we all nod. "Now, you may go and prepare for tomorrow. Everyone except Ariah."

It isn't until the door shuts that she moves off the steps and towards me.

"Tea." She continues to the other end of the room and disappears behind a wall. Taking it as a command and not a question, I rush to follow.

We find ourselves in a circular room with walls made of glass, the space overlooks one of the many gardens on the property. In the center is a table, and the one wall that isn't made of glass holds a floral print that looks overdue for a replacement.

The Queen sits and places the fox in her lap. With the slightest head flick from her, she has me rushing to my seat as she begins pouring the steaming liquid into a cup as I get comfortable.

"Cream?" She pours some into her cup and holds it up, waiting for my answer.

"Umm, yes, please." Once the cream is in, she goes for the sugar, dropping a teaspoon in hers and then holds it out waiting for me again. "No, thank you. Not a fan of it in my tea."

Whatever I say makes her smile. "Your mother was the same way. Said it ruined it." There is an instant longing for home at the mention of my mother. "Tell me Ariah, how are you getting on with the other members?"

"Chana is helpful." I blow on my tea and take a quick sip. Her eyes pierce mine, so I swallow quickly. "Sky is still a mystery and Vera is...Vera is maniacal." I'm blunt and not sure if I went too far on the Vera part.

"Vera is fiery, which is why she's so good at what she does. Her mother was a Fox, just like yours. Partners at one point."

"So, I've been told." Reflexively my hand goes to my throat, still feeling the bite of Vera's blade.

"I have no doubt Vera will share the story with you at some point." The Queen's smile is wicked, but she lets it fade away to sip on her tea. "Anyway"—she perks up and sets her cup down — "I am here to make good on one of my promises. The ball will be a masquerade and the most important people in Haymel have been invited. Fine occasions call for fine outfits." She pauses to butter a biscuit and admires the blissfulness beyond the glass wall. "Ariah, you are to design a dress for me to wear to the ball, as well as design one for each of the Foxes, including yourself."

All the tea in my mouth nearly comes flying out. "Me? You want to wear something I design to the ball?"

"That was the agreement, was it not?"

"I remember. I just didn't think..."

"That I would make good on my promise." She bites into the biscuit, wiping away any crumbs with a napkin. "I do what I say I'm going to do, and I expect the same from others. Now, remember you are still in training, and with the princes arriving tomorrow, you will need to find time to create these pieces when you're not busy. You start slacking and I'll make other arrangements." I nod, finishing up the tea in my cup. "Good. I will have Ernessa, one of my ladies-in-waiting, show you where you can find the sewing room you'll be working in." She picks up the teapot. Steam rolls up, and I catch her glance at me. "Don't disappoint me."

I might not be any good at being a Fox, but I know how to design a dress. Disappointment is something she won't feel when she sees what I have in mind.

17

IANN

It took us a few days to travel out of the mountains, and another few days later, we ended up in a village called Foxhead.

We weren't meant to stay in the village, but Deean ate old meat and ended up vomiting in our carriage, which had Esha vomiting with him. All of it was a hot, smelly mess. With nightfall coming it was best to get a place in town. Of course, we weren't as welcome as we would have liked, and found ourselves without a place to sleep that night.

Thankfully, a woman overheard the innkeeper using colorful vernacular about us being Saden. Despite the many attempts to assure him we were there to end the feud, he still wasn't accommodating. The woman, who was privy to the whole ordeal, said her name was Adreena, and she led us to her family's home. She and her husband put us up for the night.

Having two daughters who no longer lived at home meant two available beds. Marcel, who was still annoyed with Deean, took his own bed this time while I took the other one, and Deean was left to sleep on the floor. The rest of the crew stayed in the carriages or in the study our hosts kindly offered.

There hadn't been much to the room. The bed was warm and provided much more cushion than any inn we had stayed in so far. There had been a torso of a mannequin, which Deean hated, draped in an unfinished dress, along with scrapes of fabric on the floor and parchments with sketches of outfits. I assume one of the daughters must have been a seamstress or designer of sorts.

In the morning, some of Queen Cayleen's guards came for us. They were supposed to have met us at a place called Pointers Pass but when we didn't show they went searching.

Today, we are to finally arrive in the city that rests before the castle gates.

As we plod forward, I notice city streets are darker than the ones in Saden. Not dirty or tainted, but unlike the light neutral colors of Saden, Haymel looks like it is stuck in an eternal autumn. Deep reds, browns, and oranges run rampant along the streets and buildings. Golden flags with a black embroidered fox wearing a crown wave from every other building.

According to many stories, the Queen has an obsession with foxes, which is why our father sent us off with a golden fox to gift to her.

"You ready?" Deean asks me.

He wears a distracting fake beard and mustache. He thought he looked too much like Marcel and me, which he does, and to blend in as one of the crew he decided to disguise himself. He even changed his clothes and accent, for whatever reason, and has fully committed to the part.

"You look ridiculous." My vision shifts back out the window as I watch the gate open for us, anxious for the task ahead. "We could have just said you were a cousin or something."

Deean waves me off. "No relationship is best. And me being your courtier means I still have access to the important things." Esha coughs a little before taking a sip of water. "You don't mind, right, Esha?"

Another part of his grand plan is to wait on me hand and foot. Well, pretend to. Meaning Esha gets to enjoy a little time off and I'm going to end up doing everything myself.

"Also I was thinking"—Deean plays with his disguise—"maybe it would be best if you call me Eli during this trip. Having two Esha's might be confusing."

"Eli? Like your old dog?" I question the hilarity of it all.

"Figured it would do for the time being."

"I suppose it works. Although, it shouldn't be confusing because there is in fact only one Esha. The only one making this difficult is you."

Deean comes closer and grips my shoulder. "You know this will be twice as fun with me here. Just you and Marcel..." He grimaces at the thought. "How boring that would have been. You know he's no fun."

There is a little pride in knowing I'm the other fun brother, especially coming from the king of fun himself.

The carriage jolts forward, and we move up a gravel path towards the cream-colored castle, almost like a pale yellow when white flower petals die. The rooftops are a washed-out black, nearly gray, giving it an old, almost eerie feel.

From the window, I see a woman standing in front of dozens of people. Her hands are delicately folded in front of her as she waits for her guests. She wears an off-white dress with traces of olive green, Saden's colors. Her skin looks like it's been coated in amber and the strands of her hair are the orange of a dying fire, nearing a dark red. Her thin lips form a straight line, and she doesn't look excited for this visit, making two of us.

I stretch my neck and flex my fingers. The muscles in my body seemingly tense, and the thrumming of my heart finds a faster beat.

"I thought she would look older," Deean says, looking

through the window. "She's near our parents' age but looks closer to Marcel's. How is that possible?"

"Magic," Benny says with a sarcastic awe as his smile fades. "I've done a fair share of studying on the Queen, especially since I knew I was coming here. A lot of people believe she has special ties to pretty powerful enchantresses."

"Blasphemous," Esha whispers.

I've seen the workings of enchanters during my travels. Have even used some of their creations on my own trips—a secret that I will take to my grave. Their presence in Saden is illegal. Of course, I could find one if I really searched; but throughout our kingdom's history their dark magic has been known to cause more issues than solutions, so my great-great-grandfather made their practices illegal.

"Don't be so uptight, Esha." Deean is still glued to the window. "Whoever she is working with has her looking great. Or maybe she's blessed by your divinity. Did you think of that?"

"No." Immediately a floodgate of thoughts rises, all of them involving Deean screwing this up. "Whatever you are thinking, you are to rid it from your mind. You are acting as one of our workers and that's it. The Queen of Haymel is off limits to you, do you understand?"

He turns to me and draws his eyebrows together. "Why would you say that?"

"I know you. Your mind is both predictable and a mystery, and that in itself needs to be studied. You are not allowed to flirt, drink with, kiss, or sleep with anyone on this trip. I will force you to travel back with Marcel if I find out you have done any of those things."

"Flirting for some of us is like breathing. We may not even know we're doing it."

"I mean it."

"Fine." Aggressively he shuts the drapes and falls back in his seat.

The carriage door swings open, all eyes drift to me, knowing I have to exit first. I scooch past Esha and lower myself onto the steps of the carriage.

The air has a slight bite but is durable, and the sun is hidden behind a patch of clouds.

Marcel gets out of his coach, and I wait until he moves to take my first step. Eventually, we walk side by side to the welcoming party.

Marcel and Queen Cayleen greet each other first, shaking hands, and Marcel ever so slightly bobs his head.

"Thank you for opening your kingdom to us, Queen Cayleen. The dissolution of our kingdom's feud is long overdue." He steps back and it's my turn.

I copy the smooth ease he had while walking up to her. She places her hand in mine. It's silky and a little cold, despite the long-sleeved dress she wears.

She holds my hand for a few seconds, then her hazel eyes scan over me and then behind me at the rest of the bodies waiting.

"Thank you both for coming." Her vivacious tone has the people behind her smiling at us, and she speaks with precision, knowing exactly what she wants to say. "I would like to introduce you to two of my ladies who will gladly be escorting you throughout the week."

She steps aside, revealing a woman in bold colors who looks like a divinity who's returned to walk this earth. I keep my eyes on hers, which is hard, and I also catch the subtle perusal my brother gives her frame. "This is Lady Vera. She has served me a great deal of time and will be here to show you, Prince Marcel, all the finest things Haymel has to offer." Vera curtsies and gives my brother a smug look. I hear Deean whisper something behind me but ignore him.

The Queen takes another step to the side. "And this is Lady Ariah. One of my newer ladies but I'm sure she'll be able to show you a great deal, Prince Iann." Ariah curtsies and I swear I've heard her name spoken somewhere before. I know I haven't seen her, surely, I would have remembered a face like hers.

Although she's not of royal blood, that I know of, I would argue she is the most put together. I would even go as far to say her style choice surpasses the Queen's. She has the tiniest coils that are collected in a beige ribbon, where a few curls break loose and hang at the sides of her ears and over her shoulders. She too, wears a long-sleeved dress but the material running up her arms and at her neck is lace, teasing me with pockets of her brown umber skin. Her lips are a plush pink and glossy like they have been coated with oil.

"Are you ready?" Marcel whispers under his breath before he nudges my arm.

"What?" Confused as to why he's trying to get my attention.

That's when I see the Queen extending an arm up the steps. "I asked if you both are ready to explore the grounds."

I hadn't even realized she was speaking to me. Clearing my throat, I find an answer for her. "Um, yes...Yes, I am."

The Queen leads, with Marcel and I following behind.

"Your workers will stay in the east wing, with mine in the workers' quarters. Beds, meals, and recreation, when they are not working, will be available. Their only rule is to stay out of areas they are told to refrain from entering." Queen Cayleen talks as she leads us through a courtyard garden. A few foxes chase each other through maze-like walls created by rose bushes. "You two will be staying in the west wing. Vera and Ariah will show you the way. I unfortunately have a meeting with a few of my advisors, but we will come back together for supper where I can hear more about Saden. Again, I am happy you both have made the journey. Feel free to explore the grounds. What's mine is yours. Please excuse me."

"Thank you." Marcel nods, and the Queen vanishes down a distant hall, adjacent to the courtyard.

"Shall we show you to your rooms?" Vera nods to someone who takes our crew off to the east wing, leaving our courtiers and a guard for each Marcel and myself. Esha is hesitant to leave, but Deean doesn't budge, and eventually he follows the others. "Or is there something else you would like to do first?"

"The room sounds nice, doesn't it brother." Marcel taps my arm before following Vera.

The two of them take the lead, with Ariah and I following a few feet behind. They start by asking each other a few questions, joking and laughing between them.

"Was it a long trip, Prince Iann?" Ariah asks as we exit the gardens and head into a hall.

"It was." I hear Deean clear his throat a little too loudly. It must not have been a satisfactory response. "As far as journeys go it was a smooth one."

Her face brightens and her skin takes on a warm glow. "That's good to hear. I'm sure as a prince you are used to traveling all over. I hear your last visit was to Diamondhead, where you found unique stones in the mountains." She closes off part of the gap between us. "What was it like?"

"Finding the stones or the journey?"

"All of it." Her eyes widen and the enthusiasm brings a smile to my face.

"Invigorating. Every journey. Every discovery. There is always something new. The stones turned out to be black diamonds and surprisingly, they weren't on the mountain. Thanks to local stories and several days of research, we pinpointed that the diamonds would have never been in the mountain, but somewhere near the border of Shadow Pass."

"Don't bore the woman," Marcel calls back, and Vera and him share a laugh and more whispers.

My face heats and frustration forces me to end my story.

"I am not bored, Prince Iann," Ariah whispers, and the warmth of her body covers my right side. "Coming here was my first time leaving my village. A virgin to travel, some may say. You're welcome to tell me any of your stories so that I may live vicariously through them."

"It's Iann," I correct.

"Isn't that what I said?" Her face scrunches like she's said the most offensive thing in the world.

"Just Iann, Lady Ariah. You don't have to call me Prince Iann." I pull myself away from her gaze as we ascend to a new level.

"Well, that's not fair. If I drop the prince, will you drop the lady?"

"Deal."

The long hall branches off into two at the end; Vera takes Marcel, Harpen, and Marcel's guard to the right, as Ariah leads the rest of us left.

"The castle is a maze but I'm sure you're used to it," Ariah says. "I'm still trying to find my own way around. If you ever get lost, remember it's the west wing of the rose garden, down the hall with the excessive number of red items, up the stairs and down another incredibly long hall, and then left at the end. If you don't see the peacock, it means you're down the wrong hall or possibly in the entirely wrong wing." She points down towards a peacock statue with actual feathers, and Deean lets loose a laugh that he smothers with a cough. "Your room is the fifth door on the left." She opens the wide doors. It is smaller than my room back at home but it's more than enough for my time here. "Oh my!" Ariah walks around, peering out the window and then examines the bed. "This room is bigger than..." She stops herself as she looks back at Deean and me. "Sorry. Well, this is it. Is there anything you need from me right now? I can give you a tour of the grounds?"

Deean arches an eyebrow at me. "No, that's okay," I assure her.

"How about helping to unpack your belongings?"

"My courtier has that." I pat Deean on the back. "Matter of fact, you might want to go direct the others on where they can bring Marcel's and my belongings."

Deean's eyelids close in on each other, but don't fully shut. "As you wish, Your Royal Highness." He turns to Ariah and dips his head. "Lady Ariah."

He mumbles under his breath as he walks past us but it's too low for me to hear.

"Alright"—Ariah crosses the room, coming closer—"if there isn't anything else I will excuse myself. I'm sure the Queen has a list of things for me."

"Will you be dining with us tonight?" There is an eagerness in my tone that I hope she doesn't pick up on.

She smiles. Damit, she heard it.

"I might," she teases before offering a curtsy. "Pleasure meeting you, Iann. If you do think of something you need, please, let me know."

Ariah leaves and I explore what will be my room for the next few weeks. Besides the main door, there is an additional one leading to a washroom with an enormous bronze bath. There are three steps on either side of the white bed with golden trim along the frame. The best part of the room would have to be the balcony.

There is a hard thud on the floor and an exasperated breath from Deean.

"I've never had to carry my own bags, let alone someone else's." He looks around getting a full view of the room. "Not bad. A smidge too small for the both of us but it'll do."

"Both?" I frown, unpacking the trunk with all of my books. "This is my room. Your bed is in the workers' quarters."

"Ha." Deean finds the liquor cabinet and searches for something he likes. "I will pretend in public, but when those doors are closed, I am back to being a prince, and more importantly your older brother. I'll be sleeping in here with you. The bed is more than big enough." He looks over at me with his hand on a bottle. "Unless you would like someone else in your bed. Perhaps Ariah can assist you in other ways." A grin pushes upwards of his face.

"You're exhausting," I mutter, and pretend to flip through one of the books as a distraction.

I don't admit it to him, but there is something appealing about her, beyond just the looks, which were equally there. I'm not sure what it is, but one thing is sure, I will use my time in Haymel to find out.

18

ARIAH

Whispers of the two Saden princes in Haymel travel around the castle walls faster than the winds of a howling storm; and although I tell myself not to be paranoid, I can't help but feel like eyes are on me.

Everyone knows I've been tasked with escorting the young prince around during his stay. The "new girl" assigned with such a duty. No one says these words aloud, but I can't help but speculate that's what they are thinking. Most of me cares little for their opinions.

There are also whispers about the Queen's mental state for letting, not one but two, rival royals within the boundaries of our kingdom.

It's all absurd to me. What damage could the two princes do? The Queen has more allies here. People who would have no issue defending her if need be. Overall, their arrival had gone well. Quick and to the point, and I think I played my role well.

Vera's follow-up lesson that afternoon, after her attempt to murder me, was to always flirt but never appear desperate, especially when it comes to royalty. "They want to feel desired but not used, tread that line very carefully," she had warned.

From the little interaction I've had with them, I can say my interest in Prince Marcel is practically nonexistent. His smug demeanor is undesirable. I especially didn't like the way he spoke to his brother. Jaleese and I would have certainly gone at it if she spoke to me like that, attempting to be funny in front of strangers.

As for Iann, I really could have listened to more of his adventures. I am a bit jealous that he even has stories to tell, and I don't. At first, I didn't know if he was going to speak to me, but I think I pulled a decent conversation out of him.

Both brothers were given looks crafted from the divinities. Marcel is an inch or two taller and carries more definitive muscles that make his coat a bit too snug. His skin is also a shade darker than Iann's. The rich brown complementing the sage green of his outfit well, was the only thing about him I appreciated.

Iann is slender and has finer features. His eyes, from the quick view I got, are an entrapping brown with flakes of green. His smile is kind and his voice pleasant, one that made me want to listen to him long into the night. If I could hear stories read aloud by him then maybe I could actually finish a book.

"What are you smiling about?" Vera rounds the corner cutting off my path to the sewing room. I thought she was still helping Marcel; to see her here causes me to jump back, and instinctively my hand goes to a dagger hidden near my bust. She catches my hand movement. "Don't waste your time, I'm not trying to kill you...again." Her red lips twitch up. "Have you bedded him already? Is that why you're smiling? You couldn't even wait until after tonight's dinner to serve up something sweet?"

"Excuse me." Something boils within me like a kettle reaching its peak and screaming for help. "Your spitefulness is getting old. I get it, my mom did something to piss your mom off, what... thirty years ago," I say mockingly, drilling in my point. "And I get I'm new blood, but I'm sick of yours and Sky's rude initiation mind games. I'm here, not much by choice, but I will not be forced out by some woman with an attitude problem."

She folds her arms over her chest, "What does 'not much by choice' mean?"

"It was either this or be married off."

"You choose being this... a spy, assassin—damn near servant to the Queen—over marriage?" She eyes me and then shrugs. "Fair enough."

"Is that all? I actually have something to do if you're done with your questions."

She smiles. "Mahogany."

"What? What in the divinities does 'mahogany' mean?" I know it's a tree but how random to drop it in the middle of a conversation.

"The dress you were ordered to make for me, I want it mahogany in color. Similar to that of a red fox. Sky will wear gray and Chana black, with the faintest trimming of silver, as usual. We have decided you shall be our snow fox, so stick to whites and creams." She starts walking away. "Don't screw it up."

"Wait!" She stops but doesn't turn around. "I'm officially a..." I look around the vacant hall, but even without people around the word fox still feels forbidden. "One of you all now?"

"Not even a little." She laughs back. "Let's see if you can earn it by the start of the ball."

It isn't a full acceptance, but her consideration means I am fitting into this strange new place, the confirmation that I made the right choice. I cling to hope and rush to the sewing room.

The room, like all other rooms in this oversized place, is

more than large enough. Much bigger than the kitchen and sitting room of my parents' cottage combined.

The thought of them makes me remember that I really need to get their letter written. Mom has sent me three in the short amount of time I've been here. She's probably thinking the worst with my lack of reply. Same with Jaleese and Luna. But between everything I have going on I have found very little time to craft a response.

The Queen has an entire wall dedicated to bolts of fabric. There are sections for silk, satin, wool, lace, velvet, and so much more and all in hundreds of different colors and patterns. She also has designated areas for ribbons, beads, bows, buckles, hats, shoes—everything one could think of. It is my dream and nightmare all in one. Nightmare because there are so many choices, and my time doesn't allow me to be indecisive.

I force myself to focus on one outfit at a time. While I probably should start with the Queen's, hers is going to take a little more time, so I begin with Vera's. My first goal is to hunt down the mahogany color she asked for.

I find a satin bolt in a color resembling mahogany along with a copper tulle with leaf patterns on it.

Perfect.

As I search for Sky's material next, I come across an olive green material that would look good on Iann. Before I know it, the material is in my hand and on the cutting table where I try to get a better view.

If I could get the other pieces done, then maybe...

"What are you doing?" I say aloud, talking to myself and rushing to put the material back. There isn't enough time and why would I bother making him something he's never going to wear.

Before I put it back on the shelf, I decide it's best to keep it out, just in case, and set it back down on the table. It is beautiful material, maybe I'll think of something else to use it for.

An hour in and I have the material for everyone's ensembles picked out, except the Queen's, and I have Vera's sketch nearly finished.

Knowing I couldn't do it all on my own, the Queen ordered two of her helpers to assist me when needed. I make them a list of things I need cut, pinned, or sewn, but keep the more intricate and important tasks for myself.

There is the faintest scuff of a shoe on the floor behind me. In seconds, I draw a dagger and flip around, launching myself forward. I find the strangers' neck and press in as close as I can without drawing blood.

I'm hit with piercing blue eyes. "I see Chana has been teaching you well," Sky says. In a quick movement he knocks the blade out of my hand and turns us, pinning me to a table. "Too bad I have years on you."

Not willing to give up just yet, I kick my knee up and get him in the closest and weakest place I can reach.

Immediately, he lets me go to cradle the pain. His face turning red and eyes ready to pop out.

"Damnit...Ariah..." He breathes with pain. "I was just messing with you."

"I know." I fix my outfit and realize if anyone were to come in it would look like a bad scene. "I just wanted to see if I could get myself out."

"You've succeeded." He hisses and finds the strength to stand straight again. His eyes get caught on my sketch. "What is that?" He's not stupid and considering it's a drawing of a dress with Vera's name written on the top, I'd imagine I don't have to answer. But when he doesn't ask anything else I take it as a sign to reply.

"It's the dress I'm making Vera for the ball. Your outfit is up next." He eyes my drawing as if she's actually standing in it. "Do you like it? My favorite part is the split in the leg." I run my finger along the paper. "What's yours?"

He snaps out of it as soon as I tease him and changes the subject. "I intercepted these from one of our messenger boys. One is a letter to Prince Iann as well as another from someone named Luna, again."

"Already? He just arrived. How does he have letters already?"

"Kings and queens have ways of getting news around urgently. King Marcel probably sent this right after they departed Saden. Anyways, he's under your charge so you get to give it to him. After you read it, of course."

"How am I supposed to do that? Have you not seen the huge royal seal on the front?" My fingers stroke the wax.

"Chana." Is all he says before walking away. At the door he stops and pivots. "By the way, she said you're late. She's in the sanctuary." He leaves and my hands fly to a pocket watch on the table.

I had three hours to work on the dresses before my late afternoon lesson with Chana, and I am already ten minutes late.

The rafters of the sanctuary always smell of mildew and the lack of light keeps the interior cold. It is one of my least favorite places in the castle, but Chana loves meeting up here. She once said it reminds her of her home, Pivennen, in the Kingdom of Ethmay.

I've asked a few times how she ended up here but she either ignores my question or changes the subject. Eventually, I give up.

Climbing up is the easy part, getting to the small platform Chana waits on is challenging. There are beams that I must cross, without falling, and more importantly, without making a sound. Sometimes the sanctuary is filled with people, people who are not supposed to know others are lurking up high.

Having traversed the high rise several times already, I manage to get across quickly and don't fear the height as much anymore.

"You're late," Chana whispers, peering over the edge.

Below is a person, their knees planted on the gold marble, praying to what looks like a sculpture of Mathemous.

"I know. I'm sorry."

"There are twenty-five of them." She doesn't bother with questions as to why I am late. "In the letter to the Queen, King Marcel II said there would be twenty-four guests."

I follow her gaze to the man below. "And you think he's not with them?"

"I didn't say that. I've been watching each of them individually. You and Vera are to find out more. The Queen wants names and positions of every single one."

I nod. "Understood." I hold up the letter Sky gave me. "I'm told you can help me with resealing a letter."

She pulls her attention away from the man. "Have you read it yet?"

"No."

"Read it and then slide it under my door tonight. You can give it to the Prince in the morning."

"What—" I'm cut off when the doors to the sanctuary open and in comes Prince Iann, his courtier, and another man I briefly glimpsed during their arrival.

"What did I tell you?" the courtier says to the man praying. The man on his knees in worship looks irritated but keeps his thoughts to himself. "No one suspects a thing."

The courtier then sits on one of the seats and kicks up his feet.

"We get it, your plan worked," Iann says. "Doesn't mean you're any less stupid for doing it."

"Plan," Chana whispers to herself, and I can see her mind beginning to work.

"Whatever." The courtier waves him off, a little too comfortable for being in front of a prince. "I'm working on my part but what about you? When are you going to ask her?"

"We just got here," Iann snaps." I haven't even said more than a couple words to her. It's going to take time." Iann sighs. "You want me to just walk in and—"

The door opens again and Iann stops talking mid sentence. This time, it's people from the Queen's court who enter. The courtier straightens up and they all act like they are praying before they get up and leave together.

Chana is already looking at me before I turn to her. "Read that letter and find out what they plan to get from the Queen." I nod. "The Queen must be protected at all costs."

19
IANN

Deean sucks up a snore as he rushes into a sitting position, surprised I hit him with one of the extra fluffy pillows on the bed.

"Sleep well?" I let my full irritation ring as I rest my back against the headboard.

He rubs at droopy eyes before raising both arms and arching his back. The stretch sends a tremble down his body. "Not half bad. I prefer my own bed, but this one is decent. Better than the workers' quarters, I imagine."

"Why imagine when you can test the theory and try out the workers' quarters tonight, disrupt their sleep for a bit." He waves off my suggestion and makes his way into the bath chamber.

"You think it might be suspicious to have the servants draw two baths?" he calls from the other room.

"What's the point? We are about to hunt. You're destined to end up filthy, anyway." I smother the last of my words as my hand glides down my face.

He replies but his words become distant mumbles as I stop listening. My fingers ebb at a headache that is slowly intensifying. Between getting very little sleep—thanks to Deean's endless snoring—and today's early hunt, my mind is a feeding ground for restless thoughts.

At last night's dinner, Queen Cayleen insisted Marcel and I join her and other notable advisors for an early morning fox hunt.

If we were in my kingdom, I would have certainly told her no. While hunting treasure intrigues me, animals not so much, they make for better companions than trophies. I also think it strange that the Queen, who is so interested in the creatures, would suggest such a sport.

But not wanting to be perceived as rude, we both agreed to participate. Though, I suspect Marcel was happy to say yes. Hunting is not new to him and happens to be one of his favorite activities back in Saden.

A sudden knock at the door eases my hands away from my temples.

Deean comes back into the room as he makes sure his fake beard is secured tight. "Who the bloody hell is knocking this early in the morning?"

At the door he lets in Esha, whom I'm more than happy to see. "Please tell me you've come to take over for this imposter."

Esha offers a bow. "Indeed. I thought Your Highnesses might need some help this morning."

Deean smacks Esha on the back. "Great thinking. I'm about ready, but Iann can use the help."

I roll my eyes and they get lost somewhere in the back of my head. I knew Deean wasn't actually going to be of any use and replacing Esha was a folly on my part.

When I'm done dressing, Deann steps back to examine my outfit. "I'm a bit dubious of our royal host. I can spot a woman scorned anywhere, and Queen Cayleen has been burned multiple times. But I'll give it to her, she can put together one hell of an outfit. You think she has some extra for me?"

My trousers are the color of fresh sage and surprisingly, fit perfectly. Not too constricting or baggy. The beige shirt, which reminds me of the Saden sands that fill our shores, matches well with the dark russet coat, and the fur lining on the inside keeps me at a perfect temperature. It's a carefully considered outfit.

Once ready, Deean—or rather, Eli—and I make our way to one of the many courtyards, while Esha finds his way back to the workers' quarters.

"Good morning, Your Highness." A voice, bold yet tender, rings out from around the corner. Dark ringlets spill before me as Ariah offers a bow. There is a sudden, but subtle, urge to wrap one of her curls around my fingertips, but I rid myself of the thought knowing it would not only be inappropriate, but also weird. "I hope you and Prince Marcel are pleased with your outfits. Queen Cayleen charged me with picking them out."

"You're responsible for this?" I straighten the coat, all too aware of her staring.

Her eyebrows bridge upwards and I can't tell if she's offended or waiting for a compliment. "It's okay if you don't like it." There is something telling me it isn't okay if I don't and that makes me smile.

"I asked people you are traveling with about any styles and specific customs when it came to hunting in Saden." She leans in close. The scent of amber floats between us. "They told me to take extra care when it came to your brother's selection. They said you wouldn't fuss too much."

"Prince Iann, was admiring it all morning," Deean interrupts.

"Everything is perfect," I follow up before Deean can carry on, and I watch the worry melt from her face. "And you asked the right people. Marcel will certainly make a fuss if he doesn't get what he wants."

Deean mumbles something inaudible behind me just as a trumpet sounds from the courtyard.

We gather with the rest of the group in the center as Queen Cayleen makes her way to us. As usual, she carries a fox in one arm, draped over a tawny long-sleeve of her dress, and behind her are a few of her ladies-in-waiting and two hounds.

"Good morning, all," the Queen calls as she walks to the center of the group. Her smile is a rarity. She held one upon our arrival but it felt forced. Today she seems eager for the hunt. She looks as though pure excitement courses through her veins. "As you all know, we have the pleasure of being in the presence of not one, but two of Saden's royal princes. During their stay it is everyone's duty to show them the best of Haymel. And what better way to showcase this kingdom than with our customary fox hunt." The crowd claps as she spins to Marcel and me.

"If you haven't guessed by now, foxes are my favorite creatures." That much I knew about her. She is always carrying one in her arms as if it were a cat or puppy. I wonder if it serves as a type of service animal to her. Something that provides her comfort and security. Marcel and I still haven't gifted her the golden fox yet, but I know she'll be pleased with it.

"We don't kill during this hunt. We save such mercilessness for bigger game. Don't we?" People in the crowd laugh, and there is a twistedness in the way she says it with such joy. "Today will be catch and release. One point for any redtail foxes. Two for silvershadow foxes, known for their pitch-black fur and silvery strands. Then you have the instant win for the rare whitethorn fox. They are known for their pearly white coat with strands of black that look like thorns. But I must warn you, no one has ever caught the whitethorn fox. Simple enough?"

Marcel grins. "I don't think we'll have trouble with that."

"Good." Her smile takes a more sinister tone. "Now, each of you find a partner and let's get moving."

The crowd disperses, each having done this before and most already partnered up.

"Tell me, Vera," Marcel says, tightening a band around his wrist. "Exactly how rare is this whitethorn fox?"

Vera, who is in a deep maroon dress with endless buttons, like all the other dresses, with subtle patterns of flowers and stars, walks forward. She matches Marcel's coat and even carries his cocky smirk. "I've hunted these grounds many times and have never seen the mystic creature." She moves until her arm brushes my brother's. "But we have never had a Saden prince in the fox hunt, so maybe new luck graces us."

"I'm sure it will," Ariah whispers, trying to hide an eye roll.

"Did you say something, Lady Ariah," Vera asks bitterly. "Do speak up."

Ariah smiles. "I'm simply agreeing with you. Maybe the princes will be the first in all of Haymel history to capture the whitethorn."

Her sarcasm isn't lost on me and there seems to be unspoken tension between Ariah and Vera, which will make the hunt all the more interesting. Plus, the opportunity to be the first to find this special fox is hard to pass up.

"What about a competition of our own?" I suggest, and gain the attention of both Marcel and Vera. "The two of you against Ariah and me."

"What does the winner get?" Marcel raises an eyebrow.

"Bragging rights not enough for you?"

Marcel displays all teeth. "Very well. What do you say, Vera? Do you think we can beat them?"

"That's easy enough." Vera eyes Ariah, who doesn't look the least bit phased.

They leave to collect their supplies and hound.

"I hope you're okay with this?" I say to Ariah. Maybe I should have asked her beforehand instead of tossing her into the bet. She probably thinks I'm just as ambitious as the rest of them.

"Are you kidding me?" she says. "We, under no circumstances will let them win. I'm not about to let Vera get the satisfaction. We do have a slight problem though." She bites the corner of her lip. "I've never hunted before."

"Well, that's a perfect start," Deean retorts.

"Eli," I make sure to use his alias. "Make yourself useful and go gather our supplies." Deean grumbles but does as he's told. "I'm not much of a hunter for sport but finding things, particularly rare things, is my specialty. Do you trust me, Ariah?"

She squints her eyes at me until it vanishes with a grin. "I might."

"That's not a no, so I'll take it." I start walking and she follows. She listens intently as I go over the plan for the hunt taking in my every word.

20

ARIAH

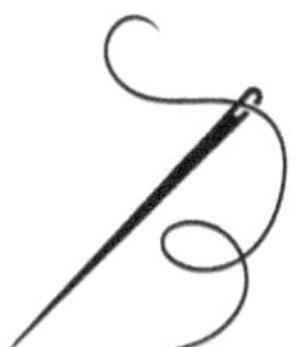

The more Iann speaks the more I realize how much he enjoys sharing his knowledge and adventures with others. He has moments of insecurities, questioning if he should continue or not, but with each hesitation I make a point to ask a question that opens him up to sharing more.

His life seems so thrilling it's hard not to get wrapped up in his stories. Oh, how I wish I had something as grand to tell him, but there isn't much to see or do in Foxhead, and my anecdotes somehow feel insufficient in comparison.

Iann theorizes different ways to catch the whitethorne. Never having hunted in my life, I listen and agree to take whatever route he thinks is best.

We bring along a hound, one Iann allows to roam ahead of us. In addition to our new four-legged friend, there is one guard, from Saden, accompanying us, as well as Iann's courtier, Eli.

Eli carries our supplies in a large sack over his shoulder along with a cage in his left hand for any foxes we can find.

"So, if you were a fox, where would you hide?" Iann asks playfully.

I clear my throat at the irony of the question. Of course, he is referring to the animal, but for a second, I think he's referring to something else entirely. I force a smile and tap a finger on my chin. "If I were a fox, I would stick to the shadows, where I can watch my prey and potential hunters."

He nods. "They are quite cunning like that. We need to find an area that's perfect for hiding."

Brushing aside a bush that blocks our path, it begins to rustle and birds come flying out. I duck my head until I realize they are only little red robins.

Iann, however, nearly knocks me into a tree in his panic.

Eli, releases a soft chuckle behind us that he smothers with a cough. "They are only robins, My Grace. Would you like me to scare them off?"

There is a quick flash of embarrassment, but Iann composes himself. "No, Eli. They startled me, that's all." He sucks in a sharp breath before putting his finger to his lips.

"Are you alright?" I take his hand without warning, causing him to flinch until he realizes I'm trying to help.

"It's a minor splinter. I think I'll survive."

"I have no doubt." From my pocket, I pull one of my many needles. "Do you mind? Removing it now will make it less painful for you later. Plus, I'll never hear the end of it if you catch an infection."

He chuckles and relaxes his hand. "Very well."

It takes a little concentration and a few seconds to extract the sliver of wood.

"Do you always carry sewing needles with you?" It isn't Iann who asks, but Eli. "Most people I know carry daggers or blades, not items intended for mending clothing."

Iann cuts him a cautious look but it only makes me smile, because I am in fact carrying both.

"Always. You'd be surprised at the many talents a good needle and skilled seamstress possess."

Eli finds humor in the answer.

"I overheard a few of the servants speak of spotting a fox near the creek this morning." My needle finds its home back in my pocket and we return to the hunt.

"Might be worth a shot, Ia—Your Highness," Eli seconds the idea.

It's not a bad idea. I haven't had much time to explore all of the castle grounds, but I do know of a spot near the creek that is a perfect hiding ground for creatures.

"This way," I direct our small group.

I lead us through the forest where leaves are transforming from their greenish hues to an assortment of yellows and oranges. The air is losing its heat from months past and holds a cooler breeze. My lungs expand with the scent of oak and loose traces of cinnamon.

The hound stops a few feet in front of me, cocking his head to the left. He listens for a few seconds before his nose is back to the ground picking up new scents. He must hear the water in the creek because after a few moments I pick up on a trickling sound.

"Do you think we'll find it?" I ask Iann, who quickens his pace until he matches my stride. "Or do you think the Queen is sending us on a wild chase?"

"You tell me." He laughs. "She's your queen. Would she send us on a hunt for something that doesn't exist?"

My immediate thought is yes. I assume Queen Cayleen would get a thrill out of watching people fight to find something she knows is a myth.

"It's hard to know with the Queen. She's difficult to read at times." I stop and question how much about her I should share with him. "It may exist, and if it does I feel our chances of finding one today might be slim."

Iann shrugs. "That's alright. It means our competition's

chances are slim as well. If anything, this can just be a mini-adventure."

He's so positive it's hard to believe his outlook is genuine, but at this moment I do. Plus, who can resist an adventure, even if it's within the Queen's back gardens.

We follow the hound to the creek and watch him sniff the rocks along the bank. Iann doesn't want to use the metal traps provided to all groups by the Queen, so we focus on a more gentle approach.

We search for hours along the creek, venturing the farthest north I've been on the castle grounds. The time fills itself with more talking, mostly how court in Haymel differs from Saden's. Iann shares stories of his family. His grandmother in particular seems to be a feisty soul I would love to meet.

The hound stops, nostrils flaring near a medium sized boulder set between the creek and a row of trees.

"What is it, boy?" Iann whispers and slows his pace.

My movements lag with him, and I signal for the others to fall back.

The hound sniffs endlessly near an opening between the rocks. I call the hound back, patting him for a job well done as Iann inspects the rocks.

"I hear something," he calls back, removing his coat and setting it on the dry rocks next to him. "I probably shouldn't stick my hand in, should I?" he jokes.

"Might get it out faster." I laugh. "Are we sure it's even a fox?" I continue to keep the hound next to me despite its eagerness to get away.

"Let me try—" He's cut short when we hear an arrow flying through the air.

It gets stuck in the trunk of the tree beside me causing the dog to become frightened. The hound pushes off the ground with all his strength, breaking my hold on him, which sends me flying back. I land right in the creek. My dress immediately soaks up all the water possible. The only thing that doesn't get wet is my head since I'm able to hold it above the shallow water.

Iann doesn't see the hound charge in his direction and he too gets knocked into the creek, the water only soaking his pants.

Eli and the guard stand with arrows drawn, but suddenly lower them, Eli taking a little longer to release the arrow's hold on his target.

Yards away from the creek are Prince Marcel and Vera who are still in position with their bows. Behind them is the rest of Prince Marcel's party.

They look to have caught many redtail and silvershadow foxes, clearly winning our little competition. I don't know if it's their obvious win or the fact it's Vera's fault that I've fallen into the creek that pisses me off more.

Iann comes into view and offers me a hand. My insides are raging but I keep my calm in front of the princes.

Suddenly, our hound starts barking, behaving crazier than before, and starts chasing something that scurries out of the cluster of rocks.

I blink triple speed at the sight. The fox running near us is not a redtail nor a silvershadow.

"You've got to be kidding me," I whisper between Iann and me.

A whitethorn fox, with the sleekest, shimmering fur, spotted with black comes running at us.

Iann pulls me in close, his dry body providing me warmth as the fox and hound race behind me.

In one quick movement Eli drops all the supplies, lowers the cage to the ground and watches the fox's every movement.

Too concerned with the giant dog chasing it, the fox runs

right into the cage, and we are the first team to capture a whitethorn.

"We did it," I say, pulling away from Iann to look him in the eyes. I start jumping and he shares in on my enthusiasm. "We caught it!"

Prince Marcel calls out to me, "Job well done, brother. I didn't think you would do it."

Vera tosses me a half smirk, and the entire hunting party heads back to the castle.

Back in the courtyard where we began the hunt, the Queen grows overly excited about our findings. It's almost as if she herself didn't believe the rumors about the fox roaming her lands.

As she gives a small speech, Prince Marcel and Iann stand up there with her, and Iann finds me in the crowd and tosses me a wink.

Someone approaches my right side. From my periphery I see Vera come stand beside me. Together we watch the Queen show off her new pet.

"Looks like the White Fox caught a white fox," Vera says.

"You shot at me," I say coldly, not looking her way.

"I shot near you, not at you. If I wanted you dead, Ariah, I would have made it happen by now. Plus, the dead aren't fun to play with." It takes me a few seconds, but I look at her as she keeps her vision on the Queen. "Don't be so bitter," she continues, "You're one of us now, you should be happy." Her gaze shifts from the Queen to the princes. "You know, I'm not one to offer advice, but I will warn you to be careful."

"Of what? You? I'm not afraid of you, Vera." My stance gets a little taller, but this only seems to humor her.

"It's forbidden for a person from Haymel to be with someone from Saden." She sees me open my mouth and stops my words by continuing on, "And even more deadly to defy a queen."

There is a sudden bird call and we both turn to see Chana hooded and standing at the edge of the crowd. She nods in our direction.

"Time to go, White Fox. We have other matters to attend to."

21

IANN

Today, the hunting is over and it is time to focus on why I'm really here.

Though my body is physically in the castle's library, my mind keeps drifting back to last night's dinner. Most of the meal was dull and consisted of Marcel and Queen Cayleen discussing politics. The other, and better half, came with the kittenish glances from Ariah at the other end of the table.

Fingers snap in front of my face. "You here to help or daydream?" Deean says, leaning on the table in front of me. "We're waiting."

He and Benny recently uncovered a symbol on the anchor and are having a debate on what it could be. Benny is certain it's a tree and Deean assures us that it's coral.

"Sorry." I take the anchor from him. On the bottom is indeed a small symbol. "Coral would make sense given the object...but it does look like a leafless tree."

Deean plucks it from my hands. "That was unhelpful. And where were you last night? And the night before? Benny and I have practically been sleeping alone in this place."

"It is true," Benny adds. "Left this library far too late both nights." He uses a magnifying glass to examine another object in his hand.

"Sorry," I say again, for the tenth time this morning. "I forgot we were meeting this morning."

"Ah yes," Deean says, "Ariah told us of your absence from the castle yesterday. You know, I find it a bit insulting that I found out your whereabouts from a woman we just met. Aren't you supposed to tell your courtier these things?"

"I would have, had he not been replaced with a fraud." I lean my head in my palms, annoyed with all these early morning questions.

"You could have at least taken Ariah. Isn't she supposed to be your guide or something?"

My shoulders tense and I roll my neck back and forth trying to rid any built-up tension. "I didn't see the point. I'm sure she had better things to do, so I suggested she stay behind."

He clicks his tongue. "A queen provides you with a woman to wait on your every need and you dismiss her. If I weren't *Eli*, I would take full advantage of every pleasantry provided."

"Well, it's a good thing you're no prince," Benny says, and he and Deean erupt with laughter. Clearly my absence has allowed them to bond. Benny suddenly becomes quiet. "On a more serious note, does anyone else get the feeling of being watched? I swear there was a figure on the roof watching me as I went back to the workers' quarters."

"Spies," Deean says plainly, and although it sounds outlandish, in this life it's not surprising. "Maybe an animal though. We did open the bottle of whiskey, you sure you weren't seeing things?"

"Spies?"

"Benny"—Deean walks past him and pats him on the back before leaning over and looking at whatever it is Benny still examines—"you don't get to be a royal without everyone wanting to know your every move. And not just you, but everyone associated with you. You think my father doesn't have spies of his own roaming these halls?" Deean gives him a cheeky smile.

"There you are!" My head snaps up at the sound of the familiar voice. Ariah curtsies at the sight of me. "Figures you would be in the one place I have yet to venture into." Unsure how she does it, but her presence lightens the room, and my mood suddenly shifts. "This arrived for you."

Today, she wears an ivory dress with an annoying number of buttons, like all the other outfits in Haymel. It's a style choice that needs to perish. I count fifteen on her dress. Fifteen isn't a desirable number but it's not impossible to work through. Her hair is down today—curls are allowed to roam freely wherever they like. A parade of sandalwood, amber, and peony moves towards me at her approach. Even the scent of her is desirable.

"Are you okay, Your Highness?" Benny asks when I bump into the table as I stand.

"I'm fine. Thank you, Benny," I reply.

Ariah hands me the letter and I recognize my father's handwriting immediately. "Thank you for delivering it," I tell her, tucking it away.

Her eyes dart away. "What are all of you up to?" She walks past me to the other side of the table where Benny and Deean are seated. She picks up an empty glass and pulls it to her nose. She sets it down with a smile and then touches pages of open books. "The Ivian Flower?" She perks up and her eyes float back to me. "Are you studying it?"

"Why would you think that?" It's Deean who speaks, plucking the thoughts out of my head.

She chuckles. "Maybe because he's an explorer and half of these books are about the flower." She takes a seat next to Benny. "It all reminds me of my father."

"Is he an explorer too?" I ask excitedly.

"No. He's an apothecary and very much believes the flower is out there."

"But you don't?"

She shrugs. "I've heard his stories but can't tell if I just don't have any interest in the divinities or if there is no belief there at all. After all, who would want to live forever?"

"I suspect someone who knows their life is nearing the end," Benny replies, and hands Ariah the anchor. "You'd be surprised what people do when they know there is little time left. "Now"—he moves the anchor in her hands to where the symbol is—"you might be able to help us settle a debate. What does that look like to you?"

She squints and then reaches for a magnifying glass on the table. "There are initials here as well. F.V. What does that mean?"

"Fraya Vellen a—" Deean is cut off by Ariah.

"Famous captain. Yeah, I know who she is. This is the anchor of Kailaric."

I rush over to her, taking a seat at the edge of the table. "The divinity of the sea," I whisper to myself.

"My father has done extensive study on them. The divinities that is. Just another thing he's shared with me. But to answer Benny's original question, I would say it's a symbol of a tree."

Deean taps on the table in frustration. "It's clearly coral."

She tilts her head. "Oh yeah, I can see that too. But given the legends I still say it's a tree."

The legend of Kailaric says he was a demi-divinity who was cruelly chased out of the waters of the Graying Sea, his home for thousands of years, by a wicked king who had gained forbidden magic. In the legend, it is written that Kailaric was forced to change into another form and washed up on Farella Isle, where his spirit rests. Many believe it is Kailaric's powers that allows the island to flourish and are responsible for the

Ivian Flower itself. They say the tree that blooms the Ivian Flower grew upon the spot he was buried.

"That would make sense," Benny says, stroking the hairs of his beard as he dives deeper into thought. "If this represents Kailaric, I wonder if it needs some kind of submergence to work."

"Ariah." I stand, and she follows my urgency, our bodies mere inches from each other. "I hate to ask, but can you have the servants draw me a bath in my chambers? No oils or plants. Only water, and preferably lukewarm."

She gives me an accusing squint and then her face eases into a smile. "I think I can do that." She curtsies and rushes out.

"You know she's going to want to stay." Deean eyes me with caution, wondering what I'm up to. "You better know what you're doing."

"She knows this is my job. I search for things. She doesn't know we are actually setting sail for it. We're no different than her father. Just men with interests in history."

"I'm sure," Deean says.

"Let's go put your theory to the test, Benny." Ignoring Deean's reservations, I take the anchor in hand and walk around the table. "I have a meeting with Marcel and the Queen soon, so we better make this quick."

The three of us head back to my bed chambers. As we make our way, I notice the castle is oddly quiet and there is a bizarre sensation of being watched. I discreetly check my surroundings, but I pick up nothing but vacant corridors and empty rooms. As soon as we reach the frame of my door, I push all worries aside and instruct Benny to shut the door behind him.

We pass the freshly made bed and move into the bath quarters where we find Ariah.

"I sent everyone away. Said you needed space for a while." She beams at the sight of me, and it is unnerving how much her joy brings me comfort. Foolish is more like it. I've known this woman all of a few days and yet I want to know so much more about her.

"Well, let's get this going." Deean snaps me out of thoughts that are on the verge of spiraling. "You have a busy day with our dear bro...prince and the Queen, sir." Deean coughs, hoping Ariah didn't catch the slip. "We wouldn't want to be late for that."

Benny hides his smile, and I pass Deean a grin of cautiousness.

"You're right, Eli." I move to the tub giving my brother one last look of warning. "Marcel will send people searching for me soon. Better try this quickly."

I submerge the anchor in the water, lukewarm just like I asked, and release it. The others remain quiet but approach the large metal bath in time to see it sink to the bottom.

"Brilliant idea but I don't think we're discovering anything from that," Deean says after waiting a few uneventful minutes.

Benny holds up a finger. "I have another idea." He crosses the room and looks through cupboards. "Salt. Where is the bloody salt?" It doesn't take him long to find a golden pot that he pops the lid off of and moves it to his nose. "If the artifact was created to represent Kailaric then naturally it will need salt water. Afterall, he is the divinity of the ocean. Here we go!" Benny holds up a jar, "Hopefully, one that's lilac infused will do."

"No!" Ariah shouts, backing away from the tub. "Let me leave first. I'm allergic to lilacs."

"You don't want to see? That's if it even works. I'm sure we can find different salts." My voice comes out disappointed at the fact she's taking her leave.

"Queen Cayleen and Prince Marcel expect you in the sundown room to meet with the Lord and Lady of Garren." Gently, she places a hand on my arm, a touch that makes me want to both pull away and lean closer. "Don't spoil your experiment because of my immune deficiencies. I'll be right in the next room." She gives me a smile and offers a curtsy before leaving.

"I thought the rule was no flirting," Deean says, nodding to Benny, giving him the go ahead to proceed.

"Not flirting. And that rule was for you, not me."

"Mmm...she's close to the Queen, so be wary." Deean nudges my arm with his shoulder.

"There is nothing to be careful about because there is nothing there."

"I believe you." He absolutely does not believe me.

Deean and I stop bickering in time to watch Benny dump the salt into the water. There is nothing at first but the scent of lilac filling the room, but as soon as the flakes of salt touch the anchor, bubbles begin rising to the top. The gold bursts with light breaking through the water, causing droplets to shower the ground.

"Is everything okay?" Ariah calls from the other side of the door.

Light rushes out of the water as beams of light, spreading out like a fan, cast an image on the ceiling to create a tree-like picture that resembles a map of Farella Isle.

"She enchanted it." My voice is so low and full of awe, I don't even think I actually spoke the words.

"Brilliant." Benny spins trying to study the image from all angles. He stops and drops his head before facing us. "You wouldn't go out of your way to enchant an image if it didn't mean something."

There is a knock at the door. "Prince Iann, Prince Marcel is *here*, waiting for you," Ariah calls, dropping the casual tone she carried this morning. "He would like you to accompany him to the sundown room."

"Sketch it, study it, memorize it." I point a finger at the ceiling. "I will work on getting the Queen to grant us access to the isle."

"How are you going to do that without telling her what we're after?" Deean keeps his gaze upwards, his eyes tracing the image.

"No idea, but I'll figure it out." I squeeze him on the shoulder. "You came through on your end of the deal. Welcome to the crew." He gives me a look, and even through the terrible facial disguise, I can tell how much he softens at the words. Words he's desperately been craving. I turn to go, but another thought stops me. "My rules are still in place."

He pushes me towards the door. "Get out of here before Marcel forces his way in."

I cautiously open the door, trying not to let the scent of lilac escape.

Ariah is several feet away waiting. "Your brother is outside. Did the experiment work?"

"Perhaps," I say with a smile to match hers.

Knowing Marcel has no issue coming in here and dragging me away, I make my way out.

As I pass Ariah, she reaches out gently, stopping me with her arm. She pulls away as if second guessing, but I make no attempts to suggest I have any qualms with her action.

"Perhaps you can tell me about it later. Lady Arranella is hosting a departure party out at the Rose House. Would you like to come? Eli and Benny are welcome to join too." She leans in before saying, "I do warn you, they aren't tame parties, but they're fun."

"IANN!" Marcel calls from outside.

"I wouldn't want to attend a party I wasn't invited to."

"I just invited you." She winks. "Plus, I'm sure she wouldn't mind a prince showing up uninvited."

I release the muscles in my jaw and give her a hesitant nod. "I would love to."

Parties have never been my favorite pastime, and often I find myself disappearing from the crowd, only to end up in a study with a book. This one time, for her, I'll make an exception.

Leaving her behind, I meet up with Marcel in the hall who is less than amused at my pace.

Today, he has on warm colors, blending in with our new surroundings, and I can't help but wonder if it's a strategic move or not.

"I hear Lord Garren is a dull man with a crude sense of humor," Marcel says, eyeing a group of people who whisper between themselves as we pass by. "He's eager to discuss opening up trade between Haymel and Saden, which could lead to potential exploration opportunities. Did you think over the ideas I asked you about?"

"I have." It's all he went on about last night. "All strong ideas. I have one of my own that I would like to propose."

Marcel stops to look at me head on. "Go on then. I'd rather hear it now than be taken aback during our meeting."

"I would like to propose that the Queen open up the lands south of the Graying Sea. Not even she explores those lands. If we could start charting more of that area there is no telling what we could find, and ultimately what could be traded."

"South?" His face pinches with hesitation. "You mean areas like Farella?" The bitterness is sucked out of his face as it molds into delight. "A fine idea. One I can see them agreeing to."

He starts walking again, wrapping an arm around me as he continues to discuss the ideas he has. My mind is split in three: what Marcel continues on about; the anchor that turned out to be a map; and the opportunity to spend the evening with Ariah.

22

ARIAH

Benny likes the bottle, cigars, and singing, both when he is and isn't intoxicated. With his short stature it didn't take much to get him drunk, but he still manages to hold his own. And he never sings around the princes though, but on occasion I can pick up on his humming. It is discreet, so much so that I don't even think many have noticed it. I suspect it to be a coping mechanism.

Benny is also wickedly smart though he doesn't show it. It is something a person has to observe from a distance. It is in the way he speaks and the instant answers he has to most questions, even if they aren't directed to him, and even if he mumbles the responses to himself. He also always carries a book in his pocket. One I caught a glimpse of titled, *The Bargain* by Thiely Devonport, if my eyesight didn't fail me from a distance. He opens it every time he finds himself alone, even when walking from one point of the castle to the next.

He is the first person Chana instructed me to follow after our observations in the sanctuary. Leading up to dinner, after the fox hunt, he had wandered the grounds and had one lengthy conversation about Farella Isle with a man I discovered to be Rolley.

Rolley's role here has remained a secret, that is, until I opened Iann's letter.

Truthfully, invading someone's privacy left me feeling guilty, but my fear of the Queen is a stronger emotion. The letter had gone on about a brother who is missing, but judging from the tone, he is a bit of a drifter—the odd one out in the family, who will eventually turn up when he needs something, or perhaps runs out of money. The King never mentioned any of that, but I felt it there, between the lines.

Another reveal, and one of the utmost importance, is that Rolley appears to be the King's confidant. His very own Fox of sorts, within Haymel's castle walls.

Chana says she will be the one to watch Rolley and my next target is Eli, the individual seemingly closest to Prince Iann.

Once Iann leaves with Marcel to the sundown room, I sneak back into Iann's room and tiptoe across the floor, pressing my ear to the bath chamber door. Footsteps draw closer, and I fling myself back just in time, before Eli swings the door open and nearly crashes into me.

"Lady Ariah," he says startled, and rushes to shut the door behind him. "I thought you went with the Prince."

"No." I point my hand aimlessly at the exit. "He left with Prince Marcel already. I was just about to go."

He squints, and I watch his eyes drift over my frame. "Hm. If you're not too busy, can you do me a favor?"

"Of course."

"Do you have any parchment and lead? Or even a pen. Anything will work."

Just his luck, I dig into my pocket and find lead and a scrap of parchment. It was meant to be for the Queen's sketch, having been the only dress I can't seem to envision, but now the supplies are his.

"You just carry these around?" He takes the items and gives me that same cautious glance.

"I am the Queen's seamstress and designer on occasion." I give him a little fib. "I'm prepared at all times. "Do you need anything else?"

"No." He shakes his head. "This will do. Thank you."

"My pleasure." I dip my head and take my leave, feeling his eyes on me from the moment I walk away to the moment I get to the doorway, I turn back one last time. "Oh, I almost forgot. You and Benny are invited to a party tonight. I'm sure the Prince will tell you more about it later."

"You got Iann to go to a party?" A smirk stretches upward and I'm uncertain if he's realized that he addressed the Prince so casually. "Maybe I do like you after all."

"Did you not before?" I squint, wondering what I could have possibly done to make him dislike me.

"I've never thought highly of a person from Haymel, including the women, and I love all women. You might be different though."

Insulted is what I should be, but his comment forces out a laugh. "I've never trusted a Saden man, but one has proved to be most kind, and now it looks like there might be two of you."

"We're full of surprises." He tosses me a wink and pushes the door open with his foot. "Us Saden men will see you tonight for a party."

Enough of the lilac scent escapes from the bath and slowly creeps its way into my lungs and disrupts my breathing. Once my shoulders start rising and air becomes harder and harder to get enough of, I dig for my spray and release two quick spritzes as I rush out of the room.

In the hall, I rest against a column and let the mixture do its job.

From afar, across a small area of grass, flowerbeds, and two benches, I spot Sky in the hall. He looks angry and argues with a figure hidden behind a pillar.

His hand grasps at the air, trying to grab whoever he argues with, but catches only air.

Moving from behind the pillar, Vera storms off angrily and wipes a hand at her face.

Coming my way, I spin along the column to face another direction. The last thing I need is to be accused of snooping on them.

Foxes spy on others, but on each other seems off limits, even if it is by accident.

Footsteps come closer and my heart races from the mixture working and the panic of coming up with an excuse when Vera finds me.

Times up, she walks past but only gets a few feet ahead before spinning.

"What are you doing?" If she had been crying, the tears are gone and sad eyes are replaced with suspicion.

"I was having trouble breathing. Just waiting for my medicinal spray to set in." I wave the spray for extra proof.

She comes closer examining the bottle in my hands. "I saw the dress you did for me."

She changes the subject much to my pleasure, and I ease off the column feeling back to normal. "And?"

Vera's dress was the easiest to make. The vision for hers was so clear.

"I don't hate it." She remains straight-faced until one side of her mouth twitches upwards. "It might be better than I pictured. I'm sure the Prince will enjoy it." The slight pleasure she holds vanishes, and her eyes become distant, lost to thought.

"Did he do something to you?"

Her eyes turn hollow, and she looks like a secret is on the tip of her tongue just waiting to be released, but she sucks in a breath and straightens her shoulders. "Don't be a sucker, Ariah. It's a role we must play. I'm sure your prince will desire something of you soon. They always do." She moves a stray curl from in front of my eyes. "They're always so kind at first. If he wasn't a prince, I would have sliced off each finger, and maybe a head, or two." Her lips curl up. "I've had worse though and can't say it's entirely without perks."

We stand there for what feels like minutes not speaking, until the sound of voices carries to us from down the hall.

"Looks like you need to go," Vera whispers.

Turning, I see Benny and Eli making their way past the courtyard. Probably heading back to the library.

When I look back, Vera is already gone, her figure dashing around the corner and disappearing.

The rest of the day goes slowly, granting me enough time to finish Chana's dress.

While working, my mind replays my recent conversation with Vera. Was Prince Marcel the reason she was crying or did something exchanged between Sky and her melt some of her stony exterior?

Vera's words echo in my mind. Iann seems kind enough, but if royals are all the same I question if Iann is as nice as he seems, or if his demeanor is just a facade.

"It's a map." A voice pulls me from working on alterations.

Chana walks up, not in her usual black, but instead a deep burgundy, a few shades off from black. There is a heart-shaped cutout, revealing flesh, just above her chest, and then more material around her neck. Gold beads decorate the fabric and form a belt around her waist.

"Thank you," I tell Dara, the woman helping me with the

dresses. "That will be all for today." She nods, never speaking as usual, and takes her leave. "What's a map?"

"The item they tossed in the bath. It's enchanted." Turning away from her I fix a button on Sky's overcoat. "And I didn't know you were allergic to lilacs."

How long had she been watching us?

"Yes, amongst other things." Finished with his piece for the day, I move back and examine the collection. Three pieces are nearly done with another to finish for the ball in a few short days. Turning to her, I see her inspecting the outfits. "I didn't know you were watching us."

The scent of fresh rainwater invades my senses, and hints of sweetness fill the air, reminiscent of watching lily pads float on the most tranquil pond. Chana never wears perfume, but tonight is Lady Arranella's party and she's treating herself.

"You should always know when someone is watching you." Approaching her dress, she runs her fingers along the feathers near the arm straps. "Tonight, I need you to figure out what the map leads to and where they got it."

"Should be easy enough, though I suspect the answer is Farella Isle."

She spins. "Your reasoning?"

"That's what they've been studying in the library. The artifact supposedly belonged to Fraya Vellen. A replication of Kailaric's Anchor."

"Have you told the Queen any of this yet?"

"No. I was waiting to collect more information."

From her pocket she pulls out a vial of purple translucent liquid. "Good. It's best to wait until we know for sure what they're after." I want to bring up the Ivian Flower, but will she mock me for mentioning the mythical object? "Sky batched this the other day. If given the opportunity, slip it into their drinks. Between this and the alcohol, they'll be fountains overflowing with secrets." Tucking it into the pocket of my dress my stomach tightens, but I give her a nod of acknowledgement. She will be attending the same party, and I know this is another test, one I can't fail, especially knowing she's been watching me. She pushes me forward, playfully. "Get changed and go get your prince. I hate people and parties, so the sooner we show up the sooner I know the night will end."

We head back to my room where I change into something more festive. I go with an ensemble more casual yet still fancy enough for a party hosted by a royal family member, well, the wife of one anyway.

Tonight, I wear pearls I selected from the Queen's collection, available in a room she provided us, filled with incentives for being a Fox. There is an abundance of other items we can select, but I've only taken the pearl necklace and a matching set of earrings. As glamorous as it all is, it's not mine. Borrowing more than my share ties me to this place in more ways than I'd like. I'll carry out my end of the deal with the Queen, but once done, so am I.

Once I'm ready, Chana and I head over to the Rose House, which is a good walk away from the castle.

Dusk sets and the sky fluffs up with fading pink-and-orange clouds, as the sound of distant instruments guides us to our destination.

"Ugh, so many people," Chana mumbles.

"It won't be so bad," I assure, squeezing her hand. "A break from hiding in dark corners and actually being in conversations, rather than listening in on them, will be good for us both."

She tosses me a look from the corner of her eye. "You think I still won't do that here?"

My grin causes her to break and it's the first time I hear her laugh. Good to know she's capable of it.

"LADY ARIAH!" A voice from behind shouts, stopping both of us.

In the dim light I make out three figures, all dressed up in matching neutral tones, a common trend I've observed of our Saden visitors.

Chana and I curtsy.

"Are you both ready to see how Saden men party? I bet you Haymelians will struggle to keep up," Eli says to Chana playfully.

"Sadens and Haymelians have nothing on those of us from Ethmay," Chana shoots back, not lacking an ounce of confidence.

Eli stops walking, caught off guard. I'm certain this is the first interaction they've shared yet both exchange words effortlessly. "And she speaks," he teases, conjuring a grin. "I've never met an Ethmay woman before." He takes a step in her direction and extends a hand. "And you are?"

"Well, now you have," she says, reluctantly taking his hand. "And you may call me Chana."

"And do Ethmay women like to drink, Lady Chana?"

"Depends on what is being offered. And it depends on the company."

The air shifts and these two linger for longer than they should.

"Why don't we continue on." Iann steps around Eli, patting him on the back and edging him towards the house. "Can't show her how Saden men party until we actually make it to the party."

I fall back, walking next to Benny, with Iann a foot ahead of us and Chana and Eli talking away at the front.

Benny strikes up a conversation, keeping it casual. We talk mostly about him and the emporium he owns back in Saden. He speaks about his son with great admiration. His son is a painter and he promises to show me some of his sketches whenever there is time. Iann also adds that Benny's son has done several murals in the castle.

We arrive at the Rose House, and as I expected people stop their conversations to watch Prince Iann make his way inside. Even the musicians slow their playing.

Lady Arranella is the first to greet us and whisks Iann away to flaunt at her guests, acting as if they are old friends.

Chana, Eli, and Benny drift off to another room, but I stick close to Iann, following behind as he is introduced to faces I've only seen in passing around court.

Food and drink are offered to us in abundance, but Iann declines it all.

Though people are excited to see him, I can tell that all the greetings and endless questions are starting to drain him. His smile becomes forced and his responses grow shorter. Lady Arranella doesn't seem to notice. She continues to escort him around the room, making sure everyone sees them together.

"Prince Iann," I say, cutting in after following them around for well over an hour. "There is something I need to discuss with you. Sorry, Lady Arranella, we'll be back shortly."

I don't give her the opportunity to protest and take Iann by the arm leading him away. We end up in a far less crowded room with a vacant sofa that we drop down on.

"I'm sorry," I say, biting the corner of my lip. Convinced he regrets coming. "I promised this would be fun and that was awful." I find a clock on the mantel across the room. "Over an hour of repetitive greetings and small talk." He laughs and rests back in the seat. "How do you do it?"

Resting beside him, he shrugs, the friction of his arm sliding across mine warms me. "I don't really know. It's just something I do now."

"You don't like parties, do you?" I ask.

He meets my gaze. The green flakes in his eyes shine brighter in this light, like jewels floating in a night sky. His smile deepens and I find myself studying the bends of his lips.

"I would prefer my time spent doing other things," he admits.

"You could have said no," I tell him.

"I know." His stare extends deeper into mine. "But I didn't want to."

The room floods with a sudden heat. "Would you like a drink?"

"I would love one."

Leaning in close I pick up the scent of a woodsy musk. "Don't move."

The room opens to a dining hall stuffed with people dancing. I find a table flowing with champagne and food and wait for the people in front of me to get their refreshments.

From where I stand, I can see into multiple rooms of the Rose House. I spot Sky and Vera pretending not to watch each other. Their feelings are blatantly obvious.

Sky distracts himself with a game of cards and Vera socializes with a group of people laughing and flirting the night away. Around her neck is a bright red stone that appears to be glowing, but it must be a trick of the light around us.

Chana appears not to notice that she's still at a party as she seems to be enjoying her time surrounded by people she was dreading to mingle with. She whispers something in Benny's ear and both point at Eli before all three erupt in laughter.

I spot Iann starring, watching me in a way that courses an inviting sensation through me. He ends the eye contact as a woman, whom I recognize as one of the Queens' ladies-in-waiting, approaches.

His leg subtly shakes, and he rubs his palms over his knees looking uncomfortable, but he still maintains a smile that's obnoxiously charming.

I grab two glasses of champagne and turn to go save him, suddenly remembering the mix Chana gave me; I suspect she consumed some of her own.

Back on the table I shield the glasses with my body and release a droplet of the mixture into one cup. Guilt grabs hold of me. What if Iann doesn't even need this? I can just ask him, find a way to sneak the topic of the flower into our conversation.

Someone bumps into me from behind and the liquid in the vial spills out onto the table.

"Where did you get that?" Sky appears, bending down near my ear and grabbing the vial. "How much did you put in there?"

"Chana said it will help me get some information out of the Prince."

He huffs. "I've told her to stay out of my workstation. It contains lorice." My dumbfounded look has him explaining more, "Has your father not taught you anything? It's a magical root. Rare and meant for dire circumstances." He shoves the vial into his pocket. "What's in there is more than enough. Do you know what this does?" I shake my head, wiping the liquid with one of the several cloth napkins placed around the table.

"Is there an issue?" Iann sends us both spinning around.

Sky dips his head. "Not at all, Your Royal Highness. Just helping Ariah out with something."

"She seemed to be managing fine without you." There is a new tone in Iann's voice. One I have yet to hear. One that makes him equal parts terrifying and attractive.

"Sky was just helping me with a spill." I find a lie quickly. "Accidentally knocked over a glass." I grab the stems of the glasses and hand one to Iann. "Here is your drink. Thank you for your help, Sky."

"Anytime." He gives Iann a taunting smirk and throws a dagger-filled glare my way.

"How about a walk?" Iann whispers near my ear.

I nod and follow his lead as we head towards the door to the back garden. Sky tries to get my attention one last time but it's too late.

Outside, a breeze picks up and luminosity beams down on the kingdom from a full moon. We walk onto a stone courtyard, stretching from the back of the house. Dozens of lanterns brighten the area, revealing other smaller groups chatting amongst themselves.

Iann takes a sip of the champagne downing it before grimacing.

"Not good?" Too much mix must have thrown off the taste.

"Champagne has never been my drink of choice."

Taking a sip of my own, I'm hit with a fizzy tartness that has me clicking the roof of my mouth. I force down a sizable gulp and set it aside. "Nor mine." Beyond the courtyard, down several steps, is a rose garden and the reason for the house's name. "Shall we continue?"

"Alright."

We continue on. Even in the dark, the garden is still vibrant, holding enough light to brighten our path.

"This might be odd, but I got you a gift." He searches through the pockets of his coat.

"For me?" Not odd, but surprising.

"A celebratory gift for the fox hunt. I told Eli what I wanted and he came back with a few options. This design is my favorite."

In my open palms he places a small vessel coated in gold filigree. Embedded into the shiny metal are flourishing designs of blooming flowers, twisting vines, and a few hummingbirds.

Without a thought, I pull the worn canister from my being and swap the needles, placing them gently inside my new gift.

"You really didn't have to, but it's perfect. Thank you."

Moving along we walk in a blissful silence, before I'm reminded of our events from earlier.

"Oh, you never told me, did that experiment of yours work?" I already know the truth, but not from him.

"It did."

"And? What happened?"

He looks around the garden, making sure no one else is nearby. "The relic is enchanted. The water allowed it to show us a map," he says with much enthusiasm. Already tasting the adventure the map can lead him to.

"A map of what?" Sharp lines cut into his face as he tightens his jaw. Maybe it is too soon to ask.

"I trust you, Ariah," he blurts out. "I'm not sure why. We haven't known each other very long, but I do. If I tell you, do you promise not to tell anyone?" I struggle with a nod. It's as if pins prick me from the inside out. Forcing up an answer. "I need you to say it."

The Queen will hate me for this but there is something within me that desires his secrets. Not to share, but to hold.

"I promise," I whisper.

"We believe Fraya found the Ivian Flower." He moves closer to me, inches away, but still too far. "I know you might not believe in it, but I do think it exists." His head leans into mine and then suddenly snaps back. "We should continue."

I'm left not wanting him to pull back. I want the kiss he clearly wants to give me. I want to taste him and feel his weight pinned against me. Suddenly my earlier threat about not wanting him to touch me is gone. It's different. He's different.

"Will you come with me? Well...not with me, with me." He flounders with his words. "Would you like to come with us? You could even bring Chana if you'd like. It is my intention to ask the Queen for access to explore Farella Isle. You could have an adventure of your own. You would no longer have to live through anyone else's story."

"Me?"

He laughs. "I know your life is here so I understand if you can't."

There is nothing I want more than an adventure. It's the reason I left Foxhead, the reason I accepted the Queen's offer. Never did I think a new opportunity would present itself, let alone from none other than a prince.

"I can't." My response is quick and I see the way it hits him, crushing any hope he holds. "Iann, I can't leave. At least not yet."

"May I ask why?"

"I'm here to pay off my parents' debt. They owe the Queen, and it was either this or getting married to Beetlerum." The verbal outpour is unwanted and unstoppable. I didn't even have a chance to sift through the words.

My body stiffens realizing Sky's warning. The enchanted mixture.

"Married?" He looks disappointed.

"Yes. My village elders like to arrange marriages. Well, only if they get something out of the bargain. They tried to do it with me, but I told them no." There is no filtering through my words, they come out as they please. "I'm sure you're familiar with such alliances. You're a prince after all. I'd bet all the families in Saden would want one of their children to marry someone of your status."

He chuckles and offers a hand as we descend a few more stairs.

"I'm sure they would. My mother included. While my parents would love an alliance, they have always allowed a union to be our choice. Always for love. Not just for political gain." He holds on to my hand and I don't pull it away. The touch feels cozy and draws me closer to him as we talk. Slowly, and ever so subtly, I inch nearer until our arms brush each other. "If it were my mother's choice though, I'd already be married. Maybe even have a child on the way. She's eager for grandchildren."

"Sounds like my mother. She was in hysterics when my sister had my niece."

He stops us and holds a stare I don't dare sever. His finger slides across my face, moving a curl that tries to get away.

"The offer will stand until my departure. You are more than welcome to join us."

I tug my bottom lip between my teeth. His eyes drift to my mouth and though I can't be sure because my head already feels like it's moving, my body drifts to him.

Pop.

The sound of a cork and a group of people laughing sends us looking in their direction. Another near-kiss completely ruined and I'm pissed.

"We should keep walking," I suggest.

"Yes—" He nods and clears his throat. "We should do that."

He offers me a smile so lovely I nearly pull him back and kiss him myself. Instead, we carry on walking for hours, late into the night—with me fighting every urge not to pull him into me and wrap myself in his being.

23

IANN

Only a fool is stupid enough to not have gone in for a kiss. Memories of her opulent, blush pink lips, which my eyes were fixed to all night, taunt me. Every blatant sign she placed right in front of me, only for me to ignore. I am a fool.

In the morning, I wake to the sound of metal scraping against clay. A painful noise to one's ears.

Shooting up, I find Deean in the corner tearing away at a piece of bread and shoveling a fork full of meat in his mouth.

"There he is." He's annoyingly chipper this morning.

I respond to him through the palms of my hands, rubbing at tired eyes. "I had one glass of champagne, why do I feel like my body has been chained and pushed off a plank into icy water?"

"I suspect benten or maybe lorice." He moves on to a bowl of fruit. "They drop concoctions into drinks down at the tavern. Makes for a better night but results in wicked mornings." He tosses the fork to the side and wipes his face. "I see you had fun though."

"And not as much fun as you. They add truth serums?" No

wonder the taste of the champagne was off. Lorice is a common mixture made by apothecaries. One I have used to get people to confess the whereabouts of hidden treasures. But never have I been on the receiving end. The thought of Ariah dropping it in my glass crosses my mind, but she also appeared loose-lipped and answered all my questions without hesitation. It must have been the man who stopped her near the table. I've seen him around watching us.

I stumble out of bed and take hold of whatever he has in his cup. The heat warms my fingers. Thankfully it's straight tea.

"You and Ariah got pretty close." Ignoring him, I plop onto the chair across from where he sits. "What do you think of her?"

I wave a hand in confusion. "What do you mean?"

"It's a pretty straightforward question."

Tapping a finger at the edge of my chair we stare at each other. "I have a confession." My mind spins and though it's against my better judgment to share, I need to unload some guilt. "I invited her to Farella with us. And I may have also told her about the flower."

His face melts into a mixture of fury and confusion, causing some turbulence of my own. "I had to twist your damn arm to get me to come, and even then, I ended up having to be a stowaway to be here. You meet a woman, you have one deep conversation with her, and then ask if she wants to go?" He throws his napkin on the table. "Absolutely ridiculous. Did you at least sleep with her?"

A pounding on the door saves me from answering and ends the discussion. Deean gets up to resume his role as courtier, a role he keeps forgetting.

We're not done, he mouths before opening the door.

To both of our surprise it's Benny who bows and rests his arm against the door frame. Slightly hunched over and profusely out of breath.

"There's a problem," he utters between battered breaths. "It's Esha."

Benny leads Deean and me across the castle and into the other wing where the workers stay and shows us to Esha's bed, where he appears to be lying on his back, lifeless. "He didn't get ready with the rest of us. When I tried to wake him, he didn't stir."

My fingers locate a slow beating against his wrist, but his skin is far too cold.

"And?" Deean asks me.

"He's alive." Leaning close I catch the scent of nightshade and newetberries. "He reeks of poison, though."

For the entirety of our stay, I've been worried that something would happen to Marcel or myself. Eating, walking through corridors, especially going into the main village comes with great anxiety. Never did I think Esha would be the one to fall victim to a blatant attack.

"Why him?" Deean whispers. He looks around as if we are being watched at this very moment. "Not to belittle him, but what value can someone get out of poisoning him? He is a servant without much to offer."

"Maybe he saw something," Benny replies.

"Possibly. Or maybe he was confused for someone else," I suggest, reeling in both Deean's and Benny's attention. "If lorice was overflowing last night, maybe more secrets were found out than intended. Benny, go share the details with Harpen and have him alert Marcel. Deean and I will see if the Queen has an apothecary who is capable of making an antidote."

Benny leaves as Deean and I search for Ariah, she might be able to help us with a cure.

Deean hits panic mode and recants details about last night. While I wouldn't be the least bit surprised if he let him being a prince slip, he swears he didn't say anything at last night's party.

Rounding one of the corridor corners, we nearly collide

with Queen Cayleen. "Our apologies, Your Grace," I say as Deean and I bow.

"Prince Iann. We missed you at last night's dinner." She strokes the flaming fur of a baby fox, and I spot the golden fox we gifted her, standing at her side. "I can't fault you, I would be tempted to attend one of Lady Arranella's parties myself, if given the opportunity."

She looks me over and then eyes Deean. "You both look flushed. Is there something the matter? I like to know all things happening within my castle walls."

"It's one of my men." I'd rather ask Ariah about the apothecary but there is no knowing where she is, and Esha may not have long. "He has been poisoned and I would like to have your apothecary assist him."

She snaps a finger and a man with the most golden hair and blue eyes steps forward. It's the man from last night, the one who stopped Ariah and potentially contaminated my drink.

"Skyleen, go with Prince Iann's courtier and help in any way possible. Guards, go ask the workers if they have seen anything untoward and track down who would do this."

I nod to Deean, forcing him to follow Skyleen. At her command the others scatter until it's just the Queen, me, and one other guard.

"I hope you don't think this is a direct act from the crown? I assure you, maintaining our newfound alliance is of the utmost priority." Black lace claws at her neck and the pearls in her earrings dangle, drooping down to her shoulders.

"No, not at all." I fill the corridor with lies.

"Good." With her free arm she interlocks it with mine and leads us down the hall. "Bad blood isn't good to have during one's visit. The last thing we need is more tension between our kingdoms." We continue strolling the corridor and that same feeling of being watched creeps up.

"I was thinking about your proposal the other day. The one

to expand trade." My attention is hers. The words make me forget about all other pressing manners. "I think it would be good for our kingdoms."

"You do?"

"Don't be so surprised. I'm not as cold-hearted as stories make me out to be. Your suggestion is a reasonable one." Letting go of my arm she stops and pivots towards me. "I've heard grand stories of the great explorer prince. And even grander stories of my precious Farella Isle. I assume it's a desired destination of yours."

I give her a pitiful smile. "I'll make you a deal," she continues, "I'll grant you access to Farella, but you must bring your findings back here and they shall be split fairly. Although, I do warn you, those lands have been closed off to travelers for a reason, and I'm certain you'll find much more trouble than treasure."

She wants the flower, and much like my father, she is counting on me to locate it. Even if there is something worth finding, my father will not permit me to come back to Haymel. Nor would I risk the return to this kingdom. But all she needs is my word, even if it is a lie.

"Fair enough." And I watch my agreement pull a smile from her, one far from joy and closer to deception.

"Well then, you have permission to travel my lands anytime you'd like." She locks her arm back with mine and proceeds into her throne room. It is far grander than the one in Saden and looks exceptionally polished and decorated for tomorrow's masquerade. Orange and white azaleas fill the room, a sight that would have my mother hyperventilating. "As one of our special guests tomorrow, I want to make sure you are ready for the festivities. Do you already have an outfit? If not, we can fashion something quickly."

"Yes, Your Grace. I brought appropriate attire with me."

"Good." Her arm slides away from mine as a servant brings

over a tray. The scent is heavenly. "Spiced pear tarts. A specialty dessert in Haymel. Do try one."

The servant lowers a tray of the flaky golden tarts. Saden is not accustomed to having pears and only receives them through trade. Most of the supply is dispersed amongst the palace and other noble homes.

My mouth waters as a parade of butter and spices floods my awareness. I resist the urge to take more. There are more important matters, and this is all beginning to feel like a distraction.

"Of course, you will need a date." She tosses her unfinished portion of the tart on the tray and pets her fox once again. "After careful consideration, I've chosen Vera to escort you tomorrow."

"Vera?" Smothering a cough with my hand, I turn my face from her afraid it will give my emotions away. Does she think I am some child who is incapable of selecting for myself? And Vera is beautiful, well spoken, clearly educated, and possesses a spiciness that is enough to keep me engaged, but her face isn't the one that comes to mind. "Isn't Ariah tasked with helping me?" I turn back, focusing to keep my face unreadable. "Surely she can remain with me during the ball and my brother can carry on with Vera."

She clicks her tongue and steps towards me. Her shoulders rise and there is a pinch between her eyebrows. "I would love to provide that option for you, but Prince Marcel insisted on having Ariah as his date. I'm afraid I must oblige to his needs first, being that he's the heir of Saden."

The fingers of my right hand fan out, spreading as far as they'll allow before curling into a fist. Blood thrums through my hand spreading a flame that ignites my body, scorching my face.

"I'm afraid I have to go." I bow to Queen Cayleen and storm

out of the throne room. She mumbles something but I don't hear the words, nor care to hear them.

Memories of an all too familiar scenario resurface. This isn't the first time Marcel has taken an interest in what's mine. He and Thana were caught by Deean years ago. In that instant, the longest and only relationship I'd ever had ended. Ultimately saving me, but scaring, nonetheless.

There were encounters after Thana, but a jaded heart makes for a terrible companion, and even worse lover.

Ariah feels different than the rest. There is a constant need to be in her presence. Excitement in wanting to share stories with her and a longing for her to reveal pieces of herself.

Though we are nothing, and I can't call her mine, it's knowing Marcel took something I desired for himself that pains and infuriates me.

I forgave him once, but I would rather a poison stop my heart before I do it again.

ARIAH

"Marcel?"

I was nearly finished with the Queen's dress when a messenger boy sent word that the Queen desired to see me.

Vera was waiting when I entered the study, her eyes falling once they met mine. It took all of thirty seconds for the Queen to share the news and for me to figure out why Vera had looked so timid.

For tomorrow's masquerade I am to be Prince Marcel's date. It comes as a surprise, and though she tries to hide it, a relief to Vera. And Vera will be the one to accompany Iann.

"I thought the arrangement you made was just fine," I say.

"Is there a problem with the change?" Queen Cayleen snaps, viciously slewing her words. "Would you like to tell the Prince, and heir of Saden, that Ariah Tyndall would rather go with his brother? That his Royal Highness is wrong in his selection?"

Vera sends me a cautionary look, one meant to keep me quiet and at the mercy of the Queen.

My head falls like a chastised child. "No, Your Grace. I

wasn't questioning you or the Prince." I force a swallow before my next words. "I will attend the masquerade with Prince Marcel as he desires."

She leans on the table with her elbows and folds her hands to rest her chin upon. "Good. Now, do you two have anything to report on the princes?"

I sense Vera's gaze go to me, waiting for a few seconds before she speaks.

"Prince Marcel has written to the King about their visit. He is worried about Lord Garren and the trade alliance, but overall considers the trip to be a success and believes the rivalry between kingdoms has come to an end."

There are circular swirling designs on the polished tile that I didn't realize the last time I was in here. They match the patterns on the curtains, and the embellishment has me envisioning countless outfits I can craft with them.

My insides flame. Distress eats away at me along with the effort to keep my mouth shut, something I'm unaccustomed to. The last time I spoke up to a higher authority, the council ended up taking it out on my best friend—a friend I desperately wish I could talk to right now. But this is the Queen. A woman with far more power, and people to use, to destroy everything and everyone in my life.

I am angry and disappointed. It was reckless to think that anything would come of Iann and I, but for one night we could have pretended.

An elbow digs into my ribs and my eyes dart up to Vera who nods her head towards the Queen.

"I'm sorry. Umm...the King wrote to Iann...Prince Iann, I mean, saying that his middle brother was missing from the palace and then stated that Rolley is his confidant." The information on the map and Farella surface, and although I should divulge such insights, I keep it all to myself.

Queen Cayleen rises from her seat and comes around to the front of her desk. "Anything else?"

"No, Your Grace," Vera and I say simultaneously.

"And what do we know of this Rolley person?"

"Chana hasn't been able to uncover much," Vera answers. "He keeps to himself. Doesn't really interact with the Saden crowd, nor ours. I believe Ariah has also been watching him." Vera's eyes slip to mine as her eyebrows raise.

"My focus has mainly been on Benny and Eli, but Rolley did have a lengthy conversation with Benny one morning. First time I ever heard him speak—"

"About?" Queen Cayleen interrupts me.

The taste of iron floods my tongue as I bite at the inside of my mouth. "Farrella Isle, Your Grace," I surrender to her, fessing up a scrap of information.

I hold tight to Iann's offer and the anchor being a map. I'm sure it's information this role requires me to give her but there is a need to cling on to the secrets for now.

Her lips purse as she gives us a slight nod. "Maybe it's the excitement of our recent guests or the training of our newest recruit, but I'm truly disheartened by the lack of competence in my Foxes. Vera spends her time crying up and down my halls." Vera's head lowers. "Chana practically lives in the shadows yet can't figure out who this extra person is. And another can't keep his poisons locked up." She walks closer until she's only a few feet away from us. "Our guests only have three more days here and I want no more distractions. Finish the dresses and accompany Prince Marcel to the ball." Her glare on me feels heavy and I can't hold it for long. "And both of you find out who poisoned our guest. Whoever is responsible acted outside of my orders and I need to know if they are ally or a foe."

"Yes, Your Grace," Vera and I sing in simulation, our voices carrying a new fear.

We turn to go but the Queen stops us. "I almost forgot." She holds up a single empty vial. "I have your first true task as an official Fox, Ariah. I want this filled with Prince Marcel's blood." I lose all control of the muscles in my face, my jaw nearly drops to the ground. Why in all the divinities does she require his blood? "And I want it in my hands by morning." Her dress glides across the floor as she walks back to her desk and sets the vial down. "Both of you can get out now." She waves a hand towards the door.

Vera has to push me forward to fetch the vial before we both take our leave.

The halls are empty as Vera and I head back towards the grand hall. I keep a lookout for Iann and wonder if I should tell him about the ball, but a bigger part of me says screw the ball.

How am I going to get a vial of Marcel's blood without him knowing, and in under a day?

Suddenly, there is a pull on my dress causing me to fly backwards, and then abruptly I am shoved into a darkened side hall.

"Keep your mouth shut," Vera says with a finger pressed to my lips.

Pulling away, I see another figure waiting in the dark. My eyes begin to adjust and I realize it's Chana.

Vera examines the necklace around her neck. The large gem is dazzling with a golden light. "She's not watching," Vera says.

"What did she want?" Chana comes closer.

"She claims Marcel wants to escort Ariah to the ball. She's also worried about the Saden man who was poisoned. She has no clue who did it." Vera folds her arms. "Oh yes, how can I forget about the part where she wants Ariah to get Marcel's blood."

"Blood?" Chana's face pinches. "I wasn't expecting that."

"Wait." I stop both of them from proceeding. "What do you mean she's not watching?"

Vera clings to the necklace. "This picks up enchantments.

Turns red when someone is using one near, or on, me. Most think it's a simple mood stone."

"Her pendant," I whisper, remembering the jewelry during Luna's wedding. She claimed it was how she kept track of her castle while being away. "Where did you get it?"

She smiles. "The Queen has her ways, and I have mine."

"She saw you and Iann in the garden last night." Chana turns her attention to me. "She knows of your feelings for each other and his offer to you." She stops and watches my eyes dart away as my gaze clings to a dark spot in the hall. "And I'm assuming you didn't tell her this or anything about the flower, so now she knows you're a liar too. She is testing you."

"Tell her," Vera adds.

Chana takes in a lengthy inhale. "She asked me to watch you. Even forced Sky to have a poison ready in case you decided to be stupid enough to leave with the Prince. She doesn't trust you or Vera."

"What did I do to make her not trust me? This is the first time we've had a conversation with her since their arrival." My insides crawl with a sudden rage and I'm about ready to go back in there and have this conversation with the Queen directly.

"She's been watching you. Between the map Iann found and the potential of you fleeing with him, it's all a bit too reminiscent for her."

"We remind her of our mothers," Vera interjects, reading my confusion. "Your mother was once her greatest Fox—her most trusted confidant. All of that vanished when your parents met and slowly their love, and then marriage, and ultimately their children, became more and more important, and further pushed away the Queen."

"It's not like I'm marrying him. If I wanted to be married, I would have stayed in Foxhead and become a Beetlerum," I shout before a hand clamps over my mouth. I push Vera's hand away. "Why are you both telling me this? Especially you?"

Vera and Chana pass each other a glance.

"We want out," Chana answers.

"We figured if we help you, then you can help us," Vera finishes for her.

I check Vera's necklace to make sure it's still yellow. "What do you want me to do?"

"Queen Cayleen has granted Iann permission to explore Farella." Chana looks at Vera once more and then back to me. "They are departing the morning after the ball. We'll protect you and help you get Marcel's blood, as long as you can get us on that ship."

"Do we have a deal?" Vera edges closer. "The alternative is to give you the poison and let the Queen have her way. Plus, your family owes mine." Chana nudges her. "What? I'd say this is a pretty fair truce."

I've only been here a brief period of time and I'm already regretting coming. I can't imagine the torment that has built up for them over the years.

"Deal," I finally get out. "I'll help you all."

"Two drops in his wine should take him out for a few hours," Sky warns me, shoving the vial of turquoise liquid into my hand. "It will give you more than enough time to get his blood and get out."

As an extra precaution, Vera gave me her necklace. She told me it is more than likely the Queen will be watching, but at least I will know when. The act of kindness also came with a threat of her destroying every outfit I own if I lose it.

The rest of the day passes at a slowly agonizing pace. I finish the Queen's dress, leaving minor details for my assistants to finish up with before the ball. It is stunning; I spend much more time on it than I should, considering she has it out for me.

On the rare occasion I see Iann, he pretends not to notice me. Even during dinner, he doesn't look my way. Marcel tries to get him to engage a few times, but he surrenders no more than two word responses. Eventually people stop trying to speak to him and I feel he prefers it that way.

After dinner I try finding him, in hopes we can speak, but he disappears before I get a single glimpse. I even go to his room, but no one answers the door.

As soon as night falls, my time is up.

The necklace stays yellow as I move about the castle, but I have no doubt the Queen will be watching me soon.

Back in my room I put on my black outfit, the same one I wore the night my mom made me sneak into the Bettelrum house. Only this time my mother is not with me, or Luna, who practically carried me through that situation.

Two knocks rasp at the adjoining door.

"Come in," I say to Chana.

She too is dressed in black. She is both helping, and acting as a spy for the Queen tonight.

Her eyes fall to the gem of the necklace. "Are you ready?"

It would be easier to just knock on Marcel's door. I'm certain I could seduce my way in, toy with him a bit and wait for the poison to carry him to sleep, but sneaking in means there will be no traces back to me. It also means not waking up to him in the morning only to convince him that something happened between us, or worse, something actually happening between us.

Iann's face comes into view, the image of him tightening my stomach. Guilt twists like a dagger in the back but I submerge the feeling.

If I ever want out of here, I need to fulfill the Queen's requests and pretend to be on her side until the opportunity to leave arises.

"Not at all." I pull out my fox mask hanging in the wardrobe. "I'm sure I don't have much of a choice though, so it doesn't matter."

"You still have one. She'll just ensure you suffer if you choose incorrectly." She gives my arm a gentle squeeze. "Let's go," she whispers before slipping on a mask of her own. One that is as black as coal with pointed ears and traces of silver. One that's perfect for her dress. "He should be heading back to his room soon."

Instead of going out of the door like normal people, we take the window. From Chana's small balcony we begin scaling the wall using the protruding stones to help us climb our way to the top. Thankfully, being on the third floor makes a very short climb to the roof. The darkness is an added bonus because it prevents me from seeing the ground. I've never been afraid of heights but would rather not look down if given the chance.

"This way," Chana says once we pull ourselves up and start running on the flat gravel roof. White light is the only thing to guide us from one end of the wing to the other.

Once we're over the west wing she leads us to the edge and looks below. "That's his room." She turns to me as I place the mask on and tie up my hair, until all curls are in a tight bun. She looks down at my chest, at the necklace, before taking a rope and double knotting it around a nearby pillar, like she's done this several times over. "Better get going. She'll be watching soon."

Wanting this night to be over, I don't hesitate to grab the rope and use it to help me lower myself onto the balcony.

Once my feet hit the ground, I linger in the corner trying to get a better view of the darkened room. When I'm sure Marcel isn't inside, I make my way through the unlatched door.

No one has lit any of the lanterns or candles that stand plentifully around the room;the only light that comes in is from the moon and the slit underneath the door, leading to the hallway.

His room is practically a replica of Iann's. Most of the guest rooms are, which makes it easier to know where I need to go.

I rush to the liquor tray and find several options to tamper with. Through the handful of dinners I've had with Marcel, never once have I seen him touch wine, so I skip that. Instead, he always has the servers bring him a glass of bourbon.

I pull out the vial Sky gave me and shake two drops inside the decanter. To ensure this plan works, I grab one of the folded napkins and soak a corner in poison. With the damp spot, I run it around the rim of both glasses on the tray.

"You are a selfish individual. Do you know that?" Nearing voices send me jumping, almost causing me to spill the rest of the poison.

The voices come closer and I hop into a wardrobe in the corner. The door slams open and two bickering souls enter before the door closes.

Through a partial slit in the wardrobe doors, I see a servant who rushes to light the lanterns in the room as Marcel comes into view. His deep brown eyes are dark, darker than usual and his face is twisted with bitter displeasure.

Trailing behind him, and the one doing all the talking is Eli. Eli?

"You've done this to him once before. Might I remind you of Thana? How can you do this again?"

Marcel goes straight to the liquor tray and pops the cork to the bourbon.

"You may go now," he says to the servant and then remains quiet until the door shuts and the footsteps trail away. "As I've stated a dozen times, I don't know what you're referring to

Deean. If our brother has an issue, he's welcome to come complain to me himself."

I sink farther into the wardrobe. King Marcel's letter is making much more sense now. The missing son. The laxed way Eli speaks to, and around, Iann, even the extra person in their party. All three Saden princes are here.

My hand flies to the necklace. It's still yellow, but now I'm wondering if it's broken. Surely the Queen will be watching me by now.

"You know he has an interest in the Queen's lady. Or are you so caught up in your own interests?"

Marcel finishes the alcohol in one sip. His Adam's apple bobbing as he swallows the poison down.

"This discussion is over some Haymelian wench? They're all fickle and of little interest to me. The Queen suggested one and I said yes without thought. As our brother should. We'll be gone in two days' time and never have to see this place or any of these people again. Why does he care so much about one girl, especially one whom he barely knows?"

"Is that what you told yourself when you slept with Thana? While our brother was out looking for riches for your future kingdom nonetheless." Deean crosses the room in three long strides. Right until he's cozied up in his brother's face. They are nose to nose and not one of them is backing down. "You are going to make a piss poor king. Your selfish ambitions will be the fall of Saden."

Marcel squints. "Better my prideful ambitions than those of a drunk." He shoves Deean back until his knees hit the side of the bed and he has nowhere else to go. "I should have sent you back when I had the chance. I didn't, for Iann, you know. He's the only one who still has hope in your pitiful ass. Like I said, I don't give a damn about whatever her name is." Rude. He steps back like he's losing his balance. Oh no, the poison is setting in and I need Deean to leave. "I'm tired. Get out of here," he orders, turning back to the tray and leaning against the table it's set upon.

"What's wrong with you?"

"Nothing, Deean. We're done here."

Deean takes a step towards him before finally deciding to wave him off and leave, done with the altercation.

Marcel's breathing deepens as he claws at his chest. A dull red light fills the space around me. He now has the attention of me and the Queen.

He lets out a lowly cry before his body gives way and he falls to the ground with a thud. I give it a minute, in case someone has heard and tries to come in, before I make my way out of the wardrobe.

Racing across the room, I make sure the door is locked before I sprint back over to Saden's future king's prone form and draw my dagger. Lifting Marcel's arm, I force a slit across the top of his forearm and watch the blood surface. The cut is oddly satisfying and comes without hesitation. Before the blood has time to hit the ground, I let it drop into the vial, filling it to the desired level as I squeeze more out.

As I wait, I watch him carefully, partially expecting him to spring up and have my head for what I'm doing, but I keep going knowing that she's still watching.

He looks so much like Iann lying there. His features cause a sudden ache in my heart. If what Deean claimed is true, then Marcel knowingly slept with a woman Iann once loved. And to Iann it looks like I'm just another woman stolen by his brother. His cold actions at dinner and avoidance in the hall is justified, but I need him to know that this is out of my hands.

Once the vial is full, I apply pressure to the wound and make sure no blood has been left on the floor.

The necklace fades back to yellow and I feel my heart slow just a tad.

I tuck the vial carefully into one of my pockets and rush to the balcony. Cool air brushes over me, sweat instantly drying with the breeze.

My body stills when the rope is gone. I check the left side of the balcony but could have sworn I dropped down from the right. Both sides come up empty. The rope is no longer there. I look over, examining the wall in the moonlight. It's not like the wall near mine and Chana's room. There is nothing to climb up on.

"Hey," I whisper-yell without speaking her name and being as loud as I can without drawing attention. "Drop down the rope." All I get is silence despite a few more attempts.

Chana is nowhere to be found, I have no way to climb up, and who knows when the Prince will be waking. This night is *perfect*.

Running out of options and time, I head towards the only exit left. I unlock the door and let my hand linger on the knob. I don't open it right away. Something tells me to snuff out the lights, so I run around the room until I'm left with only darkness. If I could carry him, I would drag Marcel to his bed and make him think he passed out, but I know I wouldn't make it an inch trying to lift him.

I remove my fox mask and tuck it into a pocket. I could explain away the dark clothes but someone sneaking around with a mask feels more suspicious. Once I slip into the hall, I take one last look back into the room before I gently shut the door.

Turning around I prepare to sprint away in search of Chana, but my world stands still. Time itself is frozen and the only thing moving is my beating heart.

Iann stands down the hall, prepared to head into his room until he notices me. His face is hollow, and he has a hard time keeping his eyes on me.

"Iann," I whisper, moving towards him, "Please, let me explain."

He puts on a fake smile. "I would rather not hear the details. You can spare me that." He taps a finger against his coat. "Plus, you don't owe me anything." His gaze is back on me, deepening, pushing forth guilt. Even though I didn't do anything I know how it looks to him. "Good night, Lady Ariah."

Lunging forward I call his name once more, but he continues down the hall and disappears into his bedroom, leaving me all alone.

I'm convinced the pounding of my heart can be heard by all of the people in the castle, as I rush back to my bed chambers. My blood is fueled by anger and worry and I can't decide which emotion should be at the forefront.

Iann didn't even give me a chance to explain. I know what it looked like to him, but had I had the opportunity to speak, the misunderstanding could have been an easy fix. Well, maybe not the fact I was hiding in his brother's room and now carry a vial of his blood. Ugh! So not an easy fix.

Finally reaching my room, I rush in hoping her disappearance is part of another test for me, and she's waiting for my return. But I grow weary when I find the room empty. I knock on the adjoining door, and after an unanswered second attempt I let myself in. Cool air instantly breezes over me from the balcony window we left open. Like mine, Chana's room is also empty.

She was meant to wait for me, where the hell did she go? Growing concerned, I head to the room of the only other person who might know where Chana is.

At the end of the hall I come to a door and hesitate knocking. It takes a good minute to drum up the courage, mainly because I know this person will make a fuss about bothering them this late, but I knock nonetheless.

The first goes unanswered, as does the second and third.

At my fourth attempt, I place an ear to the door and hear a heavy sigh. "Vera?" I whisper loudly.

There is movement at the sound of my voice and a few seconds later the door clicks open a sliver, large enough to reveal her face, forms in the doorframe.

"You damn sure better have something important."

From the crack in the door, I spot two long needles and a ball of yarn lying on her bed. "You knit?" It's not the most pressing issue at the moment but it throws me for a second. She didn't seem like the type to spend her time kitting.

"Ariah," she says too calmly. "I'm only going to ask you one more time what you want at this hour?"

"Chana is missing. She left me during our mission and she's not in her room."

She releases a heavy breath. "Wait here."

A few minutes later she comes out of her room changed out of her night dress and in full Fox fashion, leads the way back to Chana's room.

Inside she inspects Chana's bedding, items on the dresser, even pokes about in my room, then she goes to the window.

"Show me exactly where you two went," she orders.

I don't hesitate to climb out the window and scale the wall to the roof. Vera follows, much more graciously than me. Once she reaches the top, she pulls a dagger from her pants and tells me to continue leading the way.

We take the same route Chane had led me in. Approaching Prince Marcel's room I slow and then stop when I spot a shadowed figure lying on the roof.

Vera pushes me out of the way when she sees the body too, and rushes to get closer.

Under the moonlight we make out Chana's still frame.

"Is she breathing?" Vera panics. It's the first time I've seen her without composure.

Bending next to Vera, I place my fingers along Chana's neck to search for a pulse.

Suddenly, I'm struck with a scent I've smelled several times inside my father's office. I am no apothecary but I know the scent of nightshade well enough to recognize it, and the deadly poison is strongly emitting from Chana.

25

IANN

Ariah twiddles her thumbs, occasionally taking one nail and applying light jabs to the other fingers. She continues to gaze out the window, answering the few questions Deean and Benny have for her. Her responses are brief and she seems as though she has to dig deeper for answers, when normally they just roll out of her.

Her wittiness is held hostage somewhere, along with her playfulness and attractive forwardness, and I despise the tension.

Benny had already invited her into town with us before I could have an opinion. The details about last night are ones I do not feel like sharing.

In truth, I'm not even sure I have grounds to be angry. With Marcel maybe, but certainly not her. She is a pawn like so many others in court, a piece moved by my brother, or perhaps even Queen Cayleen. I have no reason to be upset with her, but just looking at her boils up my emotions and makes me want to punch a hole in the wall or tear off the coach door. Seeing her come out of Marcel's room last night has my head spinning. It makes me want to hurt him.

"You alright, Your Royal Highness?" Deean says to me, tugging my glare away from the window. When I meet his gaze, his eyes shift down to the fist on my thigh. "Do you need some cool air? Or perhaps a drink?"

"I'm fine, Eli. Thank you." I go back to looking out the window but feel a new set of eyes on me. Ones that haven't looked my way all morning.

Ariah pins me with a heavy stare and I'm not strong enough to ignore it. I give in and meet those hazel eyes of hers, ones circled with dark, puffy patches. Has she been crying? Did someone do something to her? I swear if Marcel hurt her, I will end him and make Deean the future king myself. The words are on the tip of my tongue, demands for her to tell me who upset her, but then I stop myself. A new wave of fear rushes over me when I realize that the very person who could be responsible for her tears is me.

Suddenly, the carriage jolts forward and noises of a busy city street fill the small space, spiking a bit of anxiety. Though I've been to town with the Queen, there are still a lot of untrustworthy people who dislike anything about Saden. The only reason we're here is to speak to the blacksmith who crafted Fraya Vellen's anchor. Well, not the direct blacksmith, since it's been several years, but the family that is said to have made it. With only a few days left this is the only opportunity we have.

A guard opens the door and Benny and Deean make their way out. I gesture to Ariah, allowing her to escape the discomfort first.

People in the street stop and stare, whispers bouncing amongst each other. Some get a little too close and force the guards to back them up.

"Saden shits," a faceless voice calls from the crowd.

"Aren't we loved," Deean whispers near my ear.

Someone throws a tomato, nearly hitting Ariah in the back.

"These are the Queen's guests!" Ariah shouts, causing the

crowd to go silent. "Treat them as such. If anyone throws one more thing, especially something that hits me, I'll have you locked up under the Queen's authority."

The people back away and resume what they were doing before we arrived.

"She might be my favorite," Deean says, and we follow Ariah through the door of the blacksmith's.

Inside is far hotter than what the cool Haymel weather provides. Surrounding us is an assortment of weapons, each one handcrafted to perfection.

Benny and Deean head towards the back as Ariah glides a hand over a set of daggers. Each one is encrusted with gems, and slivers of light from the sun shining through the windows ricochet off the blades.

"Thank you," I say. She spins around and tilts her head. "For the crowd. You didn't have to do that."

She shrugs. "I wasn't about to let them get food on my outfit." She curtsies. "Please excuse me, Prince Iann."

As she passes, I reach out to stop her, but she doesn't notice and slips farther into the workspace where she joins the others.

"I've never seen you here before," a boisterous voice says, and a shadow on the floor grows with approaching footsteps.

Behind me is a woman, inches taller than me with defined muscles in her arms and legs. Her raven hair holds sage green streaks and foreign markings run up and down the dark skin of her arms and neck.

"That's because I've never been here before," I reply. "My friends and I found something that we believe was made here, and we have a few questions about it."

"And where is this item?" She offers me a smirk and walks over to the others.

"I have it." Benny pulls the anchor from his pocket and sets it on the counter.

The woman rests one elbow on the table and picks up the

anchor with two fingers, examining it like she's uninterested. Uninterested until she turns it and sees something that makes her stand tall and pull a magnifying glass from under the counter.

"Where did you find this?" She inspects every inch, her focus bouncing between the item and us.

"Got it off a drunk," Benny answers. "One of the best deals I've ever made."

She places the anchor and magnifying glass down. "And I assume you know what this is?"

"I'm not sure we would be here if we didn't."

"You also realize that this item was stolen from my family years ago. Technically it belongs to me."

"Technically, he won it during a bet. So, it's his," Deean interjects, gesturing to Benny.

"Why risk coming in here? Who are you lot?"

"The name is Iann." I step forward. "With me is Benny, Eli, and Ariah. And who are you?"

"Iann? As in Prince Iann of Saden. The Queen's special guest?"

I nod. "That would be me."

She clicks her tongue. "The name is Kala. I've never had a prince in my shop before. Certainly not one from Saden. You're not particularly liked by people around here."

A smile finds my lips. "I'm well aware. And what might your opinion be?"

She shrugs. "I'll keep my opinions to myself." She grabs a rag and begins polishing the item. "What might you want to know about the anchor, Prince Iann?"

"Who enchanted it?"

"I was born after the anchor was created, so don't take all my answers as absolute truth. Stories I've heard say it was an enchantress by the name of Morrena. She owed Fraya a favor."

"So, the flower is real?" Ariah says, taking a step forward

until we're side by side. Her knuckles brush mine and reflectively my hand curls into a fist.

"I've never seen it." Kala places a hand to her chest. "But I believe most legends stem from somewhere. I'd say the flower more than likely exists than doesn't." Kala comes from around the counter. "Is that all you want to know?"

"If Fraya had the anchor made for herself, how did your family end up with it?" I ask.

Kala shrugs.

"She had vowed to come back but broke her promise." A voice from behind us causes the atmosphere to shift. Rolley emerges from a backroom. "Nice to have been invited today. Since I've been kept out of the loop most of this trip, I've done some searching myself."

Rolley has been more like a shadow during this trip. I knew he was with us but didn't pay attention to him, not once. I was meant to find out information about his family but compared to other things, his history keeps getting pushed further down my priority list.

"Fraya was a wild soul. And a gambling one as well. After she found the flower, she brought part of it back with her. With the help of an enchantress and blacksmith, she took the poorly drawn images she had mapped of the island and secured them in that device. As payment she promised Kala's great-grandfather immortality.

"A few days later, when she was supposed to meet with the blacksmith, she ended up at one of the nearby taverns with a winning hand and endless drinks laced with lorice. My great-grandfather was not so morally sound and took advantage of her drunken state. They played a round of cards and he bet a deed to land he just acquired in exchange for everything in her pockets."

"Spare us the rest," Deean says. "Your ancestor took it for himself and became immortal and I'm guessing the blacksmith went out looking for his cut and in return got the anchor back, which was later stolen from him. Sound, right?"

"Aren't you a clever one, Eli," Rolley mocks.

"So, what do you want out of this?" I ask.

"I want to remind you of the deal made between me and your father. I want to be included from now on."

"Or what?" Deean says. "No offense, but what do you have to offer us that we don't already have?"

Rolley's grin curls upwards. "You have strong opinions for a servant." I catch the wink he throws to Deean and hope Ariah didn't pick up on it. "I have more power than you think. Tomorrow, after the ball we leave for Farella. Oh, and Kala here will receive part of the prize once we find it. Thanks to all of her help, I was able to piece it all together without aid from any of you."

I hold out a hand in surrender. "Alright. We hear you. Kala will be given what her family is owed and you as well. We came to end a feud not start another."

"Sounds good to me," Kala says. "I've always wanted to live forever. Or maybe I'll sell it to the highest bidder and live out a life away from this grungy place."

"Is there anything else we need to know?" I direct my question to Rolley.

"There might be some rather useful information you need to know. But I will only share it after we depart. Consider it my assurance that you don't leave me behind."

"Are we done here?" Benny asks, caught in the middle of it all. "Bad blood is never good for an expedition, particularly one that takes you out to sea."

"No bad blood," I say. "We're done here."

"Of course." Rolley stuffs something into the inside pocket of his coat. "Thank you for your time, Kala. You'll see us again."

Rolley takes his leave and Kala distracts herself with work.

"I would like to check out something in the apothecary

across the road, if you're okay with that, Your Grace," Benny says.

"Of course. We should get going."

The crowd has completely dispersed by the time we come out of the blacksmith's, and though some catch glimpses of us, no one stops and lingers.

Rolley is by our carriage waiting. Apparently, he's coming back with us. I should make him walk for that little stunt he pulled. In time, and I don't know how I'm going to do it, but I will get the papers he shoved into his pocket and find out every secret he's been hiding.

"I'm going to start walking back," Ariah says looking up to the graying sky. "I need some fresh air." She curtsies and heads in the direction of the castle.

My body flies forward as Deean shoves me. "You'd be a fool not to escort her. You two can go back and we'll catch up when Benny is done. Rolley might be missing though."

I chuckle at his teasing and just as I start to move toward Ariah, he stops me. From the carriage Deean pulls out an umbrella. "You might be needing this."

"Have fun." Benny bows, matching Deean's humor.

For the first time in a long time, I don't think twice. There is no hesitation, no contemplating the right or wrong move. I obey my heart and chase after the woman who I may never see again.

It doesn't take me long to catch up and maintain her speed. "May I walk with you?" I try breaking some of that tension. I want to apologize but for some reason I hold back.

"You may do as you like." Her words are sour but there is something stronger there. Her mind is on other things.

We walk in silence and our leisurely pace allows me to see more of the town. There isn't much. Not too different from Saden—nearly the same shops and stalls as any other kingdom.

"Is your friend okay?" she says with genuine concern. "I heard he was found nearly dead."

"Poison. No one knows who gave it to him though." Her arm presses into mine as she moves closer to allow a woman to cross our path. Her touch is like a rush of a thousand kisses. The thought has me thinking of her kiss. The one we almost shared the other night before we were cut off. It's a moment my mind likes to revisit often. "I overheard you asking Eli about Chana this morning. Is she okay?"

"Like your friend, she too has been poisoned. Found her unconscious last night."

That makes two in less than a day, and one from each kingdom. I originally thought the culprit would be someone from Haymel, but why would they harm their own?

There is a tap on my forehead, and then another, and another. Opening the umbrella, I hold it above us to keep dry from the drizzle that steadily picks up.

We walk in silence, making our way through the town until we hit open fields. We stop as we eye the road that continues up towards the castle gates.

"You know"—she stops walking and moves from under the umbrella—"you could have told me how you felt instead of shutting me out. We aren't children Iann. Words go a long way."

The way she says my name has me wanting her to say it more. Over and over.

She continues, "Like you, I had no say and yet you've been acting like accompanying your brother is my doing."

"I know and I am sorry to have behaved as such." I move to her, placing the umbrella back above her head and wipe away a few water droplets that have collected on her face. "It's not the first time Marcel has taken someone I desire." Her face melts and she bites at her lip. "I wasn't upset with you until I saw you coming from his room last night. I know I had no right to be, but I was."

Her lips part and for the first time since I've met her, she has no response. "I'll be leaving soon, and don't expect anything, I just want to be the one to escort you. The one to dance you around all night. The one to touch you." I wrap a finger in one of the coils of her hair and watch her breathing become uneven. "Pure jealousy on my part."

"So you desire me, eh?" She finds her playfulness once again.

No words have ever been truer. I desire this woman in every way imaginable.

"I see my rudeness hasn't diminished your confidence."

"Why would it?" Her lips twitch teasingly, but there are notes of seriousness. "I assure you, nothing happened with your brother last night. And if it means anything, I wish you were the one taking me."

Her words bring a smile to my face. "It does mean something."

She straightens her stance and places a hand against my shoulder. "If we don't have tomorrow, how about now?"

"Now? You want to dance while it's raining?" I don't remember giving myself permission to drop the umbrella, but it's shut in an instant.

Extending an arm I give her a slight bow. "Lady Ariah, would you care to dance with me?"

She curtsies and her face glows with a new light, an addicting glow I wouldn't mind seeing shine for the rest of my days. Slipping her hand in mine I draw her in close, entangling my fingers with hers, then I find the small of her back for my other hand to rest upon.

Rain continues to trickle down, but at this moment, it's barely noticeable.

Right when I'm about to apologize for the lack of music she begins humming, her melody growing louder and exquisitely blending in with the sound of the rain.

Time becomes irrelevant as she places her head on my shoulder and melts into me. Our feet glide over the muddy road not caring how soggy our shoes are becoming or how drenched our clothes get.

"I'm sorry," I whisper, pulling her in closer until there is no longer space between us. Until there is nothing but each other to hold on to.

Lifting her head to mine, my mouth steals the next hum from her lips, and I'm met with no opposition as she fully embraces the kiss. Her taste is just as pinquant to my senses as the rest of her.

Thunder ripples overhead but we remain interlocked. If this is what a sliver of eternity feels like with her, then I want to dissolve into it, right here, right now.

26

ARIAH

I'm unsure how long it takes us to get back to the castle and honestly, I don't care. The thought of the Queen watching us plucks at my conscience, but I push it out and ban it from returning while wrapping myself entirely in Iann's presence.

Despite the cold brought on by the rain, my body runs warm. Every touch Iann gives me releases an intensifying heat, one that sets my soul ablaze.

We find ourselves back in the castle teasing, flirting, and devouring kisses the entire way. His lips, touch, even glances are gentle, making me want him more.

In his room, the servants already have a fire going, it sets a warm tone throughout. As soon as the door closes behind us, he finds my mouth with his again. His hands roam over the curves of my body and eventually end up in my soaked hair. Delicately he pulls at the ribbon bound around my curls and sets them free. He tugs at my hair tilting my head to the left and breaks our kiss to begin trailing his lips down my neck and over my collarbone.

Hours ago, I was worried about being in his presence and

now I want nothing more. My hands go for the buttons of his shirt and undo them with haste. Once free, my hands glide up each line of his abdomen and then grip his firm shoulders.

He begins peeling off the soaked fabric of my top and suddenly stops kissing me as he rests his forehead to mine. "Can I just say how pleased I am that you aren't wearing that outfit with hundreds of buttons on it." I raise my hands as he pulls off the layer over my corset. It smacks against the hardwood floor when he tosses it.

"I happen to like that outfit."

"I'm not saying it didn't look good." His mouth is on mine again and my tongue stops him from speaking.

Just as he begins to undo the strands of the corset there is a knock at the door.

"Can you use your princely powers to make them go away?" I say before planting a kiss on his chest, and then two more.

"Not now, Eli," he calls and pulls me back to him.

I want to tell him that I know it's really his brother. I want to tell him everything about the Foxes and that I want to go with him to Farella, but it will make for good pillow talk, so I hold it in for now.

There is more knocking, growing in intensity.

He grumbles and pulls back, buttoning up his shirt halfway and marching to the door.

"I said not—" He stops and opens the door wider. "Apologies, Lady Vera. I thought you were Eli."

Vera?

I slip the soggy top back on and go to the door.

"I apologize, Your Highness." Vera does a quick curtsy. "I came to let Ariah know the Queen is requesting her. Immediately."

Red beams from Vera's necklace and I wonder how long the Queen has been spying.

The guards close the door, locking Vera and I inside the Queen's study.

Inside I see Sky standing—waiting—almost reminiscent of my first meeting here.

The Queen writes away at her desk and the fox she usually holds is fast asleep near her feet. Vera and I stop a few feet away and wait next to Sky.

"Well done last night." She doesn't look up from the parchment. "I suspected you were going to fail but you managed to make it through." I assume her words are for me, unless she had someone else carry out another bidding for her.

"Thank you, Your Grace."

"Tomorrow is the big day." She throws her pen on the desk and rests back in her seat. "If our guests are going to attempt anything, tomorrow would be the night to do it. With Chana still unconscious I need all of you to pay extra attention. The last thing we need is for more people to go missing or be poisoned. Sky, how is the antidote coming along?"

"I'm still working on it, Your Grace. I believe I'm up against more than just poison." Sky sounds tired, and his eyes are swollen, like he's been crying or hasn't slept in days.

"I didn't order my enchantress to..." The Queen's thoughts trail off and she keeps them in her head. "Ariah, are my dresses finished?"

"Yes, Your Grace. I completed them yesterday."

"And what have you been doing today? With all your free time the servants could have used your help setting up or you could have assisted Sky in waking up your friend."

Vera looks at the ground with the faintest grin on her face knowing what I was up to. I also don't like the way she said "friend" as if it was meant to be used against me.

"I went into town with Prince Iann. He wanted to look at some of the shops."

She looks at me for the first time. Her eyes roaming over the damp clothes and wild hair, making me self-conscious.

"Did Vera interrupt you at a bad time? Or perhaps, maybe it was a good one?"

Vera's necklace was red when she knocked on Iann's door and I know with certainty the Queen was watching.

"You said, 'do what it takes,'" I answer her quickly, trying to scour for a good lie. "I know the Prince has feelings for me, so I was using them to get information out of him."

"Is that so?" Her grin is a wicked one. She either thinks I'm utterly stupid for trying to fool her or that I am growing accustomed to this new life in her court. "Information of what kind?"

I have no intentions of betraying Iann directly, but she doesn't know that. I need her on my side until we leave for Farella. "Our mystery guest—all Saden's royal sons are here, Your Grace."

Her eyes expand to twice their size, and a few fingers play with her lips as she processes the news. I even have the attention of Vera and Sky.

"You're sure?" the Queen asks.

"Yes," I answer without hesitation.

"Do you know where the other brother is?"

"Not yet," I lie. "But I can find out."

"Do that and report back immediately. I have a parting gift for our princes. We mustn't leave one of them out." She gets up and walks past Sky, then Vera, and ends with me. "All of you are to go straight to your rooms and rest up for tomorrow. Any one of you caught outside your beds, or caught in another's, will be punished."

She is doing her best to keep Iann and me apart. For now, I will play her little game until tomorrow. All I need to do now is convince Iann to leave after the ball and not wait another day. She can't stop me if she doesn't see it coming.

In the hall, we wait until we're far from everyone to speak.

I check Vera's necklace before saying, "Be ready to go tomorrow."

Vera nods. "Okay. Sky is trying to find a way to wake Chana. If she doesn't, we're going to have to leave her. Unless anyone has a clever plan to get her on that boat."

"I told you I can't wake her," Sky whispers between us. "Chana isn't just poisoned. She is in some kind of trance. One more powerful than anything I can pull off."

"Wait." Is he saying what I think he is? "Are you an enchanter?"

"Not exactly. My mother is one and she taught me a few things. Most of which I've forgotten since being here. The Queen doesn't know, or she'll use it against me, so you better not tell anyone."

I surrender both palms. "You have my word."

"There's a bigger issue," Sky continues. "The Queen isn't responsible for Chana or the Saden servant. Which means someone more powerful is and they went after one of our own. We not only have the Queen to fear but whomever is responsible for rendering two individuals into an indefinite slumber."

My clothes are still damp and starting to itch. "Great. Give me some time to think everything over. I'll have a plan come morning."

They nod and just as I'm about to walk away Sky stops me. "Here." He holds out a hand and lets a chain dangle from his fingers. "It's like Vera's necklace only in bracelet form. It will let you know when someone is watching."

"Thank you." He helps put it on me. "You got anything for blocking her from seeing us completely?"

Sky's tired eyes fall to a squint. "I might be able to come up with something."

"Good. Once we've escaped, we're going to need to ensure that she can't find us."

I think about going back to Iann's room. Not even to finish what we started, though that would be a good distraction, but just to see him. To talk to him.

Instead, I find myself in a hot bubble bath, infused with peony and lemon. My chest has been feeling tight and I suspect stress.

The bracelet Sky gave me drapes over the side of the tub and I watch it with growing intensity, afraid at any minute it might flash red.

As a distraction, I use this time to catch up on the newest round of letters I received. Starting with Luna's, she tells me of hers and Morren's travels. She says they will be going north to the village of Kemp, where they plan to stay for a few weeks. She also writes about how unimpressed she is by my last letter to her and the measly few paragraphs I threw together. She threatens to come all the way here just to make sure I'm adjusting well. I laugh at her valiancy and the irony of just how poorly I find myself fitting into this life.

Moving on to my mother's letters, she writes of two princes who stopped in Foxhead.

> To my sweetest daughter,
> There is so much to share with you, but the
> most important is of a surprise visit from two
> Saden princes. Both tall and dashingly handsome.

Don't tell your father or anyone else I said that. How dare I say such a thing about a Saden.

One, Prince Iann, has visited far more places over the past year than I have my entire life. He was much too kind to be a prince. I think you two would have found comfort in each other. In many ways he reminded me of you. He also stayed in your bed, which not many can claim a prince has been in their bed.

But enough about them, I miss you my sweet girl. I truly wish I could take your place. I know the life of a Fox and it's not one I wanted to ever subject you to. If you ever find yourself feeling homesick, just know you are always welcome home, no matter what.

P.S. I may have some enemies there and apologize in advance for any cruelty heading your way because of me.

P.S.S. Your father says hello and to not strain yourself, or your breathing condition will have its way with you.

We love you,

Mom

The warning of enemies is a little too late, but I appreciate the sentiment. Starting to prune, I wipe my remaining tears, get out of the tub, and dry myself off. The bracelet goes back on my wrist before slipping into a silk nightgown.

A light knock comes from the door of the main room. I'm certain it's Vera, but when I open it, I'm happy to find Iann.

"I wanted to make sure you were okay," he says sheepishly, seeming unsure if he should have come here.

"I am." The Queen said to stay in my room and not end up in another's bed, but she didn't mention anything about someone else in mine. "Would you like to come in?"

He dips his head and enters my bland quarters as I shut the door behind him.

"How is Chana?" He takes a seat on a nearby chair.

"She still hasn't woken. And your servant?"

"No, not yet."

I pour us each a glass of water and I sit at the edge of my bed, facing him. "Can I ask you something?"

"Anything."

I think of all the things I could share with him but there is only one thing I desire right now. "Will you stay with me tonight?"

He sets the glass down on a bedside table. "If that's what you want."

I get up and feel his eyes follow me across the room where I blow out my lanterns and set my glass on a stand. When it's dark I make my way to him and slip a hand in his, pulling him to his feet.

He grazes his nose along mine and just holds me. It's all I need right now. All I crave is to be held by him.

We move to the bed and tuck ourselves beneath the covers. My bed is far smaller than his but it's just enough for two. Our heads stay close, foreheads resting against each other.

With a fingertip he traces unseen lines over my body starting at my head and moving down to my thigh. "Can we stay like this all night?" I whisper. It's the calmest feeling I've ever known.

"Yes." His finger comes back up preparing for another lap around.

"Are you happy, Iann?"

"Yes." His answer makes me smile. "Even more when my name slips from your lips."

The beating of my heart speeds up. We tease each other, our lips drawing in on one another's but never fully connecting.

"Can you tell me about your greatest adventure?" I continue our little question game.

"No," he says flatly but then gives me his dazzling smile. "I have had many adventures, but I honestly don't think the greatest one has happened yet."

It's at this moment when I realize I trust him with everything in me, including my heart, something no one has ever held. Not a single person. It's also at this moment when I unravel.

Catching a quick glimpse of my bracelet I see it is still yellow.

"I have something to tell you." I stroke his cheek with my thumb. "A lot of things to tell you, actually. Are you ready?"

He stops tracing his finger over me and his tone is more hesitant than before, but he still holds on to me. "Anything," he says. "You can always tell me anything."

PART THREE
TURN OF EVENTS

27
IANN

Today is my final day in Haymel—that's if all goes according to plan. Although departure is set for tomorrow, I asked Benny, Deean, and Rolley to secure a ship and to prepare the others to leave tonight.

Ariah confessed to everything, and I was only partially surprised. My father has spies of his own, people paid to do his grunge work; they aren't called Foxes, but I'm sure they have a name of their own. Gran will surely gloat about her warning for me turned out to be correct. The most shocking part of it all is the extraction of Marcel's blood, which is a secret that shall forever be mine. If he finds out what she did he would have no qualms about killing her. And while she did lie, her secrets didn't do much to change my feelings for her.

The biggest challenge will be convincing Marcel to leave for Saden tonight, without disclosing all details. But I fear if Queen Cayleen finds out we have stolen a ship and taken her people she will take it out on him. Despite everything, I can't set him up like that. Instead of me informing Marcel, I send Deean to do it, which is against my better judgment but it's one of the few options I have.

After breakfast, to ensure the Queen isn't using an enchantment on Marcel, I distract her with light conversation. Most of it consists of inquiring which guests will be in attendance tonight. She seems more excited than usual, and I can't decipher if it's because she enjoys a good ball or if she's planning something nefarious. Afterall, she has a vial of my brother's blood and in the wrong hands bad things can come from it.

"He intends to leave tonight," Deean whispers in my ear. "All our men, including Esha, will disappear."

I nod and pretend to laugh, as if he's told a joke. "Good. I feel like this may revert our kingdoms back to being rivals but…"

"It's better than ending up dead," Deean finishes for me. "I've also sent word by carrier pigeon Father. He should know soon." Deean smiles at a group of women walking by as they gawk at us. "You sure Farella is worth it? We can just go back with the others. Take Ariah with us."

Having Ariah come back with me to Saden is what I desire most. It's selfish because I know her life is here, but what if she could start over somewhere else, with someone else.

"I promised our father. And for whatever reason he's desperate for it."

"You don't think someone is sick, do you?" I stare at him and watch his face twist with concern. "Who? Do you think he's dying?"

"I don't know. It's just a feeling. We've come too far now. I will find that flower."

He places a hand on my shoulder. "I'm with you. We'll do whatever it takes."

Night comes quickly and everything is in place for our departure tonight. Our bags wait, packed in the rooms, but when it comes down to it, the unimportant items will be left behind. Marcel is set to flee in a carriage but knows if he needs to go sooner, he is to go by horseback.

We all dress for the ball. Ariah surprises me with an outfit she crafted herself, one she promises will go with her dress. The mask she selects for me is sage green with a long beaked nose and covered with golden filigree.

She even assists Deean with selecting an outfit and is pleased to finally be introduced properly to my brother. While the Queen knows all three of us are here, Ariah promises not to give away his identity.

Near nightfall, Ariah slips away to get ready and Benny comes in shortly thereafter.

"I've secured us a ship," he says fiddling with the top button of his shirt.

"Don't you look nice and dapper." A shirtless Deean tosses Benny a compliment as he searches for some jewelry in one of the packed bags. "Where is the chunky gold necklace? It's my newest piece. It would go perfectly with the mask Ariah selected."

"Servants aren't really meant to wear too much jewelry," Benny says nonchalantly.

"No one asked you."

Benny grins before smuggling a cough with his hand. "Plus, I used it as a down payment for a ship."

Deean snaps a head in his direction. "You did what?"

"You told him to do what it takes. Turns out our new captain has similar tastes as you." I shrug and lace up one of my shoes. "Did you give my cartographer the image of the map we had drawn from the anchor?"

Benny nods. "Yes, he's been studying and comparing it to other maps in the library. He and a few of the others in our crew will be sneaking out as soon as the ball begins. They will grab what luggage they can and some will head to the ship while others will wait for Prince Marcel."

After tucking in a shirt he then throws on a doublet—Deean is near ready. "Everything is in motion. Let's go have some fun until then."

Together we make our way out of the left wing, to the other side of the castle where the masquerade will commence. We know we're close to the ballroom when the expansive hall starts becoming more and more decorated. The Queen doesn't shy away from abundance. Flowers and feathers stuff the halls and candelabras set the place aglow; everyone adds to the décor with the different masks they wear.

Our party makes its way into the ballroom and I hang back, waiting for a formal announcement, Deean waiting with me. I'd rather skip such decorum, but I'm certain Queen Cayleen wouldn't appreciate the lack of posturing.

"Hello, brother." Deean and I spin around to find Marcel in an off-white outfit complete with a fur surcoat that scrapes the floor and a mask similar to mine, only white and trimmed with silver. "Brought you someone."

Next to him is a woman wearing a fox mask the color of fresh snow and decorated with lace and pearls. Curls, ones my hands have laced through, are loose and hold tiny pearl-like beads. A single strap hangs off a kissable shoulder and strings along faded green and pink flowers that move down the beige dress. The flowers run up and down the ribbed part of her gown and along the bust. Further down my eyes get caught on the slit that reveals smooth ebony skin—my hands itch to touch her once again.

"Do you like it?" She moves closer, with a certain tease in her step. I meet those russet eyes of hers and only for a second, allow myself to forget that other people are around. I lean into the hand she places against my cheek, hearing the bracelet Sky gave her as protection clink as it shifts on her wrist. "Your brother has decided I simply won't cut it as his escort. He much prefers to go with Vera, and now I am partnerless."

"Isn't he an idiot." A smile tugs at my lips. "Turns out I don't have a partner either."

Marcel smacks a hand on my shoulder. "You two have fun. And Ariah—" He hesitates. "Thank you."

"I've never heard those words from you," Deean whispers under his breath.

"Funny," Marcel says dryly, and bobs his head towards the entrance, forcing Deean to follow him.

"Is now a bad time to tell him I poisoned him and gave the Queen a vial of his blood?" Ariah asks.

"Let's deal with one issue at a time."

"You're probably right." She laughs and takes the hand I extend to her.

"You truly are beautiful." Her shoulders rise and I see her push down a swallow.

"Thank you," she whispers.

Together, we take our turn in line and wait for our introduction. Marcel and Vera are up first, and I feel Ariah's arm tighten around mine.

"No fear," I say, brushing my lips against her ear.

She bites her bottom lip, a movement has been increasingly driving me mad. "Easy for you to say. She isn't your Queen, and therefore she can't punish you."

"After tonight, she won't be able to punish you either. Your parents should receive a warning letter soon and we will be long gone from here within hours." I pull at a strand of hair that has become trapped by her mask and push it back with the others. "We can do this."

She takes a deep inhale and gives me a single nod just as our names are announced to the attending crowd.

Hand in hand we walk through the curtains and come to

the top of a staircase. The floral garland-wrapped railings are too far away to hold on to and I notice hundreds of lights suspended from the high ceilings.

I recognize Benny, Deean, and Marcel instantly; the only other person who I can identify, even with a mask on, is the Queen. She is dressed in her usual blood-red color—which is all too symbolic—and her dress is the largest one on the dance floor. Both her and the gown look like they have been dusted with gold and her mask is of course, in the shape of a fox.

"Well done with her dress. You have real talent," I whisper to Ariah. "Yours looks better."

"You're just full of compliments tonight. And, thank you," she says.

We reach the end of the stairs and offer the Queen a bow before we approach.

"Don't you two look striking...together," Queen Cayleen says with arms folded across her waist. "Prince Marcel was just telling me how he preferred Vera's company over Ariah's tonight," she comments mockingly, meant to get under Ariah's skin. "I hope you're okay with the swap, Prince Iann."

"Of course," I respond without a thought. "If I'm honest I'm glad for the switch. Ariah and I have had the pleasure of getting to know one another during my stay and I can't imagine escorting anyone else."

"Everything worked out then," she snips and turns to the orchestra, giving them a signal to begin. "Please, enjoy your last night." She gives us a pathetic smile and slips away.

"A bit ominous," Ariah says.

Deean comes over with two glasses in hand and Benny beside him. "How long are we giving this? I don't have a good feeling."

As he lifts the glass to his lips Ariah stops him. "Don't drink that." She looks around to make sure no one is nearby. "Sky went around this morning dropping things into the wine bottles and anything else he could get his hands on. Something about making people drowsy so they sleep longer tonight."

Deean lets out a hefty sigh. "Great. Drinking is out too. We need to move this along then."

"I have a bottle of silver rum in my bag," Benny offers him an alternative.

Deean smacks his lips as if he can taste it already. "We'll be back."

"While you're gone, go to Sky's workshop and see if he needs any help. He's still trying to wake Chana and Esha," Ariah instructs.

"Yes ma'am." Deean gives her a wild grin and he and Benny slip away.

I'm prepared to ask Ariah to dance when Vera swoops in. The tulle of her russet brown dress sweeping over my shoes.

"I hope you don't mind me stealing her for a quick dance?" Vera asks.

"The lady does as she pleases," I say in surrender. "As long as I get a dance eventually, I have no apprehensions."

"I'm sure you would get a dance and then some if a plan was not in motion," Vera teases, and Ariah slaps her forearm with the back of her hand.

The two women disappear into a sea of people doing some sort of group dance, and I spot Marcel reaching for a glass of wine.

"You might want to skip the wine tonight," I say, approaching the table.

He continues to pick up the glass. "Vera warned me. Thought I'd play along though. Make it look like nothing is up."

I nod. "Smart." And reach for a glass of my own.

"I hate balls," he grumbles, pretending to take a sip. Now that I think of it, most of our family dislikes them."

"I know I do. Deean and Mother seem to enjoy them though."

He smiles. "Mother does. Deean just likes the drinking and women that come with such a show. He'd enjoy those in any setting."

"True." We laugh. He seems to be in an odd mood. A good one, but that's odd for him. It's been years since he and I have joked with one another. "Thank you, for letting me escort Ariah."

He meets my eyes. "Of course."

Immediately, I find Ariah in the crowd and watch the joy pass between her and Vera. If they're pretending it looks real enough. Eventually, the girls drag Marcel onto the dance floor with them. It kills time and every new song pushes us closer and closer to departure.

I'm a bit winded and a few beads of sweat roll down the back of my neck when the music takes on a new rhythm, a slower one. I swoop Ariah in my direction before anyone else can claim a turn. My left hand finds the crook of her back and the right holds her hand up.

"You know," she begins saying as we twirl about, matching the pace of those around us, "I just discovered that last night was not the first time you've slept in my bed." She can't see my forehead pinch between my brows, but she continues anyway. "My mother wrote to me, saying that two Saden princes showed up in our lowly village of Foxhead. The community wasn't very kind, so she offered to let the two men stay in our home."

My neck jolts back slightly as memories about the room surface. There had been a headless mannequin in the corner and scrapes of fabric on the ground. "I thought you looked familiar when we first arrived. You take after your mother."

"I do." She smiles. "And you should be happy to know she likes you. I'm sure my father does as well."

"They were very kind. Nice to know I don't have to agonize over meeting your parents anymore."

On the other side of the room Queen Cayleen fixes her gaze on us. The mask hides her expression, so all I have to go off of are her piercing eyes.

Suddenly, she gets up from her throne and leisurely walks in our direction.

Before she can interrupt us there is something I've been wanting to say to Ariah all night. Something I've been contemplating and have questioned over and over again.

At first, I thought the feeling was sheer infatuation, and maybe some of it is, but it runs deeper. There is a pull she has on me that I'm not ready to let go of. A pull that I have yet to feel with anyone else I have met in life.

My hand slips out of hers and trails over her elbow and glides up her arm and along her neck until it stops against her cheek. A finger thumbs over her exposed lips and I feel her shudder at the touch. "You don't have to say anything, but I need you to know that I...that I...I think I'm falling in love with you."

28

ARIAH

The words "in love with you" hit me harder than anything I've ever endured. No one, outside of my parents and sister, has said those words to me, and they certainly didn't mean it the way he does.

He did say "I think" though, which makes it a little less daunting. These past few weeks have brought a lot of joy and comfort when I've been around him. I've never known feelings as strong as the ones I've developed for Iann, but how am I supposed to know if this is love? What if these heightened emotions are just from the thrill of being here, or maybe it's all just infatuation because he's a prince.

Wrapped in my own thoughts, it takes me a minute to realize the musicians have stopped playing. Iann doesn't move, and everyone around us has ceased dancing, frozen mid-step or twirl.

"Iann?" I wave a hand in front of him and then remove his mask to find a soulless being in his place, unable to blink or move. "Iann!" I shout like the sound of my voice alone can pull him from the trance.

Clap. Clap. Clap.

There is distant clapping from across the ballroom. I step to the side, so Iann is no longer blocking my view. At first, I think it's a sick, twisted game the Queen conjured, but she stands near us, like she was about to approach, also as still as stone.

"Well done," someone says from across the room. Rolley steps away from a group of people frozen in mid-conversation. "You, Ariah Tyddel, went from rejecting a notable village boy with rather poor manners, to getting one of the finest princes I've ever been in the presence of, to admit his love for you." He steps onto the dance floor, walking over to me without fear of, or concern for, the unsettling lifelessness around us. "I personally thought you would have gone for Deean had he not foolishly disguised himself. You both have a similar personality and wit. And Marcel, well he was never really an option, was he? But Iann suits you well, I can almost see it being the truest type of love...one day."

Rolley steps behind a couple who are stone still, and when he comes back into view, he's no longer himself. His body is completely altered, having shifted into a figure with an abundance of dark curls sweeping low to their waist and bony skin that's illuminated, as though they smuggle a star in their being. "Allow me to introduce myself, my name is Morrena. I'm the Queen's fifth Fox and personal enchantress."

She is also the woman who was waiting in the coach outside my house the day the Queen showed up.

Unable to move, she comes closer to me. Two violet gems rest in her eye sockets and she wears a golden dress lined with fox fur.

When I first arrived, the Queen mentioned a fifth Fox she had sent to Ethmay on assignment. What I didn't know is that she was an enchantress.

"How old are you?" Is the first question I can summon.

She releases a baleful grin, one filled with secrecy. "Not the politest question but I understand why you'd ask it. Fraya was the second person I was tethered to. All enchanters must be connected with another soul, or our powers remain dormant. I was with her the day she discovered Farella." She stops a foot away from me. "You see, before we left the island, Fraya had me use every ounce of power I had to so that only her bloodline would be able to see the flowering tree. It drained me so much I was nearly powerless for weeks."

"Why are you telling me this?" I ask, trying to put together any missing pieces.

"Finders are only allowed to take one flower each. It can either be for yourself or another, but no more than a single blossom. Fraya took it for herself, she was selfish like that, but it also meant I could be tied to her forever. Because we were tethered, my life was hers and it was only her that could release me." She waves her hand, annoyed at the memory. "She was supposed to come back to Haymel, map out exactly how to get back to Farella, and then return for more flowers that she had promised people, like our shopkeepers' great-grandfather.

"But Fraya was fickle. She met a man, as a lot of silly women do, and fell in love. To shorten the story let's just say she ended up pregnant and then found out he was already married. Heartbroken and not the maternal type, she gave the baby to a family by the surname Tyddel. Fredrick is what they named him, he went on to have a son named Isso, and Isso became owner of the apothecary in town. Isso also had a son, Galen Tyddel. By this time Fraya grew depressed and her gambling debts increased as well. She learned of Queen Cayleen's search for an enchantress, and to relieve herself of her burdens, tied me to the Queen. Fraya then disappeared and I haven't seen her since." She leans in addressing me with a conspiratorial whisper, "Are you keeping up, dear?"

"My father is the great-grandson of Fraya Vellen?" I stop as more of her story weaves together. "I can see the tree..."

She claps. "Thank goodness you have a brain. The level of

stupidity I have to deal with sometimes is frustrating. Yes, you and your father can see it."

"Did you know I came up with the idea of the Queen's Foxes? Was pretty much a matchmaker for your parents. Vera's parents as well, but that's a more tragic story that we don't have time for."

"Why bring Iann along? He won't be able to see it?"

"True enough. But finding the island is already a difficult plight. I've tried to convince several others to take me there, but no one has been able to make it since Fraya. Your precious prince has a knack for finding things, and I believe he might be able to do what so many have failed at. Plus, he's needed for other things." Her grin is wickedly deceitful.

"And Fraya is alive?"

"Unfortunately." She tosses up a hand in annoyance. "The flower did as many claimed it does, and she's still somewhere out there. Completely unreachable and probably useless. I've searched all over Ladora for her and found nothing. So now you see why I had to move down the line."

"Why not ask my father? Why me?"

She laughs. "Your father is skilled with poisons but that's where his discoveries end. And regardless, your father was given a chance." She walks over to a boy who is mid-dance and plays with the feathers of his mask. "Are we done with all the questions? Time is really running out."

There are about a million more questions I want to ask her, but there is something about her tone that makes me suddenly feel impatient. "What do you want?"

"Finally, a question about my needs." She places a hand to her chest mockingly. "It's simple. Iann will find the island, he's just not able to help it. The chase is so thrilling to him. Plus, his mom will die if his father doesn't get a flower of his own." She pouts her lips sarcastically. "Once your boyfriend finds the island, he will lead you to the trail Fraya mapped out and then you'll be the only one to see the tree. When you find it, you are to bring a flower back to me."

"What do you need it for? You just said you can live forever as long as you're tied to someone."

"That's not part of story time." Immediately she appears before me, neither of us dropping our gaze with the other.

"Now, time will remain frozen for another thirty minutes. To unfreeze those you wish to wake up, all you must do is touch them. Including your dear friend, Chana." She strokes the back of her fingers along my cheek. "If you don't come back with my flower, I will make the Queen remember how you betrayed her and together we will come after everything you have and destroy it. Death will not be your escape. I will trap you forever like Chana and Esha—the real Esha—where you can hear and feel everything but remain an unmoving soul forever. It's a true kind of torture."

"They did nothing to you."

"They found out who I was before my big reveal. Couldn't let them go spoiling it. You're lucky I'm even allowing you to wake them." She pulls out a pocket watch and declares, "You have a thirty minute head start, before everyone wakes. I would move quickly."

"And what about the Queen when she wakes?" I touch Iann and watch his body melt back into reality.

Looking back at Morrena, she's returned to Rolley's form and is waving at a waking Iann. "I'll deal with my responsibility. You take care of yours. Unless you would like me to wake the Queen and have her serve the princes her deadly surprise."

"What's happening?" Iann pulls off his mask and tosses it to the ground.

"We have to go!" I shout and pull on his arm.

In the ballroom I touch Vera, Deean, Benny, and Marcel.

"What the hell?" Deean spins around, noticing the unmoving bodies. "Benny, what was in that bottle?"

"I swear it was just rum." He sniffs the rim to check he's not mistaken.

"I'll explain everything later. Let's go!"

We run to the workers' quarters where I touch all of those from Saden, including Esha. He's the most startled and looks to be suffering mentally and physically.

I tell Iann to have his brother's men get ready to depart as Vera and I head to Sky's workshop. We find him frozen by Chana's bedside and with one touch there is life in them again.

Chana is just as shaken as Esha, but it doesn't stop her from wrapping her arms around me. "Thank you," she cries." Pulling back, her eyes flutter to Vera and Sky. "Morrena is back."

"What?" Vera hisses and pulls a dagger.

"Chana is right. She's the one who rendered everyone immobile. But I'll explain once we're on the ship," I say.

Sky rushes to grab some bags, handing one to me and another to Vera.

"I haven't packed," Chana cries as she wobbles with her walk.

"No shit," Sky says impatiently. "You've been out for a few days so how could you? We have your stuff already."

Not wasting another second, we run through the castle and race out to the courtyards where our carriages await.

"We're ready, Your Highness," a deep voice calls—one of the servants.

Marcel comes over to us, moonlight outlining his frame. He places a hand on Deean and the other on Iann. "If something goes wrong, or you think for a fraction of a second you won't be able to make it to Farella, get the hell out and go back to Saden. Our father will be fine without whatever it is you're looking for."

A burning sensation slides down my throat when I swallow, reminding me of Morrena's warning about their mother.

"Be safe," Iann says to Marcel.

"And no stopping until you are far from here," Deean adds.

Done with farewells, Marcel gets in one of the carriages and we watch it race away.

"We're ready," Benny says, tossing a bag into our carriage.

Iann holds out a hand for Chana, who is still a bit wobbly. It takes her some time but as soon as she slides over, he holds out a hand for me.

"Rolley is the only one missing," Benny shouts, having accounted for those we planned on coming with us tonight.

"Leave him," I reply, and watch the faces around me fall. "Trust me."

"Morrena," Vera whispers. I follow her gaze up the stairs.

Morrena stands on the steps with a dubious smile on her face. Her skin still appears illuminated as if it's radiating all her power to hold the people still.

"Ariah, you need to get in." Iann brushes my cheek and gently pushes me farther inside.

Once inside we wait for Iann, Deean, and Benny. Vera and Sky move into the final carriage with three other men from Iann's crew.

Our carriage jolts forward and a hand slips into mine. It's not Iann's though. Chana holds on tight as she rests her head back.

"I've been on one adventure in my life. The day I was taken and transported from Ethmay to Haymel. They said it would be better here. It's been miserable," she says slowly. "Promise me this one will be different."

"This will be different." The answer doesn't come from me, but instead, Deean who sits across from her. "That I promise you."

She rests her head against the window and gives him a hopeful smile as our carriage charges out of the castle court-yard and down towards the town.

Most of the townspeople are stuck back in the castle,

unable to move, and the rest are tucked away for the night, resulting in clear roads and little fuss as we get to the docks.

Across from me, I lock eyes with Iann, who, despite the situation, looks to be wrapped in joy.

The last words he spoke to me before Morrena froze him play endlessly in my head.

There is an uneasiness about feeling this way so soon, but I can't deny there is something between us, something I would like to explore more of. There is hope in him. A hope that I've never known, and I both fear and crave it.

We reach the docks where a burly captain is waiting for us.

"Right on time," he says, pulling a pipe from his mouth. "I appreciate folks who respect time.

"This is for you." Benny hands him a sack, which I assume is payment. "Everyone, meet Captain Sallen. He and his crew will be working with us."

"Punctuality and payment. My two favorite things." He tips a hat and allows us to board the ship.

"Nice necklace," Deean mumbles as he makes his way on.

"Keep moving," Iann says. I look back, but he only shrugs. "I'll tell you about it later."

Once everyone is on deck, we watch Sallen's crew prepare for departure. I only count six crew members and expected more, but as long as they can get us away from here, who am I to complain.

It isn't long before the ship drifts farther and farther from the dock and floats closer into the awaiting darkness.

ARIAH

"I want to go back!" I shout, before hurling chunks of bread and something red out of my mouth and nose.

What did I eat that was red? Thinking over breakfast this morning I vaguely remember a bowl of fruit and the sweet strawberries in the blend. While they tasted heavenly going down they're wretched coming up.

Hands gather my curls and while I try to push him away, Iann doesn't leave.

I'm not the only one seasick. I hear Chana throwing up as well, but since she's been unconscious for a few days, hers is straight bile. Hearing it splatter on the wood only makes me sicker.

"Iann, go. I'll be done soon." I try pushing him away but I'm too weak to move him.

He chuckles. "I've seen worse."

He holds my hair tighter as I thrust forward and throw up again.

There is a knock at the door as I settle back into him. Having someone to lean on feels nice, so I guess it's not all bad that he's here.

Sallen comes in with a tray and sets it on a table near the bed. "A few ginger cakes and lemon-spiced ginger tea. It'll help with your stomach." He comes and squats in front of us. "I should warn you both, we will be hitting a storm in a few hours. One of the crew gets these intense headaches when a storm is nearby. He's an odd one, but he ain't never been wrong." He smiles at me. "If you think you're sick now—" He catches a look from Iann. "Anyways, you don't mind if I steal your chap for a moment? Need to speak to him about something."

I wave my hand and lift myself up so Iann can leave.

Chana stumbles in after the men get out. "Deean lied," she says and then crawls into the bed. "This is not going to be fun."

Getting myself up, I sway with the waves and try not to focus on the movement. I manage to make it to the tea Sallen left behind. The cake sounds disgusting right now, so I take two swallows of the hot liquid.

"Here. Drink some," I coax Chana, as I work my way to her without spilling a drop.

Her nose scrunches at the scent but she sips, then she and I take turns until the contents are gone. Once finished we throw ourselves into the bed and under the covers.

"How did you know his name is actually Deean?" I ask.

"I know everything." She moans and rubs her forehead. "Plus, he confessed it to me at the party."

"You knew before me?"

"I guess. I was unsure what to do with the information, so I kept it a secret. He was pretty drunk when he told me. Something about going to the Queen felt wrong."

"I understand," I whisper. "And I was worried about you."

"I was worried about me too." She laughs. "You all thought I was asleep, but I heard everything." She turns her head to look at me. "Did you know Sky and Vera like to use his workshop as a personal getaway? Imagine hearing those two going at it and you can't move. Good thing I was only out for a couple of days."

"Oh no!" We laugh together, the tea seeming to have settled our stomachs.

"You and Iann though"—her words cut out, and for a moment I think she's fallen asleep—"I approve."

"Thanks for your approval." I release a bit of a forced chuckle.

She changes the topic and tells me stories about her home. How much she misses thornberry tarts and her mother's spiced rabbit stew. Most of all she misses her family. A younger brother and sister she hasn't seen in over seven years, since being abducted. I couldn't imagine working for Queen Cayleen at such a young age. Chana started working as a servant, and when Morrena noticed how silent and sneaky she was, the enchantress offered her a position as a Fox. Even promised her a way out one day.

"Maybe this is her way of holding up her end of the bargain," she says, yawning between each word.

I don't know Morrena well, but it seems doubtful; I respond with a half-hearted, "Maybe."

Tiredness drops on me like an anchor tossed at sea. I wonder if Sallen put something in the tea because my body becomes all too relaxed, so much so that I can't move.

Chana releases a snore, and the control of my body gives way with it, until I slip away into sleep.

A continuous galling tapping pulls me out of sleep. I shoot up in bed and find Chana still passed out beside me.

The porthole of the cabin window flaps with the night's wind and there is the distant sound of water droplets colliding with the deck.

I search the cabin for a coat and find one in a small cabinet folded up with a few sweaters. There is one I packed in my bag but I don't see my belongings in here, or a sign that anyone else in our traveling party has been in here.

Leaving Chana to rest, I wander out onto the deck and instantly get hit with a light drizzle. I hear voices from around the corner and follow the sound of conversation along the side of the boat. I stop at some windows that lead into a bigger cabin resembling an office as opposed to sleeping quarters. Through the grungy windows, I see outlines of figures along with lit lanterns. When I enter, all attention seems to focus on me.

"Just who we were talking about," Deean says, leaning back in a chair that he balances on two legs.

In the center of the table is a beam of light that casts a map onto the ceiling. The map they discovered.

"We were going over plans," Iann remarks, suddenly at my side. "How do you feel?"

It isn't until he asks that I pick up on the movement of the ship.

"I may have put something in your tea," Sallen admits. "No ill intentions. Just knew you and your friend would do better during the storm if you couldn't feel it."

"It passed?" I ask.

"That and a full day," Sallen says with pride. "And you both made it through."

"We've been asleep for over a day?" I look to Iann.

"Don't be so dramatic," Vera interrupts from the far end of the table. "You two would have been vomiting everywhere if he hadn't. You're just in time though." She points to an empty seat. "We're all curious about what our dear Morrena had to say."

I follow Iann to the table and take a seat between him and Benny. This is the first time I've seen what the anchor depicts. Not only is it a map to help get us to Farella, but there are directions for when we actually get on the island.

"Anytime is good," Vera says teasingly.

"She wants me to bring her back a flower."

"If you don't mind me asking, why you?" Benny says.

I dig my thumbnail into my pointer finger, feeling a slight pressure. "Morrena pretended to be Rolley. She's capable of transforming herself to look like someone else. She got your father to agree to this journey," I say to Iann. "She also believes I'm the only one who can see the flowering tree. Fraya made her conceal it so no one outside Fraya's bloodline would find it."

"You're a descendant of Fraya Vellen?" Benny sounds confused and amazed all at once. "Are you sure?"

I shrug, not having any evidence other than Morrena's story.

"Morrena is known for her games. She lives for secrets" Sky says, speaking for the first time. "She could be setting up a trap."

With the group, I disclose all the details Morrena shared with me the night of the ball and what she is wanting of Iann.

"Father wouldn't send you here for nothing. She had to have promised him something," Deean says to Iann. "Sure, he's sent you to many places, but he wouldn't risk your safety."

"Unless..." Chewing on the inside of my lip I try to find the right words.

Iann shifts his body in my direction and probes, "Unless what? What did she say?"

I don't want to tell him, and with every ounce of hope I pray it's one of her lies. "She said your mother is sick." Cupping his knee, I lightly strum my finger over his pants. "I'm sorry."

Both Iann and Deean become pale. Their faces suddenly drain of blood.

"She could be lying," Vera whispers, offering the only words of comfort she can find.

Iann pinches the bridge of his nose and clears his throat.

"We don't know for sure, so no need to get worked up." He pats Deean on the back and his brother gives a subtle nod but keeps quiet.

Sallen, who hasn't given much input throughout this entire conversation, stands and looks to the ceiling.

With a wooden stick he points to somewhere on the map. "These are our current coordinates." He circles a spot in the vast blue area of the map before creating an invisible line that leads to more blue. "Based on your research, and after speaking with my navigator, I'd say we'll see the isle in four days or so. That's if it truly exists. For all we bloody know, this Morrena gal could have one hell of a trap waiting for you lot." My stomach turns knowing I'll be on this boat for four more days. "Once we get there, your people can go ashore and mine will stay aboard this vessel."

"How do we know you won't leave us?" Sky asks.

"You don't." Sallen smiles. "But I won't. Unless you take too long to get back. Prince Iann predicts it will take a few days to find what you're after then return to my ship. That's if the map is correct. If you're not back in a fortnight, I'll leave."

"And your payment for staying?" Vera folds her hands over her chest. "Don't tell me you want immortality too."

Sallen's face pinches like he's going to be sick. "And stay in this dreadful world for eternity? No, thank you. If the flower does indeed exist, I want no part in its power. Just don't forget me in your stories. Plus, the princes and I have already made a deal and what they are willing to give me and my crew is far more important to me."

30

IANN

Over the next four days I study the Foxes. I've watched them before, but knowing they have been keeping careful surveillance of my brothers and me over the past several days has me needing to know more about them.

I discover Vera is a sensational liar. It makes her particularly good at cards. She is an easy talker, making her not only an excellent flirt, but an even better distraction that helps her win nearly every game. The only person she doesn't toy with is Sky, and had I paid attention sooner I would have known instantly that they were lovers.

Chana is an observer and her strength is in her silence. She is also a keen listener in both conversations not meant for her ears as well as for those who confide in her. Like Deean, who managed to pour out all his tribulations to her. She doesn't seem to mind though.

Sky is the trickiest. He is neither sly or great with conversation. Introverted, but not because he's shy, because he genuinely despises most human interactions. It takes me several tries to break him, my attempts at connection are usually blocked with callousness, until the conversation becomes about apothecary—a shared passion. He is obviously much better at it than me, but I used the opportunities to have him teach me a few new poisons and elixirs.

Then there is Ariah, who I don't watch with suspicion like I do the others. Attention to her is strictly personal. Her wit and quick tongue make it easy for her to get along with others, but this I already knew. In her free time she takes to drawing, refusing to show me her designs even when I beg for a peek. Instead, she offers up a kiss, which I don't dare refuse. She is also inquisitive and goes around to the crew to learn the responsibilities of the various positions. The navigator educates her about sailing and how to stay on course; the boatswain teaches her how to rig each morning; and the arms man lectures her about everything in the weapons cabin.

Today I find her with the navigator, fixated on what she sees through a spyglass.

"Good morning," I say as I approach.

She lowers the tool to give me a kiss. "Good morning."

"Anything yet?"

"No." She starts searching again. "We should be approaching soon, shouldn't we? Do you think the calculations are off?"

I catch the navigator's grin as he excuses himself.

"Are you questioning my ability to read a map?" I tease as I wrap my arms around her waist and pull her back into me. "You do remember I have done this more than you."

Resting her head against my chest, we hold each other. "I just want to be there already." She turns her head to look at me and lifts herself up on her tippy toes to place her soft lips to mine. I inhale the faint scent of the peony and musk perfume she always wears, but it is fading. She pulls away and out of my grasp, then spins to face me. "Find the flower." She gives me another kiss before pulling away again. "And go to Saden and this can all be over."

Although her main reason for going back to Saden is for her safety, there is a kernel of excitement in knowing she'll be with me.

"I want that too." I kiss her forehead while one of my hands slyly grabs hold of the spyglass and I yank it from her playfully. Let me show you how it's done."

"Didn't know you needed to be an expert to look through a chunk of glass." She folds her arms and watches me carefully.

I smile at her dig and look through the spyglass, scanning the horizon. Nothing but endless blue for miles. It's disheartening until I catch a few birds in the sky, flying southeast and far away from any land mass. They disappear and that's when I see a small sliver in the distance.

I move across the deck to get a better view and sure enough, off in the expanse is a cluster of trees. The image is blurry and blends in with the sea, making it especially hard to see, but it's there. Farella is there. Every bedtime story and the countless books I've read are no longer just words, they mean so much more.

I give back the spyglass and point Ariah in the right direction. "Look again." Concentrating, she gives it another glance. She tries moving the spyglass, unable to see the distant isle, but I gently glide it back. "Follow the birds."

Remaining silent, she looks once again. Her head snaps back for a second, but she quickly goes back to the rim of the spyglass. "We're almost there," she whispers excitedly.

"You want to say it, or should I?"

She doesn't answer and instead, for everyone on board to hear, shouts, "Land ho!"

Come morning, Sallen steers the ship into a large mouth of the island. Enormous mountain ranges are situated on both sides of us. The land is covered in the greenest leaves and a sandy white beach waits for us at the shore.

Without getting too close to shore we anchor the ship and load one of the row boats on the starboard side. Sallen allows us to take what we need from the weapons cabin. I arm myself with a sword and a few throwing knives. Also on me is the small anchor figurine, in case we need it again, along with a few healing elixirs.

Most of the Foxes have weapons of their own but it doesn't stop them from taking more. I suggest Vera, Sky, and Chana stay behind with Sallen's crew but Vera looks ready to punch me. Dismissing my suggestion, they prepare themselves.

Leaving my carrier behind I put Deean in charge of carrying our supplies. Benny takes some of the extra stuff, but Deean takes all the heavier items.

The only other person going with us is Nico, my associate navigator and cartographer. Not only will he be our guide, but he is also in charge of creating a new, much easier-to-read map of the isle. A lot will be missing, as we don't have the time to explore the entirety of the isle, but we just need the main route to the flower.

"You should have everything you need." Sallen hikes up a leg on the side of his ship. "We packed some non-perishables and a few canteens of water for you. But I suggest killing your own food and finding fresh water so you don't run out." He waves a hand towards me. "But you're well aware."

"Thank you." I give him a nod of appreciation. "Nico is confident that it will only take us two to three days to get to the flower and then the same amount of time to get back. That's if Fraya's map is correct."

"We'll be here," Sallen assures. "And in case you need it,

there is a bit of parfa powder in there. Set it on fire if there is an emergency. We'll be able to see it from the ship and will find you. Let's just pray to the divinities it will be in time."

"Smart," Sky says. Recognizing the name for a combustible material common in Haymel. When burned it releases red-colored smoke. It also helps keep animals away and can be used in liquids to help combat infection. "Never thought to use it that way."

"Let's hope you don't have to." Sallen gives someone a cue and we are lowered to the water. Once our boat is on the surface of the crystalline water, Sky and Deean begin paddling us to shore.

Ariah's eyes are twice their normal size as she looks over every inch of our surroundings. Her vision catches on the birds that fly overhead, animals that shift beyond the trees, even the fish that appear luminous as they swim below us. It's the way I used to look too, when I first began my travels. I'm still often amazed by what I find, but some of the awe has worn off.

"It doesn't look real," Chana says, gliding a hand above the water. "It's far too perfect to exist."

There is a charm about the isle. Its lush colors bleeding and melding together in a way I've never seen before.

"That's what happens when things remain untouched by people," Benny says, scribbling away in a notebook.

"Please," Deean interjects. "People can appreciate beautiful things."

"Appreciating and maintaining are two different concepts," Benny replies with a grin, while still writing away.

As we near the shore, we hop out into the water. It's not as cold as I thought it would be. Together we pull the boat onto the sand.

Nico, who has been with me three years now, starting when he was sixteen, moves a finger over the map. His long hair, that he refuses to cut, is up in a bun and his clothes are a little baggy on his dark skin.

"You're up," I say, walking up beside him. "You got this?"

He flashes a crooked smile, one he gives all the time. Honestly, I've never seen him not happy. "Yes, sir. We are going to head northeast. According to her map we should come to a fork in our path. It's marked with a cluster of trees."

"Northeast it is." I walk in front of him and feel Ariah at my side. "Everyone, stay close."

We continue walking inland and the sand slowly turns to soil. There are puddles of water here and there. We must have just missed some rain. The air is crisp and smells of nature, fresh moss is most potent and there is a sweetness from purple flowers that bloom around us.

"Indigo orchids," Sky informs us as he snips a few flowers and tucks them away in his bag. "Rare beauties. Helps with fevers and inflammation."

"Anything that will keep snakes away?" Benny asks. "Not afraid of much, but snakes terrify me."

"We'll keep watch for some marigold. That should help."

"Mosquitoes for me," Deean chimes in.

"These orchids should help with that." Sky chuckles.

"What about you?" Ariah nudges my arm. "What's your biggest fear?"

"What makes you think I have one?" I ask, deepening my voice as if that will convince her I don't scare easily.

"Everyone does, spill it."

"Birds," I say with a smile.

"Birds?"

"It's a rational fear."

She laughs. "I kind of get it. You would like Lemon though."

"Lemon?"

"My father's pet bird. A bit of a tattletale, but still cute."

"That's it," Nico says, interrupting our quiet conversation

and pointing an arm between Ariah and me. "There is the fork."

"Does Fraya have any notes on that?" Ariah asks as Nico tilts the map towards her, allowing her a better view.

"Fraya had symbols embedded into the map and I was able to copy them from what the anchor showed me. For instance, there is an eagle over here." He moves his finger over the map. "There is a strange pattern of different shapes over here. And this is the fork."

Ariah asks, "Which way do we go?"

"To the right," Nico checks the map once more. "We should come to a bridge soon."

We go right and come to a long path arched by a canopy of trees. Vines swing from one branch to another, and bright birds fly overhead. I stop as I watch them get a little too close and immediately feel Ariah's hand in mine.

"A totally rational fear." She scrunches her nose to keep from laughing, and although she's mocking me, she doesn't let go, and I don't either.

The path through the tunnel is clear and takes us hours to make our way out of. A few claim to hear strange noises but nothing of great concern comes from it. Overall, the island is eerily quiet.

We eventually find ourselves at one end of a wooden bridge, held together with rope, that is who knows how old. Thankfully we don't find ourselves too high up and a fall would land us in a murky swamp. I'm more afraid of what's in the water than the bridge snapping.

Not one plank threatens to give way with each crossing. On the other side we find another path. This one is steep and rockier than the first.

Ariah has to take a few inhales of her spray the higher in elevation we climb, but overall, all goes well.

Hours later, the ground begins to level out and past a

clearing of trees, we see a cliff that overlooks most of the isle. A dark orange paints the sky, with lines of purple-and-pink brushed throughout. Utterly stunning.

"I've never seen a tree look so luminous," Ariah whispers. "Like it's crawling with glowworms."

There are several trees covering the land. Most of them are situated in shadows as night nears. But nowhere do I see a lustrous tree.

Deean comes forward and stands between us, squinting so he doesn't miss anything. "I see a lot. But there is no glowing tree out there."

"It's right there." Ariah points a finger off in the distance. "Just next to that waterfall."

The waterfall is practically on the other side of the isle, a good day's worth of hiking away.

Nico pulls out the map and points at something below, not too far off from the shore. "Is it just over there? Near that cluster of rocks."

"See, Nico sees what I'm talking about," Ariah says.

"I know what you're talking about but I can't *see* it. On the map it shows this is where we'll find the tree that grows the Ivian Flower."

"She really did enchant it," Chana says.

"Greedy witch." Vera continues along the path, away from the cliff.

"There is a cave up ahead." Benny states in between sips of water. "Might be a good spot to rest for the night. Given it's not occupied."

There is also a river nearby, flowing out into the sea. A chance for us all to get water and food. "He's right," I offer in response to Benny's suggestion. "Let's scout it out and see if it's a safe place to camp for the night."

The cave is clear. No animal tracks or signs of danger.

"I've been thinking" —Chana takes a seat near Deean who

bangs two nille stones together, sparking a fire—"if legend is true about the isle forming from Kailaric, the chances of there being any invasive species are slim. We might be fairly safe here."

In *The Forbidden* by Wanner, he went on about native plants. He referenced birds and snakes but not much else. Any other creatures would have to have been brought here, which is unlikely. The isle is already difficult to find. I can't imagine many discovering such a place just to bring foreign animals.

"Explains why we've only seen birds." Deean sits back on a log and passes out the food Sallen packed. "That reminds me, I know the Captain said it was for emergencies but maybe in the morning, or when we're closer to the tree, we can light some of that powder. Make them come get us instead of having to journey back."

Benny looks over to me and raises his eyebrows. Both of us are surprised at how much help Deean has been.

"I think we can definitely make it by sundown tomorrow if we get an early start," Nico says. "First light. First cavahor."

Chana's head flies up. "You're from Ethmay?"

Nico flashes the usual grin. "I am. My father worked for a number of merchant crews there, but three years ago we met Prince Iann and were allowed to reside in Saden for work."

"Can either of you explain what cavahor means to the clue-less," Vera inquires.

"It means 'to be filled.' The first up and moving are usually more filled with their day, or life in general. So Ethmaians believe."

"I enjoy sleeping in and I feel just as satisfied as any other." Deean takes a bite out of the stale bread and dried fruit we have for supper.

"Filled with liquor," I say, giving some of my bread to Ariah as everyone laughs.

"Even better." Deean tosses me a wink.

Benny pulls out his notebook and scribbles something down. "I have a question for our Haymelian guests. How did you all become secret servants to the Queen? I would like to make sure I get my notes correct."

"Are you going to put us in a book or something?" Ariah says, swatting at the crumbs in her lap, then pulls out the ribbon in her hair. Curls fall to her side, brushing over elbows I desire to kiss and nibble on. I love it when her hair flows loosely.

"Of course. Every story must be told, especially one as grand as this. No person can be left out or the story is incomplete."

"No one would know we're missing anyway." From his bag, Sky pulls out the orchids and other plants he's collected on the trail.

"We would," Benny replies and gets his writing tool ready.

"My mother was once a Fox." Vera goes first. "She got injured when her partner didn't show up to a task they were assigned to." Her eyes drift to Ariah, who is awash with sudden guilt, but Vera attempts a faint smile. I assume there is much more to the backstory, but I'll ask Ariah at another time. "Anyways," Vera continues, "she was beaten by some grifters who weren't meant to be there. Left her bloody and broken. A lord she was supposed to be spying on discovered her, along with a vial poison and a suicide note she was to leave behind to make it look like he had taken his own life. The Lord learned of my mom's identity and all Foxes are to remain unseen. Queen Cayleen knew she could never employ her again, so she exiled her to a small island on the northern shores of Haymel. It's where I grew up. But come my sixteenth birthday, the Queen sent a carriage. My gift that year was the chance to redeem my mother's name and I've been a Fox since."

Benny widens his eyes as he writes down her story. "I'm sorry. Thank you for sharing though."

Vera shrugs. "It's not what I wished for that birthday, but I suppose she could have killed us instead. If it means my mother is forever done with her, then so be it."

"Haymel and Ethmay do a lot of trade." Chana picks at her bread and continues on without giving us time to digest Vera's story. "Mostly food, spices, and material. On occasion they decide children are best. In my village we called them coratas."

"Night thieves," Nico says.

"Yes. They came in the dead of night, seven years and two hundred and twenty-seven days ago. They wanted my sister and I offered them me, instead. It was the last time I was home. The last time I saw her." We sit in silence for a minute or two. "It could have been worse though. Most don't end up in the Queen's court. There are far worse fates than ending up a Fox. Some have no fates at all."

Vera rubs Chana's arm in comfort, causing Chana to smile. Although she has every right to feel hopeless and miserable, she isn't. They both turn their attention to Sky, who immediately rolls his eyes.

"Oh, you want me to follow you two?" Sky huffs. "Mine is not as horrid as all that. No clue who my father is or where he's from. Ma has tried to tell me several times, but in all honesty I don't care to know anything about the bastard, which ironically is what I am. My mother got into trouble a few years back and to make all her issues go away she made a deal with Morrena. I was simply part of the deal and ended up working under Morrena as a Fox about five years ago."

"Your mother traded you to get rid of her problems?" Deean sounds like it's a concept too unfathomable for him to accept. Suddenly, all the trials in our life added together seem minor compared to the lives these seasoned Foxes have had to endure.

"Maybe I was the problem." Sky lets out a dry chuckle. "But that's how I got there. Any more life facts from me require stronger drinks—or cruel poisons—so that's all you're going to get."

Benny ends his interviews there, already knowing what reasons Ariah has for being here. Guilt sweeps in. According to Ariah, one of Queen Cayleen's greatest rules is to never fall in love, and I can't help the remorse I feel knowing we are repeating a history similar to Ariah's parents. But she turns to me and gives me a smile so rich that I would do anything to wrap myself in it, even if it means making enemies with the Queen of Haymel.

We sit around a fire and share more stories, happier ones, until sleep carries us away for the night.

31
ARIAH

A deafening shriek wakes me and propels my body forward.

Through the mouth of the cave, I see dawn breaking through a blurry sky. With a few blinks I notice Chana stands near the mouth of the cave with a dagger drawn. Beside her is Iann who I thought was still next to me, but he's wide awake with a sword in hand.

"What's happening?" I whisper, taking my ring blade and standing with the others.

"Started minutes ago," Vera whispers back, her shirt brushes the skin of my arm as she stands close. "Sounds like we might not be alone." She stands up from her squat, and I join her. Both armed for the unexpected.

"We should keep moving." Iann fastens the sword back in his scabbard. "Collect everything and let's get going." He comes over to me and discreetly rests his head on mine. "Good morning."

"Is it a good one?" I pull away and eye the others with caution. "What was that?" The noise didn't sound like it came from a human, but instead, a large creature of some sort.

"No idea." He gently squeezes my arm. "But I don't think we should worry. We'll just have to make sure we're extra careful."

I nod and together we pack up our things. There are another two screeching sounds before we all exit the cave. The most unsettling part is that we seem to be heading in the direction the shrieks are coming from, but it's hard to tell how far, or near, the offending creature is located.

Nico, who impresses me as he keeps the same cheerful spirit throughout the journey, continuously checks the map making sure we are always going in the right direction.

He's in the middle of telling me a story about his first expedition with Iann when he stops walking. His fingers trace over the map and then at invisible lines in the air.

"We can't go that way." He speaks loud enough for Iann and Deean, who lead us, to hear.

Deean immediately drops his bag, breathing heavily at the weight that's been strapped to his back. "Then which way are we supposed to go?"

Nico does some more searching on the map and turns to his right, facing a stone wall. Thriving green vines cover most of it and I don't want to think of what spiders hide within.

"Do you have a way of getting through stone?" Sky sarcastically throws out, before taking the opportunity to sit on a boulder and downing a swig of water.

I see Iann pick up a hefty size rock off the ground and before I can ask what he's doing he throws it into the air. It lands on the continued path, but it doesn't stay there. Chunks of mud fly up as if it's boiling and slowly pulls the rock under until it disappears, and then the terrain returns to normal, like nothing has disturbed the ground.

Deean jumps closer to the rest of us, feeling a little too close to the muddy death trap.

"The stone wall it is," Sky concludes.

"What now?" I look over Nico's shoulder to see what little

clues Fraya left. "That patterned one—maybe it's a cipher or something."

Suddenly, the ground rumbles, urging us to move faster.

Iann cuts away at the spider-infested ivy. No actual spiders come crawling out, but I'm still convinced they're in there.

Once the vines come down, tile-like rocks with symbols embedded in each are scattered across the wall.

"What language is that?" Iann takes a step back examining it more in depth.

"Kind of similar to Ethnay. But then again, it's not," Chana suggests, as she tilts her head to the side.

Benny chuckles, although no one has told a joke. He moves close and glides a hand over a few stones. "It's Herolvic. An old dead language many claim was invented by the divinities."

Great. Not only foreign to us but a dead one as well.

"What are you talking about?" Sky aims his head to the grouping of symbols further at the top. "It's Haymelian. It reads, 'What is my true name?'"

I spin to Sky prepared to tell him it says nothing of the sort but my eyes get caught on Vera's necklace. It shines with a red urgency and causes me to look down at the bracelet, which glows the same color.

"Is she watching us?" I back into Chana as fear snakes up my spine.

Sky grabs my wrist, and I see Iann lurch forward but stills before he realizes Sky is only examining it. His eyes drift back and forth from the bracelet to the wall. "The wall is enchanted." Sky's words come out in amazement, and it doesn't take me long to realize why.

The necklace and bracelet pick up on any enchantments around us. They were also created by Sky who might be more than an ordinary apothecary.

"What does this say?" Nico holds up the map to Sky.

"Ocean Ruler." Sky's interpretation carries no hesitations.

Without warning he begins to push in the stones of the wall matching that of what's on the paper. With the final stone he steps away, and the ground rumbles and the wall shakes as a chunk sinks back in itself.

Iann is the first to approach the gap in the wall. Pushing the area that has become disconnected from the rest of the wall. Once pushed to its limit, he starts sliding it over as Deean comes to help; before us is a door of darkness, continuing us on the path.

Iann grabs a few fallen sticks and takes one of the blankets we have, wrapping it around the stick. Deean searches for the nille stones and then sets fire to the blanket.

"This way." Iann bobs a head towards the entrance and slips into the darkness.

I follow first and Nico stays close behind us, clinging to the map.

The ground is solid, nothing like the muddy trap outside, and the walls are narrow. Along with the soil scent there is something powdery, almost waxy about the smell around us. There is something familiar in the peculiar odor. It's almost like being in my father's study, near Lemon's cage.

The walls begin growing wider and in the distance, I spot a light.

Iann stops and hovers the torch over Nico's map.

"Does it show us what's next?" He finds where the olden language is written and follows the route upwards, his finger freezing on the map.

"It's the image of the bird." Nico slowly pulls the map away.

In the dark I find Iann's hand and squeeze it tight.

Deean, somewhere behind us starts laughing to himself. "Sorry, it's not funny." He lets a few loose snickers slip. "Do you remember that time when you were eleven and one landed on your shoulder?"

"Not the time," Iann grumbles and continues walking.

Deean ignores his brother and continues telling us a story of how someone had gifted their parents lovebirds one year as an anniversary gift. The next day one bird had died, making the other one become quite sad. Little Iann wasn't aware of the violence a lone lovebird could cause. Iann had opened its cage, and it immediately flew onto his shoulder. Confident he could touch it, the bird bit his finger and then his nose before it started flying around the room.

"Even shit on his head." Deean is wrapped in the memory and laughs his way through the tunnel. "Poor Iann tried getting out of the room, but the door was stuck. The bird did him one good that day."

I feel Iann sigh and move my other hand up his back in comfort, tracing familiar sculpted lines. I hold my laugh in, and it's not from Iann's fear but from the way Deean tells the story. It may seem cruel to others, but the way in which Deean recounts the experience is done in a way in which only your siblings can tease you. I know it well from Jaleese, who would certainly have stories of her own if she was here. Her and Deean would probably end up in a most-embarrassing-sibling-moment contest.

Approaching the light, everyone stops talking. We walk into the openness of a cavern, under a dome-shaped room with an enormous circle cut out in the ceiling that allows in sunlight.

There is a path from one side of the room to the other and several trees that stretch up to the top of the dome. Sitting in every tree are tiny, round shadows that I think are some sort of fruit at first, until we get closer. Then I realize, thousands of birds are sleeping in the trees.

Iann grips my hand, cutting off my circulation and crushing my bones. I pull away before he has a chance to break anything.

"Sorry," he whispers unsteadily.

"We just have to make it to the other side and then we'll be done." I try comforting him but have no clue what awaits us once—or if—we make it through.

"No one move," Chana warns as she passes the entrance and sees what lies inside the dome.

"Are those..." Nico quietly tries to fold the map.

"Picos." Chana eases past Vera and Sky and looks more closely at the path. "They occupy some of the forests in Ethmay. One or two usually aren't a problem but we're looking at hundreds, if not thousands. They are particularly drawn to noise, so we need to move with silence. They are known to attack anything that disturbs them."

Foxes are to remain unheard. With one deep inhale I take the first step onto the path. Iann tries grabbing my hand, but I pull it away and place a finger to my lips and give him a smile. He's led the way most of this journey but in his fear—which I know is ever potent right now—it's my turn.

The ground seems like any other dirt path and doesn't make much sound as we walk on it. The closer we get to the trees, the more visible the birds become. Speckled among their black feathers are traces of yellow-and-orange, colors that scream caution. Their eyes remain closed and we take our time. Slowly but still steadily getting across the room. The exit is nearly within reach.

Almost there. I encourage myself to keep going. Unseen. Unheard. Untraceable. I repeat the rules over and over. Even if I have no desire to ever be a Fox, all the training had to have meant something. Every late-night watch, every poor soul I had to follow, or every gritty task ordered by the Queen, it all had to have been for something.

Just when I find my pace, my confidence is shattered by a metallic sound. My body goes rigid, and I instantly feel Iann lose all momentum behind me.

Looking back, I spot Benny gathering the lead pieces back into a metal tin, making more noise as he's going at it.

Chana bends down, placing a hand on his, forcing him to stay quiet. She looks above us, and I follow her gaze. Every bird now perches with eyes open, peering in our direction. They begin making sounds, similar to the cries we heard earlier.

"Damnit, Benny," Deean hisses. "What could you even be writing about at a time like this?"

Benny assures us it just slipped, but Chana pushes him forward before he can finish explaining. "GO!" she shouts.

The birds begin flying around, circling the space above us. Iann becomes paralyzed by the terror of it all, lost in the fear above him. It takes me a few times, but on the third tug he finally starts running with me.

"The parfa powder, Your Highness." Sky stops running to shout at Deean. "Keep going," he orders the rest of us.

The moment I have to look back, I see Deean and Sky struggling with a backpack. By the time we hit the other mouth of the cave, the birds make a final circle and then dive.

"Run!" I warn them.

Seeing the birds flying at them, Sky struggles with the sack of parfa powder as Deean holds on to the nille stones.

Leaving a trial of powder behind, Sky dumps it all and Deean stops for a second to generate sparks over the small mound. In a panic it takes five strikes before the stones spark and set the powder ablaze. Right before the birds can reach Deean they divert and fly upwards and out of the clearing at the top of the dome, rising with the smoke.

The smoke is strong and hits us in a rush. We continue running until we are in absolute sunlight and out of the cave and its adjoining tunnel.

Out of breath, I bend over and take in as much air as my lungs allow. Between the running and the strong scent of the powder, it's difficult to breathe.

A tightness in my chest begins to set in and my shoulders rise. Even though I desperately try to take deep inhales it's not enough. I dig in my pockets for my spray. My hands sweat and it's like I've rubbed them with butter because the bottle flies out of my hand and lands near me. Thankfully, it remains whole.

"We need to keep going," Deean shouts running out of the tunnel. As I bend over, he runs my way and steps on my bottle before I have a chance to retrieve it.

Crunch.

The noise sucks out any air I have left in me, and I watch the liquid soak into the ground.

"Ariah." Iann is at my side in a second. His hands lift up my face to see him. "What's happening?"

"She can't breathe," Vera says, having seen me struggle in the past. "Sky, help her."

Vera starts to rub my back as Iann tells me to drink some water.

My wheezing picks up as I watch Sky sniff the mixture on the ground.

"Twenty-five crushed elderberries, two pinches of mullein, a dash of ginseng, four leaves from an elmonk flower," I struggle to get out. "Boiled."

He gives me a look and then gives one to Iann. A look that doesn't need to be translated. We are on a deserted island and the chances of finding all those ingredients in the limited time I have before my breathing stops is impossible.

Iann lifts me into his arms and tells Sky to get moving. He sits me near a tree, allowing me to rest against it. I feel his hands brush the hair from my face. "I'm going to make it better, Ariah." He kisses my forehead and tells Vera to watch me.

There is something stronger here than just my difficulty to breathe. There is a tingling that coats me. A near-magical feeling, but not in a beautiful, majestic way. Something malevolent is at work.

My eyes grow heavy and my breathing becomes more and

more strained. People start running and shouting but it all becomes a blur.

I feel Vera's hand in mine. "I'm sorry my mom never showed up," I struggle to say and should really refrain from talking.

"No, more talking," she orders.

I don't know when, but all noise becomes mute, and my eyelids fall heavy. Breathing, the one thing we must all do to survive, becomes painful. Too painful to bear. My eyes finally close off to the panic of those around me, and I slip away to somewhere else.

32

IANN

I've only lost one man in all my days of leading expeditions. His name was Rein Cordwall and it was on my third voyage to an area just outside Diamondhead. He was bitten by a snake while hiking a nearby trail and couldn't get back in time for help. I was the one who found his cold body keeled over in a pile of autumn leaves. It is the closest I've been to death.

Dusk falls upon us and Ariah still hasn't awakened. I move her body away from the fire the others sit around, afraid the fumes will exacerbate her current state.

Sky struggled to find ingredients needed for her spray. A few couldn't be found at all and we had to make do with a few substitutions.

Getting the concoction in her system was harder. Without something to spritz in her mouth and with her being unconscious, it was nearly impossible, but Sky managed. Almost magically healing her.

Deean makes a few attempts to approach us, but guilt keeps him away.

He thinks I'm angry with him. I'm not. I'm more worried if

the mixture is helping her. I've seen others who share her ailment and never have they become unconscious from it. It's as if her body has completely shut down, and I wonder if there is something nefarious at play. Or perhaps my mind is scrambling for an excuse. Sky assures me as long as she's breathing, she'll be fine, but I won't be satisfied until her eyes open.

"You can come closer," I say to a spying Deean.

He brings me cooked fish they caught from a nearby river and berries from a bush Sky said are safe to consume.

"How is she doing?" He eyes her as he takes a seat next to me.

"Her breathing is regulated. I'm not sure why she hasn't woken up yet."

"She will. You think this will be Ariah's end?" he jokes, but I'm not laughing. "She wouldn't allow herself to go out like this." The last part makes me smile. It's true. "I'm sorry," he admits. "I didn't see the bottle."

It's hard to be mad at him. He went from saving my life, and everyone else's, to accidentally threatening the one life here with the power to crush me if she doesn't survive.

"It's not your fault." I do my best to comfort him.

He urges me to eat something. With a fire, I sanitize one of Ariah's needles and use it to better spear my food. I play with the fish until I finally take a bite. The meat hits my tongue with disgust. I forcefully chew it until it slides down my throat. The soggy meat tastes like dirty water that's been marinating for days.

From the corner of my eye, I catch Deean smuggling a smile. He knows damn well this is one of the most disgusting things ever made.

"I told Benny to find some herbs or something. Season it up, you know. Hell, he could have fried it in that berry sauce to make it taste better, but he claimed he knew what he was doing." He reaches into his pocket and pulls out some stale bread. "I don't know how you do it. Days ago, we were eating like the princes we are and now this hard bread is the best thing I've had in days."

"You get used to it." I chuckle. "Most of the time we have months to prepare and pack much better food. We also would never let Benny prepare it."

We laugh together and pick at the food. Eventually his eyes get caught in the sky, drifting away in its beauty. With little light out here the stars are exceptionally clear, thousands of them scattered above.

"She's going to be okay." He breaks his contemplation at my words.

"I already told you she would be. Ariah is a fighter."

"So is our mother, whom I was referring to." He swallows hard before looking back up. "I don't believe Morrena," I conclude.

"I don't want to, but it makes sense why Father pushed you so hard." He sets his food down and moves to the ground to rest his back against a fallen log, holding the back of his head in his hands. "We'll find out the truth when we get back. I'm not worried." Deean has always been a momma's boy, and even though she claims not to have favorites, she loves him in a different kind of way. I suppose she loves each of us differently.

"I've been thinking, how would you like to go on another expedition with me? You've done well. Benny too. I'm even thinking about asking him to be a permanent member of my crew."

With eyes still looking up towards the sky, he grins. "Are you asking me to be a permanent member of your crew as well?"

"Potentially. As long as it comes with no more embarrassing stories."

He gives me a look, one mixed with gratitude and a dash of cockiness. "I suppose that's fair. And I'd follow you anywhere, brother."

Come morning, Ariah still isn't awake. Sky says her body faced an immense amount of stress and anyone would need time to recover.

While I try not to worry, we work on building a tool that will help us carry her. According to Nico's calculations, he fully expects us to be there within a few hours. It isn't far but it's still a long way to carry someone.

With a blanket, sticks, and rope we manage to put together something that will hold Ariah. Deean and Sky lift her as I stick with Nico and lead the group.

There aren't any more hidden walls or bird surprises. The path stays clear and level, making carrying Ariah easier. There are also no more symbols left on Fraya's map, with the exception of one more near the tree.

The air shifts and a crispness prickles my skin. The scent of orchids floods my nostrils as we turn a stone corner and find ourselves surrounded by a field of the beautiful flowers. In the distance I pick up on the sound of trickling water.

"We're nearly there." Nico angles the map in my direction. "Just beyond the waterfall."

The sound of rushing water increases and just as we pass a cluster of bushes a waterfall comes into full view. Colorful rays glisten above the three-tier fall that spills over moss-covered stones.

"I can feel it," Sky says. "The tree is nearby. Whatever enchantment Morrena used is strong."

"Let's rest here," I instruct the group. It's great we're close but useless if Ariah isn't awake. We won't be able to see the tree or its blossoms without her.

The others take to the water as I sit with Ariah and use the time to document the experience so far, something I haven't been keeping up with. I get to the birds when a shadow emerges over my journal.

"I'll sit with her if you'd like to go take a dip," Chana says, and bobs her head at the water before sitting next to me.

The water has been tempting me since I first heard the rush of the falls. We haven't bathed in a few days and a musty scent has been clinging to me since yesterday.

"Thank you." I close up the journal but feel her gaze on me. "Are you okay?"

She turns her head towards the water and taps a foot against the rocks. "The others and I were wondering what will happen next?" My eyebrows pinch together. "After we get the flower. I know you are going to convince your father to pardon us, but what if he doesn't? We have done terrible things in the name of the Queen. Things against your own kingdom."

"He doesn't have to know." I place the journal back in the bag and wave away a bug that circles Ariah's face. "I know my father and he'll grant the pardon, especially with the flower in hand. Hell, if you all desire, I could probably convince him to grant you titles." That makes her smile and her eyes soften. I'm reminded of the other night when she felt comfortable enough to share her story. "I could also help you get back home. If that's what you wish for."

Her smile dissipates and she wrings water out of her short hair. "I don't even know if my family is still there. I used to think they would come looking for me. That my father would tear down every door until he found the right one. Foolish though, they don't even know where I was taken to, let alone have access to the castle."

"I'm sorry." It's the only thing I can think to say that feels right.

"Don't be." A smile returns. "It wasn't your fault. Life with the Queen wasn't all bad. I might have ended up a pathetic, silenced creature back at home. Certainly, married off by now to some man I would have had no desire for, in hopes my parents could gain some type of payment from the union. We weren't as well off as other families."

The faintest moan sends our attention in Ariah's direction. Her eyeballs move behind shut eyelids and there is the slightest twitch at her mouth.

"You should go." Chana moves to Ariah's other side. "She'll be waking soon and it's probably best if you don't smell like an unbathed mule." The comment is forward and has me second guessing if I heard her correctly. "Sorry, Your Highness. Not sure if that was too honest, but I felt someone had to say it."

"No offense taken." Stripping off my boots and top, I leave my breeches on and head to the water.

The water feels as perfect as it looks. My thirsty skin absorbs it immediately, and I waste no time using my fingernails to scrub away layers of dirt that have built up over the past few days. Eventually, I swim beneath the waterfall, letting it douse me as I wash my hair. Something about the water feels different. It layers my skin, making it feel like velvet. I scoop some up in my palm and notice it carries a sheen—almost like crushed up diamonds amalgamating into a crystal blue.

"Iann!" Deean shouts from the bank. He stands beside Chana and Ariah. "She's waking."

33
ARIAH

I wake on a hard floor— my body uncomfortably face down on what feels like polished wood or perhaps ceramic.

Lifting myself up, my hand slips in a puddle and I fall back down, my face smacking into the ground. It's another minute, maybe an hour—who really knows—before I try again. Time feels irrelevant and my mind drifts in and out of consciousness.

When I try again, I'm able to push up on my forearms, holding my head up off the floor. My blurry vision is corrected with a few blinks. That's when I notice my right hand is coated in red. There is a strong scent of iron that churns my stomach and brings about a feeling of nausea. It's *blood*.

The image of a body next to me becomes clear.

It's Chana. Eyes wide open, but no soul inside.

Scrambling to my feet I find myself surrounded by more bodies. I spot Vera and Sky. Luna and Morren. My parents aren't far off either. All are dead, lying in the ballroom of the castle.

My heart falls along with my knees when I see Iann lying there soaked in blood.

"Think you can escape our deal by dying?" I don't need to look to know whose voice it is. Morrena walks closer. "If you're dead then who will be able to see my precious flower? I suppose I could always threaten that sister and know-it-all father of yours into doing it." She kneels beside me as her face closes in on mine. "The island may look like a blissful paradise, but trust me when I say, something darker resides there. Get me my flower and leave. Now"—her lips move to my ear— "wake up." Her words fling me back to reality.

My eyes flutter open to Iann. His beautiful smile calms the nightmare I've been trapped in.

"Are you real?" My voice is hoarse and I'm not even sure the words come out until people start laughing.

"Very much so." Iann traces a finger along the curves of my face and I never want him to stop. "I told you, I wouldn't allow anything to happen to you."

Vera comes over with a canteen and makes me take a drink before I say anymore.

Chana kneels beside her. "You scared us."

"Scared myself." I get up before Vera can shove more water down my throat and find Deean amongst the group. "Nearly killed by a Saden prince," I tease and see a smile tug on his lips.

Standing up, I rise to the prettiest view. "We made it," I say with awe.

"You see it?" Chana looks around.

"I do."

"We thought it was here." Nico comes into view with the map tucked into the pocket of his top. "But it's like there is an invisible force field or something."

"Can you not see the gate around it?"

They all turn their head towards the tree. "It's just an empty field," Vera answers for them all.

Feeling suddenly normal again, I take a step forward. Iann holds on to me, but I assure him I'm okay.

Glowing like a worm in a deep, darkened cave, the tree emits a hypnotic turquoise light. Through the slits of iron bars, I catch glimpses of white petals dusted with a purple sheen. The Ivian Flower.

The hairs on the back of my neck stand straight up. A perplexing force shifts around the area. One that makes me both want to run screaming and draw closer to the tree.

I wonder if this fence appeared as part of Morrena's enchantment or if it was originally part of the isle's foundation? It's out of place and makes me a tad worrisome.

Moving along the tall iron posts that protrude from the ground and circle the tree, I search for a way in and feel the others follow. They don't ask questions or insert opinions, they simply watch and allow me to explore.

Within minutes of searching, I come to a bolted section within the gate that forms an opening. My fingers trail over the lock, tracing the keyhole. It's not a regular keyhole, this one requires a specific shape—that of an anchor.

"I think I found the way in." Like a magnet I'm pulled to Iann instantly. His eyes are eager, hungry to see the legend we've been chasing. "I need the anchor."

Deean dumps the contents of his bag on the ground. The anchor is the last item to fall out and he swoops it up so fast I don't think it even has a chance to hit the ground. He walks it over like it's the most precious thing in the world. My hand dips when he places it in my palm. I nearly forgot how much weight it carries.

Aligning the anchor to the keyhole I confirm it is a perfect fit, and then I insert and turn it, until the clicking noises come to an end.

A ripple runs along the gate, as a gust of air rushes through my hair, and I see nearby trees bend to its power.

"What was that?" Deean shouts as everyone shields their eyes.

"Magnificent," Benny says, "I can see it now."

The wind stops and the gate opens. Whatever enchantment Morrena put on the perimeter is broken or temporarily interrupted. Who knows how much magic that woman used.

"I thought only you could see it?" Iann is at my side, his eyes locked on the tree that's finally within his grasp.

My head shakes in bewilderment. "That's what she said. But maybe only until we unlocked the gate?" I rub his arm. "We found it. We can save your mom."

There is no hesitation, no disturbances, no issues as we walk through the gate. The only difference is a shift in the land surrounding the tree.

While the tree stands tall, thriving in its stance, the field around it is dry and nearly dying. I assume it's another thing the enchantment was concealing.

"The ship," Chana says, her finger pointing towards the shore.

"He must have seen the powder Deean and Sky set off." Iann holds a new reassurance in his voice. "Let's get this flower and go."

The petals shine brighter as we approach, the vibrant allure carries us closer. The flowers' scent is a sweet intoxication, like the smell wants us to devour them all.

There are hundreds of flowers on the tree, some hang low enough to pluck off and others are at the tippy top, out of reach.

No one takes the chance of reaching for one first, so I do.

Like velvet slipping into my hands, the petals are there waiting to be plucked, and with one quick movement that's exactly what I do.

You'd think after being cut from its life support it would dim, but the bloom only glows brighter and there is an urge to shove it in my mouth and consume immortality.

"Are you okay?" Once Iann touches me my mind drifts back. The urge to eat it falls away.

"Yes," I whisper. "Someone else should try." If the flower I just picked can be sent back to Morrena then Iann can keep one for his mother, meaning we won't have to choose between the two.

Iann releases a steady breath and takes a flower next. His eyes lighting up like he's holding the most precious thing in his hands.

We give it a few minutes. Waiting for the island to swallow us whole and punish us for stealing, but nothing happens.

With no disaster having ensued, everyone takes a turn selecting a flower. Whether it will be something they consume, keep, or trade is a discussion for another time.

"Imagine how great this could make Saden." Deean reaches for another flower. "We'd be an unstoppable kingdom."

"And who wants that?" Vera places hers and Sky's flower in his bag. "The rules are clear. One flower each."

Iann grips his brother's hand. "She's right. Whatever you're feeling is the flower talking, and I would not like to find out what Kialeric has in store for a punishment."

Deean holds up both hands, surrendering. "Fine."

"Sallen is waiting," Iann shouts to us all. "Let's meet him at the shore and get the hell off Farella Isle, before Queen Cayleen or Morrena sends people after us."

He leans in close, his arm brushing mine. "Are you ready to see my home?"

My heart flutters from the idea of it all, his touch alone is enough to send me spiraling, but knowing I'll be on a new adventure after just experiencing this one has me thinking my heart might explode.

"I'm ready to follow you anywhere." I lock my hand in his and don't let go until we reach Sallen's ship.

34
IANN

It takes us five days to cross the Graying Sea. We move into familiar waters, my body knowing every wave as if they are old friends. The air brings back a million memories and once we hit a crystalline shore, my fear dissolves like foam out on the surf.

Saden.

Green flags wave at the shoreline, banners rippling with the breeze, and Saden soldiers have lined the beach with tents.

Marcel or my father must have sent them, expecting our arrival, and I wonder how long they have been camped here.

"That's Saden?" Ariah holds on to my arms as I wrap her in a bear hug and rest my head on her shoulder as we stare out at my home.

"I've been to hundreds of places"—Benny takes a swig from the flask Deean hands him—"but nothing compares to Saden."

Vera peers through a spyglass. "It's nice, but I've seen better. Like the orchards near Plumming or the Fields of Evertaum in Haymel. You boys are going to have to show us more than this to impress us."

Chana gives her arm a push and snatches the spyglass from

357

her. She only looks and never comments on whether it's the most beautiful sight she's ever seen, though I suspect for her Ethmay would win every time.

"So, what now?" Sky leans against the post. "We are free from Queen Cayleen and yet we can't go home. What are we to do?"

"King Marcel will grant you pardons," Deean answers before I get the chance. "You'll be declared allies and then you'll have the freedom to choose what you do next. You can stay or you can make new lives elsewhere. That's why you all left Haymel, isn't it?"

They silently take in his words, letting them truly sink in. They've been searching for freedom for years and finally have it back.

"And what will you do?" I say low enough so others won't hear, and apply a kiss to Ariah's temple. My lips are pillowed by dozens of curls.

Her gaze hasn't left the shoreline. "I'm going to see what my parents want." She takes another minute. "But I think I would really like to stay. Or go with you on your next trip."

"Another crew member. First Benny and Deean, and now you."

She spins so she can rest her head on my chest. "You think I would stay behind while you have all the fun? Didn't I say I'm following you anywhere? You are going to be so sick of me, you'd wish you left me back in Haymel."

"Not possible." If everyone wasn't on deck right now, I'd ravish her. Trail every inch of her being until it's embedded in my mind, I don't want to forget a thing about her.

Trumpets cry out and we watch the people prepare for our rival. Just when the day couldn't get better, four figures emerge from the grandest tent. My father, mother, Marcel, and Gran wave us on as the ship comes in.

As soon as I step onto the sandy floor my mother is right

there, not caring who is in her way. She kisses my forehead and then spots Deean.

Before his kiss she slaps his arm. "What is wrong with you?" She gives him a look like she's scolding a child.

My father comes to me and grips both sides of my shoulders before pulling me in. "Your brother told us what that evildoer tried to do. I should have never sent you. Our line could have ended in one night."

I pull away, patting an arm. "Well, we had help." Stepping to the side I reveal the Foxes, announcing each by name. "They request pardons and protection. Without them, we would have never returned."

My father has no hesitation about the request and has a few guards show them to tents where they can freshen up.

The only one who stays behind is Ariah, standing close to my side.

Once Marcel and Gran take their turns with greetings, I properly introduce her to my family.

She bows to my parents. "It is a pleasure to meet you all. Iann speaks highly of all of you."

"Ariah here is the one that led us to the Ivian Flower," Deean fluffs her up for our parents, even though I don't think it's needed. "She is also the one who defied her own Queen to save us."

My father folds his arms in front of him as my mother steps forward, walking up to Ariah. "You defied your Queen to save my son?"

Ariah shifts but finds confidence in her stance as she replies, "I did. Not just for your sons, but for myself too, and my friends. I'd do it again if it meant saving him."

Gran cracks a sly smile but refrains from commentary.

My mother grabs both sides of Ariah's face. "Anyone willing to save one of my boys is most welcome in Saden." She lets go and spins around, extending an arm for Ariah to hold on to. "I would like you to tell me all about your trip and leave nothing out."

Ariah looks back, tossing me a smile before my mom throws a wink of her own.

Deean slaps my back. "That was easy enough. I'm sure she'll have Ariah planning for your marriage in no time."

"Shut up." I push him and we join the others and head to the tent.

Days later my mother throws a party, as she does best, to celebrate our return and discovery.

My father is still in shock that the tree even exists, but hasn't discussed my mother ingesting the petals or her illness. I also think he's afraid of her saying no.

I understand she may not want to be immortal, but the alternative is just as terrifying.

No one else has done anything with their flowers, and no one is too sure what to do.

Ariah, who refuses to use it, has prepared to have it shipped to Morrena. Come morning, a carrier will take it and settle the deal between them.

My mother introduces Ariah to several party goers, and it isn't until later in the evening when I whisk her away from the festivities.

"Where are we going?" She clings to her dress as I run us through the halls.

"Trust me."

Taking her to the dining hall, I rush us out of the courtyard doors and pass the fountains.

I allow us to go from a run to a light jog, leading her past hedges and down a rocky path.

When I see the carriage waiting, I know her wait is almost over.

The driver opens the door and I extend my hand for her.

"Are you going to tell me where we're going?"

My eyebrows gesture for her to get in and she does with little fuss. I climb in and slide beside her. With a tap on the roof of the carriage we're off.

She gives up asking questions and offers up a kiss instead. A hand that's cupped around my cheek slides down my neck and then to the buttons of my shirt. Her lips hold me hostage, but they can have me anytime.

I take the hand at my buttons. "I'm still not telling you where we're going."

She smiles before silencing my words by deepening our kiss that I kindly oblige to.

"You're going to hate me." I laugh as I pry myself away from her and reach for a piece of fabric on the seat across from us. "I want this to be a surprise and need you to put this on."

She squints and rolls her eyes, but spins around anyway. "Fine. I guess I can play nice."

I cover her eyes and tie the fabric around the back of her head. My lips draw near her ear and I feel her body shudder when she realizes how close I am. "Not too nice."

"That depends on how nice this surprise is."

The driver comes to a stop, and I help her down. Leading her a few feet away from the carriage, I face her in the desired direction and pull the blindfold off.

"One of my favorite places in Saden is Petal Path." My mouth moves near her ear. "I thought you would enjoy it as well."

Her mouth drops open and she walks without realizing I'm not at her side. Instead, I watch her admire it all.

Tonight, Petal Path is filled with thousands of fireflies that make needing a light of our own unnecessary.

"Iann," she says my name with amazement. I point behind her before she can continue. Spinning in the direction of my finger she spots bushes of hydrangeas. "No way."

I follow her as she moves deeper into the flower maze. "You like it?"

"Like it, I'm in love." She inhales the different varieties. "It reminds me of home."

What I wouldn't give for this to be her home. For her to know the land's wonders just as I do.

One minute I'm watching her and the next my hand is at her waist pulling her to me. I rest my nose to hers and together we remain still. Not wanting to move or speak.

A hand grips my shoulder as one moves higher, inching toward the nape of my neck.

Our lips hover closer, catching each other's breath but before we close the gap, I move my mouth to her neck planting kisses all the way down until I reach her collarbone.

"Iann," she whispers, pulling my face back to hers, and I'm greeted with a look of worry, or maybe fear. It's one I've never seen before so it's hard to read.

"Do you want me to stop?" Concern I've done something wrong sets in.

She shakes her head, and a smile eases the restlessness inside. "Absolutely not." She places a hand in mine. "I think...I think I'm falling in love with you." She repeats the words just the way I said them to her at the ball. I thought it would take more time for her to get there, which would be an excruciating wait, but one I would endure a hundred times over. In this moment that's all it takes for me to fall into her. "I've been unsure about several things in life. But not this."

"I love you too, Ariah Tyddle." I kiss her with the intensity of a thousand storms. My insides are set ablaze and there isn't a thing I wouldn't do or destroy to get to this woman. She's forever stolen the most important part of me, and without her there is no me.

35
ARIAH

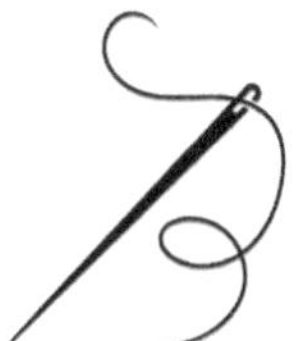

One of Queen Evies' ladies-in-waiting, Glanya, helps detangle my hair and applies oils and creams that absorb right into the curls. It's much needed after weeks out at sea—all the salt drying out my hair and skin.

Iann's parents have been kind and much too gracious. They even sent guards to the border of the kingdom to meet my family.

The servants wait on me every day like I'm some kind of princess. If it were up to Iann, I would be.

It's a foreign life that doesn't feel like mine. There were small perks of being a Fox but never quite like this. Not to mention, the vast difference between rulers.

"I'm going to go get you a few options for ribbons, ma'am." Glanya squeezes my shoulders and then steps out, closing the door behind her.

In her absence, I finish getting myself ready and move to the bed where she placed a new dress. It's far too pretty to be worn casually, but at the moment I don't have any other options.

My hand glides over the blue tulle and the tiny hydrangea

flowers sewn into the material. Iann must have selected it, knowing the blooms to be my favorite.

I slip it on and dance my way to the mirror. My body riddles with giddiness. It's hard to do anything but smile, this is the best I've felt in months.

"It's a bit pretentious don't you think?" A familiar voice stills me. The sound ices my blood and my head spins wildly.

Behind me, in a dress black as night that constricts her upper body and then puffs out below the hips, is Queen Cayleen.

My eyes shut, trying to blink her away, but when they open, she's still before me. "This isn't real."

"My body may not physically be in Saden, but I assure you this is very real." She doesn't move, only deepens the glare she pins me with. "You and I had a deal."

"You were going to kill them." I back up and collide with the mirror. Cold glass smacking into my skin. "Morrena told me of your plans."

"Morrena knows better and trust me she's being dealt with. What's it to you if I kill a few princes? Their family destroyed mine. Would you not do the same to save your own?" She looks me over and then around the room, stepping forward for the first time. "Is that not what you did with your parents? Tried to pluck them out of Haymel before I could reach them?"

There isn't much courage in it, but I straighten my stance. "What do you want?"

"My men caught your parents in a village near the Saden border." There is a sudden strain around my heart. "Along with your sister, her husband, and their child." My heart is thrown from a cliff. "They also found Luna, Morren, and her parents." My heart falls and splatters on rocky ground.

"You're lying." My head shakes violently. Her lies ignite my rage. "The King's guards are on their way to retrieve them."

"A waste of a trip. They won't find them."

My anger has me thinking irrationally. I pull a dagger tied up near my thigh and rush the Queen before she has time to think. Reaching for the material of her dress my hands come up empty and I fall right through her.

Her body spins to find me lying on the ground, the dagger landing on the wood with a thud, spinning a few times before stopping.

"You still have fight in you. You're going to need it." She walks forward, her body towering over me, shadowing my being. "As I said before, you owe me a debt. You and my other Foxes, have until the stardust moon to eradicate the Saden line. If you refuse, your families will pay for your failure." A sheen waves over her body as if she's fading away. "Let this be a reminder: there is nowhere you can run, no distance you can go, or anything you could possibly do to escape, until all you owe me is paid." She holds up four fingers. "Four cold bodies by the stardust moon." She fades away as if she was never here, and I'm not certain she even was.

Four fingers for four bodies.

King Marcel II.

Prince Marcel III.

Prince Deean.

My eyes sting—the thought of the next name alone releases a river of tears, which flows down my cheeks and lips before soaking into my dress.

And Prince Iann. *My Iann.*

ACKNOWLEDGMENTS

In the summer of 2023, I sat down to write a new story, one set in a brand new fantasy world. I didn't know exactly where it would go, only that I wanted to tell the tale of a young girl named Ariah, who longed for more than the life she knew, and a prince who often felt invisible in his own world, but had a knack for finding adventure. What started as a vague idea slowly became *Foxes & Poisons*—a book that has challenged me, exhausted me, and yet completely stolen my heart.

To my family, I thank you for always listening, even when I couldn't stop talking about my stories. To my friends and coworkers, thank you for your patience, encouragement, and constantly cheering me on.

A massive thank you to my editor, Joyce Fernandez at ReJoyce Literary Editing, for your sharp eye and kind guidance. To Natascia, Lictoria, and Dezaray—your artwork brought this world to life. Lexie, thank you for a cover that still makes me stop and stare. Hannah, your map gave Ariah's world a shape and soul. And Brindi, thank you for all your formatting magic.

This book would not be what it is without each of you. From the bottom of my heart, thank you!

And finally, I'm grateful to God—for the quiet strength to keep writing, and for the gift of storytelling.

ABOUT ADINA CHILES

ADINA CHILES has an obsession with all things; coffee, fantasy, and contemporary. She is both a creator and collector of fictional worlds and enjoys the company of a good book over peopling.

She was born and raised in Northern California, and outside of the book world, she enjoys creating new recipes for her baking business, traveling, and binge-watching shows. Find out more at *adinachiles.com*.

ALSO BY ADINA CHILES

The Queen's Favor

Foxes & Poisons (2025)

Swans & Stardust (2026)

The Enchanted Woods Collection

Unraveling Magic and Shadowed Pasts (2025)

Co-authored with Devon Thiele

Royal Blood Series

Secrets of a Rose (2022)

Eyes of a Snake (2023)

Heart of a Liar (2025)